The Swiss Conspiracy

Garrett Hutson

This book is a work of fiction. Aside from historical figures, the names, characters, events, and places depicted are the products of the author's imagination. Any resemblance to actual events, places, or persons living or dead is entirely coincidental.

Warfleigh Publishing first edition March 2021

Cover design by Steven Novak

For more information, or to book an event, please contact the author at
www.garretthutson.com

ISBN 978-1-953846-05-1 (hardcover)
ISBN 978-1-953846-06-8 (paperback)
ISBN 978-1-953846-04-4 (eBook)

For David, always.

Prologue

Wednesday, September 24, 1941 - Zurich, Switzerland

The pounding of heavy footsteps down the hall made the professor look up from his desk. He glanced at the clock on the wall. It was almost half past seven. The building would be locked up by now.

The small lamp on his desk cast light over the multitude of papers scattered there, but the rest of the office lay in shadow. He looked toward the door, where only dim light was visible beneath. Even the hall was dark at this hour.

The door flew open with a loud crack and thudded against the wall, sending splinters flying.

The gray-haired professor bolted from his chair, his brown eyes widening as two men stormed into the room, pistols drawn. They wore brown sweaters and dark brown trousers, with black leather jackets. Flat caps sat atop their heads, and their hands were hidden beneath black gloves.

They stopped in front of him with their pistols pointed at his chest.

"What do you want?" His voice trembled.

"Shut up, Jew!" one of the men said.

The other man, taller than his companion, sneered at the name plate at the front of the desk. "Dr. F. Rubenstein." He glowered at the framed sepia-toned photograph on the wall. A much younger

Rubenstein, twenty-one years old, stood next to Albert Einstein, whose hair and mustache were still dark. Their arms at their sides, they wore high collared shirts and three-piece suits.

The taller man stepped toward it and slammed his elbow against the glass, shattering it and sending the frame crashing to the ground.

"I have very little money!" the professor said, his voice still trembling. He thrust his hand into his left pocket, removed several coins, and held out his hand palm up.

"We don't want your money," the taller man said.

Dr. Rubenstein swallowed hard, and remained standing.

"Step away from the desk," the shorter stocky man said. When Dr. Rubenstein remained in place, the man's green eyes narrowed. "Do as I say, Jew." He waved his pistol for emphasis.

Dr. Rubenstein stepped sideways, looking the stocky man in the eye. "I have seen you two today, and yesterday too I think. You were unloading boxes and chairs from a truck."

The taller man smirked.

"You are not Swiss, either of you," Dr. Rubenstein continued, his voice growing stronger. "Your accents are Bavarian, I think. Am I wrong?"

"That is not important!" the stocky man snapped, but the look in the taller man's pale blue eyes confirmed he was right.

"Are you Gestapo?" Dr. Rubenstein demanded, his voice now firm and loud.

There was no response.

"Am I somehow an enemy of your Reich? Am I dangerous to your Leader for some reason I am not aware of?"

"Not another word, you stupid, filthy Jew!" the stocky man shouted, and lunged forward, striking Rubenstein on the temple with his pistol.

The professor cried out, clutching the side of his head and almost falling sideways. He regained his balance, and faced his attackers.

The taller man reached inside his jacket, fishing in the pocket, and removed a folded paper.

A large Cross of Lorraine adorned the front of the pamphlet. Dr. Rubenstein looked back at the tall man with some confusion. "There is some mistake! You have me wrong, gentlemen—I am not affiliated with the French Resistance."

The tall man said nothing, and dropped the leaflet on the floor.

"Prepare to die, Jew." the stocky man spat. "The world is about to be rid of you."

He fired his pistol at Rubenstein's heart. His tall companion fired a second later, hitting the professor in the right lung.

Dr. Rubenstein's eyes grew wide again, and he clutched at his chest with a trembling hand. The fingers covered with blood.

His legs buckled, and he crumbled to the floor. His eyes twitched around the room for several seconds, not focusing on anything, before finally stopping and staring up at the photograph of a young woman on his desk.

The tall man ran his hand across the top of the desk, sending papers flying. The stocky man kicked over the chair next to the door, and flung open the drawers of the tall filing cabinet in the corner. Grabbing at papers and folders, he tossed them into the air with abandon, scattering them like snow over the floor.

The taller one stepped behind the desk, pulling out the drawers and dumping the contents onto the floor. He threw the now-empty drawers against the wall and let them clatter across the cluttered floor. He took the rubbish can next to the desk and laid it on its side. Then he removed a single sheet of paper folded in thirds from inside his coat, opened it, and crumpled it up before tossing it at the lip of the rubbish can.

A smaller filing cabinet sat against the opposite wall beneath the clock, and the tall man kicked it over onto its side, the drawers flying open.

Once the office appeared suitably ransacked, the men strode to the open door. The taller one paused to pull a ring from his pocket. He flipped open the top to show the Cross of Lorraine inside, then let it drop to the floor next to Dr. Rubenstein.

Chuckling, he followed his companion down the dark hallway.

Sunday,
September 28, 1941

1

Lisbon, Portugal

Martin Schuller stepped out of the airplane door and onto the seawing, putting on his navy blue fedora, which matched his crisp suit. Yesterday's Wall Street Journal tucked under his arm, completing the look of a businessman, he strode onto the pier. The Lisbon pier was said to be crawling with spies, from every secret service imaginable, as well as Portuguese secret police. He'd been warned before leaving Washington.

Shouts in multiple languages from a crowd at the next pier reverberated while he strode down the quay. Perhaps as many as two-hundred people pressed forward against a line of police holding them back from the steam ship anchored there. Others rushed to join them from every direction.

Martin scanned the crowd, and noted at least a few pale-faced and fair-haired Germanic-looking types. Abwehr agents, or expatriate dissidents? There was no way to know for certain.

More uniformed police opened a narrow corridor through the roiling crowd, and through it passed a fortunate few bearing tickets for steerage—tickets for which they had doubtless overpaid. Not the most comfortable way to travel, but it was passage to America nonetheless. They wore tattered travel clothes and carried scuffed and faded suitcases, their expressions a strange combination of shell-shock, fear, and hope.

Martin turned away from the river at the next street, and hiked uphill through the commercial district, making frequent turns and glancing around to see if he was being watched or followed.

He wound through the streets for thirty minutes before he was comfortable that he was alone. He dropped the day-old newspaper into a trash can and headed back toward the river.

Martin wondered if he'd be able to tell his kids about the sights and sounds of Lisbon. If he'd be allowed to admit that he was here. And if Becky would let him see them anytime soon.

He pushed those thoughts from his mind. He had work to do.

Martin walked down a street overlooking the River Tagus. The brim of his fedora shielded his eyes from the sun as he searched the store fronts, finally locating the sign painted with the image of a bouquet of violets. He took a seat at an empty table in front of the little café.

He was glad to sit for a few moments. His stomach still felt a tad queasy. He wasn't a fan of flying, let alone over the vast Atlantic.

It had been two years since the amphibious Pan-Am Clipper—the only regular trans-Atlantic flight—had changed its route from New York-Southampton to New York-Lisbon, to avoid the war zone. His flight had been less than half-full, so Martin hadn't been obliged to make much small-talk with strangers. He hated that. No doubt the return flight to New York would be packed with well-heeled emigrants who had pawned enough jewelry or other family heirlooms to afford the $700 tickets.

Martin would have preferred to travel by ship, in spite of the U-boat risk—a fast steamer could make the passage in six days. But his assignment couldn't wait that long, so he'd taken a commercial flight from Washington to New York, followed by a long flight on the Clipper that stopped in the Azores before continuing on to Lisbon.

And in twenty-four hours he'd crossed the ocean that Columbus had taken two months to traverse. *Ah, progress.*

A man in a dark gray suit, matching fedora, and dark sunglasses appeared in front of him. "Mr. Schuller?"

"Yes, I'm Mr. Schuller." Martin stood and extended his hand.

The other man shook his hand. "I'm Rodney Babcock, from the U.S. Embassy. Welcome to Lisbon."

"Thank you."

"Please sit." There was a nasal quality to Babcock's accent. New England, probably.

Babcock took a seat opposite Martin, and motioned for the waiter. He fired off a rapid line in Portuguese, and the waiter hurried off. "You weren't followed?" Babcock asked, lowering his voice.

"No."

"You were briefed before you left?"

"A little." *Barely. Physicists, the French Resistance, and a promise of more information upon arrival.*

"This should help fill in the gaps." Reaching inside his jacket, Babcock removed a manila envelope and slid it across to Martin. "I was instructed to tell you to open that in private."

Martin placed the manila envelope inside his own jacket, but Babcock's hand remained in the center of the table. A slight motion of his fingers, and the shine of metal appeared.

Martin glanced around. Most of the tables were occupied. A pair of lovers sat at the table closest to them, their chairs close together and their hands clasped, their dark eyes locked on each other as they spoke in soft tones through broad smiles. Beyond them, a trio of old men shouted and gesticulated, arguing some point amongst themselves. Six young people sat around two tables pushed together near the door, laughing and quaffing red wine.

Assured that no one was watching, he swept his hand across and covered the key a second after Babcock's hand pulled away.

"Locker seventy-four at the train station. You'll find directions to an airfield outside of the city, a plane ticket to Zurich on a registered Swiss flight, and a train ticket from Zurich to Bern. Read the contents of the envelope before you leave. You'll find the address of the embassy there. The ambassador will meet you on arrival. Memorize the information in the envelope before you meet him."

The waiter returned and set a demitasse of espresso in front of Babcock. "*Obrigada*," he said.

"How much time until my plane leaves for Zurich?"

"Two hours," Babcock replied, setting the demitasse back on its tiny saucer with a quiet clink. "It's a five-hour flight. You should arrive in Zurich fifty minutes before your train leaves for Bern."

"Taking a train from here to Bern would be far less conspicuous," Martin said, not relishing the idea of another plane.

Babcock took another sip of espresso. "Best for you not to travel through Spain and France before you get your papers in Bern."

Martin's gut clenched. "There are no identification papers in the envelope?"

"No. The embassy in Bern is handling all that."

Martin frowned. It was bad enough entering Portugal under his own name; now he had to enter Switzerland the same way. He would have preferred more anonymity. But he shouldn't be surprised—America was unprepared for the kind of sophisticated spycraft it would need if tensions continued to escalate in the Atlantic.

Babcock stood, took one more sip of espresso, then extended his right hand. "Good luck, Mr. Schuller." He laid a few coins on the table and walked away.

Martin walked into the café, and found the washroom in the back. Locking the door, he pulled out the manila envelope.

There were four pieces of paper inside. He read through them, then folded them and stuffed them down the front of his pants. A wad of Portuguese escudos he put in his pocket. He returned the empty manila envelope inside his jacket, unlocked the door, and strode toward the exit.

The taxi stopped at the end of a gravel lane, a short distance from a hangar, and the driver turned around and said something in Portuguese.

Martin assumed he wanted payment. He fished inside his pocket and removed the escudos Babcock had provided. He forked over the cash, not sure if he was overpaying. The driver appeared satisfied, but didn't offer change; he pocketed the money and exited the vehicle to open Martin's door.

Martin hadn't been surprised when the driver didn't speak English; he'd recognized the name of the airfield, so no real disadvantage. And a driver who didn't speak your language wouldn't feel the need to get chatty.

A small passenger plane stood in the grassy field beyond the hangar, with three men standing near its nose. A red Lockheed Orion single-engine with one large propeller on the nose, and three windows along each side, the plane had a horizontal white strip down the sides, and the word "Swissair" in white on the tail.

Two of the men wore crisp Swissair uniforms, the third a pair of greasy coveralls. One of the uniformed men stepped forward to greet Martin, a clipboard in his hand.

"Good evening, sir," he said in German. "May I have your ticket, please?"

Martin handed over the ticket.

"And your name, sir?"

Martin's gut tightened. The ticket Babcock had reserved was under his real name. "Martin Schuller." He used its Pennsylvania Dutch pronunciation.

The accent seemed to work. The man checked off his name, wished him a good flight, and didn't ask to see his passport.

The cabin contained six seats, and Martin took one of the back ones. The front pair of seats was occupied by a well-dressed middle-aged couple, conversing quietly in Swiss German. The man nodded as Martin boarded, then turned his attention back to his wife.

Martin was relieved to see no one else on board. With any luck, he wouldn't be obliged to make conversation.

The pilot and copilot came aboard, closing the cabin door, and the pilot announced that they were about to take off. A moment later a loud roar shook the cabin as the engine started, and they rattled across the bumpy field.

Martin gripped the sides of his seat, his knuckles white. He hated this part most of all. The bump of the wheels across the uneven ground rattled his jaw, but at least this take-off from land lacked the sudden jolts of the Pan-Am Clipper skipping across the waves as it took off.

The plane ascended, and Martin's stomach dropped. He stared straight ahead, not the least bit interested in watching the ground slip away. This was his third flight in two days, and he didn't like the experience any better than the first time.

It wasn't that he lacked bravery—he willingly put himself into dangerous situations for his work, and had been shot at a couple of times—but flying was simply not natural.

His grandfather Schuller had refused to ride in an automobile to the day he died, calling them "dangerous and unnatural." Martin loved automobiles—and no matter how dangerous they were, you were in control of your own destiny when you were behind the wheel. In an airplane you were forced to put your trust in the pilot. Martin never put his trust in strangers. He supposed it was the same with a cruise ship or a train, but ships and trains just *felt* safer.

If Colonel Donovan hadn't told him on Friday afternoon that he needed to be in Switzerland by Monday morning, he would have happily lived his life never riding in an airplane.

But he hadn't been given the choice.

He'd been looking forward to driving up to Philadelphia on Saturday to spend time with his kids. Instead, Donovan told him he was needed in Europe.

Europe. That had come as a shock. State Department Counter-Intelligence personnel worked inside the United States, not overseas. He'd asked the reason, but Donovan had been vague, saying he'd learn what he needed to when he arrived. Very strange indeed.

Martin could still hear Becky's voice, furious when he called to cancel his weekend with the kids.

"What is it this time, Martin? A woman? Or work again?"

He hadn't answered.

Her voice grew derisive. "I'm sure it's work. It's always work. And what woman would tolerate you never being around?"

"Stop it, Becky."

"No, I won't. You can't keep doing this, Martin. It was bad enough when you used to leave me high and dry for work, but your kids don't understand. They'll be devastated, you know—not that it matters to you."

He seethed. "Are you finished?"

"Oh, we're finished." And the line clicked off.

The memory made his blood boil all over again. Why could she never understand? He had a duty, for God's sake, a duty to protect their country from Nazi infiltrators. He couldn't step away from that.

He took a breath. It was dark inside the cabin. He should try to get some sleep. He leaned his head back and put his hat over his eyes.

2

Zurich, Switzerland

Ernst Zubler listened with a forced smile to his wife's enthusiastic chatter about the upcoming debutante ball for the Heinzes' sixteen-year-old daughter, Gretchen.

"You must be very proud of your daughter, Mr. Heinz," he said to the gentleman sitting two seats to his left.

"Indeed we are," Erich Heinz said, with a hint of smile.

Zubler took another bite of chocolate cake while Mrs. Heinz detailed the preparations for the ball. He barely listened.

Eight people sat around the long mahogany table, each with a piece of chocolate cake on a small china plate. A long lace tablecloth showed the rich color of the dark wood underneath, which matched the mahogany paneling on the walls. The four men wore white dinner jackets and black bowties, their wives evening gowns and elbow-length white gloves.

Zubler sat at the head of the table, opposite his wife Sophia, who listened in rapt attention to Mrs. Heinz. He set his silver fork onto the plate beside his half-eaten piece of cake, pushed back his carved chair, and stood. Every face at the table turned to him.

He addressed himself to his wife with a polite nod. "If you'll excuse us, my dear, the men and I need to discuss some business, before it becomes late. We shall retire to the study, and let you ladies continue your socializing over coffee."

A slight scowl crossed Sophia's face, quickly changing to a rueful smile meant to look indulgent. "Didn't you gentlemen discuss finance several times at dinner? Must you conduct business at this hour, on Sunday?"

"I'm afraid so, my dear," Zubler replied with a cool half-smile and a polite nod. "We have much to discuss from my trip to Frankfurt." He turned to the butler standing beside the door. "Anton, please bring a decanter of port to the study."

"As you wish, sir."

Zubler turned back to the table, where the three other men had also stood. Bowing to the ladies, he gestured the men into the hallway.

His study sat at the end of the long hall. It was half the size of the dining room, but the high paneled ceiling gave it a feeling of spaciousness. Bookshelves lined three of the walls, and heavy green drapes covered the large window on the outside wall.

The butler came in a moment later, and set a crystal decanter onto the top of a mahogany desk in the corner. He poured four crystal glasses half-full, and turned toward his employer.

"Thank you, Anton. Please close the door behind you."

When the butler had left, Zubler turned toward his guests with a thin smile, and motioned toward the upholstered chairs. "Please sit, gentlemen." He handed each a glass. "I'm sure you have surmised by now that my trip to Frankfurt last month was not primarily motivated by banking business."

Erich Heinz grunted. "When you call us into a private meeting to discuss your recent visit to the Reich, it is not difficult to infer that you attended to nationalist business."

Zubler nodded. "Indeed. The meetings with Deutschebank were a useful cover."

All of the men present had joined the League of Swiss for Greater Germany earlier that year, frustrated that the other far-right parties in

Switzerland merely pushed for greater cooperation with the Third Reich. This new organization called for Switzerland's inclusion in the Reich.

Zubler stepped behind his chair, clasping his hands behind his back as he spoke. "While there, I met with Mr. Franz Burri, our founder-in-exile, and presented him with my ideas for implementing Switzerland's future."

"What ideas, Mr. Zubler?" Dietrich Hagen asked.

"Trying to persuade the people politically is a fool's game, gentlemen. Mr. Burri agreed with me. Political arguments would have been more persuasive three years ago, after the Austrian Anschluss, and before the Leader became aggressive about invading the Reich's neighbors. But once the Wehrmacht began blitzing across Europe, the public's sympathies turned. We saw the enthusiasm with which our countrymen embraced national mobilization. What is needed now is action to re-educate public opinion."

"How do you propose to do that?" Dietrich Hagen pressed.

"We have already begun!" Zubler said. "I shall come to your role in a moment. While in Frankfurt, I learned that the Leader and the High Command had a plan of invasion prepared for Switzerland last summer, after France capitulated—Operation Tannenbaum, and it was nearly put into action. Our country's mobilization gave the High Command pause—with every Swiss man armed and organized into militias, the high alert of our army at the border, and our mountainous terrain, they know that the Wehrmacht would lose too many men and tanks in an invasion. Though successful occupation of our cities was assured, they knew that the remnants of our army would retreat to mountain redoubts, and could cause trouble for months, or years.

"The Leader wanted to turn his attention to Britain last summer. Then this summer the Reich's invasion of Russia tied up the remainder of the Wehrmacht's resources. The point is, a military-enforced Anschluss is not going to happen. If Switzerland is to take her rightful place within the new world order as part of the Greater Germany, it must be voluntary. And this is where our plan comes into play."

"Are you going to tell us?" Friedrich Zindorf asked, not disguising his impatience.

Zubler nodded and gave Zindorf an indulgent smile. "There are a great many on the right who betrayed us last year, organizing the mobilization against invasion, instead of doing what they could to welcome it. All of the major leaders of the SVV, in the military and in government, called upon the people to fight to the last man to defend Switzerland's independence. They betrayed us, and they must be punished. And in so doing, if the Gestapo can make it look as if they were assassinated by the Bolsheviks or the French Resistance, it will create a feeling of panic that we can capitalize upon. The Gestapo will remind our leaders that they have the most experience rooting out Bolshevism and anarchism, and will offer the Reich's assistance."

Friedrich Zindorf's mouth opened, and the color drained from his face. "Do you mean to tell us, Mr. Zubler, that you are involved in the recent wave of assassinations that have terrorized the country?"

A cold smile spread across Zubler's small mouth. "Not just involved, Mr. Zindorf. I am commanding them. I choose the targets, I choose the method—bombing, shooting—and I choose whom to frame. The Gestapo takes care of the rest. They are quite efficient."

"You mean that the Gestapo is already here?" Erich Heinz asked, his eyes widening.

Zubler waved a hand dismissively. "The Gestapo has been operating in Switzerland for more than a year, reporting to Berlin about the situation here. I offered my plan to my handlers in Frankfurt, and the local Gestapo cell here in Zurich contacted me upon my return, prepared for me to give them assignments."

"What do you need our assistance with, Mr. Zubler? Why did you call this meeting?" Dietrich Hagen asked.

"Financing, gentlemen. Bombs and propaganda cost money, and I'm afraid what the High Command has committed to the operation is insufficient to meet our needs on a grand scale."

"You want our *banks* to finance a terror campaign? You can't be serious!" Erich Heinz said.

"Don't be ridiculous!" Zubler snapped. "My bank has not contributed a cent to the operation, nor will it. I would not be able to embezzle sufficient funds without drawing the attention of auditors, and we cannot have this known. I have been contributing from my own resources, and I ask you gentlemen to open your pocketbooks tonight and make a contribution for the cause."

"How much do you want?" Erich Heinz asked.

"Ten thousand francs apiece should finance the operation for the next month."

"How long do you expect this operation to last?" Dietrich Hagen asked.

Zubler made a half-hearted shrug. "Not much more than a month. If public opinion has not turned sufficiently to influence the government by then, we will escalate matters by taking the terror campaign to the highest levels."

"I will not be a part of this!" Friedrich Zindorf leapt from his seat. "I cannot support the killing of our leaders and the terrorizing of our countrymen, Mr. Zubler. We must continue political efforts to advance our cause."

"The killing of traitors is a patriotic duty, Mr. Zindorf." Zubler's voice was as cold as an alpine wind, and froze everyone in the room, except its target.

"I will not be party to it! My wife and I are leaving."

"As you wish," Zubler replied with an indifferent shrug. He opened the door, and watched as Friedrich Zindorf stormed down the hall toward the dining room.

"My hat please, Anton!" Zindorf snapped as he turned into the dining room.

A hard look had settled on Zubler's long face, and he closed the door and turned toward Erich Heinz and Dietrich Hagen. "Please stay a moment, gentlemen—I'd like you both to hear this."

They watched Zubler walk to the desk, pick up the telephone receiver, and place a call.

Zubler sat alone in his study forty minutes later when the phone rang.

"It has been done, Gauleiter," the voice on the other end said in a Bavarian accent. "We forced them into a wall, and after their crash our second car rammed the driver's side, hard and fast. Mr. Zindorf was crushed, but his wife survived, just as you instructed. The ambulance arrived twenty minutes ago and took her away."

"Excellent work. A widow is more sympathetic, and we need her to tell the press that it was a deliberate attack, not an accident. And the car?"

"It looks like a tank hit it."

Zubler exhaled in exasperation. "I mean did you mark it as I instructed?"

"Oh, yes, sir! We painted a hammer and sickle on both sides in red paint."

"Excellent. I'm sure the High Command will reward your diligence when we rule Switzerland. Good night." He hung up, a look of satisfaction on his face.

Monday,
September 29, 1941

3

Bern, Switzerland

Jason Bachman sat on the corner of the desk with his ankle crossed over his right knee, a newspaper spread across his lap. He wore a light-gray argyle v-neck sweater vest over a blue dress shirt, with a slate-gray necktie that matched his pressed slacks. He liked that it made him stand out from the other grunts in Consular Services, in their plain white shirts and black ties.

"You know they have an English-language paper you could read," Amanda Overstreet said from her seat behind the desk, flashing him a teasing smile.

"Yeah, I know," Jason replied without looking up. "This gives me good practice with my German, though."

"Anything interesting?" Amanda asked, stapling two pages together and setting them at the side of her desk for the ambassador to sign.

"Yeah, a big-time banker got killed in a car crash last night in Zurich. His wife's at the hospital. They got T-boned by another car. It was gone by the time the cops got there. But before they left they put a big hammer and sickle on the side of the banker's Mercedes."

"I thought they'd outlawed the Communist party," Amanda said.

"They did. But lately there've been several attacks on military officers, and the Reds have always painted a hammer and sickle. Kind of their calling card, I guess."

Amanda said no more, and Jason continued reading. Every few minutes he stopped to take a bite of the pastry sitting on a napkin next to him.

Since he'd arrived in Bern two months before, Jason had taken to leaving his apartment early each weekday, and stopping at the bakery a block away. He bought a pastry for breakfast, and took it with him. He walked the rest of the way to the U.S. Embassy, stopping to buy a newspaper along the way.

He wasn't due at work until eight-thirty, but he liked to arrive around eight and go upstairs to Amanda's desk. She'd always started a pot of coffee by then, and he could pour a cup, eat his apple or cherry turnover, and read the local news in German before he had to go downstairs to his desk in Consular Services.

"Saturday night was lots of fun," Amanda said as she got up from her desk with a stack of papers and walked to a large filing cabinet. "Thanks for dancing with me."

"Anytime!" Jason looked up from the paper long enough to glance her way with a big smile.

"You're a far better dancer than any of the other fellas," Amanda said, rifling through the files and inserting papers. "And I can always trust you to keep your hands where they ought to be."

Jason's grin widened, and he shifted on the desk to turn towards her. "I love to jitterbug, and I'm glad I found a swell girl to let me dance with you and not expect me to buy you dinner."

"You know the fellas all think we're doing more than dancing," Amanda said, closing the drawer.

"Really?"

She sauntered back to the desk. "I don't mind letting them think that, do you?"

"Not at all," Jason replied, turning his gaze back to the newspaper.

A knowing smile crept across her lips. "I figured as much, sweetie."

"It's nice of Brad to let us come over and play his records," Jason said, staring at the photograph of the mangled Mercedes on the front page.

"He's the only one of you grunts that owns a record-player. I don't know how the other fellas think they're gonna make a play for any girls if they don't even have a record-player."

"Ha!" Jason said, looking up from the paper with a grin. "Like you'd share the attention. If any of them ever *did* bring a girl along, you'd probably lock her in the bathroom."

"Honey, I wouldn't have to," Amanda said, glancing down at her bust and running her hands down the side of her form-fitting pink sweater, tracing the hour-glass curve.

Jason laughed out loud. "You're a real piece of work, you know that? A super swell gal, but a piece of work."

Amanda shrugged in exaggerated fashion, batted her eyelashes, and turned toward the typewriter. "You need to get out of here and let me do my work."

A bell dinged down the hall, and the elevator door opened.

"Oooo, here comes that dreamy marine you like," she murmured. "And he's bringing a handsome hunk of man along with him."

Their eyes both locked on the tall blond in the dark blue suit. He walked with a purposeful stride, arms swinging in rhythm to his pace, fedora in one hand, his back straight and his head high. His intense pale green eyes seemed to take in the whole space. His square jaw was set, giving him a serious look.

A young marine corporal in black dress uniform marched beside him, coming straight at Amanda's desk. Jason covered a smile with his hand when Amanda thrust her bust forward and flashed a dazzling smile.

"A Mr. Schuller to see the ambassador, Miss Overstreet," the corporal said, his posture rigidly straight, arms at his sides.

"Of course," Amanda said, her blue eyes twinkling as she smiled at the handsome visitor. "The ambassador is expecting you, Mr. Schuller. This way please."

"Thank you," Mr. Schuller replied in an American accent.

Jason nearly laughed out loud at the exaggerated way her hips swayed as she led Mr. Schuller down the hall toward the ambassador's office. He turned toward the marine corporal who was pivoting to leave.

"Good morning, Corporal Lawrence!" He couldn't help but grin.

"Good morning, sir," the marine replied with a nod.

"You have guard duty all day?"

"Yes, sir," the marine replied, his steel-blue eyes unblinking as he faced Jason.

"Then I guess I'll see you when I leave for lunch later."

"Yes, sir." The marine turned on his heels, and marched toward the stairs.

Jason watched him the whole way. He was a little shorter than Jason, maybe five-foot-eight, with a waspishly narrow waist contrasting with broad shoulders that were accentuated by the gold braiding of his uniform. His light blond hair was buzzed so short it was barely visible, except on the top. His black dress pants hugged a round backside, which he held tight as he marched. He turned at the stairs, and Jason listened to the rhythmic clack of his dress shoes as they echoed from the walls of the stairwell.

"Damn!" he breathed.

The squeak of Amanda's chair wheels behind him made him jump. He laughed to cover his embarrassment. "You were gone a little long for just escorting the ambassador's visitor."

"It was a little strange," Amanda replied, cocking her head to the side. "I announced Mr. Schuller, and the ambassador asked me to go tell Mr. Witherspoon right away. Mr. Witherspoon isn't usually in before nine, but I went to his office and he was there. He must've arrived before me. I sure never saw him come in. I told him that a Mr. Schuller was here to see the ambassador, and he jumped right up and hurried the other direction. What do you make of that?"

Jason shrugged. "Who knows?"

"It's just strange, that's all."

"American businessmen call on the ambassador all the time."

"Yes, but Mr. Witherspoon never joins them."

"Maybe this one's extra important," Jason said with a shrug. "Maybe he knows the President or something."

"Maybe. He sure was handsome, though, wasn't he? And no wedding ring."

Jason laughed. "You *would* notice that right away, wouldn't you? Not that it makes a difference to you."

"Does so! Hush!" she replied, swatting his arm. The slight smile on her lips belied her false anger. "Now go on downstairs and let me get to work. I've got to type these letters for the ambassador before ten o'clock, and I've got a lot of them today."

"Alright. See you at lunch time?"

"If I'm not out with Mr. Schuller."

"Ha! Fine. I'll come up and see you later."

4

"It's an honor to meet you, sir," Martin said when he was introduced to the ambassador, trying not to be awestruck. Leland Harrison was legendary at State as the man who initiated and led the department's encryption and decryption operation during the Great War. *They're calling it the First World War now.* Martin wasn't sure he'd ever get used to that.

"Have a seat, Mr. Schuller," Ambassador Harrison said, indicating one of the chairs in front of his desk. He spoke with a polished lockjaw accent, refined over years at Eton and Harvard. His salt and pepper hair was slicked back from his long face, and he wore a stylish black suit and tie, with a white silk handkerchief folded in the breast pocket, gold cufflinks at his wrists. "Mr. Witherspoon will join us in a moment. He's a Third Secretary, our Information Officer."

"I'm familiar with the role," Martin said. He'd held that exact position at the embassy in Buenos Aires until June.

"He's fetching Colonel Legge, the military attaché," Harrison said. "You understand our entire conversation is classified."

"Of course." Martin might ordinarily be irritated at such an obvious statement, but Leland Harrison was a legend.

A fussy man of about forty rushed into the office, tall and lanky with dark hair slicked back from his long and narrow face. He wore a white shirt and black necktie, but no jacket. Behind him entered an Army man in dress uniform, about fifty, with a dour expression. Martin stood.

The ambassador remained seated behind his desk. "This is Mr. Ronald Witherspoon, our Information Officer. And this is Colonel Barnwell Legge, Military Attaché. Gentlemen, this is Martin Schuller, from the Office of the COI."

"How do you do?" The words tumbled out of Witherspoon's mouth, and his hand was clammy when he shook Martin's. He plopped down in a chair.

"Agent Schuller," Col. Legge said in a pronounced southern drawl, with a firm handshake. His stare seemed to size up Martin for several seconds.

"Thank you for coming at such short notice, Mr. Schuller," the ambassador said, folding his hands on his desk. "You read the information given to you in Lisbon?"

"Yes."

Harrison nodded. "Good. I'll let Colonel Legge take it from here. Colonel?"

The military attaché sat stiff-backed, his mouth set in a straight line. He stared at Martin for several seconds before speaking. "I'm sure Bill Donovan has the highest trust in you, since you're the one he sent. But for my own benefit, before we discuss classified information, I'd like to review your qualifications."

Martin tensed. "By all means, sir."

"I asked Donovan to send someone thoroughly fluent in German," the colonel said. "Are you fluent enough to blend?"

"Yes."

Legge continued to stare at him. "You're certain?"

"Yes."

"Colonel, Washington sent us a cable with Mr. Schuller's background." The ambassador opened a file and put on a pair of glasses. "They assure us that he speaks German like a native. Sixth-generation American, of one-hundred percent German ancestry, and raised in a bilingual family in Reading, Pennsylvania. Attended a church that conducted services in German until 1926, when it switched to English."

Martin shifted in his seat, resisting the urge to squirm. "I stopped attending the church in '25." He hoped they wouldn't ask why. He never spoke of it, and it wasn't pertinent, anyway.

Legge cleared his throat, and his brows drew closer together. "Being German-American, raised in a German-speaking family, do you have any sympathies for Germany?"

Martin held the colonel's gaze. "No more so than any country."

"Do you feel Germany was treated unfairly at the end of the last war?"

Martin was familiar with this line of questioning. He'd been drilled on the subject when he interviewed for the Foreign Service eleven years ago, and then again three years later when he transferred to the Office of the Chief Special Agent.

"I don't make policy, and don't care to."

The ambassador resumed reading from the file. "Mr. Schuller attended the University of Pennsylvania, where he studied Political Science and German. He earned all A's and B's in his courses."

Legge continued to stare at Martin with narrowed eyes. "Why did you take German in college if you spoke it at home as a child?"

Martin's patience wore thin. "Didn't you study English in school, even though you spoke it at home, colonel?" He'd given that answer once to a skeptical congressman; he wasn't intimidated by an army colonel.

The ambassador interrupted again by reading from the file. "Mr. Schuller joined the Foreign Service in 1930. He was assigned to the embassy in Vienna, 1931 to '33. Then he returned to Washington to work in the Office of the Chief Special Agent. His work was instrumental in the arrests of several Nazi spies on American soil."

"How did you like Austria, Agent Schuller?" Colonel Legge asked.

"Very much, sir."

"What do you think of Austria joining the Third Reich?"

Martin was silent for a second, keeping his face expressionless while he considered what to say. "It was probably inevitable."

Legge scowled. "I'd say it's quite regrettable. Would you agree?"

"Yes, it's regrettable."

"You were in Austria for two years. Why would you say it was inevitable?"

"For one thing, it was Herr Hitler's home country. Also, until seventy years ago, Austrians considered themselves Germans. They had no reason to think of themselves otherwise. The only reason they weren't included in German unification was because of their own empire. Even after they lost it at the end of the last war, the first temporary name of their new country was the Republic of German-Austria."

"I know the history!" Legge snapped. "I want *your* perspective. From your experience with the Austrians ten years ago, would you say there was a rise of pro-German nationalist feeling?"

Martin hesitated, wary. "Yes—especially among the young people."

Legge nodded, apparently satisfied. "And what is your experience with Switzerland?"

"I traveled through Switzerland a few times while I was stationed in Vienna."

"Would you say you know the country well?"

"Not as well as Austria."

"Humph," Legge grunted. Martin couldn't read his expression. "You also visited Germany during that time?"

Martin took a deep breath. "Yes, I did. Twice. Once in 1932, and once in '33."

"Both before and after the Nazis," Legge mused, the tiniest hint of smile cracking the thin line of his lips. "During your travels in Austria, Switzerland, and Germany, were you ever mistaken for a local?"

"Not as a *local*, no…"

Legge's eyebrows rose. "But not as an American?"

"No."

"Explain."

Martin relaxed a little. "In Austria and Germany, I was sometimes mistaken for Swiss. In Switzerland they were never sure where I was from."

"Why was that?" A glint of interest shown from Legge's eyes now.

"I've learned that the Pennsylvania Dutch dialect I grew up with is much like the German dialects of Switzerland."

The ambassador pushed his glasses down his nose and looked over the rims. "Mr. Schuller worked undercover in sting operations aimed at Nazi falsification of American passports. And he earned good reviews from his superiors."

Martin was glad Harrison hadn't mentioned the incident of insubordination in 1939 that got him transferred from the Office of the Chief Special Agent, and shipped to Buenos Aires.

The ambassador took off his glasses and set them on the desk beside the file. He looked at Legge. "So Mr. Schuller's been able to fool the Abwehr's agents, Colonel."

Legge snorted. "I've been told that Abwehr agents are pretty stupid, by and large." He stared at Martin again, his eyes narrowing. "If your work here takes you inside Germany, would you be able to fool the Gestapo?"

Martin's stomach fluttered. Why would he have to go inside Germany? "Yes, I could."

Legge regarded him for several seconds before nodding. "I hope so, for your sake. We may not be at war yet, but that doesn't mean they wouldn't shoot one of our agents if they caught him spying inside Germany."

Martin nodded but said nothing. There was a big difference between catching spies, and becoming one himself.

Harrison and Legge shared a look, and the ambassador nodded once.

Legge cleared his throat. "When I cabled Bill Donovan last week, I'd hoped he'd send someone with military experience—but I can see why he's placed his trust in you, Agent Schuller. I will, as well."

Martin waited in silence.

"Swiss Military Intelligence reached out to me on Thursday, asking our assistance in a delicate matter pertaining to Swiss national security. I'm not sure if you're aware, but Swiss Military Intelligence has only been in existence for a few years—they're inexperienced, understaffed, and underfunded. The situation we're about to discuss has stretched their resources."

Martin contemplated that. While America's Military Intelligence Division—MID—dated back almost sixty years, the United States was barely more experienced than the Swiss in covert operations. "Why us? Why not the British?"

Legge's lips pursed for a second. "While we are no longer officially neutral, we're still a non-belligerent nation. It's crucial to Swiss neutrality that any help they request should not come from one of the warring parties."

Martin nodded. "Understood."

"In recent weeks there has been a wave of violence against certain military figures connected with right-wing Swiss political organizations."

"So I read," Martin said. That much had been in the brief Babcock had left for him in the locker in Lisbon. What he didn't know was the connection to the murdered physicist.

The ambassador shifted in his seat. "Switzerland has a history of opening its arms to political refugees of all stripes—Russian anarchists and Bolsheviks especially—until recent years when right-wing elements here have persuaded their Assembly to restrict immigration. Last year, the Communist Party was outlawed. The Reds took their operations underground, of course. Over the last two months, several of those right-wing officers have been killed assassination-style, and their attackers have always left a painted hammer and sickle at the scene. You're probably not aware that there was another such attack last night—this time on a prominent banker in Zurich. Naturally, we're concerned."

Legge leaned forward. "The Swiss haven't been able to identify the criminals responsible. We kept tabs on the situation, of course, without interfering. Since there was no threat to the United States, MID saw no reason to share this with the COI—until last week. Because the Swiss asked for assistance, I contacted Bill Donovan."

Martin frowned. This didn't fit what Donovan had told him. "In Washington, I was told the mission concerned a physicist in Zurich, a college professor, who was shot in his office. The police found documents and paraphernalia linking it to the French Resistance."

Legge grunted and nodded. "The Swiss believe it's connected. Apparently this Dr. Rubenstein was working R&D for them. They won't say more."

So that's what I have to help find out.

Ambassador Harrison motioned toward Witherspoon. "Ron, explain your information for Mr. Schuller."

Witherspoon sat up straight, and his cheeks flushed. "Of course. My contacts in the Swiss Government say they're allowing the local police in Zurich, Bern, Basel, Fribourg, and so on to handle the individual investigations, while sharing information with FedPol—the Swiss Federal Police force, similar to our FBI. So far the only obvious connection is the Communist calling card—and until last night, that all of the victims, except Dr. Rubenstein, were members of the SVV."

"The SVV?" Martin asked.

"The *Schweizerischer Vaterlandischer Verband*," Witherspoon explained, taking an air of authority. "It's a far-right Nationalist organization founded after the last war, with the aim of ending immigration. It echoes the anti-Semitic language coming out of the German Nazi party, and it's made calls for close cooperation with Germany—even though its members include French-Swiss and Italian-Swiss as well as German-Swiss. Much of the top brass in the military belong to the SVV, including General Guisan, the head of the Army. Though they never attempt electoral politics, they've exerted a good deal of influence on government policy in recent years, as the ambassador said, due to the high position of many of the members. They have not been outlawed, unlike other pro-Nazi organizations. The SVV's membership is a closely-guarded secret, but my contacts in the Foreign Ministry know who the prominent ones are."

Martin listened in silence. On the surface, this reminded him of The Cowl, the secretive Fascist organization in France that had been busted four years earlier for bombing Socialist politicians, and blaming the communists—only here it wasn't left-wing figures being killed. And one other thing didn't connect, and he leaned forward with a slight scowl. "What about the murder of Dr. Rubenstein? Aside from his secret connection to the military, nothing else fits the pattern."

Witherspoon stiffened. "Yes, that incident made us question the theory."

"How so?"

"Dr. Rubenstein was shot by a Glock pistol, which is not a weapon favored by the Soviets, who tend to be the ones to arm Communist elements around the world. It's also not used by the French Resistance, though the police investigation has pointed the finger at them."

"Because of the French Resistance paraphernalia found at the scene," Martin said. He was already wondering who might have the capacity to fabricate those items.

"Yes. A secret ring worn by members of the Gaullist Resistance. Also a letter from the Resistance was found in the trash, asking for Dr. Rubenstein's assistance with 'technical issues.'"

Martin nodded, but said nothing.

Legge cleared his throat again. "The intelligence brief in Lisbon informed you that Dr. Rubenstein was once a pupil of Dr. Albert Einstein while he was a professor in Zurich. Also, Dr. Rubenstein taught a class on propulsion ten years ago that was taken by Wernher Von Braun. He's a top engineer for the Wehrmacht."

Martin took a deep breath, and looked up in thought. "So maybe the Germans were concerned that Dr. Rubenstein would provide the French Resistance with rockets that could be used against occupation forces?"

The ambassador spoke again. "Perhaps the Germans, perhaps right-wing elements in Switzerland—we're not sure. That's what we want you to find out. That, and if this is connected to the recent assassinations of Swiss officers."

"Understood," Martin said. He looked at Colonel Legge. "Where do I start?"

Legge chuckled. "Swiss Military Intelligence has given us identification papers for you to pass as a FedPol inspector named Max Schmidt. You'll also have a Swiss passport under the same name. We only need to add your photograph. You'll need to memorize the vital statistics." He looked at Martin with one brow arched, as if expecting confirmation.

Martin stared back at him. "I have experience."

Legge ignored his tone. "You'll be given a German-made Ford sedan, along with a book of gasoline rations, and four-thousand Swiss Francs in cash. They've also secured you an apartment in Bern, close to the train station, not too close to the embassy. I have the address and the key in my office."

"You may have the use of a spare office down the hall," Ambassador Harrison said. "Ron will give you the key, which also opens the back door of the embassy. We trust you'll use the back door."

"Of course," Martin replied.

"You'll have a secure phone line. Ron will provide you with more detailed intelligence to read through before you leave for Zurich. I'm sure you're eager to get started."

"Yes." Martin's whole body tingled in anticipation.

"Do you speak any French, Mr. Schuller?" Ron Witherspoon asked.

"No."

"Italian?"

"No."

"That could be a problem," Witherspoon said with a sigh. "Educated Swiss can speak all three languages. We'll have to see that you learn some, and quickly. Enough to pass, anyway."

Hardly my top priority right now. "Do FedPol inspectors dress plain-clothes, like American detectives?" Martin asked.

"Yes," Witherspoon replied. "The suit you're wearing will work, if we remove the American label and have a Swiss label sewn in its place. Same goes for the hat and tie. If you'll pardon me—even your undergarments and socks need to be from a Swiss store. And you'll need some European accessories. We'll make sure you have a Luger pistol, a Swiss watch instead of that Timex, and French cufflinks."

It had been a couple of years, but Martin remembered how to prepare for undercover work. Ron Witherspoon seemed to be enjoying this, though.

"What size shoe do you wear?"

"Eleven." Martin didn't remember the European equivalent.

"I'll have some delivered in an hour from a cobbler we trust." He sounded excited.

Martin suppressed his amusement. He nodded and stood. "Will you show me to my office?"

Witherspoon jumped from his seat and opened the door. "Right this way. And I'll take your coat, hat and tie. So the seamstress can get started on them."

Martin nodded to the ambassador and Colonel Legge, then followed Witherspoon out. In the hall, he removed his coat and his tie, and handed them to Witherspoon. The excitable fellow draped them over his left arm, and lead Martin to the spare office.

"There are files in the drawer that I've left for you—the additional intelligence the ambassador mentioned. If you need anything sensitive, my office is down the hall on the left, across from the ambassador's. Anything else you can get from Miss Overstreet."

"I was surprised that your secretary is an American, and not a local hire," Martin said. While it seemed that might be a good security measure for American embassies in Europe to implement, he wasn't aware that any had.

Witherspoon flushed, and Martin detected a nervous twitch in his eyes. "Miss Overstreet was recommended for the job. By a congressman. She's worked well for us."

Helps to have connections in high places. "Thanks." Martin closed the door and locked it.

5

Jason stepped off the elevator on the fourth floor and walked down the hall toward Amanda's desk.

"Hi there!" he said with a big smile. "Did you work your wiles on Mr. Schuller, or are you still free for lunch?"

Amanda gave him a conspiratorial look, and motioned for him to lean closer. "Mr. Schuller's locked himself in one of the spare offices all morning, ever since his meeting with the ambassador and Mr. Witherspoon," she said in a low voice.

"You don't say?" Jason replied, sitting on the corner of her desk. "What do you make of that?"

"Well, he's no businessman here for commercial reasons, that's for sure. I'll let you draw your own conclusions."

"Something top secret?" Jason grinned at the idea.

"All I'll say is there's been an awful lot of activity up here this morning." She got up and walked to a filing cabinet. "How was your morning?"

Jason shrugged. "The usual—processing visas. I got to speak some French, though."

"Oh?"

"Yeah. A Romanian couple with three kids. They walked a thousand miles to get here, following railroad lines at night. The husband and wife both spoke French."

Like most of the grunts in the embassy, Jason processed visa applications for foreign nationals wanting to get to the United States.

Sometimes these were temporary travel visas for Swiss businessmen. More often than not, though, the applicants were refugees, hoping to relocate permanently and escape war-torn Europe.

The businessmen almost always spoke to him in English, usually quite good English, and it made Jason a little embarrassed that their English was better than his German or French. The refugees rarely spoke English, but could usually get through a conversation in either German or French.

"So, are you coming to lunch with us?"

"Can't today," Amanda said without looking up from her filing. "I told you, it's been busy up here. Bring me back a pretzel, though?"

"Ok," Jason said, and walked back toward the elevator.

Jason exited the embassy with five other young men. He smiled and waved at Corporal Lawrence at the guard-stand, who replied with a nod and said "Have a nice lunch, sirs." The group turned right and walked up the street a short distance toward the bridge, laughing and chatting.

There was a Wurst stand on the next corner, where a street vendor sold sausages as a sandwich between warm rolls, with hot mustard. Jason liked the burn of the horseradish sweeping through his sinuses, so he ordered his bratwurst with extra mustard. He also ordered a pretzel for Amanda, but left the mustard off.

The conversation turned more serious as they strolled back toward the embassy, eating their sandwiches.

"How can you say President Roosevelt isn't one of the greatest presidents we've ever had?" Devon Wolcott said, giving Jason an incredulous look.

"I don't see what he's done that's so great," Jason said with a shrug.

"He's gotten us out of the Depression!" Devon's voice rose with indignation.

Jason shook his head. "No, the war in Europe got us out of the Depression. The president had nothing to do with it. Two years ago, we still had fifteen percent unemployment—and that was *seven years* after Roosevelt was elected. Since then, production of planes and tanks has gotten the factories hiring. The military draft hasn't hurt, either."

"How could he get elected three times if he's not a great president?" Devon pressed.

The truth was, Jason and most of the people he knew had wondered the same thing the year before, when FDR won a third term. "I don't think greatness has anything to do with popularity," Jason replied, echoing what his elders had said.

Jason had little experience with Democrats prior to joining the Foreign Service. He'd never met one before college. His parents, and the parents of all of his friends, universally despised the president.

"You Republicans are just bitter because your taxes went up." Devon countered.

Jason shrugged. "Who should have to pay seventy percent?"

"*You* don't pay seventy percent," Brad Harris pointed out.

Jason scowled. "Well, no—but my father does."

"You don't live with your parents anymore, Bachman."

Jason let that one go. "If Roosevelt's such a great president, why does the Supreme Court keep striking down his programs?"

"Because they're a bunch of rich old Republicans, that's why," Devon said, with a tone that suggested it was the most obvious thing in the world.

Jason shook his head and smiled. "Maybe we should stop talking politics."

They rounded the corner, and the white façade of the U.S. Embassy with its geranium flowerboxes welcomed them.

A black Ford sedan pulled out of the parking lot south of the building, its polished hood shining in the sunlight, and accelerated past the embassy. Jason recognized the face behind the steering wheel.

"That's Mr. Schuller," he said, more to himself than anyone else.

"Who's that?" Devon asked.

Jason's cheeks flushed, and he covered his embarrassment by waving it off. "Just someone who met with the ambassador this morning."

He made a mental note to share this with Amanda later.

Martin drove out of Bern and took the highway toward Zurich. The Swiss highway system, like the Swiss railway system, was oriented as spokes all centering on Zurich, the largest city and financial center of the country. It wasn't difficult to find his way. The highway wound northeast from Bern through a hilly country of green pastures and tidy little villages, with the imposing presence of the giant snow-capped Jungfrau always visible in the distance to his right.

Nervous excitement filled him. He was glad to be back doing undercover work, but this was different.

Concerned that Nazis and Bolsheviks were using forged U.S. passports to operate inside the United States—not only for spying, but also for recruiting Americans to their causes—the State Department used its authority to issue passports to put its Office of the Chief Special Agent to work breaking up the rings. Using agents fluent in German and Russian, it infiltrated the clandestine organizations.

It was dangerous work, and Martin always felt nervous apprehension whenever he started a new assignment—but this task was different. He was working in unfamiliar territory, taking on an unfamiliar role.

He was also alone. No Joe Hansen as back-up.

He'd rehearsed all morning the role of Swiss Federal Police inspector, how he would act, how he would speak, what questions he would ask. He didn't want to come off as Dick Tracy. He thought of Inspector Javert from *Les Miserables*, and decided to take elements of his aloof coldness, but not to that extreme.

After reading through all of the intelligence that Ron Witherspoon had left for him, Martin doubted the French Resistance had anything to do with Dr. Rubenstein's death. There was no direct evidence that the Resistance had operations in Switzerland, though they certainly had sympathizers, especially among the left-leaning youth. So if that were a deliberate red herring, who planted it?

The letter could have been forged by almost anyone, and placed on the scene by the killers. The insignia ring was more perplexing—few outside of the Gaullist Resistance had access to one.

But... Resistance operatives who fell into the hands of the Gestapo would have been stripped of any paraphernalia they had on them. Might the Gestapo have sent the clues to the killers? And if so, to what purpose? That hypothesis lacked motive.

At least, no motive yet.

6

Zurich

Sonia Rubenstein scowled in response to the loud knock at the door, and set down the flask of organic acids. She tugged a loose strand of black hair away from her face and tucked it behind an ear, wiped a tear from her eye, then marched to the lab door and threw it open.

A tall man in a dark blue suit stood in the hall, his blond hair visible below the rim of his hat, which he removed when she opened the door. He had a handsome square face with a prominent brow and square jaw line.

"Miss Sonia Rubenstein?"

"Yes."

"I am Inspector Max Schmidt. I'm here to speak to you about your father."

Another one? This one was young, early thirties, and his speech carried a tiny accent. He was not from Zurich, but she couldn't place the accent. Perhaps Bern or Luzern?

"I have already spoken to Inspector Frisch." *The condescending bigot.* Her lips pursed.

"Inspector Frisch is with the Zurich police. I'm FedPol."

Her heart did a double beat. "Why is FedPol interested in my father's murder?"

"May I come in, please?"

She hesitated a second, irritated at the non-answer, then stood aside. He closed the door behind him.

"My condolences at the death of your father."

Sonia was silent, and stared at the inspector, preparing for the hostility she knew was coming.

"You lived with your father, correct?"

"Yes."

"And your mother?"

Her frown deepened. "My mother died nine years ago."

"I'm sorry to hear that."

Are you? She made no reply.

"You're a student?"

"A doctoral candidate," Sonia replied, emphasizing the words.

"What do you know of your father's work?"

"Very little."

"But he worked here at the Polytechnic. And you lived with him."

"Yes."

"Wouldn't you know what he was working on?"

Her lips tightened. "My father was a physicist. I'm a chemist."

"Did he ever discuss his work at home, over dinner perhaps?"

"Rarely."

"Did he ever bring work home with him?"

"Occasionally."

Martin regarded Sonia Rubenstein for a moment. Everything about her oozed hostility. Her shoulders were squared, her narrow chin was raised and thrust forward, her black eyebrows bunched, and those dark eyes could burn a hole through him.

"Have I done something to offend you, Miss Rubenstein?"

"Not yet."

He raised an eyebrow. "But you expect me to?"

Her eyes narrowed, and her voice became bitter. "Yes. My father was Jewish, and so am I. But my father was a great scholar, a great scientist, and a respected professor. His murder deserves better than a perfunctory investigation that ends as soon as it begins."

"I'm still investigating," Martin said. He turned away from her and walked toward the stainless steel table where a flask of orange liquid sat a foot from the Bunsen burner. "What are you working with here?" He turned around to face her.

"Vitamin K. The components of it, that is."

"Vitamins, eh?"

She seemed to relax a little. "Yes. Dr. Karrer won the Nobel Prize in Chemistry four years ago for his work on the components of Vitamins A, C, and B2. I work with him."

Martin nodded. "Your father also studied under a Nobel laureate at this very institute, didn't he?"

Sonia said nothing, and her posture stiffened again.

"Were you aware that your father studied under Dr. Albert Einstein in 1909?"

"Yes."

"Are you familiar with the name Wernher von Braun?"

A puzzled look came to Sonia's face. "The name sounds familiar."

"He's from Germany. He was a student in a propulsion class your father taught ten years ago."

She nodded, silent.

"Von Braun is now a lead scientist in the Third Reich's development program."

A sharp laugh came from her mouth. "And you think my father had anything to do with *that*? You police really are stupid. He would never have worked with Nazi scientists! They pervert science in the name of their twisted ideology. It is unthinkable."

"Would he have worked with the French Resistance?"

"That arrogant Inspector Frisch already asked me that."

"And?"

"I don't know why the police would think that."

Martin paused a moment, thoughtful. "Why did you call Inspector Frisch arrogant?"

Sonia stiffened further, and her chin rose higher. "He acted as if he already knew all the answers. He treated me like a stupid girl—a stupid Jewish girl, beneath his dignity to have to interview. He was brusque and condescending. And I never heard from him again. I called the police several times to ask about my father's case, and they will only say they are still investigating. But they haven't done anything since the first day."

Although she was hostile and evasive, Martin didn't get the feeling she was lying. Her gaze was steady, and there was no tell-tale sweat on her brow or lip. He could trust what she said, the little there was.

She stared at him for a moment, her dark eyes seeming to bore deep. "Why are you here, Inspector Schmidt?"

"To find out who killed your father, and why."

"You aren't interested in justice for my father. What is the reason for these questions?"

He couldn't tell her the real reason.

"I want you to leave," she said, marching to the door and throwing it open. "Good day."

Martin nodded without a word, put his hat on, and closed the door.

Martin took the tram the short distance to the city center across the river, and brooded. That hadn't gone as well as he would have liked. He felt uncomfortable with this role. He had little experience with interrogation, and it didn't come naturally.

He grew more nervous thinking about his next task, but he sat upright and still on the tram, his outward appearance calm. He rarely suffered from lack of confidence, but he felt less prepared than he would have liked.

It was one thing to impersonate a Federal Police inspector to a civilian, but quite another to do it to the police.

He stepped off the tram at Bahnhofstrasse, and walked a few blocks to the police station. He showed his FedPol identification, and asked to see Inspector Frisch.

Several minutes later, he was shown into an office. A brass name-plate on the desk read "Inspector Georg Frisch." A thin man with brown hair and brown mustache stood behind the desk, looking annoyed.

"Inspector Max Schmidt, FedPol," Martin said, extending his hand.

Inspector Frisch gave it a perfunctory shake. "What is it that FedPol wants, Inspector Schmidt?"

"I'd like to ask about the investigation into the killing of Dr. Fritz Rubenstein at the Polytechnic Institute."

Inspector Frisch's scowl deepened. "That is my case. What interest does FedPol have in it?"

Martin ignored the question. "Tell me what you found when you arrived at Dr. Rubenstein's office."

"It is all in my report."

"Of course. And I trust you'll provide me with a copy of it. But first, please explain to me what you found."

Inspector Frisch stood straight, as if at attention. "The room had been ransacked. Drawers had been emptied, papers and folders were scattered on the floor. Cabinets and rubbish cans had been knocked over. The deceased lay on his back on the floor behind the desk, shot twice in the chest. We found no fingerprints anywhere in the office other than the deceased's own. On the floor we found a ring with a French Resistance insignia inside. In the rubbish can was a letter from the French Resistance, asking for 'technical assistance.'"

Martin pretended to jot down notes. "And what of the murder weapon?"

"None has been found," Frisch said. "Given the scarcity of clues, I doubt one ever will be."

"But you were able to identify the make of the gun, were you not?"

"Yes, of course. It was a 9mm Glock pistol."

"Odd weapon for the French Resistance, wouldn't you say?" Martin asked.

Frisch tensed. "Who knows what weapons those terrorists use?"

"What did you do after collecting evidence from the scene?"

"We interviewed the custodial staff, and the professors who had offices in the same hall, but none of them had seen anything unusual."

"Did you speak with anyone else?"

"Yes, I interviewed the deceased's daughter."

"Sonia Rubenstein?"

Frisch's green eyes narrowed. "Yes."

"What did you learn from Miss Rubenstein?"

Frisch's long face took on a haughty look. "She claimed to know nothing."

"What did you do after that?"

"What more could we do? There is little evidence, no witnesses. It is a dead-end."

"Then, what conclusions did you draw from the evidence, Inspector?" Martin asked.

"That unknown French underground operatives requested assistance from the physicist, were denied that assistance, and killed him in retaliation."

Martin looked the inspector hard in the eye. "That is a big assumption given the 'scarcity of clues,' as you put it."

Frisch smirked. "Did you know, Inspector Schmidt, that Sonia Rubenstein is part of a secretive leftist group with ties to the Resistance in France?"

Martin was taken aback. "Oh?"

A satisfied smile spread across Frisch's lips. "Yes. If the Resistance were looking for a physicist to provide technical assistance, they had a channel to reach Dr. Rubenstein. We've had the group under surveillance, but they have not met since the attack. I can provide you with a list of names, though we haven't identified all of them. Some of the members are Russians, of course."

Martin made a mental note to find out if Inspector Georg Frisch was a member of the SVV. He talked like one.

"Yes, I would appreciate that list. Thank you. You said you've had the group under surveillance—do you have photographs?"

"Of course. And complete dossiers."

"I would appreciate copies of those as well."

"I will get them for you right away." Frisch stuck his head into the hallway and called to the sergeant. "Karl! Bring Inspector Schmidt a list of the known members of the underground group in The Niederdorf, with their dossiers."

"Of course, Inspector."

Frisch turned back to Martin with a stiff smile. "Why don't you wait out front while Sergeant Altmann gets that list for you? You'll be more comfortable there. Unless there's anything else you want?"

"No, thank you." Martin gave Frisch's hand a stiff, formal shake, and walked toward the lobby.

**

Frisch closed his door as soon as the FedPol inspector disappeared around the corner. He picked up his phone receiver, and gave a number to the operator.

"Zurischer Kredit," the voice of a receptionist said.

"Mr. Zubler, please."

"Mr. Zubler is unavailable at the moment."

"He'll take my call. This is Inspector Georg Frisch."

"One moment please, Inspector."

Frisch's fingers drummed on his desk.

Ernst Zubler's voice was sharp with irritation. "I've asked you not to call me at the bank. What is the purpose of this call?"

"I've just had a visit from a Federal Police inspector, looking into the killing of that Jewish professor."

"Federal police?"

"Yes, FedPol damn it! What am I to do?"

"Nothing. Act as you normally would with a Federal inspector. I shall take care of this. What was his name?"

"Max Schmidt."

"Don't worry," Zubler said. "I shall take care of this Inspector Max Schmidt. He will be dealt with."

7

Heidelberg, Württemberg, Germany

"More coffee, miss?"

This was the fourth time in a half-hour that the waiter had come to Ilsa Schuber's outside table and asked her that. This time, she smiled and said, "Yes, thank you, Axel."

Axel bowed, and hurried away. He came back a moment later with a steaming cup of ersatz coffee. "Anything more, miss?"

Ilsa was used to the waiter's over-attentiveness. She knew she looked like she'd stepped out of a propaganda poster. Her light blond hair was thick and wavy, and her blue eyes were large. She was tall and willowy, with long slender arms and legs. Her face was long and delicate, with a slender chin tapering to a fine point. At twenty-one, her skin was flawless and white. She was by any measure a beautiful young woman.

"No thank you Axel, this will be fine." She pretended to look at the large book she held open. She returned her gaze to the troop of Hitler Youth that marched across the cobblestoned square, wearing tan shirts and light brown shorts, with red armbands displaying black swastikas. Their shiny black boots clacked on the stones and echoed around the square.

The café at the corner of the Marktplatz in the old quarter was her regular mid-afternoon resting place, after her last class. It was a moderate distance from the university buildings, and there were other cafés closer, but she liked this one for the unparalleled view of the square. She never complained that they no longer served real coffee due to war shortages, and made ersatz from ground chicory.

The goose-stepping teenagers across the square illustrated the contrasts in this ancient university town, which boasted one of the most respected institutions of learning and culture in all of Europe—and also one of the most enthusiastically pro-Nazi populations in Germany. Seeing the intense stares on the handsome young faces brought an ache to Ilsa's heart.

The rumble of motors echoed off of the wooded hills behind the town, and steadily grew louder. Ilsa peered to the right and spotted a convoy of dark green Daimler-Benz trucks with brown canvas covers bouncing down from the direction of the Bergstrasse. They rumbled past, then turned at the far end of the square and stopped in front of the Rathaus.

The five-story Rathaus was one of the finest examples of baroque architecture in western Germany, and its stately appearance hadn't changed in almost three centuries—except for the giant red flag with the black swastika that hung from its roof.

Soldiers in khaki uniforms scrambled out the backs of the trucks, stopping to stretch before milling around. A few went into the Rathaus, but most stood near the trucks in small clumps.

Ilsa counted eighteen trucks. There seemed to be about ten soldiers from each, so a quick estimate told her this was two companies.

She closed her book and stood, laid two coins on the table, and stepped into the sun-lit square. She strolled across, moving generally in the direction she would go to get back to the university, but making sure she passed in front of the nearest group of soldiers.

Glancing at them from the corner of her eye, she made sure they were watching, then stopped and bent over to straighten her stockings.

Several of the troops whistled, and she stood and flashed them a smile. They returned eager smiles of their own.

She sauntered over to a man with sergeant's stripes on his shoulder. He wasn't much taller than she, a balding young man of about twenty-five, whose hairline sat all the way back at the crown of his head. His dark hair was buzzed short, but his green eyes were bright, and his long face had a nice tan. His lips were terribly thin, but Ilsa supposed he wasn't unattractive. She could fake it.

"Good day, gentlemen," she said, locking eyes with the sergeant.

"Good day, miss!" the sergeant replied with a toothy grin.

"Are you staying in Heidelberg long? Or passing through?" She opened her eyes wide in a slightly exaggerated quizzical expression.

"We're passing through, miss, stopping for a rest and a chance for some of the boys to relieve themselves—begging your pardon, miss!"

She smiled at the sergeant. "That's too bad. We won't have the chance to become acquainted then, will we?" She started to turn away.

"We have a little time, miss. You don't have to run off yet."

Ilsa turned back, and let a slight smile come to one corner of her mouth. "But you haven't introduced yourself to me, sergeant."

"Oh! I beg your pardon, miss. I'm Anton Thurau." He spoke with a northern accent—Hannover or Braunschweig, she guessed.

"My name's Ilsa."

"I'm pleased to meet you, Miss Ilsa."

"Where are you from, Sgt. Thurau?"

"Hildesheim, miss. Near Hannover."

She smiled at her own accuracy. "Have you been in the army long?"

"Five years, miss."

"Then you've probably seen a lot of action, haven't you? How exciting!"

"We're not combat troops, Miss Ilsa," Sgt. Thurau explained. "But we have been sent in with the invasion forces to secure the cities and restore order behind the front lines."

"Oh, that sounds dangerous!" Ilsa feigned concern.

"It can be sometimes."

"Where have you been?"

"I was in the invasion of The Netherlands, and was stationed there a while. Then after a bit they sent us up to Denmark. We've been back in the Fatherland for a while now. We've just come from a tour in Frankfurt."

"Are you staying in Germany?"

"No, they need us in France, I'm afraid."

"Oh." she faked a slight frown. Of course she knew that—what other reason would a large caravan of army trucks have for going south down the Bergstrasse? It was the best route from Frankfurt toward the French border. "Is that where you're going tonight?"

"I'm afraid so. We're due in Strasburg before nightfall, and then tomorrow we're going west to Reims. Do you know where that is, Miss Ilsa?"

She gave him a sweet smile. "My family visited Reims on holiday when I was a little girl. It has an amazing cathedral." She was telling the truth.

"I didn't know that."

Ilsa wasn't shocked that the sergeant hadn't heard of one of the most famous pieces of gothic medieval architecture in all of Europe. She forced herself to keep smiling. "I'm afraid Reims is awfully far away."

"It's over four-hundred kilometers from here, Miss Ilsa."

She knew that, too, but she let the sergeant take the role of the expert. "Is that too far for a visit?"

A surprised look came to his eyes, and his grin widened. "Yes, I'm afraid it is too far for me to visit on my days off. But you could write to me."

She had to smile at his eagerness. "Yes, of course I'll write to you. You'll give me the address?"

His face lit up. "Wait right here!" he practically bounced to the back of one of the nearby trucks, reached inside, and removed a piece of paper and a pencil. He scribbled furiously for a moment, then sprinted back to her.

An officer blew a whistle. "Load up!"

Sgt. Thurau thrust the paper at her with a breathless grin. "You can write to me here, Miss Ilsa. I promise to write you back right away."

Ilsa read the address, then folded the paper and gave him a dazzling smile. "Thank you, Sergeant. It's been so lovely talking to you. Be careful in France." She slipped the folded paper into her book, and turned to walk away.

"Good bye, Miss Ilsa!" he waved, then scrambled into the back of the truck.

She walked to the corner of the Marktplatz, and waited while the rumbling trucks drove past, turning south toward Baden. As the fifth truck roared past, Anton Thurau grinned and waved. She smiled and waved back.

While she watched the caravan roll past, a tall blond man in the black uniform of an SS officer appeared beside her and stood watching the trucks as well. Or pretended to watch them.

Ilsa only glanced at him, and pretended to be interested in the passing trucks.

"That was nice of you to chat with our brave soldiers," the officer said in a deep voice.

Ilsa turned to see the tall officer staring at her with an intensity that made her uncomfortable. His collar bore the twin silver lightning bolts and four silver pips of a *Sturmbannfuhrer*—Storm Troop Leader—the rank of SS Major.

"Oh! Thank you, sir."

"I'm sure our troops appreciate the attention of a beautiful German girl before they leave the Fatherland for occupied territory. You must be very patriotic."

Ilsa couldn't tell if the officer was being complimentary or sarcastic. His face lacked expression, except for the intensity of his pale blue eyes. She gave him a faint smile and a slight nod.

He continued to stare at her for several seconds as the last of the trucks drove away. Then he clicked his heels together, gave a sharp nod, and extended his right hand. "I am Major Volger."

She took his hand with her fingers only, and allowed him to kiss it.

"And you are?"

"I'm Ilsa." She realized he would be more suspicious if she didn't give a surname. "Ilsa Schmidt," she lied.

"Be careful, Miss Schmidt."

She gave him a quizzical look.

"Don't get run over crossing the square."

"Oh, yes—I'll be careful. Thank you." She looked down the street, which was devoid of vehicles, and hurried across. She glanced over her shoulder when she reached the other side; Volger was watching her. She gave him a nod and hurried away.

Ilsa walked down a side street, checking occasionally that no one was following her. She had turned several corners, just in case—but she saw no one behind her, so she hurried on.

She came to a bakery on the next corner, and went inside. The shelves sat half-bare behind the glass, thanks to the rationing. The only one there was the plump woman behind the counter, her blond hair streaked with gray and pulled back in a bun. "May I help you, Miss Schuber?"

"I'd like some Challah please, Mrs. Lange." Ilsa always found it ironic that the secret password was the name of a Jewish bread that could no longer be found in German bakeries.

The plump woman nodded, and hurried toward the kitchen door, holding it open for Ilsa. "Günter! We have a request for some Challah," she called, then closed the door behind Ilsa.

A tall, thin man wearing a dirty apron nodded. "Good day to you, Ilsa. What is it?"

"I need to get a message to Emmantaler."

Günter nodded toward a desk along the far wall, and she sat down and composed a paragraph.

Two flocks of geese flying south for the winter turned west
at Strasburg, and roosted at the cathedral in Reims.

She paused and consulted the address outside Reims that Sgt. Thurau had given her, and concluded her message. She folded the paper into quarters, and gave it to Günter. The baker walked to the back door and stepped into the alley, where a stocky man in a brown jacket swept flour dust out the back of the delivery truck.

"We have a last-minute delivery for Emmantaler," the baker said, handing the paper to his driver.

The driver slipped the paper into the inside pocket of his jacket. "I'll see that it's delivered as soon as possible." He jumped down from the truck and closed the doors, then climbed into the front and started the engine.

Günter stepped back into the kitchen. "The delivery is on its way."

"Thank you, Günter."

She went back through the store, waved to Günter's wife, and slipped out.

8

Zurich

"This is Dr. Rubenstein's office, Inspector," the dean said, unlocking a door and stepping aside.

Martin noted that the room had been cleaned; the papers put into neat piles, the furniture set upright. "Were Dr. Rubenstein's files put back together?"

"Yes, sir. As soon as Inspector Frisch told us he was finished with everything here, he gave us permission to clean it up. I came in personally with two other professors to put things back together as best we could."

"Did you remove anything?" Martin asked, his eyes narrowing into a stern stare.

The dean looked startled. "No. I mean, I'm sure we didn't remove anything. Except for the crumpled papers, that is, which we assumed had come from the rubbish can."

"Thank you. I'll have a look around." He closed the door and left the dean outside.

Martin walked to the largest filing cabinet and opened the top drawer. He went through each file, looking at each piece of paper. It was painstaking, but he took his time and was thorough.

After a few minutes he took out his miniature 35mm camera and snapped a photo of a document describing propulsion systems. From time to time he took more photos.

After the filing cabinet he moved on to the professor's desk drawers, and finally to the small filing cabinet beside the desk. When he was satisfied he had found everything of value, he hid his camera back inside his jacket.

He glanced at the clock. Two hours had passed, and it was now quarter after five. He put his hat on, stepped into the hall, closed the door, and hurried toward the exit.

Sonia Rubenstein walked out of the science building shortly after five-thirty, and the tall figure of the FedPol inspector approached her. She turned her gaze ahead and quickened her step.

"Miss Rubenstein! A word please," he called after her. She stopped and turned toward him with an inpatient stare. The late afternoon shadows stretched across the sidewalk, and she clutched her shawl tighter around her shoulders, against the coolness of the fall evening.

"Yes, Inspector?"

"Miss Rubenstein, was your father working for the French Resistance?"

She scowled. "As I told you earlier, I doubt it, Inspector."

"You doubt it? Wouldn't you know?"

This inspector was going to be a problem. "My father didn't discuss his work with me, as I told you. But I have no reason to suspect that he was working with, or for, anyone in France, Resistance or otherwise."

"But you know people in the French Resistance, I've been told. Did you put them in contact with your father?"

Icy fingers seemed to grip her heart. Her face flushed, and her tone came out sharp. "Who told you I know people in the Resistance? That Inspector Frisch?"

"You didn't answer my question, Miss."

"Don't believe everything Inspector Frisch tells you. I know no one in France."

"Do you deny being a member of a group that has ties to the French Resistance?"

Yes, this inspector was definitely going to be a problem.

She was silent for several seconds, but her expression relaxed. Martin thought how much more attractive it made her when she didn't scowl or frown.

She stared directly into his eyes. "Universities are centers of learning and culture, two things Fascists fear most. In Zurich we are blessed with two such institutions—the University, and the Polytechnic Institute. There are many people at these institutions who are alarmed at the way Fascism has marched across Europe, and I do not deny being one of those people. So was my father. We are determined to keep learning, culture, and freedom alive in Switzerland."

"But you are also part of an organized group that meets at the Café Alden, in the Niederdorf district."

Her silence was her only answer.

"Are there any Communists in this group, Miss Rubenstein?"

She smirked. "Communists fear learning as much as the Fascists do, Inspector."

That was a partial truth, meant to dissuade him. "Do you know any Communists, Miss Rubenstein?"

Her dark eyes narrowed and her lips grew tight. "Am I under investigation, Inspector? Do you suspect me of any wrongdoing?"

"No."

"Then I do not wish to answer any more of your questions. Good evening." She stomped away.

**

It was a mile to the apartment she had shared with her father, but Sonia rushed home and made the walk in twenty minutes. As soon as she got inside and put her books on the table, she marched straight to the telephone on her father's desk. She gave the operator a number, and drummed her fingers while the line rang.

"Hostel," a middle-aged female voice answered.

"I need to speak with Elena Krasnakovich, one of your residents. Is she available, please?"

"Let me see if she's in."

Sonia heard the receiver come down on a hard surface, then silence. She paced for more than four minutes while she waited. Finally, a young female voice said, "Yes, this is Elena Krasnakovich."

"Elena, this is Sonia. I'm sorry to call you, but you're the only one with access to a telephone." Her voice was breathless.

"Is something wrong?"

"Perhaps. A Federal Police inspector asked me about the group. I didn't tell him anything. He knows we meet at the Café Alden, so how much more might he know? He says he's investigating the murder of my father, but I get the feeling he's after much more."

"You think he's a Fascist pig?" Elena asked, her voice full of alarm.

"Perhaps. I don't know. Until we find out, we need to find another meeting place. The Alden might not be safe."

"But our next meeting is tomorrow evening."

"I know. Another café? Can you arrange it?"

"Yes, I think so. You want me to contact the others?"

"Please. Then send me a note at the lab. Also, I think Franz should know about this. He should come to our meeting tomorrow if he's able. Can you reach him?"

"I can try."

"Do your best. I'd try to reach him myself, but you…" she let her voice trail off.

"Yes."

"Thank you, Elena. I'll see you tomorrow." She hung up the receiver.

Bern

Martin went to Ron Witherspoon's office the moment he arrived back at the embassy that evening. The information officer was waiting to hear from him.

"Is there any way we can have their phone lines tapped?" Martin asked after showing him the list of student "leftists" that Inspector Frisch gave him.

Witherspoon shook his head. "Only if you can place the wiretap yourself. There's no way I could justify it to the Swiss authorities."

"The police are already keeping tabs on these kids, according to the inspector…" Martin let his voice trail off, and he leaned back in his chair. "But I don't trust Inspector Frisch. He has an agenda, I just don't know what it is."

"I'll see what I can find out," Witherspoon offered. "I'll go through official Swiss channels, but I've also got a couple of contacts at the German embassy that I could ask, to see if we strike gold."

Martin scowled. "Abwehr officers?"

Witherspoon shrugged. "Not officially. Contrary to Colonel Legge's opinion of them, they aren't stupid. The agents they send into Britain and the United States have been poorly trained." He leaned forward, and a slight smile came to his lips. "What makes them useful to us is they're all career military types, who distrust the Nazis about as much as we do. They're patriotic, but they're no more Nazi than you and I."

Martin frowned. "I thought the Fuhrer always put loyal Nazis in important positions."

"He does, by and large—except for the military. He can't afford to. He needs good officers, and he can't apply a political litmus test and still get the best officers. The Wehrmacht is pretty well free of political appointees—other than Himmler's SS. It's as thoroughly Nazi as you can get. But not the rest of the military—its officer corps is still dominated by the old aristocracy, particularly the Prussian aristocracy, and that's the one segment of German society that has proven most impervious to Nazi ideology. The Abwehr is part of the Wehrmacht, and like the rest of the military they remain ideology-free."

"So they could be turned into double-agents."

"I don't see why not," Ron said. This seemed to excite him.

Martin stood. "I think my next step is to trail Sonia Rubenstein, and see if she leads me to this anti-Nazi group. I'll regroup with you in the morning."

"I'm off to a cocktail party at the Swedish embassy. I should be able to speak to my German contacts there. Good night, Schuller."

9

Frankfurt am Main, Hesse, Germany

The sky was nearly dark when the black Mercedes sedan eased down the gravel alley and stopped in front of a large brick garage. Rudolph Volger stepped out of the vehicle and opened the doors, then drove into an empty parking bay.

He closed the doors, removed his gloves and consulted his watch. Twenty past six. He'd told his wife he wouldn't be home until after seven o'clock. He unlocked a door in the side wall, and mounted the stairs on the other side.

There was light under the door at the top of the stairs. Volger opened it without knocking.

A black-haired youth lay on his stomach across the bed in the middle of the small garret, propped up on his elbows, reading a comic book. He looked up when Volger entered. "Good evening, Major." There was a distance in his brown eyes.

"Good evening, Michael."

He set his hat on top of the dresser and strolled to the window, which had the heavy black-out curtains drawn. He peeked between them toward the house. A full one hundred meters of manicured lawn and gardens stretched between here and the kitchen door, so he was confident his early arrival would not be noticed. He turned toward the youth still lying in the same place.

"Has Cook brought you your supper yet?"

"No, sir," Michael replied, his eyes wary.

"Good." Volger unbuttoned his black uniform coat. "Take off your clothes."

Michael stood and disrobed without a word, first pulling off his shirt, then dropping his trousers and boxer shorts. Finally he removed his socks, then stood and waited.

Volger unbuttoned his shirt, and ran his eyes up and down the seventeen-year-old's body. He was slender, but had good definition and smooth skin, and a circumcised penis. Michael stood still, expressionless.

Once he had removed all of his own clothes, Volger stepped around behind Michael and pressed against him. He rubbed his erection on the soft skin at the top of the boy's buttocks. He ran his hands down the boy's chest and belly, to his groin. He kissed Michael's ear and down the side of his neck.

After a minute of caressing, Volger pushed the boy onto the bed face-down and spread his legs. He spit several times, and penetrated.

Michael's hands clenched around the bed-cover. He made no sound.

Once Volger had finished, he lifted his weight off Michael. The boy continued to lie motionless.

"That was very good, Michael," Volger said from the dresser, wiping his hands on a ragged towel. He tossed the towel to the youth, who got up and scrambled into the shadow of a corner to clean himself up.

Volger plopped onto the small bed, propped himself up on a pillow, and beckoned Michael to join him. "Come, come—lie with me."

Michael lay on the bed beside Volger, who put an arm around his shoulder and hugged him to his chest. He kissed the boy's forehead, and ran his fingers affectionately through the tight black curls on his head. He kissed the end of the boy's nose, and caressed his cheek, then nudged the boy's head onto his shoulder. He put both arms around Michael and held him close.

"I was in Heidelberg today," Volger said, stroking Michael's back. "A beautiful town. I should take you there when the war is over. It's south of the state boundary, but I was scouting the area for Colonel Schneider. Once we finish relocating the Jews of Hesse, we shall continue south down the Bergstrasse."

Michael barely listened to the rest. As often happened when Major Volger spoke of deporting Jews to Dachau, Michael's mind drifted back to a day in the spring of 1940 when several soldiers had come to their house in Frankfurt am Main, shouting orders to pack their bags.

The deportations of Frankfurt's Jews had begun a few weeks before, and at first they hardly believed it was happening—concentration camps were where the regime sent criminals, Communists, and homosexuals, not law-abiding Jews. Then they had all wondered how long it would be until their turn arrived. Now it had.

His father, Simon Kaim, had run into his bedroom, and returned holding up the Iron Cross that he'd received from the Kaiser himself during the last war. "Is this how the Reich treats those who have served the Fatherland?" he shouted at the soldiers.

The house fell silent. Michael huddled in a corner with his mother, his two older brothers, and his older sister, barely breathing. The soldiers said nothing, and looked down. Only the SS officer watching at the door moved. He stepped into the center of the room, an amused smile on his face. He glanced at Michael, and their eyes locked for a second before Major Volger turned back to Simon.

"You and your family may stay—for now." As he turned to leave, he gave fifteen-year-old Michael a lascivious look.

Six months passed, and it seemed that the atmosphere in the Kaim home was so thick with tension it could be sliced like bread. One by one, every Jewish family they knew was deported to Dachau. By late fall 1940, Michael's class at the Jewish high school was nearly empty.

His father tried to get them out of the country, but exit visas were now forbidden to Jews. At the dinner table, Michael's parents agonized over whether or not to seek out smugglers—but the smugglers wouldn't risk taking out more than one or two at a time, and the cost was too much for them to afford.

Finally, on a cold night in December 1940, Major Volger had returned with a squadron of soldiers. They were given twenty minutes to pack a single suit-case apiece. As they were escorted from the house at gun-point, Volger ordered one of his men to hold Michael back.

Berthe Kaim shrieked and cried, and the soldiers struck her across the face several times until she fell into silent whimpering.

When Simon Kaim protested at the treatment of his wife, a soldier struck him on the head with the butt of a rifle, knocking him down, and then tugged him back to his feet.

"What are you going to do to my son?" he shouted at the soldiers, but they knocked him on the side of the head again with a rifle butt and pushed him down the street.

Michael's family marched away at gun-point, shaking with fear. Then the soldier holding him dragged him to a black Mercedes and shoved him into the back seat.

He was driven to the garage behind Major Volger's house. The major pulled out his pistol and ordered him up the stairs.

Michael closed his eyes at the memory. The major locked the door, checked that the heavy curtains were drawn across the tiny window, then removed his hat and gloves and set them on the bedside table. He turned to Michael and removed his belt and coat, then unzipped his pants. Michael's stomach had fallen into the pit of his belly. Volger ordered the then-sixteen-year old to strip naked, and when Michael refused, he chased him into a corner and ripped his clothes off. Volger slapped him across the face several times as he struggled, then knocked him hard on the back of the head. Michael wished later he'd blacked out, but he hadn't. Volger forced him down onto the bed face-first, beating him across the back. He clamped a hand over Michael's mouth as he violated him.

For the last nine months, this had been Michael's lot. He cleaned the garage and waxed the cars, and whenever the major was in the mood he used Michael's ass. In exchange, Michael was fed and clothed, did not wear the yellow Star of David, and was safe from deportation to the camps.

If he kept quiet and did as he was told, he wasn't beaten, and the major brought him American comic books. But on the inside he burned.

"Michael? Have you been listening to me?"

Michael looked up to see Volger's face inches away, scowling down at him.

"I'm sorry, Major. What did you say?"

"I asked if you would like to go on holiday with me this fall, the two of us, to a nice hotel in the Alps. You didn't answer."

"I'm sorry, Major. I think I dozed off. I've been very tired this evening."

Volger slapped him on the cheek, just hard enough to make a sound without really stinging. "See that you don't ignore me again."

He sat up, pushing the boy away. He stood with his back to the bed and tugged his trousers on. He dressed with his back to Michael, then strode to the dresser to retrieve his hat, and stomped out.

The lock creaked from Volger's key, followed by the heavy thud of the major's boots down the stairs. Michael wondered if Cook was going to be allowed to bring him dinner. He'd probably go hungry this evening.

He got dressed and returned to his comic book.

Louisa Volger was coming down the stairs, dressed in a blue evening gown, when Rudolph strode into the central hall. Her light brown hair was pulled back into a stylish knot of braids.

"Good evening, my dear," Rudolph said, giving his wife a kiss on the cheek.

"Good evening." Louisa's smile was polite, cool.

The butler walked in from the dining room, where he had been setting the table. "Welcome home, sir," he said, taking Volger's hat and gloves.

"Thank you, Hans."

"A delivery man stopped by ten minutes ago, and left an envelope for you. He said it was an invoice from the baker. I placed it on your desk."

Volger's jaw clenched. "Thank you, Hans. I shall see to it."

He strode into his study and closed the door. The envelope sitting on the desk bore only his name handwritten across the front. He tore it open and unfolded the paper inside.

My Dear Major Volger,
The next payment on your account is requested, due
Thursday, 2 October
Thank you.

Lange's Bakery,
32 Rohrbacher Strasse
Heidelberg

PS: We expect a delivery of Emmantaler from Switzerland that evening. We know you're interested.

"Damn!" Volger struck a match and watched the note burn.

10

Bern

Martin sat at the desk in his temporary apartment, collar open, reading for the third time the dossiers that Inspector Frisch had given him. He'd already studied their photographs for an hour, committing each face and name to memory. Now he memorized the details of their lives.

He set down the one he was rereading and sighed, slumping back in the chair. The stress of the day had exhausted him. He wasn't comfortable portraying a law-enforcement officer. It was stressful enough pretending to be Swiss all day, let alone pretending to perform an occupation with which he had no experience.

He was not an interrogator. In the past, his job had been to go undercover as a Nazi sympathizer, and then arrest the Abwehr's secret agents as soon as he could ascertain that they were using a forged American passport. Once he apprehended them, he turned them over to U.S. Marshalls.

He shook his head at the irony. Usually he had to pretend to be as averse to law enforcement as his targets. He was always the cat in mouse clothing; now he felt more like the mouse in cat's clothing, wondering when the costume would unravel.

He walked to the sink, and poured a glass of water. There was a loaf of coarse bread and a wheel of white cheese in the ice-box, so he made himself a cheese sandwich. He stood at the counter and ate, deep in thought.

He looked around the little apartment. *Not much bigger than a hotel suite.* The main room had a couch, a desk and chair, and a little kitchen area with sink, icebox, and small stove. A radio cabinet stood in the corner, but he had yet to turn it on. *I should probably listen to the news at ten.*

The other room held a full-size bed, small dresser, and a wash basin. There was a small bathroom with a tub and toilet off the bedroom.

Nothing personal adorned the plain space—no photographs, no books, no knick-knacks. He wasn't allowed to bring personal affects. They might compromise his identity. He was used to that, but this time felt different…

It had been two months since he'd seen the kids. That wasn't unusual, but he'd been supposed to have them for the whole summer.

He could picture their faces beside him on the National Mall, looking at the sky in wonder at the fireworks exploding above the Washington Monument, painting everything in colorful illumination. The rambunctious threesome had fallen into silence. For those precious moments he'd felt no distance between them.

But then in August, Colonel Donovan had sent him and three others to an isolated cabin in the Catskill Mountains, where a Canadian named Stephenson had taught them spycraft. He'd had to send the kids back to Philadelphia early.

He sat back down at the desk, pulled out a blank sheet of paper, and began to write.

> *Dear Marty, Jackie, and Stevie,*
> *Hi kids! How are you? How are you doing in school this year?*
> *I'm well. I can't tell you where I am, but it's not in the United States. I'm doing important*

work for the country, but I miss you. It may be a while until I can come back to see you.

I got your letters last month. Thank you for writing to me! I'm glad you had such an exciting summer.

He sat back and took a deep breath. He was terrible at writing letters. He always had been. He sat for several minutes, trying to think of more to say to his kids, but nothing came to mind.

Finally, he just decided to keep the letter brief. *Short and sweet.*

If you want to write back, I can't give you my address, but you can write to me c/o the United States Department of State in Washington, D.C., and they'll get your letters to me. Your mother knows the address.

Be good, and I'll see you when I can.

Love,

Dad

He folded the letter in thirds, and placed it inside an envelope. He'd send it tomorrow with the diplomatic pouches going back to Washington. That way, there would be no tell-tale postmark until it got to the States. He didn't bother sealing the envelope, knowing the letter would be read by security before it left the embassy, and that it would be read again by Counter-Intelligence in Washington—his old collegues at the Office of the Chief Special Agent—before it was sent on to the Postal service.

He put the envelope into the inside pocket of his suit jacket, hanging on the back of the chair, and returned to the dossiers.

Jason's hair was still wet from the public swimming pool when he climbed the steps to his apartment on the third floor, which would be the fourth floor to an American. He walked halfway down the hall, and turned the key in the door of Number fourteen.

"Hey!" he called to his roommates.

"Hey yourself," Mark Hodges said from the kitchen table, where he sat eating a frankfurter wrapped in a roll with mustard.

Jason walked into the bedroom, and set his bag on one of the three twin beds. His other roommate, Devon Wolcott, looked up from the bed on the far side of the room, where he lay on his stomach reading a magazine. An image of Veronica Lake was pinned to the wall above him.

"Did you have a good swim?" Devon asked.

"Yeah, I did. Thanks for asking." Jason unpacked his bag, removing the wet towel and swim trunks.

He'd been a competitive swimmer in high school and college, and he still enjoyed swimming laps for an hour several nights a week. It was relaxing, and let him clear his mind, bringing him an almost meditative sense of calm. And it was great exercise. He'd been thrilled to learn that Bern had a public pool only a twenty-minute walk from his apartment.

Jason's stomach growled as he hung his towel on a rack in the bathroom. "Have you eaten?" he asked Devon.

"Yeah, a little bit ago. Mark boiled some frankfurters. There's still a couple left."

Jason went back into the main room and headed for the stove, where a pot sat on the burner. He took a plate from the cabinet and forked out one of the frankfurters. Then he took a bottle of beer from the ice-box and sat at the table next to Mark.

"A telegram came for you earlier," Mark said. "It's over on the desk."

"Thanks." Jason retrieved the telegram, marked from Evanston, Illinois. "It's from my folks." He tore it open, retaking his seat.

> DEAR JASON
> RENTED CHALET IN INTERLAKEN FOR
> CHRISTMAS STOP
> WILL BE IN SWITZERLAND DECEMBER 20 TO
> JANUARY 3 STOP
> UNLESS THE DAMNED DEMOCRATS GET US INTO
> WAR STOP
> DAD

"My parents are coming for Christmas!" Jason beamed at Mark.

"That's swell," Mark said. He didn't sound enthused.

Crestfallen, Jason folded the telegram and set it aside, and ate in silence.

Tuesday,
September 30, 1941

11

Bern

"What did you learn at your cocktail party?" Martin asked Ron Witherspoon at eight-thirty the next morning.

"Very little. My German contacts claim to know nothing of Dr. Rubenstein or his work, and when I hinted that he was working for the military, they assured me they would know if he were working on anything substantial."

"Do you believe them?"

"I think they were being sincere—though I don't agree that they'd have known if Dr. Rubenstein's work were a threat to German interests."

"What about Inspector Frisch?"

"They said they'd never heard of him, and I believe them. I placed a call to a contact in the Swiss Federal Department of Justice and Police, to see what he can tell me. He said he'd look into Frisch's records for me. I expect him to call later today."

Martin scowled. He'd hoped to learn more this morning. Unproductive meetings irritated him.

"Then my only choice is to go to the Rubensteins' apartment today while Sonia Rubenstein is at the Polytechnic Institute, and convince the portierfrau to let me inspect it."

"She might demand a search warrant, if she's at all educated. The Swiss take their personal liberties seriously."

"Can you have one forged for me?"

"Colonel Legge's contacts could get one for you," Witherspoon said.

Zurich

"Miss Rubenstein's a very private lady, I'm sure she won't like that the police have been in her home," the plump Mrs. Schlachet said as she waddled up the stairs in front of Martin. Her fair hair was streaked with gray, and pulled into a tight bun at the crown of her head.

"It's important to our investigation."

"Of course," Mrs. Schlachet said as she reached the landing, slightly breathless. "Poor Dr. Rubenstein! He was a very gentle man. Always so kind. I can't imagine why anyone would want to hurt him. Over here, Inspector." She unlocked a door at the end of the hall and stepped in ahead of him.

"Thank you, Mrs. Schlachet. I shall take it from here."

"Of course," she said, looking disappointed. She gave him a nod and stepped out, closing the door behind her.

Martin locked it.

He stood in a short foyer, with a door to his right, and a combination living room/dining room ahead. He opened the door and found a small coat closet. Dr. Rubenstein's dark gray overcoat hung in the back, and a woman's heavy woolen coat hung in front of it, with a gray scarf draped around the collar, but otherwise the space was empty.

He walked into the living room. A plain green couch sat along one wall, its cushions looking a bit worn and flat. There was a brown armchair in the corner, also looking a little bit ragged.

The Rubensteins were clearly not a wealthy family.

A dark wooden credenza stood farther down the wall in front of the dining table, with several framed black-and-white photographs on top, around a brass menorah in the center. But there were no candles in the menorah. *Observant enough to own one, but not to use it.*

He tugged on a leather glove and picked up one of the photos. A short man with a dark mustache, wearing a suit of a style that was common in the 1920s stood beside a smiling woman with black hair in a plain dress that hung to the middle of her calves. Next to her was a little girl of about ten with long dark hair, short bangs, and a crooked smile. The little girl had large round cheeks and mischievous eyes. He hardly recognized Sonia Rubenstein, but one look at the woman standing with her and he could see echoes of Sonia's face.

He knelt and opened the doors of the credenza and found stacks of dishes, rows of wine glasses, and a neat pile of table linens.

He turned his attention to the dining table. It was rectangular, with four chairs. A rose-colored table cloth covered the entire surface, with a white lace laid on top. Two places still sat with plate, bowl, silverware, and wine glass. Two candlesticks stood in the middle, holding tall white candles with charred wicks.

Seeing nothing of interest, he moved on to the desk on the opposite wall. The surface of the desk was tidy, with a small lamp and a telephone on one side, and a pad of paper and a fountain pen on the other.

He opened the top drawer, where dozens of papers lay strewn around.

He removed the pages with both hands in a disorganized heap, and laid them on the table. Then he leafed through them. Most were invoices that had a handwritten "Paid" on the top. There was a letter from the synagogue confirming his reservation for two seats at the Rosh Hashanah services Sunday night and Monday of last week.

That was two days before he died.

He found nothing else of interest—nothing mentioning the Resistance, or Communists, or anything else. He carefully returned the papers to the drawer as they were.

There was a larger file drawer beneath, but Martin found it locked. He searched under the desk for a key secured to the bottom, but didn't find one. He considered picking the lock, but the wood around it was dry and brittle and would easily splinter.

He scanned the room, searching for a possible hiding place for the key, but nothing stood out.

He stepped into the tiny kitchen. He opened drawers and cabinets, but found only silverware, pots and pans. He rifled through the trash, but found nothing out of the ordinary.

He crossed the living room again and entered the small hallway— more of a tiny square of space, four-foot by four-foot at most—with a bedroom on either side, and a small bathroom at the rear.

A yellow cat dashed under the bed as he entered what he presumed was Sonia Rubenstein's bedroom. The curtains at the window were white and lacy, as was the quilted bedspread.

He felt strange opening the drawers of Sonia Rubenstein's dresser, but he needed to find that desk key. Instead he found himself rifling through undergarments, stockings, and a few folded sweaters. The only other item was a small, inexpensive-looking wrist-watch.

The image of Rosa Linda Bianchi searching his drawers accused him. He frowned and slammed the last drawer shut.

The top of the dresser was bare, except for a single framed photograph of Sonia in a polka-dotted dress, standing next to her father, holding a parchment that appeared to be a university degree. Both of them were beaming.

He stared at the picture a bit longer than he needed to. It was amazing how much different Sonia looked when she smiled.

A small table next to the bed had a single drawer, but it contained only a pad of paper, a few pencils, a large eraser, and a fountain pen. Still no desk key.

A book-shelf stood in the corner, and he flipped through every book on all four shelves, but the only thing he found was a gold necklace with a Star of David pendant hidden behind a book of poetry.

He moved on to the other bedroom, but had no more luck there. Frustrated, he marched back into the living room and stood in the center, turned and scanned the whole room. Still no potential hiding place.

Damn!

He could think of no reason to prolong his search, and left. The portierfrau's door stood open, and violin music came from the radio cabinet.

A Beethoven sonata. Becky had always loved Beethoven…

"Mrs. Schlachet, I've finished. You may lock up now."

She waddled out from the kitchen, a ring of keys dangling from one hand. "I'll lock up right this minute, Inspector Schmidt. What shall I tell Miss Rubenstein when she arrives home this evening?"

Martin couldn't care less. "You may tell her the truth if you'd like. Good day."

Martin found a telephone booth near the Polytechnic Institute, and gave the operator the number for the U.S. Embassy in Bern. The Swiss receptionist transferred him upstairs to Amanda Overstreet, who put him through to Ron Witherspoon.

"Have you heard from your government contacts?" Martin asked.

"Yes, about an hour ago. He said Inspector Frisch of the Zurich police has an exemplary record, and a closure rate of nearly ninety percent on his investigations—which doesn't sound like someone who would do a perfunctory investigation of a homicide."

I can come to that conclusion on my own, thank you. "Did he say if Frisch is a member of the SVV?"

"Well, *officially* Inspector Frisch belongs to the Party of Farmers, Traders, and Independents—which is the conservative party in the German-speaking cantons. It's more conservative than the center-right Free Democratic Party, but not far-right. You could think of it as the equivalent of the conservative wing of the Republican Party in the States, whereas the Free Democratic Party is more akin to the moderate Republicans."

Get to the point. "You said he *officially* belongs to the Farmers something-something Party—but the SVV isn't an official party, is it?"

"Correct. The SVV doesn't participate in electoral politics, preferring to work behind the scenes, using influence to affect government policy. And the membership is a secret—although everyone knows certain high-ranking military officers are part of it, such as General Guisan, for instance. My contact said there's no evidence Inspector Frisch is part of the SVV, but it can't be ruled out."

"That's somewhat helpful. Thanks for checking on that." Martin hung up.

There wasn't much more he could do in Zurich at this point, except wait for Sonia Rubenstein to lead him to the anti-Nazi student group. He drove back to the Polytechnic Institute, and parked near the Science building, but not close enough to be spotted from the door. He leaned back in the seat and waited.

12

Zurich

Franz Lemiel strode into the Schiffman tavern as if he'd been there a thousand times, though this was his first visit. He caught the eye of the bartender, a sandy-haired young man a couple of years older than he, and motioned him toward the end of the bar.

"I believe there is a meeting here, my friend. The Freethinkers. Where might I find them?"

The bartender looked Franz over, a guarded expression in his brown eyes. "And who would you be?"

"I am Emmantaler."

The bartender smiled at the name—Switzerland's most common cheese. "Yes, they are expecting you. Follow me."

He led Franz into the storeroom, then up a flight of stairs to a heavy wooden door. He knocked once, then turned the knob and let Franz in.

"Franz, I'm glad you got our message," Sonia Rubenstein said, standing.

They kissed each other's cheeks, and Franz whispered, "We'll have a word after the meeting. I want to hear about this Federal inspector."

Franz greeted the others one by one, shaking hands until he came to Elena Krasnakovich. Her expression was stony, but he flashed her a broad grin anyway. "Elena my dear! Wonderful to see you!" He put his hands on her shoulders and kissed her pale cheeks.

The corner of her mouth turned up, and an amused twinkle came to her gray-blue eyes. "Franz." She tossed her coal-black hair and resumed the stony expression.

"What news have you, Franz?" a red-haired young man asked, leaning forward in his seat, his eyes wide with anticipation.

"The Wehrmacht is on the move into Occupied France again," Franz said, taking a seat. "Eagle-eyes in Heidelberg and Stuttgart have spotted convoys moving toward France, to Rheims in particular. I haven't been able to get into France in a while, but I've passed along the observations to the Resistance in Rheims via a friend in Colmar, Alsace."

"How?"

"We've exchanged original poetry for years, and lately I've been moved to write about the gray clouds gathering over the Cathedral of Rheims."

"I recall being on the receiving end of some of your bad poetry, Franz," Elena said. "I feel for your friend in Colmar. Hopefully she doesn't mind it so much."

"He," Franz corrected.

"Ah, I see," Elena said, leaning back in her seat with a smug look.

"Perhaps we should begin," Sonia said, flashing Elena a look. Elena shrugged.

"We have much on our agenda," Sonia continued. "First, if Elena hasn't already told everyone, the police are monitoring the group, so everyone needs to be extra careful. Be vigilant about being followed— always be aware of the people around you and behind you. And remember that while they cannot touch us for anything we say, they can for what we write. So be extra cautious when distributing literature. Franz is here to help us learn to cope with the scrutiny."

Franz nodded and sat forward. "If anyone needs advice on how to evade a tail, there are many techniques. Vary your routes as much as possible, try not to be predictable. Change directions even when you don't have to. If you are being followed, go into busy stores that have a side door, or try to move through a dense crowd. But above all, keep calm and don't look afraid. Learn to observe people from the corners of your eyes. And remember that the person following you may not be the only one watching."

"Will you stay and help us, Franz?" The red-head asked.

Franz shook his head. "I am only in Zurich for tonight."

"Thank you, Franz. We all appreciate that you came here this evening when you weren't expecting to." Sonia looked to the young man sitting next to Elena, his back as straight as a board. "Peter, you have a report for us?"

"Yes," said the well-groomed young man wearing a gray tie, sweater-vest, and slacks, with thick but neatly-combed brown hair. He had a deep voice, and appeared uncomfortable speaking. "There's been ever-more business coming into the bank from Germany— mostly gold—and lots of movement amongst accounts. You understand I'm violating the Banking Secrecy Law by reporting this…"

He proceeded to give a dry account of numerous financial dealings between Nazi businessmen or SS officers, and the Zurischer Kredit bank where he worked as an accounting clerk. Franz struggled to maintain interest.

"Thank you, Peter. That was very thorough," Sonia said. "Does the group wish to debate what response we should make?"

"I still don't understand why we can't confront those damned bankers!" the red-head exclaimed. "Demand that they stop laundering money for Nazi murderers."

"We must be sensitive to Peter's position," Sonia soothed. "He's broken the law by revealing these secrets to the group."

"I understand your feelings, Bernhardt," Franz said. "And ultimately we will need to confront the bankers for their one-sided dealings. But we must proceed with caution, build popular outrage first—otherwise our demands will fall on deaf ears, they'll have us arrested for trespassing, and will continue as before. We'll have accomplished nothing."

"So more leaflets?" Bernhardt asked, a doubtful look on his face.

"Leaflets and boycotts," Franz said. "Educate the public, and they will do the right thing."

He leaned back, and placed his hands behind his head. "I have word from Germany that the deportation of Jews to concentration camps continues. On my next trip into the Reich, I hope to come back with photographs of the deplorable conditions at Dachau. There's a journalist I know in Augsburg who's made it his mission to sneak as close as he can to the fence-line and capture photos, a few at a time. He's built a damning collection, and needs a way to sneak them out of the country. I have an avenue to assist him."

Sonia's face lit up. "We have printed countless leaflets about the imprisonment of the German Jews like common criminals, and we've gotten precious little response—but if we can prove to the public that the concentration camps in Germany are not like Swiss prison camps, we may convince more people to cry out for justice."

"Oh, and speaking of leaflets," Franz said, sitting up. "Not to take the glory from Peter's report, but I have a new list from my father of Swiss businesses that have provided goods and services to the Third Reich." He chuckled. "As always, if he's not able to publicly shame them in his newspaper, he's content to let us shame them with anonymous leaflets. As the largest number of offenders are here in Zurich, I shall be happy to leave them to your scrutiny."

"Wonderful!" Sonia said. She turned to a skinny young man with thin brown hair and black-stained hands. "Eckhardt, will you see to the printing for us?"

"As always."

"Well, then! Let's compose something," Franz suggested.

Martin stood at the phone booth on the corner, pretending to use the telephone for twenty minutes, while watching everyone entering and leaving the Schiffman tavern. He had memorized the photographs, and noted the arrival of each. There had been none entering for ten minutes, so he replaced the receiver on its cradle and crossed to the tavern.

Ignoring everyone at the bar, Martin walked toward the closed door of the storeroom. The bartender stepped out in front of him.

"Do you know the password, sir?" he said in a low voice.

"No." Martin showed his FedPol badge instead.

"I'm sorry sir, but do you have a search warrant?"

"No."

"Then I cannot let you in, sir."

Martin hated for it to come to this, but making sure his back was to the bar he pulled back his suit jacket to reveal the 9mm Luger in its holster. "How's this for a warrant?" he whispered.

The bartender took one look at the expression in Martin's eyes, and broke out in a cold sweat. He swallowed and said, "That will do very well, sir." He opened the door and stood aside.

Martin shook his head. "No, you lead the way."

The bartender nodded without a word, and walked toward the staircase. He stepped hard on each stair.

Martin scowled; the meeting was alerted to their presence. He concealed the Luger before being shown into the upstairs room.

The bartender looked to a pale, dark-haired young woman. "Federal Police," he murmured. "I'm sorry."

"It's alright, Herrmann," the dark-haired young woman said.

Martin showed his FedPol badge. "I'm Inspector Schmidt of the Federal Police. I'm here to ask some questions. Do not be alarmed."

"We aren't, Inspector," said a scruffy young man with a cocky half-smile, his arms crossed.

Martin glanced at the faces in the room, and knew most of them. There were two faces he didn't recognize, however—the cocky one, and another young man. That one looked terrified, his eyes wide, with perspiration beading on his forehead and upper lip.

The other lounged in his seat as if this were a lark. This one had a tan complexion, a square jaw with round cheeks that could almost give him the appearance of a baby-face except for the dark five o'clock shadow. His thick brown hair was parted carelessly, not neat and tidy like the nervous one. This one up was a potential trouble-maker.

"Miss Rubenstein I'm familiar with"—she glared at him—"but the rest of you will need to identify yourselves." Martin removed Inspector Frisch's list from his pocket and read the names aloud, pausing as each person identified themselves.

Three people on the list were not present. And the two unknown young men had not identified themselves as any of the names Martin had—the tight-buttoned and horribly uncomfortable one, and the shortish bohemian type who sat back as casually as if he were in his own home.

Martin looked the nervous one in the face. "And who are you, young man?"

"I'm Peter," he said, swallowing hard.

"Peter who?"

Peter hesitated, looking to Elena Krasnakovich beside him. She shrugged. He turned back to Martin with a deer-in-headlights look.

"Peter Kraus. I'm just a visitor here."

Miss Krasnakovich rolled her eyes and turned slightly away from Peter.

Martin turned to the scruffy one. "And you?"

He leapt from his seat and extended his right hand. "Franz Lemiel, also a visitor here, from Basel."

Martin ignored Franz's proffered hand, and the young man shrugged and returned to his seat.

"Why are you visiting all the way from Basel?"

"I was asked to join this evening, and I was able to oblige."

"For what purpose?" Martin asked.

"I might have learned had you not interrupted the meeting, *Inspector*." He put heavy emphasis on the last word.

"Have you joined this group before?"

"On occasion."

"What is it you want from us?" Sonia demanded.

Martin ignored her and spoke to the group at large. "Who among you have met Dr. Fritz Rubenstein?"

He got surprised looks from most of them.

"Is that Sonia's father?" a red-haired young man asked.

"Yes. Have any of you met him?" Martin repeated.

His question was greeted with head shakes from everyone except Sonia, who thrust her hand into the air. "I have!" she declared, raising her chin.

Several of them snickered.

"I will speak to each alone," Martin said. "When I have finished, he or she will leave the building."

He stood in front of the door and called Elena Krasnakovich. He waited while the rest of the group huddled together on the other side of the large room—all except Franz Lemiel, who didn't move from his seat, where he watched Martin with an unreadable expression.

Martin motioned for Elena to join him in a corner, far from the others. He spoke in a quiet voice. "Miss Krasnakovich, how long have you been part of this group?"

"A year and a half."

"Was the group already in existence when you joined?"

"It was new."

"Who formed the group?"

"Franz and Sonia got it started."

"How did you come to know of it?"

"Pavel brought me."

"Pavel Minskayev?"

"Yes."

"Who is not here tonight, it seems."

"No, he couldn't make it."

Martin looked at her dossier. "Miss Krasnakovich, you were born in Russia, were you not?"

"Yes."

"How long have you been in Switzerland?"

"Nineteen years."

"And you are how old?"

"Twenty.'

"You came to Switzerland with your parents, then?"

"Yes."

So far, she was answering honestly, what Martin knew from her dossier. "Are your parents Communists?"

"Certainly not!" Elena practically spat the words. "My father fought in the White Army against the Bolsheviks. That is why we had to emigrate. He took a bullet in the leg." A decided note of pride came to her voice.

"Do you know any Communists?"

"No, I do not."

"And what is your political persuasion?"

"I am an activist for women's suffrage."

Martin cringed. That was a stupid mistake, forgetting that Switzerland was one of the last western European countries where women still could not vote.

"Are you certain you know no Communists?"

"Absolutely certain."

"Do you know anyone from France?"

"No."

"Have you ever met anyone from France?"

"I don't know. Possibly, but I don't recall."

Martin believed her. She gave no sign of lying. Her gaze was steady, she didn't fidget, and she didn't sweat. "Thank you, Miss Krasnakovich. That is all. You may leave."

He called the next name, but Franz Lemiel stood from his seat and motioned to Martin. "May I have a word with you, Inspector Schmidt?" Then lower, "Or should I call you Mr. Smith?"

13

Martin stared into Franz's twinkling brown eyes, keeping his own eyes hard and narrow. He motioned for Franz to step aside, and stood close to him. Franz was several inches shorter than he, so Martin leaned his head down to speak quietly.

"What can I do for you, Mr. Lemiel?"

Franz had an amused smile on his lips. "I know people in every canton, and I can identify every accent and dialect in Switzerland. You're accent is good—very good—but you are not Swiss."

Martin stared at him without a word.

"I must compliment you, Mr. Smith—you seem to have everyone else fooled. But as I said, I know people all over Switzerland, and I can tell you are not from this country. English or American, most likely. Am I wrong?"

Martin's first instinct was to clam up—but it could be dangerous to let Franz assume he was British. "American," he conceded.

"Your secret is safe with me, Mr. Smith. But I ask myself, why would an American impersonate a FedPol inspector? There must be more to Dr. Rubenstein's death, something that interests the United States. What would that be?"

"I think you should leave that to me, Mr. Lemiel."

"I can help you, Mr. Smith."

"How?" Martin asked, skeptical.

"I can get information for you. I know the leaders of a few Resistance cells in northeastern France. I also know members of the underground inside Germany itself."

Martin's interest piqued. "And the others here?"

Franz shook his head. "No, I am the only one with contacts outside of Switzerland. Most of them don't know anyone in the other Swiss groups. Sonia Rubenstein alone knows a couple of members of the Bern group, but that is all."

Sounds like the classic cell structure. "Modeled after the French Resistance?"

"Not exactly. There is no organized network. And no sabotage here, Mr. Smith."

"What is the purpose of these groups?"

"Each is unique," Franz explained. "They are fully autonomous—much like our cantons—and they each have their own mission. In Fribourg, for example, they focus on smuggling banned books over the Juras and into Occupied France. In Geneva, they work to smuggle political refugees out of France. In Bern they challenge Swiss politicians on the uneven nature of our neutrality. And here in Zurich it is about shaming Swiss businessmen, and exposing their collaboration with Nazi thugs."

"And you run the whole thing?"

"Hardly!" Franz chuckled. "I'm a facilitator, Mr. Smith. When needed, I get them in contact with sympathetic individuals in Occupied France, and I bring information from Underground operatives inside the Third Reich. I am both courier and advisor."

"You are a national organizer, it seems."

Franz shrugged. "You could call me that, yes."

"How did it start?"

"That is a long story. Perhaps we should continue this later. I'm sure you don't want the others to grow concerned at how long we are conversing."

Martin couldn't disagree. "We'll speak again—tonight. I'm going to pretend to dismiss you now, but please wait downstairs in the tavern while I speak to the others."

"Of course," Franz said. "We mustn't blow your cover. Best if everyone else believes you are a FedPol inspector. Safer for them that way."

"Thank you, Mr. Lemiel. You may leave." Martin said at a normal volume.

As Franz walked out the door, Martin called Peter Kraus's name.

Franz sat at the bar and ordered a beer. He looked around the tavern as he waited. Elena Krasnakovich was sitting at a table in the corner, watching him. She looked away.

Once he had his beer, he walked to Elena's table. "May I sit with you?"

She gave him a cool look. "If you'd like. It doesn't matter to me. What did you think of the FedPol inspector?"

"Harmless enough," Franz said.

"Why is he investigating the group?"

"He's investigating the murder of Sonia's father."

"He thinks one of us knows something?"

Franz shrugged. "Why are you waiting?"

Elena hesitated before replying. "I'm waiting for Peter."

"The banker?" Momentary sheepishness crossed her eyes, and realization dawned. "Really? Elena, he hardly seems your type."

"At least he sticks around."

He leaned forward with a grin. "Elena, did you seduce him to get him into the group?"

Her eyes narrowed. "You're hardly one to judge."

He waved a hand dismissively. "You know I don't judge like that. On the contrary, I'd compliment you on your resourcefulness."

Elena took a drink of beer and leaned back in her chair. "Why are you waiting here, Franz?"

"I need to speak to Sonia."

"Yes, I suppose you do."

Franz reached his fingers across the table to touch hers. "Maybe later I could come by your room. I need a place to stay tonight."

Elena pulled her hand back. "Find somewhere else. I told you, I'm waiting for Peter."

"Invite him along! I'm sure the three of us could enjoy ourselves."

She gave him an exasperated look. "Have you forgotten what happened last time? And do you think it's a coincidence that Pavel hasn't been at the meeting the last three times you've visited us?"

He scowled and looked down at his beer. "That was a misunderstanding."

"You can't eat your cake and still have it, Franz. Sooner or later you'll have to choose one way or the other."

"I don't *have* to do anything." He took a long swig of beer.

They sat in icy silence for a few minutes, and avoided looking at one another. Peter appeared from the storeroom door, and Elena stood as he approached.

"Am I interrupting?"

"Not at all," Elena said, giving Peter a kiss on the cheek and making sure Franz saw. Then she slipped her arm through his and said, "Let's go. Franz, I'll see you next time you visit."

She looked back over her shoulder and gave him a cold smile as she left.

**

Sonia Rubenstein emerged thirty minutes later, and Franz waved her over. She wore a deep scowl, and Franz smiled in an attempt to lighten her mood some.

"How was your conversation?" he asked, offering her a seat.

"Non-existent. I refused to answer any of his questions, and then asked to be allowed to leave. He agreed."

Mr. Smith emerged from the storeroom door, and locked eyes with him. Franz shook his head almost imperceptibly, to which the agent replied with a tiny nod. He stood at the bar, ordered a beer, and watched them.

Sonia's back was to the bar, and she hadn't noticed. Franz leaned close and whispered, "Sonia, I have something important to tell you, but you must not repeat it to anyone. Do you promise?"

She cocked her head, puzzled, but agreed.

"Inspector Schmidt is not really a police inspector," Franz continued, still at a whisper. "He's with American Intelligence, and they believe there is something troubling about the circumstances of your father's death. He has been impersonating a FedPol inspector to find evidence of a conspiracy."

Sonia stared at him, open-mouthed. "How do you know this?"

"He told me."

"And you believe that?"

"I suggested it. His accent is not Swiss, though it is very good. He admitted it." Franz paused for a few seconds to allow that to sink in. "And I think we should cooperate with him, you and I."

She sat up straight, her dark eyes hard and her jaw set. "No! Out of the question."

Franz cringed at her volume. "Shhhh! Keep your voice down."

"Why in God's name would you suggest that?" she whispered.

"Because he's working against the Nazis, too. I suspect there are pro-Nazi elements behind your father's death, but we need evidence to disprove a connection with the Resistance." He placed a hand on her arm. "You could help him with that, Sonia. It's important."

She was silent for a full minute, and Franz waited. "I still don't trust him, or his motives," she said.

"Does that mean you'll cooperate with him?"

She shrugged. "For now."

Franz grinned at her. Then he waved Mr. Smith over. Sonia looked startled as he took a seat between them.

"I let Sonia in on our secret, Mr. Smith," Franz said quietly. Seeing the agent's pale green eyes narrow, he raised his hands in reassurance. "There is no one more trustworthy than Sonia Rubenstein. She is one of the few people I would trust with my life."

Mr Smith nodded, but continued giving Franz a stern look. "If we're going to work together, Mr. Lemiel, I must make myself clear again that you cannot reveal my identity or role to *anyone* without my permission."

"Absolutely!" Franz said with a grin, sitting back and taking a long drink of his beer.

The agent turned his gaze to Sonia, who still wore a scowl. "I'm sorry to involve you in this, Miss Rubenstein."

"I'm already involved."

"Sonia is willing to cooperate with your investigation, Mr. Smith—to find out who killed her father and why." Franz gave him an I-told-you-so look. "You would have never won her cooperation pretending to be a FedPol inspector."

Mr. Smith turned back to Sonia. "Miss Rubenstein, I need to know what your father was working on. It could be the key to learning who wanted him dead. I know that you aren't aware of what he was working on, but the evidence might be locked in his desk drawer at your apartment. I need you to unlock it for me."

Sonia's face flushed. "You've been inside my apartment!"

Franz cringed again at her volume, but Mr. Smith's expression was stony. "Please keep your voice down. Yes—I was in your apartment today, trying to find your father's work papers. The drawer was locked, and I couldn't locate a key."

"Did you break in?" she hissed.

He shook his head. "No, I had a warrant. Mrs. Schlachet let me in."

"A warrant? I'm sure it was as phony as your identity, *Inspector*!"

Mr. Smith ignored her sarcasm. "This is important, Miss Rubenstein."

"Sonia will cooperate, Mr. Smith. Won't you, Sonia?" Franz looked her in the eyes.

Her expression softened. "Yes, I will."

"Will you let me look this evening?" Mr. Smith asked.

Sonia hesitated. Franz understood—Yom Kippur began this evening. He squeezed her hand. "God will understand, Sonia. This is important."

She nodded. "That will be fine."

Franz relaxed. "Good, that settles it. What more do you want to know, Mr. Smith?"

"Tell me about these groups you coordinate. How did they get started, and why?"

"My involvement goes back several years," Franz said with a smile. "When I was at art school at university, we used to have lots of discussions, my fellow students and I—philosophy, religion, politics. None of us liked the Nazis. The enemies of art and culture, not to mention personal liberty. They gave us much to be outraged about, with their book burnings and their Nuremberg Laws."

"When was this?"

Franz looked up in thought. "Probably 1936 or '37. We took long visits to Paris, too, and the Sorbonne students at the cafés in the

Quartier Latin were of like mind." A gleam came to his eyes. "Some of the best times of my life were spent in Paris. Such a wonderful city! Passionate young men and women. And wonderful art!"

He grew serious again. "And now our beloved Paris is occupied by Nazi pigs who hate art, hate culture, and hate the French."

Mr. Smith pulled him back on-topic. "From these discussions, when did you organize?"

"Two-and-a-half years ago, when the Germans invaded Czechoslovakia."

"Not until then?"

Franz shook his head. "We didn't see any reason for alarm until then. None of us were happy about the Austrian Anschluss, but most Austrians were ambivalent. Many wanted it. And it was Hitler's home country. Most of us decided it was inevitable.

"Six months later when Germany annexed the Sudetenland, we had mixed emotions again. It was terrible for the Czechs to lose so much of their country against their wishes—but the Sudeten-Germans clearly wanted it." He shrugged. "And now the Sudetenland is the most Nazi state in the Reich."

Franz's lips pursed, and he sat back. "It wasn't six months when Hitler sent troops across the rest of Czechoslovakia, without provocation. *That* was when we knew the world was in danger, and we decided to organize. Basel is like a finger between Germany and Alsace, so it was easy to make contact with student groups over the border. We had to be cautious with what was said—the Reich is like being inside a cage of paranoia, and one never knows who to trust— but we found students like us, who felt the same way about their regime. Swing Youth mostly, and other non-conformists.

"I like to travel around, so I took it upon myself to go to the other universities around Switzerland and help them organize as we had. I met Sonia and Pavel here in Zurich two years ago, and they got this group started."

"Pavel Minskayev?" Mr. Smith asked

"Yes, that's right."

"He was not here tonight. I'd like to speak with him."

Franz exchanged a quick look with Sonia. "You may have to wait until another time, Mr. Smith, but I'll take you to him," Sonia said.

Mr. Smith frowned, eyeing them both. "Perhaps we can go look in your father's desk now."

"If you wish," Sonia said, her eyes wary.

"I shall leave you two, then," Franz said, standing. "I must be off to find a place to stay tonight. I shall call on you at your embassy tomorrow, Mr. Smith."

"I'll meet you inside the door. Can you be there at two o'clock?"

"Yes, I shall be there at two," Franz said with a grin.

14

Zurich

Ernst Zubler took a sip of brandy, and a knock came at the door. "Come in!"

His butler entered, his expression dour as ever. "Excuse me sir, but the men in leather are here to see you."

"Thank you, Anton. Show them in, please."

Zubler looked to the diminutive man sitting across from him. "The Gestapo always make their presence known by their attire, don't they Mr. Krinke? Anton and I have come to call them 'the men in leather.'"

Wilhelm Krinke made a series of deep guttural sounds that passed as his laugh. "Yes indeed, always black leather coats!" he said, bobbing his head up and down.

The door opened, and Anton entered with two men dressed all in black, including black leather jackets.

"Messrs Karol and Tischer, sir," Anton announced, and backed out of the room, closing the door.

"Thank you for coming, gentlemen," Zubler said, standing to shake hands. "You remember Mr. Krinke, one of our Under-Secretaries in the Ministry of Justice and Police?"

"Yes," Tischer, the tall one said.

"Take a seat," Zubler said, motioning to the chairs next to Krinke. "Mr. Krinke was telling me that he has thoroughly reviewed the

111

ministry's records, and there is no Inspector Max Schmidt at FedPol, nor has there been one by that name going back many years."

Zubler looked to Wilhelm Krinke, and raised his eyebrows.

"Yes, that is so," Wilhelm Krinke said, bobbing his head. He had thin brown hair and an even thinner mustache. His cheeks were sunken, and his gray eyes closely-spaced. A small nose and narrow chin gave his face an almost mousy look. "Max Schmidt is a common name, and FedPol has several officers by that name. We are in the process of interrogating all of them to find out if any have been impersonating an inspector."

Zubler found Krinke's sing-song Bernese accent almost as annoying as his mannerisms. "My suspicion is that none of them is our mystery man. That is why I have asked you gentlemen here—to find out who he is and what he's after."

"You have a description for us, Mr. Zubler? Or are we to start checking every street in Zurich for men named Max Schmidt?" Karol, the shorter and stockier of the two, asked with a sarcastic sneer.

Zubler found the guttural working-class accent of the two Bavarians even more grating than Krinke's Bernese sing-song cadence. And their manners matched their lowly accent.

"Inspector Frisch of the Zurich police has a good description," Zubler replied, holding his patience. "I shall provide you a copy, but I recommend you speak with Frisch yourselves, as he is the only one to have met this Max Schmidt in person."

"You have an idea who he might be?" Tischer asked.

Zubler gave him a thin smile. "Nothing concrete. Soviet intelligence, perhaps? Or British intelligence? Maybe a member of the Communist underground? Or some damned Jew on a vigilante mission. If he's any of those, I want you to find him, interrogate him by any means necessary to find out what he knows and what he wants—then kill him."

Wicked grins spread across the faces of both men. "That's what we do," Tischer said.

"Yes, and you do it well. That's why I have you here in Switzerland. Now go find this spurious Inspector Max Schmidt. And don't let me down."

The Gestapo men left, and Zubler turned back to Wilhelm Krinke. "Have there been any new inquiries at the ministry?"

"None that I haven't been able to quash."

Zubler sat back with a satisfied smile, swirling his brandy. "Good! You'll keep me informed, of course?"

"Of course." More head bobbing.

"We're stepping up our campaign soon," Zubler said, and took a long sip from his glass. Krinke sat forward, his eyes wide and eager. Zubler let him wait a moment while he savored the brandy.

"In the next few weeks there will be a grand gesture, comparable to Berlin in '33, and you are to make sure the ministry doesn't ruin things. I'm sure I can count on you, as always."

"Yes, of course!" Krinke said, beaming. "What kind of gesture will it be?"

Zubler's thin smile grew. "Best to keep that secret for now. But you will know when the time comes."

After Krinke left to return to Bern, Zubler picked up the telephone and gave a number to the operator. After several rings, a female voice answered.

"Mrs. Frisch, I presume?"

"Yes."

"May I speak with your husband, please?"

"Who's calling?"

"This is the Gauleiter."

"Of course, sir! One moment please, I will fetch him right away."

Zubler smiled to himself. Mrs. Frisch didn't know his name and had never met him—for security reasons—but she knew who her leader was.

A moment later, Georg Frisch answered the line. "Good evening, sir. What may I do for you?"

"The Gestapo will call on you shortly. They have been tasked with identifying the man who calls himself Inspector Max Schmidt."

"You don't know who he is, then?"

"Not yet. We only know that he is not a FedPol inspector. Probably not police at all. But don't worry—the Gestapo will get to the bottom of this. They need your cooperation, of course."

"Of course, sir. I will assist in any way I can."

Zubler smiled. "I know you will. You are a loyal and good son of the Fatherland, and you will be rewarded when the Reich is finally whole. Good night."

Martin sensed their presence before he saw them.

He walked with Sonia toward her apartment building, and glanced over his shoulder. A man dressed in black sat inside a dark green Opel Kapitan across the street, half a block from Sonia's building. He was smoking a cigarette and reading a newspaper, not an unusual sight, but still troubling.

The car faced toward Sonia's building, giving the man a perfect view. Martin wondered if it was one of Frisch's goons, but decided they would drive something cheaper than a four-door Opel Kapitan.

They reached the building, and Martin held the door for Sonia. He took a quick glance down the street. There were a few people going about their business—a middle-aged woman carrying a bag of groceries on one arm, a loaf of dark bread sticking out the top; a young couple strolling arm-in-arm the opposite direction. All seemed harmless enough. Only the dark figure in the Kapitan concerned him. He followed Sonia inside.

"Miss Rubenstein, I'm glad you're home. There was a police inspector here this afternoon—oh! Good evening, Inspector."

"Good evening, Mrs. Schlachet." Martin touched the rim of his hat.

"Everything is alright, Mrs. Schlachet," Sonia said. "But thank you for your concern." She touched the older woman's arm, then turned and climbed the stairs.

Martin nodded at the bewildered-looking portierfrau as he passed.

"I'll open the desk for you," Sonia said when they were inside the apartment, without looking at him. She removed the key from her purse, opened the drawer, and stood back.

"Thank you," Martin said. He stood at the desk with his back to her, and flipped through the files inside.

On top sat a copy of Dr. Rubenstein's Will. Martin laid that on the desk and continued. There were several important personal records—a copy of his life insurance policy, a bank book for an account at the Zurischer Kredit Bank, his and Sonia's passports, a copy of Mrs. Rubenstein's death certificate from 1932.

Then he found a check stub for twenty-thousand francs from the Swiss National Bank, drawn from the account of the Ministry of Defense. The date on the stub was September 1, 1941. Martin reached for the bank book and flipped through it. Amid the neat entries and carefully lined-up ciphers was a deposit for twenty-thousand francs the first week of every month, going back to July 1940.

He spun toward Sonia, who stood a few feet away with her hands folded in front of her. Her expression was unreadable as he held up the check stub.

"Miss Rubenstein, were you aware that your father was on the federal government payroll?"

She didn't respond immediately. "I found that after he died. He never mentioned it to me. And he never spent a rappen of that money, either. He put it all into a bank account and never touched it."

Martin thought he saw her eyes go moist. He did the math in his head, and figured that 240,000 Swiss francs was almost $60,000. Sonia Rubenstein had lost her father, and then suddenly found herself rich. From the look in her eyes, she hadn't expected it.

"Do you know what these payments were for?" he asked, more gently.

She made a tiny shrug, then shook her head. "Not really. There are papers in there, but I don't know how to read them."

There was a tremor of emotion in her voice, and Martin turned back to the desk, as much to give her a moment of privacy as for his own purposes.

He found a large file at the back of the drawer. It contained dozens of pages of schematic drawings—mostly round cylindrical things, usually drawn horizontally, but also occasionally on the wings of an airplane. But the planes always lacked a propeller. Numerous mathematical equations were written all around the drawings, some seeming to go on endlessly.

"Have you looked at these, Miss Rubenstein?" Martin asked without turning around.

"A few days after he died. I only looked through the first ten or twelve pages, and put them back. I don't want to know too much."

He half-turned toward her, holding some of the pages in his hand. "You know what these are?"

She shrugged. "I can make an educated guess. Some type of air propulsion system that doesn't use propellers."

Martin stared at her a moment, and their eyes met. He held them for a moment before she looked down in embarrassment.

"Your father was a patriot, Miss Rubenstein."

Her eyes moistened again, and she nodded. Her heart-shaped face was soft, her mouth quivering, and for the first time since Martin met her, she looked truly beautiful.

"I'm sorry, but I'm going to need to take photographs of these pages. More educated men than you or I will need to see these."

She nodded her ascent, then turned away and walked into her bedroom.

Martin had no doubt that this was only a small part of what Dr. Rubenstein had been working on. He'd probably kept most of his papers at his office in the Polytechnic Institute, but Frisch's goons had likely removed everything.

He took his 35mm camera from his inside jacket pocket and snapped photos. Twice he had to change film before he finished.

He walked to the open door of her bedroom. She sat on the end of the bed, looking out the window.

"Thank you, Miss Rubenstein. I'll show myself out."

She nodded without looking at him. He slipped away.

The Opel Kapitan was parked in the same place, but it was unoccupied. Martin hoped his instincts had been wrong earlier. The street lamps were spaced far apart, and the sidewalk was fairly dark. He kept his hand close to the concealed Luger.

He reached the corner and checked the street before crossing. A tall man dressed in black, with a black leather coat, sat on the stairs of an apartment building, reading a newspaper. Martin kept him in his peripheral vision, and the man folded the newspaper and stood when Martin crossed the street.

Martin slipped his right hand into his jacket and put his fingers around the handle of the Luger. He kept a brisk pace, but not fast enough to seem hurried. He took a right at the next corner, and glanced behind him to see the tall man in black following some thirty yards back.

Momentarily out of sight, Martin broke into a run for five seconds to put some distance behind him, but dropped back to a brisk walk before his tail had a chance to round the corner.

At the next corner Martin crossed the street and went left, casting a quick glance back. The man in leather was now forty-five yards back, but had picked up his pace and now appeared to be hurrying.

Martin's eyes darted from store-front to store-front, settling on a small French bistro at the next corner. He crossed the street again, and stopped in front of the menu posted on the window. He stood there for a minute, pretending to read. Out of the corner of his eye, and saw the tall man in leather stooped down twenty yards back, tying his shoe.

There was a good crowd inside the bistro. Martin stayed near the door until a waiter emerged from the kitchen with a bottle of wine. He watched the waiter present it to a table, open it, and pour some, then wait for the gentleman to smell and approve. Martin glanced back at the man in leather, who was strolling away, pretending to look up at the stars.

As soon as the waiter finished pouring the glasses, Martin dashed inside. He reached the kitchen door at the same time as the startled waiter. Standing between him and the kitchen door, he pressed a fifty-franc note into his hand and flashed his FedPol badge.

"Stay out here a moment. If anyone asks, I went into the washroom."

Martin hurried through the kitchen, ignoring the angry shouts from the sous-chefs. He pushed his way through to the back door, and found himself in a dark alley beside large trash cans. He sprinted past several doors, turning right at another dark alley leading away from the bistro.

This alley led to the next street, a narrow lane lined with apartment buildings. After glancing around and not seeing the man in leather, Martin hurried across the street and dove through a thick hedge lining a garden beside one of the buildings. Jumping over flower beds, he rushed to the alley behind the building, and sprinted north.

He followed the alley at a run for several blocks, pausing to check around before crossing streets, and eventually came to a wide avenue. The automobile traffic was light, but the pedestrian traffic was heavier, and after pausing for a moment to catch his breath and find his bearings, he walked west in the general direction of the train station, keeping to a crowd as much as possible.

A dark Opel Kapitan sedan passed going the other direction, a tall figure in black at the wheel, a second figure in black in the passenger seat. Martin turned his face away.

He picked up his pace, not daring to look back to see if the Kapitan had stopped until he'd gone another block. The car was nowhere to be seen, but the face of the tall man in leather bobbed above the crowd two blocks behind him.

Martin faced forward again and picked up his pace still more. A busy intersection loomed ahead, and he searched around for an empty taxi. Not seeing one, he checked out the storefronts. His gaze fell on a busy chocolatier to his left, and he hurried to the door and went inside.

He stood behind a shelf of boxed chocolates, pretending to check out a collection while keeping an eye on the sidewalk. Several moments passed before the two men in leather walked past, peering into the window at the shoppers. Martin kept behind the shelf, and they moved on.

"Are you going to buy?" a rail thin woman with hair more gray than brown asked, nodding toward the box of chocolates in his hand, a friendly smile softening the long and rather severe lines of her face. "It is very good, your wife will be pleased."

"No, thank you," Martin said, handing her the box and walking to the door.

He looked around; no sign of either of the men in leather. He walked back the way he had come, and saw a tram picking up passengers half a block ahead. He sprinted through the crowd, apologizing as he bumped into people, but reached the tram as it pulled away. He jumped on-board, paid the fare, and took a seat.

As the tram roared to full speed, he spotted the men in leather on the other side of the street, still looking in store windows. He chuckled as he pulled his hat down over his eyes.

Wednesday,
October 1, 1941

15

Bern

Lt. Colonel Legge stood when Martin entered his office, and shook Martin's hand. "Excellent work, Mr. Schuller. Seems Bill Donovan's trust in you is well-placed."

Martin took a seat, but not before glancing at the colonel's desk and seeing copies of his photographs front and center.

"I'm not sure if you're aware, but my office knew that Dr. Rubenstein was working with the Swiss military. We weren't certain how far his work had gone, which these photographs of yours confirm for us, but we were fairly certain the Swiss development of jet propulsion systems was behind our own. These photographs tell us that it was a bit further than we imagined, but still behind ours. You understand, this information is classified. Not even the Ambassador has need to know of this." His eyes seemed to bore into Martin.

"Understood, Colonel. As I'm sure you understand that the Office of the COI will share it with Assistant Secretary for Intelligence at State, Mr. Berle." Legge's eyes narrowed, so Martin added, "State's Intelligence bureau has different interests than MID. We're concerned with the diplomatic and geopolitical implications."

The colonel's expression showed mild distaste. "'We?' You work for the COI."

Martin matched Legge's stare, unblinking. "Yes—as the liaison for State."

The military Attaché looked down. Martin felt a tiny tug at the corners of his mouth, and suppressed the smile.

"I'll have to report to my superiors in Washington, assuring them that the situation is under control. I don't have time to get involved in turf wars with State."

Martin fought the irritation that welled up in response to the attack, with only partial success. "That's what the COI was appointed for. We're on the same side, Colonel. It serves us both to share information."

The colonel was silent for quite a while. Martin wondered if the officer was going to respond at all. Finally, the colonel grunted and nodded, looking down at the photos on his desk. "We made inquiries each time a high-ranking officer was killed, but found no Soviet involvement. MID is not concerned about underground Communist groups venting their grievances."

"State is more concerned than the War Department with the possibility that armed Communist cells are operating in Switzerland, and killing high-ranking officials—whether military or civilian." Martin watched the colonel's face.

Legge chuckled. "I have no desire to tell you diplomats what your priorities should be. I only ask that you keep me informed before you meddle in matters that have a military component."

Martin nodded. "We're in agreement. As representative of the COI, I will keep you informed personally of any findings that have military bearing."

The colonel stood, and Martin followed suit. "Then we understand each other," the colonel said, shaking his hand.

Martin didn't feel entirely positive about the encounter. As he walked to Ron Witherspoon's office, he braced himself for the reaction he'd get to what he had to say.

"Good morning. I'll need to meet with your German Embassy contacts as soon as possible."

Witherspoon looked startled. "But you're—that's out of the question."

"It's important."

Witherspoon straightened, taking a deep breath. "You have to understand how the information game is played outside of the States. In my classified role as Information Officer, I make contact with foreign agents who are much like me. We exchange promises of confidentiality whenever we exchange information. And we all have diplomatic immunity. A covert operator such as you couldn't meet with a foreign attaché without risking exposure."

Martin felt his blood pressure rise while he listened to Witherspoon describe the job that he had literally done himself in Buenos Aires just months ago. "I understand all of that, and I understand the reasons. But I need to infiltrate certain right-wing organizations that are quite secretive, and I can't do that cold. I need a mutual contact to get me inside, and your contacts are the best candidates."

Witherspoon blanched at his tone. "It's a huge risk."

"I know."

"I'll have to arrange a meeting far from the embassies."

Obviously. But that sounded like agreement. "I'll meet them wherever you say."

Withespoon sighed. "Let me see what I can arrange."

Franz sauntered up to the US Embassy, and a blond marine held up his hand.

"Can I help you, sir?" he asked in English.

Franz hadn't anticipated an armed guard. He'd assumed he could walk inside and find Mr. Smith waiting. Since when did the embassies of neutral nations have armed guards?

"I am meeting Mr. Smith, two o'clock," he replied in halting English.

"Mr. Smith?" The marine's eyebrows bunched in doubt.

"Yes. Mr. Smith expects me." He didn't know enough English to explain that Mr. Smith was waiting for him inside the door. In frustration, he pointed at the door. "Here."

"Come with me."

Jason sat at his desk on the ground floor, reviewing a visa application for an Italian couple. The annual quotas for Italians had already been met this year and next, and the best he could do would be to grant them a visa for 1943. It broke his heart to have to tell them that.

The husband spoke some English, but Jason still had to repeat the year and hold up three fingers for emphasis. The man seemed to deflate before having to turn to his wife and translate. Her eyes grew moist as she replied in Italian, her voice rising and falling with emotion.

"What can we do?" the man asked.

Jason had heard this same question from others who had fled Fascist Italy. They were only allowed to stay in Switzerland for a short time while they sought permanent asylum elsewhere. If they couldn't find a way out, they were sent to a detention camp with other stranded refugees.

"You could try the Brazilian embassy, or the Argentine embassy. I've heard many of your countrymen are granted visas there."

The man nodded. "Thank you."

"I'll give you the addresses," Jason said, opening a drawer and flipping to a file labelled "Italians." He'd asked Amanda for the addresses of the Brazilian and Argentinean embassies in Bern, and had stapled them to the inside of the front cover of his folder for easy access. He copied the addresses and handed them to the man.

"Here, see if they can help you. Good luck, Mr. and Mrs. Giordano." He stood and shook Mr. Giordano's hand, nodded to his wife, and walked with them to the door.

Reaching the foyer, he noticed Martin Schuller standing by the elevator, watching the front door. He smiled, but Mr. Schuller responded with a nod.

Jason bid the Italian couple goodbye. Corporal Lawrence stepped aside to let them pass. Behind the corporal stood a handsome young man about his own age, with dimpled round cheeks that might have seemed baby-faced if it weren't for the shadow of dark beard that made the face look rugged. Thick brown hair under a newsboy cap, a dingy white cotton shirt, and a worn-looking brown corduroy jacket gave him a bohemian air that wasn't unappealing.

His warm brown eyes met Jason's, and for a second Jason stood immobile. The young man grinned, and Jason found himself smiling back and blushing. He looked away. "Hello, Corporal Lawrence."

"Good afternoon, sir," the marine replied while marching past.

Jason walked back toward his desk, but heard Martin Schuller's voice from the foyer saying, "Thank you, Corporal. Mr. Lemiel is here to see me."

Jason decided he'd have to go upstairs and visit Amanda later.

16

"Thank you for coming, Mr. Lemiel," Martin said, in German.

"I am glad to offer you my assistance, Mr. Smith—although I know that is not your real name."

Martin nodded. "Safest for us if you don't know my real name."

"But you know mine."

"Yes." *That's how this works.*

Franz shrugged. "I was planning to be in Bern today anyway, even before I was called to Zurich last night. So meeting with you now is convenient for me."

"You have a meeting tonight?"

"Yes. The local group is meeting tonight. They have grown concerned, as have I, that there is something afoot in Switzerland."

"You refer to the recent assassinations, with Communist symbols?"

Franz nodded. "It is not the Communists, though. Of that I'm certain."

Martin grew suspicious. "How?"

Franz smiled. "I know several individuals whose thinking used to go that direction, before the Stalinist purges alienated them, and convinced them that democracy is best. Some spent time in the Soviet Union fifteen years ago, when they were idealistic and hopeful. Now they are Socialist realists, but they still have ties with individuals who were in the Communist Party until it was outlawed. They are all in agreement that the Communists are a scapegoat, and someone else is assassinating the colonels."

"How well do you know these people?"

"Some of them I have known my whole life," Franz said, sitting back in his chair. "You see, my father runs a left-leaning newspaper. He is the owner, publisher, and editor. Father is a Social Democrat, but his friends include the whole spectrum of socialists and communists. I have been around such people for as long as I can remember. I trust them, Mr. Smith."

Martin scowled. "So we are clear, Mr. Lemiel—you yourself are not, and have never been, a Communist?"

"Correct," Franz said with a firm nod. "I believe in freedom and democracy."

"Have you ever spoken with anyone from the Soviet embassy?"

Franz shrugged. "Not to my knowledge."

"If approached, would you ever consider working with the Soviet intelligence agencies?"

Franz paused, and seemed to be sizing Martin up for a moment. "In my opinion, Mr. Smith, Stalin is as dangerous to Europe as Hitler. But Switzerland is not surrounded by Soviet-occupied territory. The Fascists are the more immediate threat."

Martin nodded. It wasn't a direct answer, but he was satisfied enough. He'd studied Franz long enough to determine that he was truthful, if not always forthcoming. "If not the Communists, then who do you think is assassinating the colonels?"

Franz smiled. "The real question is, who is framing the Communists? Who do you think would want to frame the Communists, Mr. Smith? Who hates Communists the most? The Nazis, of course. It's the only sensible answer. Surely you've come to that conclusion?"

"But the officers who've been killed have all been members of the SVV, which is pro-Nazi."

"*Mostly* pro-Nazi, Mr. Smith. There are others in Switzerland who are more so."

Martin frowned. "Explain what you mean, Mr. Lemiel."

"You may call me Franz."

Martin waited in silence.

"Last summer, when the threat of German invasion was real, General Guisan and the colonels rallied the country behind national defense. Every man between sixteen and sixty mobilized. We Swiss may be peaceful, but we are not cowards. For months the country was armed and ready. Most of the officers organizing national defense were—are—members of the SVV.

"The country was galvanized. We are passionate in our national pride, willing to lay down our lives to defend our freedom. But, there is a tiny minority in Switzerland—maybe one percent of the people, two percent at most—who think that we should be part of Germany. These Nazis would have every reason to assassinate the officers who mobilized us against invasion, and to blame the Communists. Have you noticed that after every assassination, the newspapers have been quick to condemn the 'Marxist terrorists'?"

Martin shook his head. "I haven't been in the country long. Do you have any proof of this?"

"No proof, but it is only logical."

Martin decided to try a different subject. "Why do you have connections with the French Resistance?"

"As I told you last night, I knew artists and writers in France during my university days. After the fall of France, I made inquiries, learned that there was a Resistance movement forming, and that many of my friends were part of it. I decided to do what I could for them."

"Which is?"

"I pass along information from sources in the German underground, mostly."

"Do you attend meetings of the Resistance cells the way you attend meetings of anti-Nazi groups here?"

Franz laughed. "It is not so easy to get into France, Mr. Smith."

That wasn't an answer. "Have you been inside Occupied France?"

"Yes." Franz leaned back, an enigmatic smile on his lips.

"How often?"

"A few times. Not often."

"How did you get there?"

"I was smuggled across the frontier from Alsace. I have Alsatian friends who are sympathetic to the Resistance. There is limited travel allowed between Alsace and Occupied France—for Germans. The Nazis administer Alsace as part of the Reich, so that makes it easier for my Alsatian friends to, um, 'visit relatives' in Occupied France. They must be cautious about how often they request visas, of course. It is not easy."

"I see." Martin checked his notes from the night before. "Tell me about the Resistance cells you know in France."

Franz's smile tightened. "It would not be safe for them if I told you much, Mr. Smith."

Martin forced a disarming smile. "I'm not going to tell the Gestapo."

Franz didn't laugh at the joke. "If you are captured, they can make you talk. Under torture, everyone talks eventually. Best if you let me be your liaison."

"Tell me what you feel you can, then."

Franz explained how he'd come into contact with the leaders of cells in Besançon, Dijon, Nancy, Epinal, Troyes, Saint Dizier, Châlons-en-Champagne, and Rheims. He could only estimate the strength of each cell. No, he had never met most of the members. He knew the leaders by their code names. The only ones he knew by name were his old friends from his days in Paris. No, he was not privy to most of their activities.

Yes, he had a code name, it was Emmantaler.

"What kind of information do you pass to the Resistance?"

Franz shrugged. "It varies. Troop movements, mostly. I hear from underground operatives in Germany if Wehrmacht convoys are moving toward France, and I pass along the details."

That's an act of war by any measure. "You are aware, I'm sure, that such information is used to set bombs and ambushes. Men die because of the information you pass along."

Franz's face grew serious. "Yes. It is regrettable. Most of the soldiers killed are not Nazis. They are just German patriots. Or conscripts. And most of them are young. But their side is wrong, and it must be stopped. Sometimes that means men have to die who are not guilty of anything more than being a soldier on the wrong side."

Franz looked down for a moment, and Martin waited in silence. Franz looked up and stared him in the eyes. "If the Americans join the war against the Nazis, I would be able to help you contact the Resistance in France, and even underground groups in Germany itself."

Martin's eyes narrowed. "But not until then?"

Franz shrugged, and stayed silent.

"How often have you been inside the Third Reich, Franz?"

"Many times."

"How do you get in?"

"Sometimes I go by train. Swiss nationals are allowed to travel inside the Reich. We are a neutral nation, and they try to keep relations as normal as possible. But the security agencies keep track of how many times we come and go, so I'm careful not to make official border-crossings too often. I don't want the Gestapo doing more than routine questioning of my business."

Martin checked his impatience at the partial answer. "How else do you get in?"

"The border is guarded, and fenced with barbed wire, but there are many places where the patrols are light, and it is possible to sneak under the barbed wire at night."

"Do you use the same crossing each time?"

Franz smiled. "That shall remain my secret, Mr. Smith."

Martin let that go. "Have you ever been stopped by the Gestapo?"

"Never on my unofficial visits," Franz said, his smile widening. "I have an insurance policy, shall we call it. But I have been followed during some of my official visits. I am careful to ditch them without seeming that I am."

He leaned far forward, and Martin instinctively leaned forward as well.

"I believe the Gestapo are operating in Switzerland, Mr. Smith," Franz whispered, which was odd, since they were alone. "There is something sinister happening, and the Gestapo are behind it."

Martin arched one eyebrow, doubtful. "Why would the Gestapo be in Switzerland? It's not occupied territory."

"But they would like for it to be."

Martin shook his head. "Now that Germany has invaded the Soviet Union, Hitler can't spare any troops for an invasion of Switzerland. It makes no sense."

"Perhaps that is why he is using the Gestapo instead."

Martin frowned. "What reason do you have for suspecting the Gestapo?"

"I was followed last night by men in black leather coats, and I haven't crossed any borders for several weeks. My tails were not

Swiss, Mr. Smith. I've been inside the Reich often enough to know the Gestapo's pattern."

"More likely they were Abwehr. Or British Intelligence," Martin said.

Franz shook his head. "No, they were Gestapo. I'm certain. The Abwehr have no use for me—I know no military secrets. And British Intelligence doesn't need *me* to make contact with the Resistance; they do that on their own."

Martin shook his head. "The Gestapo could have you followed inside Germany and Occupied France, hoping you'll lead them to their enemies. That makes perfect sense. But they have no reason to follow you in Switzerland."

The corner of Franz's mouth turned up. "How did you learn about our little group in Zurich, Mr. Smith?"

Martin hesitated a second, weighing whether or not to reveal his source. *What harm could it do?* "From Inspector Georg Frisch of the Zurich Police."

"He knew all of the members, didn't he?" Franz paused, but Martin didn't acknowledge. "Why would the local police be interested in that group? Because of anonymous leaflets that haven't been cleared by the censors? No. They wouldn't hesitate to arrest anyone caught distributing such literature, but they wouldn't bother to closely monitor the group. They don't have the time for that. But if someone important—say an inspector—were working for the Gestapo..."

Martin's instincts had told him there was more to Inspector Frisch—could that be it? Could he be working for the Gestapo? It seemed incredible; and yet, the pieces seemed to fit.

He looked hard at Franz. "Are you, or anyone else you know, smuggling weapons to the French Resistance?"

"No! I do not fight wars. I work only to pass information, not weapons or ammunition. That is what the British are for."

Martin allowed an amused half-smile to spread across his lips. Everyone knew the British armed the French Resistance, it seemed. Some secrets were anything but.

"Are you sure no one you know is smuggling weapons or ammunition out of Switzerland to the Resistance?"

"Absolutely certain. We Swiss are not afraid to fight if we are attacked—I mobilized with the rest of the country when we feared the Germans would invade—but we do not fight wars *unless* attacked. That is a national honor."

"Then why would the Gestapo be interested in following you inside Switzerland?"

"That is what we must find out," Franz replied.

Martin led Franz down the hall. "Wait here while I go over everything you've told me. I may need to speak with you more today, so please do not leave. He indicated a padded chair near Amanda Overstreet's desk. "Miss Overstreet will get you anything you need while you wait."

Martin turned to Amanda and said in quiet English, "Herr Lemiel is going to wait here while I meet with Mr. Witherspoon. Please get him something to drink if he asks, and please see to it that he is not disturbed by anyone."

"Absolutely!" Amanda said with a gleaming smile.

After Mr. Schuller left, Amanda looked at the ruggedly-handsome young man sitting a dozen feet away and flashed him a smile, which he returned. She leaned forward, and arched her back enough to thrust her breasts out; his smile broadened and his eyes dropped toward her bust.

"Would you like anything to drink, sir? Some coffee, perhaps?"

He looked back at her face, and cocked his head.

"Do you speak English?"

A sheepish smile came to his lips, and he held his fingers close together. "A little. Not so good. *Sprechen sie Deutsch?"*

Amanda sighed. *"Nein,"* she said, shaking her head. *"Nicht zer Gut."*

"Parlez vous Français?"

She shook her head. If only she'd paid attention that year she took French in high school.

Herr Lemiel shrugged and leaned back in his seat.

"Coffee?" she asked, holding one hand up in imitation of holding a saucer, while making a motion with the other to imitate drinking from a cup.

"Kaffee? Yeah, thank you," he said with a thick accent.

She walked toward the coffee pot, exaggerating the swing of her hips. She glanced back as she poured a cup, and smiled to herself when she saw him staring at her backside.

She leaned down a bit farther than necessary when she handed the cup and saucer to him, allowing him a glance at the cleavage beneath the collar of her tight pink sweater.

He gave her a wicked grin as she straightened back up, then stared at her over the rim of the cup.

She sauntered back to her desk, and saw Jason rounding the corner from the top of the stairs. His heels echoed on the tile floor.

"Shouldn't you be working?" she teased.

"It's three o'clock, time for a coffee break."

"Don't you grunts have coffee downstairs?"

"Yeah, but you make the best coffee. And you're the best company."

"Flatterer!" she said, swatting the air, but smiling. Then she motioned him to come close. "You can't stay long. I have to babysit that Swiss man over there. He's meeting with Mr. Schuller."

Jason cast a quick glance at Herr Lemiel. "I saw him come in an hour ago. Mr. Schuller was waiting for him."

"I'm supposed to see that he's not disturbed by anyone," Amanda whispered.

"Hmm. Must be something top secret!"

"Could be," Amanda said, straightening back up. "Now get your coffee and go back downstairs so I don't get in trouble."

"Can't I at least say hi to him?" Jason said, not waiting for her to answer.

"No!" she said, too late. Jason was already half-way to the man, extending his hand and greeting him in German.

"*Guten Tag*," Herr Lemiel said in return.

"My name's Jason Bachman," he said in German, shaking hands.
"Franz Lemiel."

"Pleasure to meet you." Jason stared into Franz's warm brown eyes. He held the handshake a bit longer than was polite, but Franz didn't pull his hand away.

"The pleasure is all mine, Mr. Bachman." Franz didn't break the stare. His eyes seemed to be smiling.

Amanda's voice broke the reverie, and Jason pulled his hand back. "Jason Bachman! If you get me in trouble, so help me I will tell everyone you are not my boyfriend and never have been. I might even say you're my best girlfriend."

His stomach dropped. He spun toward her. "You wouldn't!"

"I might."

"I'll only be a minute, for Christ's sake!" He turned back to Franz with an apologetic smile. "Sorry about that," he said in German.

"It's quite alright. She probably thinks you're going to steal me away from her."

Jason's heart fluttered. Franz stared into his eyes with an intensity that made Jason blush and look away. "You're waiting for Mr. Schuller, I understand."

Franz looked momentarily surprised. "Mr. Schuller? Ah, yes! We have met already, and he wishes me to remain so that we might speak again."

"I don't know him well," Jason said, grasping for a way to keep the conversation going.

"Bachman—that is a German name, yeah?"

Jason's heart swelled with pleasure that Franz had noticed, and he nodded. "My grandfather's parents emigrated from Germany almost ninety years ago. I guess that makes me a quarter German."

"You speak German well."

"Thank you!" Jason beamed.

"Perhaps we will have an opportunity to speak again. For longer, I hope."

Jason's smile widened so much his cheeks ached. "I hope so, too!" His mind raced. "There is a tavern up the street, called the Sulgenkeller. My friends and I go there after work for beer. Perhaps you could meet us there?"

"Yes, perhaps so," Franz said with an enigmatic smile that Jason found mesmerizing.

He blushed. "I'd best be on my way. Very nice to meet you, Mr. Lemiel."

"Franz, please."

Jason grinned and nodded. He turned with a wave. He gave Amanda a big excited grin as he passed her, but she scowled.

"You never got any coffee!" she called as he walked toward the stairs.

17

"Russian Relations Office," a young woman's voice answered, sounding as if she were talking through a pipe.

Martin asked for a name, and waited while the line clicked. It sill amazed him that he could talk to someone halfway across the world. Bill Donovan made trans-Atlantic calls from London whenever he traveled there, and the President had given his office a generous budget, which the COI made thorough use of; Martin was directed to spare no expense on this mission, if he could justify it.

And he could justify this.

"Ken, it's Martin Schuller."

"Martin, good morning!"

"Afternoon."

"Ah—I heard you were on assignment in Europe. Switzerland, I'd guess, based on your cable last night."

"Did you learn anything about those two Russians?"

"Yes. Elena Krasnakovich checks out exactly. Born Elena Maria Krasnakova in Kiev 1921, parents were both Russian, not Ukrainian. Her father Boris Krasnakovich was a captain in the White Army, and he was wounded in battle. Our friends at MID confirmed that. The family escaped to Switzerland in 1922, just before the borders were sealed."

"And Pavel Minskayev?"

There was a second's hesitation. "A little bit, yes—but it doesn't really add up. Very strange."

"I'm listening."

"The Swiss Embassy here confirmed that Pavel Minskayev immigrated to Switzerland in 1928 at the age of nine, with his mother Irina Minskaya, thirty-two, and his younger brother Mikhail Minskayev, age six. But that was all they'd say. Acted pretty strange about it."

Martin thought hard for a moment. "How difficult was it to get out of the Soviet Union in '28?"

There was a snort at the other end of the line. "Easier to try to get out of Hell."

"What was happening there at the time?"

"Well…that was toward the end of the big power struggle in the Politburo, between Stalin and Trotsky. The United Opposition, as Trotsky's people were called, was pretty much finished."

"What happened to them?"

"A lot of them were sent to Siberia. Some were 'rehabilitated' and eventually released, only to be killed in the purges in the mid-thirties."

Martin's mind raced. "Ken, see if you can look in your archives, and find out if there's anything about Irina Minskaya there."

"Jesus, Martin! You know how long that could take? How am I gonna justify that kind of time? What am I gonna tell the chief?"

"Tell him to talk to Bill Donovan. Thanks Ken." Martin hung up before Ken could argue.

"Hey, a bunch of us are going to the Sulgenkeller for beer, and maybe dinner—you wanna come along?" Jason asked Amanda at quarter past five o'clock.

"No thank you." She barely glanced at him as she tidied up her desk for the night.

"Aw, you're not still sore at me for earlier, are you?"

She stopped what she was doing and looked at him, her eyes not holding any anger. "You could've gotten me into serious trouble. I still could, you know—Herr Lemiel's been in Mr. Schuller's office for the last hour, and God only knows what they've been talking about. If he mentions that I let someone talk to him, I could lose my job!"

That startled Jason, but he recovered quickly. "I'm sure you won't get sacked for a little thing like that."

"I might!" She leaned forward and motioned him closer, then continued at a whisper. "You know as well as I do that they're being very secretive. And I'd rather not be accused of compromising national security or anything. I've got connections, but I don't know if they could help me if I let someone talk with a secret agent!"

Jason had always wondered how Amanda got a job that was normally held by local women, with nothing more than a high school diploma and a certificate from a secretarial school in Newark. Especially since she spoke only English. And at a plum assignment like Switzerland, no less.

He took a reassuring tone. "It's probably not like that. Herr Lemiel didn't seem like a secret agent, now did he?"

Amanda shrugged as she sat back and resumed straightening her desk. "How should I know? And I don't want to, either."

Jason let it go. "You wanna join us at the Sulgenkeller?"

"I can't—got a date tonight." She gave him a wink and a smile.

A pang of jealousy shot through Jason's chest as he pictured her on the arm of Franz Lemiel. He hadn't noticed if any American businessmen had come in to see the ambassador today. "Anyone I know?"

Amanda shook her head. "No, not a repeat. An importer from New York who's in town for a few days; forty years old, handsome, in a nice suit and silk scarf. Big gold watch. He's taking me to a nice French restaurant."

Jason breathed a sigh of relief. "Have a great time!"

Franz left the embassy after five-thirty. His second meeting with Mr. Schuller had been a long one. The American agent was none too thrilled when Franz addressed him by name upon reentering his office. But Franz had sworn secrecy, and they'd moved on to the serious business of logistics.

They'd determined that Franz would send messages to the embassy using a code they developed together from the opening page of Kafka's *Amerika*, which Franz knew word for word. Mr. Schuller, not surprisingly, had not read it, but promised to get a copy.

Now Franz hurried across the street. He spied the Sulgenkeller tavern a couple of doors down. He had an hour-and-a-half until the meeting in the University district, plenty of time for a drink or an early meal.

A group of ten young men stood around the back of the room, with ties loosened and steins of beer in their hands, all laughing loudly and conversing equally loudly in English. He nodded to Jason Bachman in the middle of the group.

Jason grinned and raised his beer stein in salute.

Franz turned his attention to the bartender. "What are the house specialties?"

"Food or drink?"

"Both."

"Mrs. Neumann makes an excellent Schnitzel Cordon Bleu, and we have a fresh batch of Mr. Neumann's black cherry schnapps."

"I'll take a glass of the schnapps now, and a plate of the Schnitzel Cordon Bleu with a side of Rosti in a half-hour."

A moment later he took his glass of schnapps and sat at a table in the corner, where he could observe the room. Half of the tables were occupied by men in business suits, conversing in English and drinking beer. American businessmen, no doubt. One table near the door hosted four middle-aged Swiss men, speaking in quieter voices than the Americans around them, and all huddled toward the table as if to lean as far away as possible from the ubiquitous foreign presence.

Three stools at the bar held men in their thirties wearing white dress shirts and dark slacks, speaking French. Probably Federal government employees. A world away from their home cantons here in German-speaking Bern.

And then there was the bunch of young workers in the back, the only ones around Franz's age. He watched them for a while, and chuckled at the overtly masculine way they interacted, standing not too close together and never touching, each trying to be louder and manlier than the others. Like overgrown adolescents. So typically American.

Only Jason Bachman appeared natural in his posture and manner. He wore a genuine smile, and he laughed often. His companions seemed to like him, talking and laughing with him—but on closer look, they leaned away almost imperceptibly if Jason got too close. Jason put his hand on the shoulder of one companion as they all laughed at an apparent joke, and the other man responded to the touch with a tiny flinch that could have almost been imagined.

The corners of Franz's mouth curled up in amusement.

The group migrated to the bar, and Jason meandered through the tables toward Franz. He greeted Franz in German with a big grin. "Hello! I didn't know if you'd come. Why don't you join us?"

Franz shook his head. "Thank you, no. I'm comfortable in my little corner, where I can people-watch."

"May I join you, then?"

"Of course." Franz motioned to the seat across from him.

"You must have had a lot to discuss with Mr. Schuller," Jason said.

"Yes, but we shouldn't speak of that here. I mustn't break any confidences."

"Oh, of course! I'm sorry if I seemed nosy."

"Don't apologize. I don't mind questions. I have no secrets of my own, but I'm good at keeping others' secrets." He stared into Jason's eyes and took a drink.

Jason held his gaze for a second and then looked away, flushing. He nodded toward Franz's glass. "What's that you're drinking?"

"Schnapps. The house specialty, and it's quite good. You should order some."

"I've never had Schnapps before."

Franz's eyebrows shot up. "Oh? Try some, then." He pushed his glass toward Jason.

"You wouldn't mind?"

"Of course not. Please have a taste." A teasing smile spread across his lips. "Anyone can drink beer, but true Germans drink Schnapps."

Jason returned the smile, held the glass to his lips, and took a sip. "Mmm!" he said as he handed the glass back. Franz took hold of the glass, and their fingertips brushed together at the exchange.

Jason looked away. "Are you from Bern?" he asked, looking toward his friends while they walked from the bar with full steins.

"No, I'm from Basel."

"Really?" Jason looked back at Franz, his blue eyes lighting with curiosity. "I've never been there. Is it nice?"

Franz smiled. "Yes, it's a beautiful city. There is a large square overlooking the Rhine, which is an excellent place to paint. We have a good artistic community in Basel."

"You're an artist?"

"Yes, a painter mostly."

"I've never met an artist before. And I've not traveled out of Bern yet."

"Well then, you must come visit me in Basel soon," Franz said as he raised his glass in a toast. "*Prost!*"

Jason blushed again, raised his stein and clinked it on Franz's glass, then drained the last of his beer.

"What do you paint, Mr. Lemiel?"

"Please call me Franz. I paint almost anything—landscapes, cityscapes, people, either alone and in groups, clothed or unclothed."

Jason's face turned crimson, all the way to his ears, and he looked down at his empty stein. "Are you in Bern to paint?"

"No, I have a meeting tonight near the university."

"Oh? What kind of meeting?"

Franz explained the anti-Nazi student group, and his work with such groups all around Switzerland, careful to leave out any mention of underground groups in Germany and France. Jason sat forward, listening in obvious fascination.

"Wow! That sounds so exciting."

Franz shrugged. "It can be."

"We never had anything like that at the University of Chicago."

"It is important for educated people to stay engaged with events outside of their own little corner of the world," Franz said.

"Oh, I agree!" Jason added quickly. "I started reading the newspaper after my father finished with it when I was twelve or thirteen, and I used to sit with my parents and listen to the news reports on the radio. I knew all about the Depression, the Spanish civil war, and everything else. We just didn't have any activist groups or anything where I went to college."

Franz nodded. It was what he would expect from American youth. "Perhaps you could come with me to the meeting tonight. You may learn things you can't read in newspapers. Unless, of course, you have things to do with your friends." Franz motioned toward the group of American young men by the dart board.

"No, I'd love to join you!" Jason's eyes twinkled.

"Excellent!" Franz said, grinning.

The bartender brought over a steaming plate and set it in front of Franz. "Anything else, sir?"

"Another glass of the schnapps, please, and one for my American friend."

"And I'll have a plate of what he's having," Jason said.

Jason sat with Franz for the next half-hour, enjoying the food and the conversation. The schnapps had moved him somewhere beyond a little bit tipsy by the time Franz said it was time to go. He forgot to say goodbye or wave to his friends.

They strode west down Marktgasse, and there was a definite spring in Jason's step. He was animated as he told Franz about his family, his childhood in Evanston, and learning to dance at the North Shore Country Club.

Franz put his hand briefly on the small of Jason's back to guide him as they rounded a corner, and continued north toward the university district. The warmth of Franz's touch radiated through his midsection. Or was that the schnapps?

"I have read that most American country clubs do not allow Jews," Franz said. "Is this true?"

A wave of embarrassment swept through Jason; he'd never given the matter any thought. There were certainly no Jews at the North Shore club. He wondered why he'd never noticed.

"I don't know," he said, quietly.

"Do you know any Jews, Jason?"

"No, I don't. Do you?"

"Yes."

An uncomfortable silence fell between them. Jason's mind raced for something to say that might rescue the situation. "I think it's terrible what the Nazis have done to them—the Jews, I mean."

"Do you know all that they've done?" Franz turned his face toward Jason, and his eyes seemed to penetrate right through him.

"I know they took away their citizenship, and fired all of the Jewish men who had government jobs, or management somewhere. And there was that night a couple of years ago when mobs attacked Jewish businesses and synagogues. I saw the images on the news reels—it looked horrible."

Franz was silent for a few seconds. "Yes, they did all of those things. But then a year-and-a-half ago, they started rounding up Jews in the cities, and shipped them to concentration camps. The same camps where they lock up criminals, communists, and men like us."

Jason's heart fluttered. He was afraid to ask what Franz meant by 'men like us.' Maybe he meant men who criticized them. Or maybe he meant men who…his cheeks and ears burned hot, and he shook his head to clear the image. Instead, he asked why the Nazis would lock up the Jews.

"Hatred can make men do all manner of terrible things," was all Franz said.

Martin kept a good distance behind the two young men.

When Franz had left his office, Martin had rushed down the stairs and gone out the back door, coming around the side of the building in time to see Franz crossing the street. He'd stood on the corner and watched him go inside the Sulgenkeller, and sit alone in the corner, until one of the embassy grunts sat with him.

The last thing Martin wanted was his new agent chumming around in public with U.S. Embassy staff. It carried far too much risk.

They'd sat together for more than an hour, even eaten together, and Martin had grown more irritated by the minute. Then they left together. Martin had planned to follow Franz to his group meeting anyway; now he had double the reason.

He had to stay far back, nearly a hundred yards, since Franz was likely experienced at detecting and evading a tail. To further complicate his task, they kept to a single street for more than a kilometer. And the pedestrian traffic was not particularly heavy.

They reached the university district before seven, and turned right off of Schazeneckstrasse. Darkness was falling, and Martin risked shortening the distance between them. He nearly missed them making a couple more turns, and finally rounded the last corner to see them entering a café.

Warm light emanated from the picture windows at the front of the café, where a waiter was busy bringing in chairs from the sidewalk tables, empty in the chill of the fall evening. Martin took up position in the doorway of a building across the street, and raised his binoculars.

The café was about half-full, but a large group of young people gathered around four adjacent tables in the rear of the room. Martin counted eighteen of them, not including Franz and the embassy grunt.

He watched Franz greet each of the young people gathered, and introduce his American companion. Martin took his 35mm camera from his inside pocket and snapped several shots, then settled in to wait.

A young man appeared at the corner of the street and stood against a wall, looking at the café. Martin stepped back farther into the shadow of the doorway.

The young man appeared to be mid-twenties—older than the students in the café, so not likely a lookout. He wore a stylish gray suit, and had dark hair that curled under the rim of his hat. He was attempting to look casual as he lounged against a brick wall, but he stared at the café without looking away.

In the deepening twilight, Franz and the others inside the café wouldn't be able to see the newcomer watching them.

After a while, the young man strolled down the street, keeping his gaze on the well-lit interior of the café. He passed in front of the doorway where Martin hid, but never glanced that way.

An amateur.

The man stopped at the other end of the block and lounged again, watching the café from the new angle.

Martin stared at him from the shadows. Who was he? A police informant? Or something more sinister?

Whoever he was, he wore his hat set back on his head, making it easy for Martin to study his round face and memorize it.

After several minutes, the young man turned and hurried away into the darkness.

Jason shook hands with each of the young men and women as he was introduced, repeating their names as he did, but by the time he got halfway through it was hopeless to try to remember them all.

They each gave him a friendly but wary smile. Jason imagined they'd never had a foreigner at one of their meetings, least of all an American. But in true Swiss fashion they were gracious and welcoming.

"I'll buy you a beer before we start," Franz said, going to the bar. Jason almost protested that he'd had enough to drink, but became embarrassed and kept silent. Franz returned with two tall glasses of dark beer.

The group mingled while the tables cleared one-by-one. Franz leaned close and whispered in Jason's ear. "The □aître'd is sympathetic to the cause, and he only allows certain regulars to sit inside on meeting days—but we still prefer to wait until the room is empty before we begin discussions.”

The warmth of his breath sent a tingle down the back of Jason’s neck, and he hoped Franz hadn’t noticed the goose-bumps that followed.

Finally the last couple got up to leave, and the group took their seats. They discussed the German army officers who’d visited Bern “on holiday” recently, including plenty of SS officers. Some grumbled about government ministers being too quick to grant tourist visas to Nazis.

“Plenty of them are here for no good,” said a dark-haired young man with a pale complexion. “They make secret deals for timber and hydroelectric power, and they spy on dissidents.” He had a small mouth, and his face tapered to a narrow chin. He had long and narrow fingers, which Jason thought should be made for piano playing.

Other similar accusations flew around the room, but none of them offered any proof of their claims.

One chubby blond boy with large round pink cheeks and big round brown eyes claimed in a high and slightly feminine voice that Luftwaffe pilots who ejected from planes and drifted into Switzerland, were given bigger and better food rations at the internment camp for Germans than were RAF pilots at their camp.

More grumblings circled the group about repeatedly confronting government officials with evidence of favoritism toward the Germans, only to be rebuffed.

“They say they are only being *practical*, that our situation is ‘tenuous’—I say they are cowards!” one tall young man with a mop of curly brown hair and a large hooked nose said.

“They never stand up to the Germans!”

“They always cave to Nazi pressure!”

Franz raised his hand. "There's little doubt that Nazi pressure is behind the censorship of our newspapers. They are terrified that the outside world will learn the truth of their activities from our little island of tranquility—as long as we remain outside of the control of their Propaganda Ministry."

Franz took a glance at Jason before continuing, his voice low. "There is a journalist I know in Bavaria who has proof of the inhumane conditions at a certain concentration camp. We're working on a way to get that proof out of Germany. If we succeed, we will be able to demonstrate to the outside world—to the Americans especially—that the Nazis are nothing more than common criminals."

The dark-haired young man with the piano-player fingers brightened. "We could throw that evidence in the face of our government ministers who welcome Nazi 'tourists,' but deny entry to anyone with a 'J' on their passport."

That caught Jason by surprise. He turned to Franz and asked "Is that true?"

"Yes," Franz confirmed, his voice and face grave. "It was at our government's request that Germany began stamping Jews' passports with the letter 'J' so that our customs officials could identify them, and deny them entry."

"But if what you told me is true, that they've started locking them up in concentrations camps—that's terrible! They have no way to escape."

Franz patted Jason's shoulder the way an affectionate uncle would to an inquisitive child who'd just realized the world wasn't fair after all. "That's why we have to expose their lies for all the world to see."

Franz spoke at length about German journalists he'd known over the years through his father, men who had been locked in concentration camps one by one for criticizing the regime. Jason listened closely, awed at the ease with which Franz spoke, and mesmerized by his passion.

The discussion moved on to planning ways to confront Federal officials in the coming weeks. Jason's attention waned, as the whole group seemed to know every official they discussed by name, and he'd never heard of any of them. He found himself watching Franz, though Franz did little speaking at this point. Once, he caught Jason's eye and winked.

Jason's breath caught, imagining that the group could see him blush, but their discussion continued unabated.

The meeting ended around nine-thirty, and Franz turned to Jason. "Thank you for being here. I hope that you learned some things."

"Yes, definitely! I had no idea." He hesitated, and waited until they'd passed out the front door before asking, "May I walk with you?"

"Yes, but I must hurry—my train to Basel leaves in thirty minutes."

Jason walked with Franz toward the station, keeping up with his fast pace. "I listened to all you said about the injustice inside the German Reich, and I wonder what I can do."

"I think you do your part already. You said that you grant visas to refugees."

"But I have to refuse most of them, or give them visas that they can't use until 1944."

Franz shrugged. "You do what you can. You don't make the policy that sets quotas for entry to the United States."

"But I think it could change if more Americans knew the things that you know," Jason said, feeling a wave of enthusiasm and passion. Like the students at the meeting. "I just don't know who to tell."

"I'm sure if you think long enough, you'll know what to do. You have a pure heart, that is obvious. You could do much good in the world—and I will help you. You should come see me in Basel. We can continue this conversation, I could show you the city, show you my art…maybe even paint you."

"Really? You'd like to paint me?"

"Of course. Write to me when you get home tonight, and we'll make arrangements for you to come to Basel."

Jason's stomach fluttered. "Where should I write?"

"My address is on a piece of paper in your pocket," Franz said with a grin. He stopped in front of the train station entrance. "I must go now. Until next time, my friend." He leaned forward and kissed Jason's cheek, then ran inside.

Jason stood there for several seconds, a dopey grin on his face. He put his left hand in his pocket and felt the piece of paper that hadn't been there before. He touched his cheek where Franz had kissed it, and his grin widened. He turned toward home, barely noticing his surroundings, or the evening chill.

He didn't notice Martin Schuller walk right past him, looking down at a newspaper.

Thursday,
October 2, 1941

18

Basel, Switzerland

Franz snuck out the front door of the apartment building in the early hours. He took a glance down the dark street, slung his bag over his shoulder and walked toward Klingelbergstrasse, the main avenue through the university district. He wore a black shirt, black pants, black socks and shoes, black leather jacket, black gloves.

A distant church bell chimed three times as he passed the university buildings. The streets were empty, and every window was dark. Klingelbergstrasse was well-lit, but there were no cars out, and no other pedestrians.

He crossed the Rhine at the Johanniterbrucke. From here it wasn't hard to see where the border lay a few kilometers to the north, where the lights ended—Germany enforced a strict blackout, while the Swiss were less strict with precautions.

He continued east along the wide Feldbergstrasse until he had to turn on the Riehenring, then east again on Riehenstrasse over the railroad yard. After a kilometer the edge of the city fell away, and empty fields sprang up alongside the road. It was only a half-kilometer to the turn-off after the village of Baumlihof, but then another three kilometers to the town of Bettingen. Dark woodlands stretched south toward the Rhine, and another kilometer of farmland stretched to the east between the town and the German border.

He left the road and took a path through the woods. The border with Germany zigzagged through these woods before encountering the Rhine a kilometer to the south-west.

He silently cursed the gibbous moon that wouldn't stay hidden behind the patchy clouds. Still, he was not about to abort this trip.

The path passed near a small farm at the end of a dusty road. Franz prayed that the isolated little farm's dog was sound asleep at this hour, as the border was less than a hundred meters away.

This was his least favorite place to cross, precisely because of the farm so close by, but it was too late to change plans. His escort would be waiting on the other side. Plus, it had been a while since he'd crossed here.

The border fence appeared ahead in the moonlight, and he stepped off the path into a thicket to wait for the next large cloud. Several small wispy clouds teased him for the next twenty minutes, but he remained outwardly calm, in spite of the pounding of his heart.

The church bell in Bettingen tolled four times, and as its chime faded away he caught the sound of footsteps and a dog's soft panting. He crouched as low in the heavy cover as he could. A soldier patrolled the other side of the fence, less than ten meters from where he hid. Holding a German Shepherd on a leash. When they passed, the dog began to whine, looking through the wire fence at the brush on the Swiss side.

The soldier stopped. Franz held his breath.

"What do you smell, Schotzie?" the soldier asked, squinting at the woods on the Swiss side of the fence. The dog continued to whine, so he got out his electric torch and shined the light around the base of trees and bushes.

Franz kept still, praying that the thick cover would hide him, and that his black clothing would conceal him if the thick grass didn't.

The soldier moved his torchlight slowly back and forth across the area for more than a minute. Then a rabbit broke from cover and dashed across the path some ten meters behind Franz. A fox sprinted across a few seconds later.

The dog's whine intensified and was broken by a single high-pitched bark. The soldier laughed, switched off his torch and tugged at the dog's leash. "Come along, boy," he said, patting the dog's neck.

Franz waited several seconds before allowing himself a sigh of relief. If a Swiss patrol came along he wouldn't be so lucky, with no fence to separate them. But the Swiss patrols were light along this stretch of border, especially at night.

A thick cloud passed in front of the moon, and Franz glanced at the sky to see its outlines glowing silver, verifying that it was a large one. He looked around, then sprang from cover. He took a quick look both directions down the fence-line, tossed his bag hard enough to get it over the high fence, and then scrambled up. He carefully navigated his way across the twin reels of barbed wire that topped the four-meter high fence, then dropped to his feet and took a roll on the German side. Glancing around again and assuring himself that no one was near, he reached for his bag a few feet away and ran from the fence at a low crouch.

The woods led downhill on this side of the border, and he tread carefully through the dark. He had to cross two dirt roads through the woodland.

Soon the landscape flattened and the woods gave way to darkened fields. He crept along fence-lines, keeping low. There was a curfew in the Third Reich, and if caught he wouldn't be able to explain his presence outside at this hour.

He knew the town of Grenzach was below him, a kilometer away, but it was blacked out. Whenever the moon reappeared and bathed the landscape in silvery light, he recognized barns and farmhouses and got his bearings.

He reached a particular cattle barn and sat beside a haystack to wait.

The soft purr of a car engine, followed by the crunch of tires over gravel, drew close. The dark shape of a car pulled off the road, dimmed headlights visible through slitted blackout covers, and pulled alongside the barn.

Franz rose from his hiding place, and strolled to the black Mercedes. He opened the door and plopped onto the passenger seat, tossing his bag to the back seat.

He turned to Rudolf Volger with a grin. "Thanks for the ride, Major!"

The blond SS officer did not return the smile.

"As always, your assistance is much appreciated," Franz added, still grinning.

"Your silence is much appreciated, Mr. Franz, so kindly be silent now," Major Volger replied, his voice icy.

"As you wish," Franz said with a shrug. "To Augsburg, please." He settled back in the seat, laid his head back, and closed his eyes. He was sound asleep by the time the Mercedes roared eastbound through Grenzach.

19

Bern

As soon as Jason sat at his desk at eight-thirty, his supervisor appeared beside him. "Mr. Bachman, come with me please," the Senior Foreign Service officer said, his voice more gruff than usual.

"Yes, Mr. Higgins," Jason said, unsure what was happening. He followed his supervisor to the foyer and waited for the elevator with him. He grew concerned when Mr. Higgins pressed the button for the fourth floor.

Upstairs, Higgins marched down the hall without pausing to acknowledge Amanda Overstreet at her desk. Jason followed, and gave a shrug to Amanda's questioning look. He was taken all the way to the end of the hall, where Higgins knocked on a closed door. A muffled voice said to come in, and Higgins opened the door, but then stepped aside.

"In you go," he ordered.

Jason stepped into the office, where Mr. Schuller sat behind the desk. Jason jumped when the office door banged closed behind him.

"Have a seat, Mr. Bachman," Mr. Schuller didn't rise or offer a hand in greeting. Jason took the seat in front of the desk and waited, his fingers trembling.

"Last night you spent the evening with a Swiss national named Franz Lemiel. Why were you speaking with him?"

Jason was stunned, and for several seconds could think of nothing to say.

"Why were you speaking with Franz Lemiel, Mr. Bachman?" Mr. Schuller repeated.

"I saw him at the Sulgenkeller, and we just started talking."

"Why?"

Jason's stomach seemed to fill with butterflies. He remembered Amanda's warning from the day before, and faked a shrug. "I saw him sitting by himself, and I invited him to join me and the other fellas. He said no, so I sat down to talk with him."

Mr. Schuller's pale green eyes narrowed. "Why did you eat with him?"

The wind rushed from Jason's lungs, he felt as if he'd been punched in the gut. "I don't know…he'd ordered food, and it looked good, so I ordered some to."

Mr. Schuller leaned forward and gave Jason a stern stare for several seconds. Jason shifted in his seat. When Mr. Schuller spoke, his voice was quiet but penetrating. "You went with him to a meeting—a political meeting. Why would you go to a Swiss political meeting, Mr. Bachman?"

Jason's mouth dropped open. How much did Mr. Schuller know? Had he followed them? Why? His mind raced for possible excuses, but decided his only chance lay in telling the truth, while leaving out his personal motivations.

He folded his hands in his lap to hide their trembling. "He told me about his work with student political groups around Switzerland, while we ate dinner. It sounded interesting, and he told me he was going to a meeting here in Bern, and he invited me to come along."

"Why did you go?"

"I told you already—it sounded really interesting. I wanted to learn more, so I went with him."

"What was discussed?"

Jason shrugged. "I don't know, mostly stuff about the Swiss government favoring the Germans more than the British, and how they let Nazi officers come to Switzerland for vacation, but won't let Jews come in to escape the Nazis—stuff like that."

Mr. Schuller leaned back and stared at him for a long moment. Jason got the feeling that Mr. Schuller's eyes could see right into the depths of his mind. His mouth went dry.

When Mr. Schuller next spoke, his rich baritone voice was relaxed and inviting. "Jason, I want you to tell me everything you heard at that meeting last night, and be as detailed as you can. It's important to American security."

"Okay," Jason said with a nod, and recounted everything he could remember. Mr. Schuller jotted down a few notes while Jason relived the meeting, but mostly listened. When Jason finished, Mr. Schuller asked if he could tell him the names of the Swiss students who were there.

"I can only remember a few of them."

"That's okay, just tell me the names you remember."

Jason complied.

"Thank you, Jason. You may return to work."

Jason walked to the door, but paused with his hand on the door knob. "Mr. Schuller? What was all this about?"

Mr. Schuller stared into his eyes for a few seconds. "National security. Please close the door on your way out."

Martin perused his notes, but there were no real surprises. The young man had obviously been rattled at first, and started out evasive, but he seemed to be telling the truth.

Martin turned his attention to the decoded cable from his superiors in Washington. The State Department's Intelligence bosses agreed with the War Department's assessment of Dr. Rubenstein's jet propulsion work. They also agreed with Martin's assessment that the Communists were probably being blamed for attacks that pro-Nazi elements were carrying out. He was instructed to find out why and report back.

Time to see what Ron's arranged for me. He got up to see the Information officer.

"National security, huh?" Amanda said.

Jason nodded. "That's what he said."

"I'd leave that alone if I were you, brother," Amanda said, giving him a warning with her eyes. "You don't know *what* kind of trouble you might find."

Jason shrugged, and then his shoulders sagged. "Yeah, I guess you're right. But I really liked him."

Amanda gave his forearm a sympathetic squeeze. "Sweetie, he's not that kind."

Augsburg, Bavaria, Germany

Franz walked down Frauentorstrasse, and entered the square in front of the Catholic cathedral. Groups of tourists stood in clusters, wondering at the massive stone foundations of the Romanesque Jungfrau Maria Cathedral, or gazing up at the spire.

With his sack thrown over his shoulder, Franz hoped he blended with the tourists. At least one group was speaking a Swiss dialect; Appenzellers, from their accent. They hadn't come far—it was less than a three-hour drive, but Franz imagined they'd spent at least an hour at the border crossing. It wasn't unusual for Swiss to still make day-trips into Germany, though no one wanted to stay overnight any more. Getting caught in a British air-raid wouldn't be a good vacation activity.

He continued south on Karolinenstrasse. These days there were few automobiles, so he walked down the center of the street. Only government officials and Nazi party big-wigs could afford the fuel rations.

His route took him past the Rathaus, with its huge Nazi flags billowing in the breeze. He wondered for a moment if Major Volger was there, or if he'd driven back to Frankfurt. There were several black Mercedes 260s parked in front, all the same.

He wound through narrow medieval streets for a few blocks before he arrived at the gothic Church of St. Ann. Originally a 14th century Carmelite church, it was now the largest Lutheran church in this mostly-Protestant city in the center of Catholic Bavaria.

Franz took a look around before walking through the front doors.

Inside the sanctuary, he spied the ginger-haired young man sitting midway up the aisle, facing the altar with his hands clasped on top of the pew in front of him. This was Kurt Weber, a twenty-nine-year-old journalist that Franz had met once before.

Franz sat beside him. "Peace be with you, my brother."

"And also with you, friend."

"Come to me, all ye that are heavy-laden, and I will give you rest."

That was the code they'd agreed upon to signal that Franz had not been followed. Kurt slid a hand inside his jacket, and set two film canisters next to Franz. After Franz had slipped them inside his sack, the young journalist turned to look at him.

"The burdens are indeed many these days." His pale blue eyes locked Franz in an intense stare. "But we shall walk in the ways of the Lord."

Franz nodded at the signal, and stood. That was the code to go outside and pretend to be on a stroll through the old quarter. He was not surprised—most large churches in Germany were bugged. The Gestapo had ears everywhere, it seemed.

They exited a side door into a narrow cobbled street, and Franz saw no one near. Kurt walked with a pronounced limp, which was the main reason he wasn't away serving in the Wehrmacht. An old *futbol* injury from his school days, he'd explained the first time they met.

"I've written many stories that wouldn't get past the censors," Kurt said. "I've locked them in a drawer at my home and kept them there. I have to write the truth, for my own sanity. Someday, when the current regime has gone, I'll pull them all out."

"You have something you want me to report for you?"

"Yes. Can you remember what I tell you?"

"I'll do my best," Franz said.

"The Propaganda Ministry won't release official casualty counts from the eastern front. They only report on the victories, and not the cost. But the cost is apparent if one looks around. Every family I know has lost someone—a cousin, a nephew, a brother, or a son. For the first time, there are grumblings that the Leader has gotten us in too deep. People are careful what they say, but more open than they would have been before.

"My own brother is serving on the eastern front right now, somewhere in the eastern Ukraine. We haven't gotten a letter in almost two weeks, and my mother is beside herself."

Franz was sympathetic, but brought him back to the point. "You know something the Propaganda Ministry doesn't want reported?"

"Yes. I know a colonel who passes me information off the record."

Franz nodded. Fifth Columnists could be found at the highest levels these days. "What has he told you?"

"The casualties have been 'nearly catastrophic,' as he put it. The numbers are like the last war, though we continue to advance this time. He said tens of thousands of dead, and far more wounded. Can you pass that along to your father?"

"Of course," Franz said.

"My wife and I have risked listening to the BBC several times at night, down low so the neighbors won't hear, and only for ten minutes at a time. We switch it off if a car passes. The Gestapo have listening devices in their cars. The BBC reports confirm the victories in Russia and North Africa that the Propaganda Ministry trumpets, but they also hint at what my colonel intimated about casualties."

"I'll tell my father," Franz said.

"Also, I have information on that Jewish family you asked about, at Dachau," Kurt continued.

"What did you learn?"

"Berthe Kaim died in March. Complications from pneumonia, officially. The truth is that she was never treated, no medication. The rest of the family continue to work. Hard workers, I'm told. The guards like those. They have less chance of being beaten that way."

"Thank you," Franz said. "I know someone who will want to know."

"Do you return to Switzerland tonight?"

"Yes, late. First I must go to Heidelberg."

"Heidelberg?" Kurt stopped and turned to Franz. That was deeper inside the country. "You may be searched on the train, or at the stations. If they find that film…"

Franz raised a hand in reassurance. "I'm not taking a train. I have an official escort."

Kurt nodded. "Say no more."

Franz himself didn't know all of the connections. A servant in Major Volger's home—which servant, he had no idea—had Socialist roots and was sympathetic to the Underground. This servant knew of the Jewish youth Volger kept above the garage, and passed the information to a local police inspector who had an ax to grind against the SS. That inspector—Franz didn't know his name, either—had broken into the garage one day six or seven months ago, and placed hidden cameras, including views of the room where Michael Kaim lived. A little inside information about when the major visited his young paramour, and the inspector had photographic evidence.

Somehow, through unknown links, the photographs got from that anonymous inspector to members of the Frankfurt underground, who informed Emmentaler—Franz—that they had a way for him to blackmail an SS officer into providing assistance.

So one chilly March evening, Franz had gone to Major Volger's home. Telling the butler that he had urgent SS business to convey to the major, he was shown into the study.

Volger arrived a few moments later. "Who are you?"

"My name is Franz. Just Franz." He presented Volger with a manila envelope, and the major snatched it from his hand and removed the black and white photographs. The color had drained from his face. "What do you want with me?"

"Several things. First, let me assure you that there are many copies of these photographs in Switzerland, entrusted to several people there, and the negatives are also well-cared for—so don't even consider shooting me."

"Understood, Mr. Franz. Now tell me what you want." Volger's voice had grown surprisingly calm.

"The underground opposition will conduct certain activities in Frankfurt in the coming months, and you are to turn a blind eye to any such activities that you witness. If you thwart one operation, or arrest any of the operatives, we will see that copies of those photographs are delivered to your commandant immediately, and to the Gestapo as well. I don't need to remind you, Major, of what the Reich does to men who fuck boys up the ass."

Volger's lips pursed, and he swallowed hard. "No reminder is needed. Is that all?"

"No. From time-to-time, you will receive a message that a certain shop is expecting a delivery of Emmentaler from Switzerland on a certain day. This is my code name, and it is your signal to drive to the town of Grenzach, a kilometer from the border, and wait for me at a pre-arranged location. That location will change each time. You are to arrive at the arranged location in Grenzach at five AM on the day indicated. Then you will drive me to wherever I ask. You will also be required to return me to Grenzach at a time and date that I give you."

"If I refuse?"

Franz smiled. "Then your commandant will find out that you like to fuck sixteen-year-old Jewish boys."

The sour expression on Volger's face deepened, but he nodded his acquiescence. "How often will my chauffeur services be required, Mr. Franz?"

"Not often. Perhaps once every four to six weeks. I'm sure you can accommodate that, can't you?"

"I'm sure that I can. How much notice will I receive?"

"How much notice will you require?"

Volger had sat back in his chair with his fingers pressed together in front of his mouth, his face taking on a calculating expression, though his blue eyes never wavered from Franz. "At least three days, if you'd please, Mr. Franz. More if you can."

"I believe we can give you that, Major. And thank you for your willingness to assist the cause!" Franz flashed Volger a broad grin as he stood and extended his right hand.

Volger gave the offered hand a hard, perfunctory shake.

Franz started toward the door, then turned back. "Oh, one more thing, Major—don't think of giving my name or code-name to anyone at the SS or Gestapo. Believe me when I say that I'll know it if you do, and these photographs will be on their way to your commandant. Good night, Major. Pleasant dreams!"

The arrangement had worked well for the last six months. This trip was the fifth time Franz had used Volger's assistance, and it could be quite handy having access to a Mercedes and an SS escort.

He and Kurt Weber paused at the next corner. "Is there anything else you'd like me to take back?"

"No, just what you have. That is enough, believe me. Wait until you see them."

"How bad is it?"

Kurt stared him in the eyes with such sorrow it broke his heart. "Truly horrible. You will hardly believe your eyes. Men and women so skinny you will wonder how they can live, and how long they have gone without food. The rags they wear wouldn't keep a polar bear warm in the winter. And yet, that is all they are given. You'll see." He glanced around before continuing. "I'm taking a terrible risk, you know. My wife and I have two small daughters. If that film should be found before you get out of Germany—"

"It won't be," Franz assured him.

Kurt clasped Franz's hand between both of his and shook it. "Good luck, Franz. I can't stress enough how vital it is that someone outside the Reich learns what is going on at Dachau, and surely at other camps as well. God go with you." He turned and walked away.

Franz went the other direction.

20

Frankfurt

"You asked to see me, sir?" Rudolph Volger said, poking his head around the door.

"Volger, it's about time you got here this morning," the SS colonel growled. Col. Schneider was a heavy-set man of about fifty, with thin pale blond hair streaked with white, round pink cheeks, and small blue eyes.

"My daughter fell ill, and we were awake much of the night with her," Volger lied.

"Yes, that can happen," Col. Schneider said absently, shuffling through papers on his desk and not looking up. "The Gestapo raided St. Paul's Lutheran church this morning on a tip from one of the neighbors. They found four families of Jews hiding in the basement. Twenty-two in total. The Gestapo have arrested the pastor and his wife. They'll be tried for harboring the Reich's enemies. I want you to go to Gestapo headquarters and take possession of the Jews. Prepare them for deportation."

"Yes, sir. Are they expecting me?"

"They know I'm sending someone. You'll have no trouble."

"Thank you, sir. Heil Hitler!" Volger spun on his heels and exited, stifling a yawn as he went down the hall.

Bern

"Come in," Martin said to the knock on his office door.

Amanda Overstreet stuck her head in. "I got the information from PTT, Mr. Schuller."

"Yes?"

"The telegram was delivered this morning, but Herr Lemiel didn't sign for it."

"Who did?"

"A Frau Statweiler. Probably his landlady."

Martin's expression remained stoic, though on the inside he hoped the portierfrau wasn't nosy enough to open a telegram. "Thank you, Miss Overstreet."

"You really owe me for this one," Ron Witherspoon announced.

"Oh?" Martin arched an eyebrow, hoping it was as good as Witherspoon implied.

"I got you a meeting tonight with one of the Abwehr's local informants. I don't know much about him, except that he keeps them informed of the activities of a certain group called the League of Swiss for Greater Germany. And his code name is *Korkenzieher*."

"Corkscrew," Martin said.

"Yes," Witherspoon said with a chuckle. "Interesting code name, eh? Makes you wonder what his job is."

"Where and when?" Martin asked.

"Ten o'clock at the Miesenheimer wine shop, in the Lindenhof district of Zurich. Here's the address. They said ten o'clock sharp you're to buy a bottle of Chablis, and when you exit the shop you'll approach a man loading cases of wine into the back of a Rolls Royce. You'll ask him if he has a corkscrew. He'll reply that he has one inside the car that he'd be happy for you to use, if you'll help him load the wine first. You'll help him with that, then join him inside the car."

Martin put his hands together and tented the fingers in front of his mouth, thinking it over. "How do we know that he knows something useful?"

"My contacts at the German embassy offered his services when I inquired about pro-Nazi groups in Switzerland, and possible links to the recent assassinations. They didn't want to speak themselves, and that's why they offered this contact. They did say you'll need to bring cash. Apparently, *Korkenzieher* offers more information if you keep feeding him franc notes."

Butterflies tumbled in Martin's gut. Every encounter carried risk, but he felt extra apprehensive about this. "Do you trust them?"

"Can we ever really trust anyone outside of our own service?"

I know that already. Martin shook his head.

Witherspoon leaned forward, and added in an almost conspiratorial voice. "My contacts won't tell me why the Abwehr's keeping tabs on this League of Swiss for Greater Germany. There are all sorts of rivalries between the German intelligence agencies, and I suspect this League must be working with one of the Abwehr's rivals. Perhaps the SD. So be careful."

"Thanks, Ron," Martin said. He would be every bit as careful with this *Korkenzieher* as he was when meeting with German spies in New York or Philadelphia.

Zurich

Ernst Zubler regarded the nervous young man sitting across from him with a mixture of disdain and enjoyment at his discomfort. "Mr. Kraus, I'm disappointed in you."

Peter Kraus swallowed hard. "Did I make a mistake, sir?"

"A serious mistake." He pulled a leaflet from his desk drawer and slid it across the desk.

Kraus blanched.

'*Swiss Bankers on the Payroll of Organized Crime!*' read the headline in big, bold type. Beneath the headline ran a few lines denouncing Swiss banks for taking gold from the Reichsbank in exchange for currency that could be used to build tanks and guns—gold that was stolen from the regime's enemies, it claimed—and laundering dirty money for the Nazis. The leaflet ended with a list of banks in Zurich and the Nazi "thugs" they had done recent business with.

On the list was the Zurischer Kredit Bank.

"Do you recognize that piece of trash, Mr. Kraus?"

Kraus swallowed hard again. His forehead and upper lip beaded with sweat. "No, sir."

"You're lying to me, Mr. Kraus. How disappointing," Zubler said, a mocking smile spreading across his lips. "Inspector Frisch here brought this to me this afternoon. Someone has spread them all over Zurich."

"Which is illegal," Inspector Frisch said from where he stood a few feet behind Zubler.

Zubler flashed him a quick glare, and he deflated.

"It is true that distributing these is illegal. They have not been vetted by the censors. But what disappoints me, Mr. Kraus, is your involvement."

"I've never seen that before!"

Zubler's eyes narrowed. "While I have no doubt that what you say is technically true, I have no interest in technicalities." He pressed a button on the intercom, though his secretary had long since departed for the day. "Gentlemen, please join us."

The door opened, and two men in black leather coats entered, one tall and the other stocky.

Zubler kept his eyes on Peter Kraus. "Inspector Frisch saw you at a meeting of a subversive group on Tuesday night, Mr. Kraus—a group that has been known to produce and distribute seditious trash such as this." He jabbed a finger at the leaflet on the desktop, and his lips pursed.

Kraus's face drained of the last color it had left. "It must have been someone else."

"No, it was you. The police followed you back to your apartment from the meeting. They identified you yesterday. And now we have this leaflet full of the most nasty accusations."

He motioned with his hand, and the two men in black leather coats took places on either side of Kraus. The young man visibly tensed.

"You had access to the kind of information that is printed in this thing," Zubler hissed. "You violated the bank's trust. And you are a danger to the Fatherland. Our friends from the Gestapo will take it from here."

"Gestapo?" Kraus's voice faltered as he said the word.

The men in leather coats seized his arms and wrested him from the chair. He struggled, knocking the chair over and kicking the side of Zubler's desk. The banker remained seated with a placid expression while the men in leather dragged the young man away.

The sign on the door of the Miesenheimer wine shop said that it closed at ten o'clock, so Martin picked out his bottle of Chablis, and pretended to browse around the store until closing time. The store had a large selection from France, Germany, and Italy, mostly expensive. Martin had picked the least expensive Chablis he could find.

A tall, thin man in a black tuxedo jacket came in at nine forty-five, and greet the woman behind the counter. "Good evening Mrs. Miesenheimer. I'm here to pick up the week's order for Mr. Zubler."

"Yes, we have that ready. I'll have Kristopher bring it out and load it for you."

"If you please, Mrs. Miesenheimer, I'd prefer to load it myself tonight. I could use the exercise."

The plump little woman behind the counter looked momentarily startled, but recovered and said, "Of course. Whatever you'd like, sir. I'll have Kristopher meet you out front in a moment."

The tall man gave her a crisp nod, and turned toward the door. He caught Martin's eye as he turned, and a scowl pursed his lips. It disappeared quickly, and a stony expression returned.

Martin waited until the cuckoo clock on the wall said nine fifty-nine before approaching the counter with his bottle.

The plump Mrs. Miesenheimer followed him to the door, and the lock clicked behind him. A black Rolls Royce limousine sat ten meters away, and the tall man in the black tuxedo jacket was lifting cases of wine and putting them into the trunk.

Martin paused beside the cases. "Pardon me, sir—do you have a corkscrew?"

"Yes, I have one inside the car that I'd be happy for you to use, sir—if you'll be so kind as to help me load this wine first."

"Of course." Martin squatted and lifted a case of Champagne, and placed it inside the trunk.

When they had finished, the tall man turned to him and bowed his head. "Thank you for your assistance, sir. Please join me inside the car, and I will locate that corkscrew for you."

Martin glanced around, but there was no one near. He put his hand on the grip of his Luger, opened the passenger door and took a seat.

"You were early," the man snarled.

"I didn't want to be late." Martin didn't mention that he'd been early on purpose, to hopefully overhear something useful—such as the fact that *Korkenzieher* was picking up a wine order for a Mr. Zubler.

"You were given specific instructions for a reason."

Martin held out a fifty-franc note with his left hand—about twelve dollars—keeping his right hand on the grip of his Luger. "What can you tell me about the League of Swiss for Greater Germany, and the recent assassinations?"

The tall man stared at Martin for several seconds before taking the note. "The banker who was killed on Sunday night, Friedrich Zindorf, was a member of the group."

"Do you know anything about the attack?"

Korkenzieher was silent. Martin held out another fifty-franc note.

"Mr. Zindorf was at a meeting of the group on Sunday evening, all of them bankers. There was a dinner party, and the gentlemen held a meeting after dinner. The Zindorfs left early, and Mr. Zindorf was quite agitated."

"Who were the others at the meeting?" Martin asked, holding out another fifty-franc note.

Korkenzieher snorted. "I wouldn't tell you those names for all of the money in Zurich! My safety is worth more than that."

"Then tell me more about the League."

Korkenzieher took the fifty-franc note. "We shouldn't stay here, it looks suspicious." He put the car into drive and pulled away from the curb.

Martin's mouth went dry, but he kept a calm demeaner.

"Mr. Franz Burri started the League earlier this year in Luzerne, to advocate for unification with Germany. Mr. Burri moved to Frankfurt this summer, and started publishing a newspaper called International Presseagentur, which the League disseminates throughout Switzerland."

A picture took form in Martin's mind. "Besides the attack on the Zindorfs on Sunday, was the League involved in the other assassinations—of Dr. Fritz Rubenstein at the Zurich Polytechnic, or the colonels who belonged to the SVV?"

"Perhaps."

Martin held out another fifty-franc note, and *Korkenzieher* took it. "Yes. The leadership of the League of Swiss for Greater Germany feels that the leadership of the SVV betrayed the cause last year when they led the mobilization against the rumored German invasion. The assassinations are revenge for that betrayal."

"Are there other assassinations planned?"

"That I do not know," the tall man said. "But it would not surprise me."

"Are you a member of the League?"

Korkenzieher shook his head. "No, but I am trusted by the group's leadership." He made a face. "I would have preferred a Greater Germany under the rule of the Kaiser, not an angry Austrian corporal with dreams of world domination."

The monarchist reference surprised Martin, but he kept his face expressionless. "Oh?"

"I'm a nationalist, but that doesn't make me a Nazi."

The distinction was too subtle for Martin's taste. "And the group members know of your, uh, 'nationalist' feelings?"

"Yes."

"Are you the chauffeur for one of the members?"

This was greeted by a snort. "No, the butler."

"How do you know these things?"

Korkenzieher chuckled. "I've been a butler for more than a quarter century. I know how to learn things that I'm not explicitly privy to."

"Have you shared all of this with the Abwehr?"

"Yes."

"Why?"

The tall man was silent for a moment. "I know someone. My younger brother crossed the border to serve in the Kaiser's army during the last war, and his lieutenant is now a colonel in the Abwehr. He recruited me. They already knew of my employer's former involvement in the SVV."

"Can you provide any evidence of the League's involvement in the assassinations?"

Korkenzieher didn't look at the fifty-franc note Martin held out. After a moment, Martin added a second, which elicited a haughty raising of the butler's chin. Martin added two more notes, and the butler's hand reached over from the wheel and snatched the two-hundred francs away.

"There are Gestapo officers in Zurich, at least two that I've seen in person, who have been tasked with carrying out the attacks that are ordered by the Gauleiter."

Four hundred francs spent—almost a hundred dollars—and Martin finally struck gold. "Who is the Gauleiter?"

Another chuckle came from Korkenzieher. "There isn't enough money in Zurich to get me to reveal that. I'll pull over at the next corner, and you can get out."

"Thank you," Martin muttered, his mind turning over possibilities.

The Rolls pulled up to a quiet corner of two residential streets and stopped. Martin exited the car, glanced around to be sure no one watched, and closed the door. The car pulled away, and he noted the license plate number.

"The wine has been taken to the cellar and racked, sir," the butler said after entering the library.

"Thank you, Anton," Ernst Zubler said from his seat at the desk. "Did you make contact with the American agent?"

"Yes, sir."

"What did our American friend look like?"

"He was fairly tall, short blond hair, square face. Wide shoulders on him, a former athlete, I'd say, sir."

Zubler tapped his finger against his cheek as a smile spread across his lips. "I wonder…" he said, and got up from his seat. He marched to a bookshelf, and removed a large volume—the Complete Works of Sir Arthur Conan Doyle, in English. Opening the book, he removed a loose sheet of paper and handed it to the butler.

"Look at this sketch, Anton. Is this the American agent you met tonight?"

Anton took one look at the sketch and nodded. "It is, sir."

Zubler chuckled as he returned the sketch to the middle of the big book, and returned it to its place on the bookshelf.

"That was a composite sketch that the police made of our spurious FedPol Inspector Max Schmidt, from descriptions provided by Inspector Frisch and a sergeant who also saw him." He paused while he poured a glass of port and took a sip. "Now we need to find out who this American agent is."

Anton's expression turned sour. Zubler knew he was uncomfortable each time he encountered the Men in Leather.

"Will that be all, sir?"

"Yes, Anton, thank you."

Anton bowed his head and backed out of the room.

Zubler picked up the receiver of the telephone on his desk and dialed the operator. "Long distance, please…Yes, I'd like to place a call to Frankfurt."

21

The streets of Heidelberg lay in darkness. *One benefit of the black-out*, Franz thought. It made it far easier to slip through the streets undetected after curfew. But it also made it harder to see if anyone was following. Franz crept along the familiar route, alert to the sound of footsteps. It was a cloudy night, which meant no air-raid danger, and little light from the moon.

He walked around the side of a large warehouse. It sat behind another large warehouse which faced onto the main road to Mannheim. As he approached a set of steps leading down to a side door, a figure emerged from the shadows and raised a hand.

"Heil Hitler," a young man's voice whispered.

"Never, as long as I take breath!" Franz replied.

"Then welcome, friend," the young man said, accepting the pass-code.

"I am Emmentaler."

"We've been expecting you. Please go in."

The young man cracked open the door, and Franz slipped inside. He went down the corridor, and emerged into a storeroom with a twenty-foot ceiling. At the far end of the enormous space was a small area lit by candles, where a group of almost twenty young people sat on wooden crates in a semicircle.

"Franz! You're here!" Ilsa Schuber jumped from her seat and rushed forward to embrace him.

He returned her warm hug, and then they kissed each other's cheeks. They were nearly the same height. He held both of her hands as he stood back and smiled at her. "Ilsa, darling, you grow more beautiful every time I see you. It's been too long this time."

"I'm so glad you made it!" she beamed. "Come sit with me." She kept one of his hands and led him back to her crate. She sat on the end, giving him just enough space to sit alongside her, their legs touching. She held his right hand in her lap.

"Tell me what's happened since I was last here," Franz said to the gathering at large.

"After the last time Erich and I cut the telephone lines to the Gestapo office, they installed cameras along the back wall of the Rathaus," said a young man with shiny brown hair, starched white shirt and flashy gray zoot-suit pants. "So yesterday, we hitched a ride to Mannheim on a delivery truck and cut the phone lines to the Gestapo office there."

"Our timing was good, too," added the pale, thin blond sitting next to him, wearing a similar outfit. "There was a street brawl about then between the Edelweiss Pirates and the Hitler Youth. We didn't get to see it, though. The Gestapo didn't learn about it until it was over, and by then the Pirates had gotten away. A bunch of the junior Nazis got their faces bashed!"

Everyone laughed. "Edelweiss Pirates" was the name given to street gangs of working-class teenagers who dropped out of school in reaction to the rigid Nazi discipline, grew their hair long, refused to join the Hitler Youth, and followed their own rules. They enjoyed taunting the Hitler Youth, and got into street fights with them in industrials cities across western Germany.

Franz surveyed the group of young faces. "Where's Joschi?"

"Joschi got called up six weeks ago," Ilsa explained. "He knew it was only a matter of time after he graduated. He got his conscription notice, and was on a train to Berlin within two days."

"He's probably on the eastern front by now," speculated a young freckle-faced boy who couldn't be more than eighteen.

Franz nodded, silent. Joschi was twenty-two and had graduated in June, so it was inevitable. Franz had a hard time imagining him in a uniform with short hair. Joschi had been one of the leaders of the local Swing Youth before the crackdown three years ago, wearing flashy clothes and floppy hair. After the crackdown he'd moved this group underground, and now they held illegal intellectual discussions instead of jitterbugging to American swing records.

"Shall we begin?" Ilsa asked. Several of them reached inside knapsacks and removed tattered books in various stages of disrepair.

"I haven't got any new ones," a tall and rail-thin blond boy with wire-rimmed glasses explained, his expression and tone apologetic. "When I went into Kessler's on Monday to buy some more, they didn't have any. Mr. Kessler explained that the supplier in Bonn that he used was denounced to the Gestapo a couple of weeks ago. He hasn't found a new one. He reminded me how careful he has to be, as if I didn't understand that."

"I know people in Switzerland who could arrange to get banned books into Germany for you," Franz offered.

The bean-pole smiled. "That would be wonderful! Thank you, Emmentaler."

They swapped the books that they had, explaining them to one another in private conversations, and what the author wanted them to learn.

Franz took the time to look around the group. All of them were younger than him these days, between eighteen and twenty-one—just old enough to remember when ideas could be freely exchanged. They would have been between ten and thirteen when the Nazis took control and clamped down on the press.

He let the book discussions go on for some time before he cleared his throat and got their attention. "I have news that needs to be disseminated. Does the group still produce leaflets?"

An uncomfortable silence fell.

Ilsa broke it. "Joschi was our main writer of the leaflets, and he could get them printed. None of us know who his printer was."

"I could ask Mr. Kessler if he has a way to print some," bean-pole offered.

"What's the news?" the brown-haired zoot-suiter asked.

"I have come into possession of photographs which prove that the prisoners at Dachau concentration camp in Bavaria are being starved to death."

The uncomfortable silence returned.

"It sounds a bit far-fetched, doesn't it?" the thin blond zoot-suiter said. "I mean, if thousands of prisoners were being starved to death, people would be talking about it."

"Only if someone told them," Franz said. "That's why we need leaflets."

"It sounds like a pretty wild accusation," added a chubby young woman with pink cheeks, curly blond hair and bright green eyes.

"It does, but it is true," Franz replied. "The outside world must learn what is going on, and we in Switzerland will work to see that they do. But it is more important that people inside the Reich learn what is going on. That is where you come in."

Even Ilsa looked doubtful. "I don't know, Franz. How can we be sure it's true? It could be some story made up by a former prisoner to make the regime look worse. Did you hear this from a communist?"

"No, he's not a communist," Franz said, not trying to hide the note of irritation entering his voice. "I trust him."

"Alright—but what if we did put this into a leaflet and left them around town? I don't know that anyone would believe it," Ilsa said.

Franz's face flushed. "People had no trouble believing that the regime was euthanizing mental patients! And handicapped people. There was an outcry against that, and they stopped. You could get them to stop again."

Ilsa put a hand on his knee. Her voice was soothing. "The outcry started with the relatives of the victims, who were all upstanding citizens, so the government admitted to the euthanasia program. And the criticism was joined by the Catholic bishops from their pulpits."

Franz gave up. He'd faced this kind of disbelief before, last year when he'd told them the Luftwaffe was guilty of bombing Rotterdam in violation of the truce after the Dutch surrendered. "That sounds like BBC propaganda," they'd said.

He crossed his arms and scowled. "Then I'll to talk to a churchman I know."

Ilsa lingered while the others filtered out, keeping hold of Franz's hand.

"Joschi is a big loss," Franz said. "He wasn't afraid to take action. He built the connections, and he recruited the operators. You included."

"I know how to contact the network," Ilsa said. "You received the message I sent on Monday about the two companies going to Rheims?"

"Yes."

She stood in front of him and looked into his eyes. "Are you staying in Heidelberg tonight?"

"No, I have to get back to Switzerland under cover of darkness. I've made too many open crossings lately. I don't want to draw suspicion."

"Can't you stay at least an hour?" She stroked his temple and cheek with her fingertips.

He smiled. "An hour, no more." Then he leaned forward and kissed her.

He held her in his arms, lying naked between two dirty blankets they had scrounged from the warehouse shelves. She ran her fingers across the dark hair on his chest, and he nibbled on the side of her neck. She squirmed and giggled.

"Stop! You know how that tickles."

He chuckled, and continued to nuzzle his nose on the soft skin of her neck. His hand cupped her breast and gently squeezed, and he smiled as she let out a low moan.

"I wish I could see you all the time," she sighed. "I can't get a visa to go to Switzerland, though."

Franz didn't reply, just moved his hand slowly down her taut belly and down between her legs. She was still damp from their earlier lovemaking, and he grew hard again as he worked his fingers inside her. She caught her breath. Her nipples stiffened as he flicked one with his tongue, then put his lips around it and lightly took it between his teeth. She moaned again.

He rolled on top of her. "I don't have much time," he whispered.

"Then don't," she replied, closing her legs. "I don't want it to end that way. We had a lovely time—let's not end it in a rush."

He shrugged and rolled off her. She laid her head on his shoulder and hugged herself to his chest.

He stroked her back between the shoulder blades and stared at the distant ceiling.

They'd had that conversation before. He'd warned her more than once not to get too attached—they couldn't be together like that. He would always have to leave in a hurry. It frustrated him that she still wanted more than he could give.

"I must go," he said, and moved to sit up.

She put a hand on his cheek and turned his face toward hers. "Be so careful."

"I'm always careful," he said with a smile. He pecked a kiss on her lips, then threw the blanket off and stood.

He walked a few steps to where he'd piled his clothes, his back to her. He sat on a crate to put on his socks and shoes, while she dressed under the blanket. When he was finished he sat and watched her put on her shoes—a pair of worn-looking blue velvet pumps that had been stylish a couple of years before.

When she was fully dressed, she looked at him sadly. He gave her a faint smile, and held out his hand to help her up. He pulled her to him and gave her a quick kiss, then held her hand as he grabbed his knapsack and they walked to the door.

"When will you be back?" she whispered while he stuck his head out the door and looked around.

"I'm not sure. I'll send word."

He motioned for her to follow him, and they hurried toward the road. He gave her one last quick kiss, then flashed her a broad grin as he sprinted away toward his rendezvous with Major Volger and his Mercedes.

Friday,
October 3, 1941

22

Frankfurt

Michael Kaim jolted awake as his bed-springs creaked, and a heavy weight depressed the mattress beside him. The room was dark and his mind was foggy from sleep, but he turned his head, trying to see anything that would make sense.

A warm hand took hold of his shoulder and pulled him back down.

"It's me, go back to sleep," a masculine voice whispered close to his ear.

It took him a moment to register Rudolph Volger's voice. He felt the warmth of the major's body pressed against him from behind, and the major's arm reached around and hugged his torso.

"What time is it?"

"It's three-thirty. Go back to sleep."

"Why are you here in the middle of the night?"

"I got back from my trip a little early, and I didn't want to wake anyone in the house," the major said, stroking Michael's side. He reached the waist band of his undershorts. "Take these damn things off, for God's sake!" he whispered, tugging them down.

Michael kicked them off without a word. The major snuggled behind him, his body wrapping around Michael's like a snake, his arm hugging the boy to him.

Michael felt the soft touch of the major's lips to the back of his neck. "Now go back to sleep," the major said.

Michael lay awake for a while pretending to sleep. Soon the major's even breathing told him the man was sound asleep. There was something about the situation, with the warmth of the major's body wrapped around his like a blanket, that felt like resting in the embrace of a sleeping bear.

A tear escaped the corner of his eye.

Bern

"I got the registration on that license plate," Ron Witherspoon said when he entered Martin's office. "It's for a 1939 Rolls Royce limousine owned by an Ernst Zubler in Zurich. The address is listed." He handed the paper to Martin.

"Bingo," Martin mumbled to himself, looking at the registration.

"What?"

"That's exactly the information I needed, Ron. Thanks."

"Any time." Witherspoon turned to leave, and almost bumped into Amanda Overstreet. "I beg your pardon, Miss Overstreet."

"A telegram arrived for you a few minutes ago, Mr. Schuller," Amanda said, handing him a Swiss PTT telegram.

"Thank you." He waited for her to leave before tearing it open.

GOT YOUR MESSAGE STOP
CAN MEET THIS AFTERNOON STOP
GRAND HOTEL LES TROIS ROIS BASEL STOP
BRASSERIE RESTAURANT LUNCH 2:00 STOP
FL

Martin checked his watch. It was after eleven. He pulled a map of Switzerland from his drawer and consulted the route. The drive north to Basel would take ninety minutes at least, more if he got held up by any sheep or goat flocks going through the hills. And he would need time to locate this hotel. The train would be faster.

He gathered several things from his office and stuffed them inside his attaché case, and tugged on his suit coat as he locked the door. He took the back stairs and exited the back door.

It only took ten minutes to drive to the train station. He parked the Ford along the side of the Banhofplatz and hurried inside. He checked the boards, and found a train to Basel departing at 12:08, arriving at 13:02. That should give him enough time to find Les Trois Rois Hotel before two.

He purchased a ticket and went into the bar to order a beer while he waited. He took a seat at a table that allowed him to watch the people hustling about in the main terminal. For a few moments, he allowed himself to relax.

He noticed their dark leather coats first. He didn't look at them for more than a couple of seconds, pretending to still be people-watching, but kept tabs on them from the corner of his eye.

They were watching him.

He recognized both of them. These were the same men who had followed him in Zurich a couple of nights ago. Martin took a few moments to gather his thoughts, and to take a fortifying quaff of beer. Then he casually stood, laid a couple of coins on the table, and walked into the terminal.

The men followed him.

He took a quick look at the boards—there was a train to Fribourg leaving a few minutes before the train to Basel, and from the next platform. He pretended to consult his watch, and then hurried toward the Fribourg platform.

It was filling with people making their way to the train, and conversations in both German and French rang through the air around him. He glanced behind him, pretending to check the clock extending from the wall. The two leather-coated men followed a short distance behind.

He took a glance at the train cars, noting the windows, and set a course for one of the cars near the rear.

He climbed in, and took a seat facing back the way he had come in. There were several passengers in the car. An elderly lady in a woolen coat sat opposite him, with her hands folded atop the handbag in her lap. A young couple occupied the seat in front of him, whispering in French.

A moment later the two men in leather coats entered the car, looked at him, and took seats several rows away, but close enough to watch.

Martin checked his watch—almost noon. The train would be pulling away in a couple of minutes. He turned, craning his neck in exaggerated fashion as he looked back toward the restrooms at the rear of the car. He took his attaché case and walked toward the men's room.

The door was closed, so he waited. From the corner of his eye, he saw the two men in leather watching. *Hardly subtle.*

A moment later the door opened, and a young man in a wool sweater stepped out. "Oh! *Pardon monsieur*," he apologized in French, stepping around Martin.

"That's quite alright," Martin replied in German, touching the rim of his fedora and giving the young man a nod as he took a step back to allow him through the narrow corridor.

Once inside the restroom with the door closed, Martin looked up to the window. It was high and narrow, but he could get through it. He climbed onto the sides of the sink, testing its sturdiness as he shifted his weight onto it, and then set his attaché case on top of the light fixture.

He couldn't stand upright, and had to bend his knees low to keep balanced on the sink. His head brushed the ceiling, and his face was directly in front of the window. The window opened toward the inside, and Martin swung it all the way to the ceiling, leaning back carefully as he did.

Grabbing his attaché case off of the light fixture and smelling a slight scorch, he tossed it out the window, then put his arms through and leaned his head out. Up ahead, the engine expelled steam out off its wheels, and the engineer blew the whistle. As long as the men in leather were still in the same seats, they wouldn't be able to see him at this angle.

With his knees already bent, Martin heaved himself up from the sink, ignoring the cracking sound from it. He hung for a second balanced on his stomach, half in and half out, then turned himself to the left so that he could squeeze his right leg out, knee first. From there he was able to slip his other leg through as he placed his hands on the window sill. Then he hung vertical for a couple of seconds with his feet dangling four feet above the gravel, before dropping.

The engine chugged up ahead, and the train car lurched beside him as he jogged away between the tracks. The rear of the Basel train was less than fifty yards ahead of him, and he sprinted toward it.

Rounding the rear of the Basel train, he looked back at the last car of the Fribourg train. The only one standing at the railing looking out was the conductor, and Martin exhaled in relief.

He only had a couple of minutes to get on the correct train, and he scampered onto the platform, then rushed toward the nearest car door. Climbing inside as the engine whistle blew, he caught his breath before strolling up the corridor to an unoccupied seat. He scanned the faces of everyone in the car, but detected nothing suspicious in any of them.

Taking his seat, he leaned back and placed his fedora over his eyes.

Basel

Franz lifted the photographs from the trays of chemicals, and hung them to dry. In the dim red light, he examined the black and white images and shook his head in disbelief.

Kurt Weber must own a good telephoto lens. So many of the shots seemed close-up, and crystal clear. On most of the prisoners he could see the six-pointed Star of David, and sometimes he could read the word "*Jude*" beneath it.

The sunken cheeks and eyes were haunting in their starkness. These prisoners were so emaciated, he could count the ribs on any man not wearing a shirt. More startling, he could see the bones of their arms.

The photo that kept grabbing his attention, even after he'd moved on to others, was a shot of an old man with a stubbly beard lying on the ground, holding his arm above his face as three guards beat him with clubs.

As soon as the photographs were dry, Franz stacked them and opened the door, then marched them down the hall. "Papa, you have to look at these," he said, setting them on his father's desk.

The older man set aside the copy he was reviewing, pushed his glasses down his nose, and leafed through the photos. "Good God!" he muttered. When he had finished, he set them on his desk, pushed his glasses back up his nose, and looked at his son with grim eyes. "Where did you get these?"

"From Kurt Weber, in Augsburg. He asked me to get the film out of Germany for him."

Dieter Lemiel shook his head. "You take too many risks, son."

"It's important, Papa. Someone has to do it."

"What do you intend to do with these?"

"To begin with, I hope you'll print some of them in your newspaper."

"I doubt that I could get them approved by the censors. Even mentioning them might get cut."

"You could run them anyway."

Dieter stared into his son's eyes for a moment. His eyes were the same warm shade of golden brown, but they carried a world-weariness that Franz's did not.

"They would shut me down tomorrow, and it would be next year before I could get an appeal heard. How would your mother and I eat?"

"You told us to always challenge authority, Papa."

The older man nodded his graying head. "Yes, I did. And I hope you always will—but there are smart ways to do that, and stupid ways. Losing my livelihood would be a stupid way."

"People have to learn of this!"

"I agree."

"Then what can we do?"

His father leaned back in his seat, his chin in his hand. "Those leafleteers you know in Zurich and Bern could print them; pass them around places where people would see them. Then perhaps, just perhaps, we could find a way to get them into the hands of the BBC. There are British journalists around—the best place to find them is at the British embassy in Bern, at the daily press briefings. You could wait outside and approach one as he's leaving."

Franz perked up a bit. "Are there similar briefings at the American embassy? Would American journalists print them?"

Dieter Lemiel shrugged. "I would suppose so. But the BBC would be far more respectable than the Americans' NBC."

"It's just that I know someone at the American embassy. A couple of someone's, actually."

"Oh?"

"Yes." At the questioning look in his father's eyes, his brow furrowed. "Don't worry, Papa. I know what I'm doing."

"Be careful that your enthusiasm doesn't get you in over your head, young man."

"I have a meeting with one of the Americans in a half-hour. Thanks for letting me use your dark room." He kissed the older man on the top of the head and grabbed a manila envelope from the desk on his way out.

The Grand Hotel Les Trois Rois was easier to find than Martin expected. It stood on the west bank of the Rhine, beside the Kleinbasel Bridge in the heart of the old quarter. The gilded statues of the Three Wise Men hanging on the façade removed any doubt, and he entered the high colonnaded lobby before Franz arrived at two o'clock.

"Good afternoon, Mr. Schuller," Franz said with a grin.

"Please keep your voice down if you must say my name."

"Of course. Shall we get some lunch?" He motioned toward the restaurant on the far side of the lobby.

"This seems an expensive place for you, Franz," Martin said after they sat at the formal table, with a stunning view of the Rhine out the large picture windows.

"That's why you're buying, Mr., um, Schmidt," Franz replied without looking up from the menu. "The Rouladen here is said to be excellent, and the veal chops as well."

"You've never eaten here?"

"Of course not! I'm a poor artist."

Martin suppressed his irritation; he'd pulled the same stunt on FBI Special Agent Sloan at the Willard in Washington a couple of years ago.

The lunchtime rush was over, and most of the tables sat empty. A blond man in the uniform of an SS Captain sat a few tables away with a voluptuous blonde woman in a stylish blue suit, and two blond children of about five and seven. *On a day trip into Switzerland?* "We must be careful what we say here," Martin said in a low voice.

"I already noticed them," Franz replied, equally quiet. "They're eating dessert."

The waiter took their orders, and Franz asked for a bottle of '39 Mosel Riesling. Once the waiter departed, Franz looked at Martin with a smile. "The wine will make the meal so much more pleasant. Now, why did you ask to meet me?"

Martin eyed the table of the SS Captain, where the waiter was removing the dessert dishes and setting the bill in front of the officer. He kept his voice low.

"I need to make a visit to Germany, and you said that you know people there."

"Yes, I know plenty of people in Germany."

"People who would assist me?"

"I know people who would be happy to assist you—if they thought you were Swiss."

"That's not a problem."

"You have papers?"

"Yes."

"They must be very well-done. They will be requested frequently."

Martin remembered how often they'd been requested the last time he had visited Germany, in 1933. It could only be worse now. "I understand."

"What is your reason for visiting the Reich? You will be asked when your train crosses the border, and likely every time a policeman asks to see your papers and learns that you're 'Swiss.' You should have an answer ready."

Martin frowned. He knew he needed a cover, damn it. "What reason do you use?"

Franz shrugged. "It varies. Sometimes I'm going to visit friends in Stuttgart. Once I was going to see the cathedral in Strasburg. Another time I said was going to the concert in Munich on Beethoven's birthday. Once I even said I was going to see Wagner's Gotterdammerung in Nurmburg! The Germans will believe any admiration expressed for their music."

Franz laughed, but Martin only nodded. "I'll think of a reason."

The SS captain and his family departed, and Martin watched them all the way out the door before turning his gaze back to Franz. By now the restaurant was nearly empty. Still he kept his voice low.

"I need your help to access the underground groups that you work with. Will you accompany me, provide me with introductions?"

Franz nodded. "I just came back from the Reich, actually. That's why I didn't get your telegram until this morning. I would be willing to go back in, if you can wait at least a couple of days—I do have to earn a living."

It was less than ideal, but Martin had little choice. "Monday, then?"

Franz considered a moment. "Agreed, Monday. Is there a specific agenda?"

Martin considered how much he wanted to reveal. "There are certain right-wing groups in Switzerland who have contact with Nazis inside Germany. I need to learn more about them and their connections. Do you know anyone who could assist with that?"

Franz leaned back and looked up in thought. "I'm not sure," he said at length.

"Would you be able to send word through the network?"

Franz shook his head. "It doesn't work that way. There is no *organization* of the various underground groups—nothing to compare to the organization and coordination of French Resistance cells, or the Polish and Czech resistance movements. Inside Germany, only the Communists have an organized network. Everyone else operates on their own. Even the Socialists are little more than an informal association based on old acquaintances."

His eyes took on an unexpected somber note. "I had one contact who was working to build a communication network. He was partly successful, but then he got his conscription notice and was shipped off."

That made things more difficult than Martin had anticipated. "Is there anyone who could pick up where he left off?"

Franz shrugged. "You have to understand how it is there. A great many people in the Reich are waiting for the day when the regime is gone, and they're keeping their heads down until then. They passively resist—'forgetting' to enroll their sons in the Hitler Youth, or not getting out of the way when the Gestapo are chasing a leafleteer—but they are afraid to do more, afraid someone will denounce them and they'll be hauled off to a concentration camp, or shot, or tortured in the Gestapo's basement. It's hard to reach such people.

"Only a brave few are willing and able to do something *now*. It's just difficult to find them. Always one must be extremely careful of what one says. The Gestapo have eyes and ears everywhere—which is why everyone is afraid to do anything."

Damn! That could be a problem. "You get your information from somewhere—why don't we start there?"

Franz nodded. "Then what?"

"We'll see when we get there."

"How long do you expect this visit to last?"

"A few days."

The waiter approached with their food, and they fell silent while he set their plates on the table and opened the wine. He poured a small amount for Franz, who swirled it and took a sniff. He nodded, and the waiter poured their glasses, set the bottle down, and walked off with a slight bow.

"Why don't you come with me after lunch and see this man I know? A pastor. He has connections with anti-regime clergymen inside Germany. Perhaps one of them could help you."

Martin scowled, for only a second, a visceral reaction. "I doubt that any clergyman is going to know the kind of information I need."

Franz shrugged. "You might be surprised at what they hear. Anyway, I have to go see him myself. I want to show him some photographs I brought back. You might be interested in them yourself."

"Photographs of what?"

Franz explained.

Martin sighed. "While I'm personally appalled, there is nothing I can do."

"You could tell your government. It might help bring them into the war against the Nazis."

Martin shook his head. "There is a strong reluctance in the United States to get involved in European wars. It's a deeply-held fear."

"I don't understand," Franz said. "America is not pacifist. You spent most of your history at war with the Indian tribes. You came to Britain's aid against Germany in the last war."

"Yes, and President Wilson paid a political price for it." Martin took a deep breath, leaned forward, and tried to explain. "You have to understand, for a hundred and seventy years, we were British colonies, and every time Britain went to war with France, our ancestors had to defend their frontiers against the French-Canadians. Once we won our independence, American policy was to *never* get involved in European wars again."

Franz frowned. "Surely this is a better reason to fight than anyone had in the last war! The Nazis are evil, and a greater threat to the world than the Kaiser could have ever been."

Martin shook his head. "My job is to protect the interests of the United States government, not to influence policy. We are not at war with Germany, but my government does have a vital interest in keeping Switzerland neutral. I've been tasked with identifying and preventing any threat to that neutrality."

"You're still welcome to come with me to meet with Reverend Kuntz."

Martin considered the possibility that the two men in leather could be waiting for him back at the Bern train station, and decided a longer stay in Basel might be in order. Perhaps they wouldn't wait around all night. "I'll go with you. Now let's talk about the people and groups you know inside Germany."

23

The sky threatened rain as Franz and Martin bicycled north from the heart of Basel, two kilometers to the northern edges of the city. Dark clouds rolled in from the west, and a chill wind whipped up.

Their route ran northwest past the edge of the Kannenfeld, the large manicured park surrounded by a handful of gigantic mansions and long rows of elegant townhouses. Three blocks past the park, Franz turned off in front of a large white church with a gray roof to match the day's sky, broken in the front by a tall white steeple. *Sankt Johanns Kirche*, the white sign by the street announced.

Martin followed Franz, dismounting in front of the bicycle rack near the entrance. He was out of breath, but Franz seemed no more winded than if he'd walked for ten minutes. Martin was embarrassed that his legs felt a little wobbly.

"Are you alright, Mr. Schuller?"

"Yes, I'm fine." Martin didn't mention that he hadn't ridden a bike since he left Austria, eight years before. "Let's get inside before it rains."

The Reverend Gerhard Kuntz was not at all what Martin expected. The thirty-eight-year-old pastor smiled when he shook Martin's hand, and it dimpled his cheeks. His pale blue eyes shined with genuine warmth. Martin had expected a dour, severe-looking man, like the German pastors he had known as a boy in Pennsylvania.

Martin introduced himself as Max Schmidt.

"Welcome, Mr. Schmidt. How do you know my young friend here?"

"You can trust Mr. Kuntz," Franz whispered.

Martin never trusted clergymen. "I met him through a mutual acquaintance—Miss Sonia Rubenstein in Zurich."

"I am not acquainted with Miss Rubenstein." Gerhard Kuntz turned to Franz. "Did you bring a supporter along, for the next time you can't explain yourself out of a corner?" He gave Franz a teasing smile.

"Not exactly."

The minister turned back to Martin. "My young friend likes to commence deep discussions. We agree on a great many subjects, but on others we don't hold the same opinions. We sometimes find ourselves in the middle of the most stimulating debates! Quite enjoyable."

"Not today, Mr. Kuntz," Franz said. "We've come to ask your help, and I'll let Mr. Schmidt explain." He looked Martin in the eye and added, "I think you should begin by telling Mr. Kuntz who you are."

Martin stared back, seething.

Gerhard Kuntz glanced between his two visitors. "Perhaps we should sit?"

"You can trust Mr. Kuntz," Franz repeated once they'd all sat. "He's a good man."

"Thank you, Franz. I do my best."

Martin looked hard into the minister's pale eyes for several seconds. Kuntz returned his gaze, but his eyes were softer, wondering, perhaps even worrying.

Martin opted for partial truth. "I'm investigating right-wing elements in Switzerland that have killed several people recently. They have ties to the Nazis in Germany."

"Oh, I see…" the minister looked out his window, where the border crossing into Alsace could be seen down the road, a kilometer away. Guards marched back and forth across the road on both sides of the red-and-white barricades. "I've heard rumors that the army has Intelligence officers now, like the great powers. How can I possibly help you?"

Martin took encouragement that Kuntz thought he was with Swiss Intelligence.

"I brought Mr. Schmidt here because he needs to get inside Germany, and you know people there who might be willing to help him," Franz said.

"Yes," Gerhard said, still looking out the window.

"You know ministers in Germany who would help," Franz prompted.

Gerhard Kuntz turned back to his visitors, his expression serious. "Yes, I do—but it would put them at terrible risk. Speaking to a foreign agent could get them shot."

"It's important to the freedom of Switzerland that I travel safely through Germany, Mr. Kuntz," Martin said. "I fear the groups that I am investigating mean to impose a Nazi regime on Switzerland. Mr. Lemiel and I are working together to prevent that."

Kuntz seemed startled, but then his expression relaxed, and a hint of smile came to his lips. "I hardly see how they could succeed in that! We are a freedom-loving people, far too independent to take much direction from Bern, let alone from Berlin."

"These people are killing off their opponents one-by-one, and will continue to do so until we can stop them." Martin glanced at Franz before adding, "And, we have reason to believe they have already brought Gestapo agents into the country."

"Good heavens!" The minister looked truly startled.

"There is more," Franz said, and leaned down to pull a manila envelope from his knapsack. "A journalist in Augsburg photographed these images of the Dachau concentration camp. They are disturbing, but you should see them."

Kuntz laid the envelope on his desktop, and pulled out the prints. As he slowly flipped through the images, his face grew pale, and his eyes filled with moisture until a single tear ran down his right cheek.

"Dear God," he whispered, tossing the stack of photographs to the other side of his desk. He stared out the window for a moment, his chin in his hand and his fingers covering his mouth. Tears flowed down both cheeks now, but he sat still and silent.

A lump formed in the pit of Martin's stomach. It was an unexpected reaction, and it disoriented him. He had no sympathy for moralizing preachers and their like. But they were supposed to be stern and hard-hearted; this Reverend Mr. Kuntz was not keeping up that end of the bargain.

The minister cleared his throat a moment later, and wiped at his cheeks before turning back toward his guests. He looked at Franz, his eyes red and heavy. "There are many men I know in Germany who would risk their lives, and their families' lives, to stop this kind of cruelty." His voice was quiet, but firm, and his jaw was set. "If you promise me that you will show each of them these photographs, I will give you a hundred names."

Wariness tightened Martin's stomach, and he raised his hand to signal caution. "Mr. Kuntz, I know you're eager to spread the word about these things, and I understand why—but we must be careful that you only give us the names of men that you can trust completely." And he was not about to carry those pictures into the Reich. He wasn't stupid.

"I understand the sensitivity of your position, Mr. Schmidt," Kuntz replied, his voice still not much more than a whisper.

"Surely there are some in the Confessing Church that you would trust with your own life," Franz suggested. "Those are the men we need to meet."

Martin frowned at the unfamiliar term. "Confessing Church?"

Kuntz nodded, and the sadness in his expression changed to calm. "That is the name given to many Protestant pastors in Germany who have left the main churches in opposition to government efforts to impose Nazi ideology, and the appointment of Lutheran bishops by the regime. Like our Catholic brethren, they preached against the regime's euthanasia of the insane and handicapped; but unlike our Catholic brethren, they could not call upon outside support. Many were arrested, sent to concentration camps. But the movement is still alive and well."

"If they learned that the regime is starving prisoners in the camps, would they still be willing to speak out?" Franz asked.

"I have no doubt."

"Can you provide letters of introduction for us?" Martin asked.

"Of course. But how shall I introduce you, Mr. Schmidt?"

"I will travel under the name of Max Schmidt, and that is the only identity I will use."

"But why should I say that I am referring you? You are bound to be asked the reason for your trip at many check points. The reason you give should match what I say in my letters."

Martin shifted in his seat. "I haven't determined my story yet."

"Then let me say that you are a divinity student in Basel, doing a tour of German churches. That was common not so many years ago, you know—I did it myself in 1927, and again in 1931—though I fear it might not seem as harmless now as it once did."

"I think that will be perfect," Franz said.

Martin scowled. "I suppose it would be the most reasonable explanation." The idea of impersonating a prospective clergyman seemed as unlikely as impersonating a police inspector. And less appealing.

"I fear that the names I give you will be known to the local Gestapo."

Damn! Martin should have anticipated that. "I can deal with that when the time comes."

"If you are going to Berlin, Dietrich Bonhoeffer would be the most obvious choice, of course—though I'm afraid his name is known all over Germany as an anti-government agitator."

"I doubt we'll need to go as far as Berlin," Franz said.

"Impossible to say at this point," Martin corrected.

"Oh, I see…" Gerhard looked troubled. "That does make it difficult to provide you with names. Understand, I wouldn't want to provide you with any name if you don't think there is a reasonable chance that you will call upon that person. If you should be arrested by the Gestapo with a list—"

Martin cut him off. "I understand your concerns, Mr. Kuntz. If you could provide us with a few individuals, we could ask them for additional names if the need should arise."

Kuntz hesitated for a few seconds. "Yes, I suppose that is reasonable. Where will you begin?"

"I need to go to Frankfurt," Martin said.

"I think we should start in Stuttgart," Franz said. He turned to Martin. "I have an associate there." He held Martin's eyes in an intense stare for a moment, as if to say "I'll explain later."

Martin nodded. "Stuttgart, then Frankfurt."

"I'd suggest Stuttgart, to Heidelberg, and then Frankfurt." Again, Franz's eyes locked onto Martin's and held them.

"If you think it best." Martin hated letting someone else call the shots, but in this situation he had to concede. It was aggravating to feel less than completely prepared for a mission, and he was not accustomed to that feeling.

Kuntz watched the exchange with his head cocked. "Very well. I shall write the letters of introduction this afternoon. Where are you staying, Mr. Schmidt?"

"I'm returning to Bern this evening."

"Why don't the two of you join my family for dinner?"

Martin's jaw clenched, but he forced a smile. "That's not necessary, thank you."

"Please! It would be my pleasure. Besides, that will give me time to write more thoughtful letters to my German brethren." His expression brightened. "And, you can practice your upcoming role as a divinity student in front of my family. I promise I won't give away your secret. If you can fool my wife, you can fool the Gestapo."

A broad grin stretched across the minister's face, amused with the idea of pulling one over on his wife.

Martin's chest constricted at the idea, but he nodded and thanked the minister for his hospitality.

"Splendid! I shall send word to my wife to prepare for dinner guests."

Frankfurt

Something felt different as Rudolph Volger strode through his back gardens from the garage. He didn't know why, but his gut tingled with apprehension when he entered his house.

His wife Louisa stood waiting for him in the back hall. "Cook's been arrested."

"What?"

"Two hours ago. The Gestapo came to the door. They asked to speak to him alone in the kitchen, and then they escorted him out and drove away. I haven't had time to engage another cook, so we're going to Johann's house for dinner. They're expecting us in an hour."

Volger cringed. "I'll go upstairs and change clothes." At home he would wear his uniform, but his older brother would expect him in a white dinner jacket.

"And there are two SS officers waiting for you in your study," his wife added, walking away.

His belly tightened, but he told himself they just wanted to discuss Cook's arrest. When he entered the main hall, the butler approached and took his hat. "There are two officers to see you, sir."

"Yes, in the study. Thank you." Volger turned toward the door, straightened his coat, and strode forward.

Three men in his study had helped themselves to chairs, and none of them stood when Volger entered. Two of them wore black SS uniforms, and the collar of one bore the insignia of a *Standartenfuhrer*—Standard Leader, an SS colonel. This one motioned toward Volger's own leather chair behind the desk. "Take a seat please, Major."

Volger sat, folded his hands on his desk, and attempted to look calm.

The third man wore no uniform, but the black leather coat and permanent scowl gave little doubt that he was with the Gestapo. He stood and positioned himself by the door.

"What can I do for you gentlemen?" Volger asked, struggling to keep his voice steady as his pulse raced, and a vein throbbed at the side of his neck.

The colonel put on a polite smile, but his steely blue eyes were cold. "I am Col. Schakenberg, of the Sicherheitsdienst. This is Captain Axthelm, also of the Sicherheitsdienst. And over there is Captain Rohrman of the Gestapo. As you may know, Major, the Gestapo arrested your cook today on charges of espionage, and working with the Reich's enemies."

"I had not heard the charge," Volger replied. Why were the Sicherheitsdienst—the SD—involved in what should have been a simple Gestapo sting oper was operation? The SD were the intelligence branch of the SS.

"He was part of a network of Socialist spies, working with the terrorists in France," Captain Rohrman said from where he stood a few feet from Volger. His voice was as sour as his expression. "We have suspected for some time that someone in this household was providing state secrets to the Resistance—secrets to which you were privy, Major."

Volger couldn't miss the heavy tone of suspicion in the Gestapo officer's voice. "Surely you gentlemen do not believe that I am responsible for such breach of security!"

Col. Schakenberg chuckled, and gave Volger a disarming smile. Still, his gaze remained intense. "I'm sure there are other explanations, Major. One of your servants could have access to things left carelessly out in view, for example..." His voice trailed off.

"I would never allow the Fatherland's security to be compromised by carelessness, Colonel. I swear it."

"I am sure that is true, Major," the colonel said, still keeping that humorless smile. "Traitors to the Fatherland keep getting craftier, and no doubt they found ways to get around your reasonable precautions. We understand your cook has been in your family's employ for ten years—plenty of time to break the combination to your safe, for example."

"Yes...that must be it," Volger said. "Is there anything else? I hate to trouble the SD with my domestic problems."

"As a matter of fact, the SD has a mission for you. And to insure your acceptance of this most important mission, we have something we'd like to show you."

Col. Schakenberg motioned to Capt. Rohrman, and the Gestapo officer removed a manila envelope from inside his leather jacket, which he handed to Volger.

Volger took the envelope, and glanced at the SD officers sitting across from him. Both wore cold expressions. He opened the envelope, and peered inside. His blood turned to ice at the sight of the black-and-white photographs inside.

It was like déjà vu. Six months before when he'd entered the home and greeted his wife, the butler had told him that a visitor arrived a few moments before and asked to speak to him—a young Swiss man who said he had important SS business.

When he entered the study that March evening, Volger faced the young visitor, dressed in dark clothing, with carelessly-combed brown hair.

"Good evening, Major Volger," the young man said with a cheeky grin.

"Who are you?"

"My name's Franz."

"Franz who?"

"Just Franz."

"What do you want, Mr. Franz?"

"Your assistance, Major." And Franz had reached inside his coat and pulled out a manila envelope—an envelope that contained photographs of Volger having sex with Michael Kaim on the little bed in the garret above the garage.

Now he beheld those exact same photographs, in a similar manila envelope—only with a Gestapo agent standing beside him, and two SD officers sitting across from him. His stomach dropped.

"We should arrest you now for violating Paragraph 175, you miserable pervert!" Rohrman said. His thin lips were pursed, and his pasty white skin glistened as if he'd broken out in a cold sweat. "You should be locked up in Dachau camp with the other perverts."

Col. Schakenberg held up a hand, and the Gestapo officer fell into a sullen silence. "Captain Rohrman, the state does not lock up men under Paragraph 175 if the pervert will demonstrate sexual conformity. Major Volger is married and has two children. Furthermore, judges will almost always release anyone arrested for homosexuality if the pervert displays obvious signs of Aryanness and manliness—as indeed Major Volger does. *Every* SS man does, Captain."

Rohrman flushed dark red, but kept silent. The warning had been obvious.

"Of course, we have a complete dossier on you, Major," Col. Schakenberg continued. He turned to Captain Axthelm, who handed him a small leather-bound notebook. "Between 1925 and 1931 you visited Hamburg no less than twenty-seven times, and each time you spent your evenings at decadent cabarets and homosexual sex clubs. During the same period you visited Berlin eleven times, also frequenting cabarets where men dressed in women's garters and stockings. You paid street ruffians to let you sodomize them."

Volger's palms turned clammy.

The colonel looked up, shook his head in mocking reproach, and said, "Tsk, tsk, Major." He returned to the notebook. "But you got married in 1932, at the advanced age of twenty-six, to Louisa Jaeger, the daughter of one of your father's business associates. You joined the Party in 1931, two years before your brother, and three years before your father—well done! You joined the SS in September 1933, and I see you excelled at your duties. High marks from your superiors. You were placed in charge of operations to round up homeless beggars, the retarded and insane—and of course, homosexuals—and deport them to the camps at Breitenau and Dachau. Last year, your duties were expanded to include the deportation of the Jews."

"I believe the boy in your garage is Jewish, is he not, Major?" Captain Axthelm asked, the first time he'd spoken. He was the youngest man in the room, perhaps thirty.

Volger didn't respond. His mouth had gone dry.

Col. Schakenberg gave him an indulgent smile. "At least Major Volger puts the boy to work, Captain. He doesn't allow him to indulge in the laziness of his race."

"It is against the law for a Jew to have sexual relations with an Aryan!" Capt. Rohrman of the Gestapo sputtered, his face flushing redder.

Volger looked directly into Schakenberg's eyes, and held his gaze. "Colonel, we both know that there are secret SS brothels all over the Reich where SS officers can indulge in sexual relations with young Jewesses who are kept inside at all times. That is essentially the same thing."

"Well, not exactly the same, now is it, Major?" Schakenberg replied, fixing Volger with a cold stare. Then he waved a hand. "But do not think me so naïve as to believe you are the only man in the SS with your predilections."

"What are you going to do?"

"We have a mission for you, Major, and we will not reveal your secret if you accept the mission and complete it successfully."

"I meant what are you going to do about the boy?"

Col. Schakenberg waved his hand again. "I don't care a thing what you do with a Jewish boy, Major. That is your business. Complete your mission, and it will remain your business."

"And what is the mission?"

"You will learn that soon. In the meantime, you should get some rest—much will be expected of you. Take a holiday…Switzerland is quite nice this time of year."

24

Basel

The Kuntz home rang with laughter and the clatter of dishes as everyone but the guests set the table, chattering and joking with one another.

"I was going to serve Rosti, with cabbage—but since we have company I've cooked a mutton roast," Louisa Kuntz beamed at Franz and Martin.

"That's kind of you, Mrs. Kuntz. Thank you!" Franz said with a broad grin. When he and Martin went back to the living room, he whispered, "Meat has gotten expensive since the war started, so this is a sacrifice for them. If you want to pass as Swiss, be grateful for their generosity, but don't acknowledge the hardship of it unless they do first."

"Understood."

Martin knew that Switzerland imported most of its beef and pork from Germany, and after the war started those imports had all but stopped. Only the wealthy regularly ate beef or pork now. Mutton was domestic and still available, but even its price had shot up with the absence of competition from German beef and pork.

Still, the tip from Franz on the proper response was a God-send.

While Mrs. Kuntz and their daughter cooked in the kitchen, and the two boys went outside with Franz to kick around a "futbol," Gerhard Kuntz joined Martin in the living room and offered him a seat.

Kuntz's voice was friendly but quiet, though the empty dining room and the kitchen door stood between them and the others. "So, Mr. Schmidt, do you attend a church in Bern?"

"No."

"Oh dear, that could make it difficult for you to believably pretend to be a divinity student."

"When I grew up, my family attended church every Sunday, so I have some experience with ministers."

"That's good. Tell me though, if you were raised in the church, why do you not attend church now?"

Martin stiffened. "I'm not much of a church person."

"When did you stop going?"

Every muscle in Martin's body tensed. "When I was seventeen."

"Did something happen then that caused you to stop going?"

"Yes." He regretted the sharpness in the reply immediately.

Kuntz looked stung. "I apologize if it seems that I'm prying into your private affairs. I'm only trying to understand your background."

Martin nodded, but said nothing.

"Tell me about the pastor at your church when you were a child."

Martin took a deep breath. "He wore black robes, and he was stiff and formal."

"Was your church Reformed? Or Anabaptist?"

"It was Reformed."

"Wonderful! The Protestant churches in Basel are almost all Reformed."

"Yes."

"Perhaps you'll join us at church Sunday? We would love to have you."

Martin stiffened again and shook his head. "Thank you, but no."

Kuntz seemed to read his discomfort. "Perhaps some other time, then."

They gathered around the table at seven-thirty, and the noise temporarily came to a halt as the family bowed their heads, closed their eyes, and sat silent. Franz and Martin followed suit, but Martin kept his eyes open.

Gerhard Kuntz's rich tenor voice filled the room. "Heavenly Father, we thank You for the food You have provided for this table, and for each person gathered around it. Keep us ever mindful of Your mercies, this day and always. In the name of Jesus Christ, our Lord and Savior, Amen."

"Amen!" his wife and three children echoed, and then each reached for a dish of food. The chatter resumed.

Martin watched them in silence, marveling at the easy way in which they interacted, even in front of a total stranger. Louisa Kuntz's round cheeks flushed pink as she threw her head back with laughter at something her eldest son said, clapping her hands with delight. Gerhard's deep laughter joined hers, and he patted his son on the shoulder.

Martin and his ex-wife Becky had three children, like the Kuntzes; but family dinners at their house had never been like this. Becky would have never tolerated anything as impolite as a joke at the dinner table, and laughter from children was kept to playtime, not mealtime.

Martin had always detested the stiff, formal manners that Becky insisted on at mealtimes. It was even worse at her parents' home in Philadelphia. Martin could only imagine how tough it must be for his kids, living there now in their grandparents' big, cold, WASPish townhouse, with furniture that looked like it had never been sat upon, and fragile glass and crystal things everywhere.

His own family had never been as formal as Becky's, but neither had they been as warm as the Kuntzes. They'd lived in rooms above the small grocery in Reading that his father David owned. His father had been stern, demanding hard work from his six children from early ages, and praise was aberrant. Sundays alone were free from work. But Sundays also lacked play-time, as the children were expected to remain pious and quiet, listening to their parents read from the Bible in German.

Conversations in their house frequently switched between German and English—a fact which had come to embarrass Martin by the time he was in high school; most of his friends on the football team came from English-speaking families. He could still remember the shame he hid when his buddies mocked his father's Pennsylvania Dutch lilt after leaving his house before a game—an accent Martin himself had shed early as a public school student.

He also remembered well the deep disapproving scowls and stern lectures his father had delivered each time he'd overheard Martin laughing and joking too loudly with his friends on the sidewalk in front of the store, or for using "impolite" language such as "gosh darn it."

Martin wondered if Reverend or Mrs. Kuntz would scowl in such a way if young Albrecht said something slightly off-color. Watching them now, he doubted it.

But would they not react with the same disappointment and shame as his parents if young Albrecht came home one day in a few years, and told them he had gotten his girlfriend pregnant? Would they not respond with the same moralizing and Bible-quoting? Martin was certain that they would.

Ministers were to be barely trusted.

Saturday,
October 4, 1941

25

Murten/Morat, Fribourg Canton, Switzerland

Police Sergeant Wernecke listened to the bilingual argument with ill-conceived irritation. He stood back a few feet, big arms crossed, scowling at the two middle-aged biddies shouting at each other across a wooden fence, wagging their fingers in each other's faces.

"Those apples came from *my* tree! You have no right to them, you filthy thief!" Mrs. Schrand shouted in German. Her gray hair was pulled back in a tight bun at the crown of her head, but strands had come loose around her face as she shook her head violently at everything the other woman said.

"They fall on *my* side of the fence, you uncharitable miser!" Mrs. Racine shouted back in French.

"You lie!" Mrs. Schrand accused, still in German.

"Look for yourself," Mrs. Racine said, still in French, motioning at a handful of half-rotten apples lying in the grass of her yard, under a low-hanging branch. The branch extended several feet across the fence into the Racines' yard.

"Liar!" Mrs. Schrand shouted in German. "How do you explain those footprints through my garden? You trampled my potato patch! I'd recognize those short, fat footprints anywhere."

"My feet are not fat!" Mrs. Racine, in French.

"Fat as a pregnant sow!" Mrs. Schrand, in German.

Police constable Berger stood beside Mrs. Racine, trying hard to sooth the tempers. He reached his hand between them, trying to separate the wagging fingers, but they both slapped his hands away.

Good luck with those menopausal bitches. The last thing Wernecke wanted was to get in between two angry old windbags who had cultural and linguistic prejudices.

The quiet little town of Murten—or Morat, in French—sat in the north of the bilingual Canton of Fribourg, near the border with the German-speaking Canton of Bern. Situated to the east of the River Saane gorges, the nominal language border, most of the three thousand inhabitants spoke German, like Wernecke himself, and Constable Berger, and Mrs. Schrand. But about fifteen percent of the town's residents were French-Swiss, or *Romands*, who had moved here from nearby Francophone villages to the west.

The two groups were usually polite and accommodating, but occasionally a dispute such as this one brought out cultural resentments that lay buried.

Personally, Wernecke wished the *Romands* would go back to their side of the Saane where they belonged.

Constable Berger tried his most soothing voice. "Now Mrs. Schrand, I'm sure Madame Racine will pay you a few rappens for the apples, or maybe share her tarts with you."

She replied with a "Humph!" and folded her arms. "I wouldn't want any tarts the way *those* people make them."

Berger turned to the other lady and said in French, "Mrs. Racine, wouldn't you be willing to share your tartes with Frau Schrand, as a sign of good-will?"

The two women shouted at each other again in their own languages, and young Constable Berger threw up his hands and turned to his sergeant with a pleading expression.

"Enough!" Wernecke shouted in German, loud enough that it hurt his throat. Both women fell silent, their arms held still with the fingers pointing at each other, and looked to the sergeant open-mouthed.

Wernecke marched along the fence to Mrs. Racine. He addressed her in German, though he was perfectly capable of speaking French. "Mrs. Racine, go into your shed at once and bring me your husband's saw. I'll take care of this problem."

The middle-aged *Romande* just stood there, apparently still stunned at the police sergeant's menacing posture and tone.

"Now!"

She shuffled backwards several steps before turning and rushing toward the shed at the back of her narrow property. The clanging of metal objects came from inside, and then the short woman with silver-streaked black hair hurried back, carrying a rusty saw.

Wernecke grabbed it from her, and marched to the offending apple branch. He lined it up over the fence-line, and began furiously sawing.

Sawdust flew in every direction, and the two middle-aged ladies stepped back, keeping their eyes on him. Sweat dripped down his face, and his breathing came hard and fast, huffing from his mouth and projecting tiny drops of spittle a great distance.

The branch cracked and broke at the fence-line, dropping onto the pickets, scratching the whitewash on Mrs. Racine's side as it tumbled to the ground.

Wernecke marched back to where the two ladies stood in open-mouthed silence, and he thrust the saw toward Mrs. Racine. "Problem solved," he hissed in German, and stomped toward the street.

Constable Berger stared at him with wide eyes as he strode past. Turning briefly to the ladies, he stammered in German, "Um, Madame Racine, see that Mrs. Schrand gets at least one of your apple tarts, and, um, Mrs. Schrand, see that you and your husband eat it." Then he hurried after his sergeant.

"Damned *Romands* should go back where they came from and leave us in peace," Wernecke grumbled when the younger policeman caught up with him on the street.

"These types of arguments aren't common," Berger said, but fell silent at the scowl his sergeant gave him.

"I'm going by home," Wernecke muttered. "I'm late for lunch as it is."

It was a five-minute walk to home from there, and he grumbled to himself the whole way.

Wernecke blamed religion for Murten's bilingual problems, such as they were. Like the other German-speaking towns and villages of the Lake District, they had been jointly ruled by Bern and Fribourg for centuries, until the Protestant Reformation divided them—Bern became Protestant, Fribourg stayed Catholic. Murten and the other communities of the southern Lake District stayed Catholic and aligned with Fribourg in spite of the language difference, while the northern Lake District went Protestant and aligned with Bern. Denominational differences were deemed more important than linguistic ones, so Murten found itself part of a canton that was three-quarters *Romand*. Inevitably, some of those *Romands* had moved in.

Joseph Wernecke had been raised Catholic, but he hadn't been to Mass in twenty-one years. The last time had been his wedding day. His split with the Church began three months earlier, when it was discovered that his girlfriend was pregnant. Maria had done her penance, but Wernecke refused. Saying dozens of Hail Mary's was bad enough, and a colossal waste of time in his opinion—but the real clincher had been the priest's demand of a half-month's wages as a "donation" to the church. Twenty-year-old Wernecke had refused.

Then that damned French-speaking bishop in Fribourg had gotten wind of it, and excommunicated him. Finally, three months later, his parents and Maria's father had prevailed on him to do his penance and beg for forgiveness, so they could have a proper wedding. He did as they instructed, went to the wedding, and then as soon as the papers were signed and he and Maria were at the doorway, he turned and gave the priest his middle finger. He hadn't been back since.

He took off his jacket and hat as he stepped into the little stone house in the medieval quarter. His light brown hair streaked with gray at the temples was matted down from sweat where his hat band touched his scalp, and he ran a hand through it, then wiped the sweat on the side of his shirt.

His wife hurried toward him from the kitchen, wiping her hands on her apron. "There have been three telephone calls for you in the last fifteen minutes," she said, breathless. "The gentleman won't leave a message."

Just then, the telephone rang. "I'll take it," Wernecke mumbled, and strode to the telephone on the dining room wall.

He recognized the voice on the line. "Sgt. Wernecke, this is the Gauleiter."

"Yes, sir?" He'd never met the Gauleiter before, and knew only that he lived in Zurich, but he'd heard the man's commanding voice on the telephone several times.

"I have an assignment for you."

Wernecke listened in silence as the Gauleiter explained the task that he wanted the policeman to carry out.

"Can you do that for us, Sergeant?"

"Yes, sir!"

"Good. The Fatherland is depending on you."

There was a click as the line went dead.

Wernecke stood against the wall, stroking his chin with his right hand, trying to think of how he could do what the Gauleiter had asked. Then he remembered Mrs. Schrand and Madame Racine, and a faint smile came to his lips.

26

Basel

Rudolph Volger did not immediately get up from his seat when the train came to a stop inside the station. He stared out the window at the platform, scanning the faces. His contact would recognize him, he'd been told. No need to know who it would be. But he still wondered.

Taking a fortifying breath, he stood straight and tall, head high, smoothed his black SS jacket, and strode toward the exit. He stepped down onto the platform, looked all around for a few seconds, then walked toward the terminal.

He was approached almost immediately by a young man of medium height, thin brown hair, and pale skin. His face bore a few pock marks that had not been obvious from a distance, and his nose was big for the rest of his features. He wore dark trousers and a black leather jacket.

Just like the Gestapo to make their identities obvious even in neutral territory. Volger had little patience for idiots with short tempers and fat egos, but he feared and respected their power.

"Major Volger, welcome to Switzerland," the young man said with an undisguised Bavarian accent. "I trust you had a pleasant trip? Your train was only twenty-five minutes behind schedule—not bad these days."

Volger was in no mood for insincere pleasantries. His reply was as stiff and formal as his posture. "Yes. We were stopped once, south

233

of Stuttgart, to allow a military train to pass. And you would do well to disguise your accent, young man."

The Gestapo officer stiffened. "You may address me as Lieutenant Schultz, Major. Come with me please."

"Where are we going, Lt. Schultz?" Volger asked, walking alongside the young man in leather.

"I am to escort you to Zurich. Then another escort will take you to your destination."

"How are we to travel to Zurich?"

"By train, of course. It is only a ninety-minute trip. I have your ticket."

Volger raised an eyebrow. In Germany, the Gestapo would never risk escorting a person of interest on a passenger train. The back of a black Mercedes Benz sedan was always the way.

Passengers exiting the train from Bern streamed down the ramp from that platform as Volger and his escort pushed their way toward the next one, where the train to Zurich waited. In this crowd, moving against the stream as they were, it would be all too easy to ditch the young tough in leather. But there would be no gain to doing that, so Volger tried to stay close.

A brown-haired young man in an argyle sweater, carrying an expensive-looking leather suitcase and gawking up at the ceiling of the grand hall rather than watching where he was going, bumped into Volger.

"Oh, pardon me! I'm sorry, sir!" the young man said as he turned around, and then his blue eyes widened in surprise at the sight of Volger's uniform. He turned back around without a word and hurried away.

His accent was foreign rather than Swiss—English, perhaps? Not quite, Volger thought; more nasal. Canadian or American, more likely. Damned foreign tourist.

Another man in leather awaited them at the ramp to their platform. He was older, closer to forty, with wispy thin hair barely covering his scalp. He was of medium height and build, but with a pronounced paunch. He also wore the tell-tale black leather coat. "Greetings Major. I am Captain Engelhardt." Another guttural Bavarian accent.

"I didn't realize the Gestapo had such a presence in Switzerland."

The captain cringed. "Please keep your voice down in public, Major."

"Your accents give you away the moment you open your mouths," Volger retorted with undisguised contempt. "If your leather coats don't give you away first, that is."

Captain Engelhardt colored. "You'll come with us please. This way." Once they were seated in a half-empty car, with no one nearby, Engelhardt said in a hoarse whisper, "Of course we have men in Switzerland. The Gestapo had men in Austria more than four years ago, ahead of the Anschluss, and we have had agents in Switzerland for over a year now."

Volger raised his eyebrows. "Oh? Is another Anschluss planned?" he whispered.

Engelhardt sat back in his seat and pretended indifference. "You will learn what you need to know when we get you to Zurich." He turned away, crossing his legs and facing the aisle.

Volger stared out the window as the train whistle blew. He had ninety minutes to ponder the puzzle pieces he'd been shown.

Jason got directions from an elderly porter, thanked him with a franc coin, and set off toward the University district. It was a little more than a kilometer, the old man had said.

The sun shown bright, and he walked with a spring in his step, looking around at the friendly Swiss faces and exchanging smiles with those who glanced back.

He had no idea that he was being followed.

Martin had already bought his ticket back to Bern when he was stunned to see Jason Bachman coming down the ramp from one platform, carrying a suitcase.

There was no reason he could think of that an embassy grunt should be in Basel all by himself, and his suspicion was aroused. Pocketing his ticket, he followed the young man out of the station.

His irritation grew twenty minutes later when they passed by the University buildings on Hebelstrasse. He had little doubt where Jason was going.

If he continued following, he would miss his train. But he couldn't go back to Bern without knowing. He silently cursed Jason and stayed behind him.

Jason grinned in anticipation at the sign for Petersgasse on the corner of two narrow streets. He checked the address on the paper Franz had slipped him the other night, found the building, and entered.

He hesitated in the hallway for a second, then walked toward the staircase at the far end. A plump middle-aged woman stepped out of the open doorway on his left, and startled him. "May I help you, sir?"

"Yes, I'm here to see Mr. Franz Lemiel, in number sixteen. He's expecting me."

The woman gave him a curious look, glanced down at his suitcase and frowned, then nodded toward the stairs. "On the fourth floor, last door on the left."

Jason inwardly groaned. Fourth floor to a European meant the fifth floor to an American. And there was no elevator in sight.

He was nearly out of breath when he reached the fourth floor, which proved to be the top floor. He paused for a few seconds to regain his composure and wipe the sweat from his forehead, then set off down the hall. The last door on the left bore the number sixteen, as the portierfrau had indicated.

He took a deep breath in a vain attempt to suppress the butterflies in his stomach, and knocked.

Franz greeted him with a huge grin. "Jason, welcome! I'm glad you agreed to come."

Jason returned the smile. "Thanks for the invitation. I was excited to get your telegram yesterday."

Franz waved him in. "Come in. Please make yourself comfortable."

The apartment was bigger than Jason had expected. One large room was at least as large as the apartment he shared with two other guys, and there was a tiny kitchen that opened off the far side of the main room to his right. A doorway closer on the right presumably led into the bedroom.

Large windows on his left ran the length of the main room, facing west so that the apartment was bathed in afternoon sunlight. A big cushioned couch faced the windows, with a small table next to it that held a stack of newspapers. There was no coffee table or ottoman in front of the couch, but in their place sat two wooden crates.

Along the far wall rested several painted canvases of varying sizes next to an empty easel, and Jason made straight for them as soon as he'd placed his suitcase beside the couch. "Did you paint all of these?"

Franz appeared at his side. "Yes."

"May I look at them?"

"Please!"

Jason leafed through them one by one, leaning them against his legs. There were beautiful paintings of old stone buildings, one of a big bridge over the Rhine, a few of boats and barges sailing the river, and several of park-like settings. The colors were muted—dark shades of green for the trees and shrubs, and only slightly lighter shades for the grass; grays and browns for the buildings, and dark blues for the river. But all of them had the feel of paintings Jason might see for sale in a gallery in downtown Chicago for a hundred dollars or more.

"They're wonderful!"

Then he came to the nudes, and his pace slowed. In these, the colors were vivid, almost life-like.

There were both men and women, alone and in groups, doing all manner of activities, mostly outdoors, either in a park or in the countryside. Some stood beside bicycles. Others lay on blankets on the grass, next to picnic meals. Six young people—four men and two women—splashed naked in thigh-deep water. Two voluptuous young women stretched out on a dock, sunning their bare breasts. One young man leaned back against the trunk of a tree with a seductive smile.

"Friends in Paris," Franz explained. "I paint them from my memory. Happy times, trips to the French countryside, or bicycle rides through the Bois de Vincennes."

The one that most caught Jason's fascination was the last one—a slender young man sitting on a wooden stool in a barn, milking a cow in the nude. His face was almost angelic in its relaxed expression, and the only visible tension was in the muscles of one forearm as it pulled on an udder. His smooth skin was the same color as the milk streaming into his metal pail, and his head was topped with a mass of blond curls. The youth's stool faced at an angle toward the viewer, so that his torso was fully visible, as was a hint of blond pubic hair behind one delicately muscled thigh.

"Ah, that is one of my favorites," Franz said, his voice low and reverential. "I painted it two years ago, but can't bring myself to sell it. The model was a Mennonite boy on a farm outside of Thun. Eighteen years old. A sweet boy—and very willing."

Jason felt a pang of jealousy, and set the paintings back against the wall. "It's beautiful," he said, his voice quiet.

Franz responded to Jason's quietness by squeezing his shoulder and giving him a big smile. "Come sit, relax. Put your feet up, and I'll open a bottle of wine."

Franz put his hand on the small of Jason's back and guided him to the couch. Jason sank into the deep cushions, and allowed himself to relax. He kicked off his shoes, and put his feet up on one of the wooden crates.

In the corner of the room, partly hidden between a radio cabinet and the wall, leaned a rifle. Next to it sat an unopened box of cartridges. *That's curious.*

Franz returned from the kitchen a moment later, carrying an open bottle of wine and two wine glasses. He set them down on the other crate, and poured both glasses.

"An Alsatian Riesling, a '38. I got it a few weeks before the Nazis marched into France. Now I'll share it with you."

Jason thanked him as he took the proffered glass. Then he nodded toward the rifle in the corner. "Do you hunt?"

"The gun? No, it's my army rifle. A K-31."

"You're in the army?"

"All Swiss men between age twenty and thirty are in the reserves. We keep our weapon and ammunition at home, so that we can use it in the event of a national emergency. I have an army knife as well. I keep it in the kitchen." Franz grinned and added, "That's how I opened the bottle of wine."

"I didn't realize." Jason took a sip, then nodded toward the stack of paintings by the wall. "Do you sell a lot of them?"

"Sometimes, sometimes not. I sold two this morning."

"How often do you paint?"

"Every day that I'm home—though sometimes I draw in charcoal instead."

"You're not working on anything right now?" Jason nodded toward the empty easel.

"I have not been home much this week. I just returned from Germany yesterday, and then I had to meet with your Mr. Schuller."

Jason's eyes widened, and he sat forward. "You were inside Nazi Germany?"

Franz shrugged in apparent indifference. "Yes."

"What were you doing there?"

Franz chuckled and waved a finger. "Uh-uh-uh! That is my business."

Jason felt his cheeks flush. "I'm sorry. What's it like there?"

Franz spent the next ten minutes describing life inside "the box"—the paranoia, the food shortages, the air raid sirens at night, and above all else the constant knowledge that the Gestapo could be listening or watching.

Jason listened in silence, awe-struck. "Wow, I can't even imagine," he said when Franz had finished his tale.

"It is always a unique experience."

The sardonic smile gracing Franz's lips made butterflies flit through Jason's stomach. He looked away and shook his head. "You must be *really* brave!"

Franz laughed, and patted Jason's knee. "No more brave than eighty million Germans."

He left his hand resting on Jason's knee.

Jason's stomach leapt, and his mouth went dry. He stared at Franz's hand for a moment, then looked up to find the handsome young man leaning close, staring at him with those warm golden-brown eyes.

"You may think me brave if you'd like," Franz said, his voice soft and low.

He leaned forward, and his lips met Jason's and immediately parted. Jason was too startled to react for a second, but then his own lips parted and Franz's tongue entered his mouth. Their arms found their way around each other.

A moment later Franz was leaning him down onto his back, his hand going up Jason's shirt and tweaking a nipple. The sudden tingle made Jason's breath catch. Then Franz bolted upright, and lifted his shirt over his head in one swift motion.

Jason stared up at his bare chest, with its firm pectoral muscles and sun-browned skin covered by a dusting of black hair. Beneath it was a taut belly, with a trail of dark hair leading down the center, growing thicker beneath the navel, and disappearing beneath the top of the trousers.

He reached up and ran his fingers across Franz's chest. Franz took hold of his hand, pressed it against the center of his chest, then slowly pushed it down his flat abdomen, over his trousers, and pressed it against his erection.

Jason's breath came fast, and his hand trembled.

"You have done this before, yes?" Franz asked, his voice still soft and low.

Jason swallowed hard and nodded. "A few times."

Franz gave him a warm smile. "I'll be gentle with you." He leaned down and kissed Jason again, softly this time. He unfastened the front of Jason's pants, slipping his hand inside.

**

On the roof of the building across the street, crouched in a corner of the fire escape, Martin Schuller lowered his binoculars. He'd seen enough. He'd known enough homosexuals at the State Department over the years that this didn't bother him personally—but for one of his secret agents, it was an unwanted complication. *Just like Javier, damn it.*

But worse, Jason Bachman had wantonly ignored his instruction to stay away. His jaw clenched, and he held his mouth tight. He spun away and started down the fire escape.

And he stopped; a movement in the next dormer window caught his eye. Someone leaned out, also watching the activity in Franz's apartment through binoculars.

It was the same curly-haired young man Martin had seen watching the meeting in Bern that Franz had attended with Jason Bachman.

27

Zurich

Rudolph Volger said nothing at the Zurich train station when he was transferred to two different men in leather. The tall one introduced himself as Captain Tischer, and his shorter and stouter companion as Captain Karol. Rudolph merely nodded in acknowledgement, and followed them to a waiting Opel Kapitan.

"We're taking you to the Gauleiter," Tischer said from the driver's seat after the doors had closed.

Volger didn't look at his escorts, but watched Zurich drift past through the window. He outranked every Gestapo officer he'd encountered that day, and he spoke far better German than their guttural working-class Bavarian slop. And he'd grown weary of their foolish obviousness.

The car wound its way through the northern districts of Zurich, eventually turning into a driveway that lead behind an enormous stone house on a low rise above the street. Volger's curiosity was peaked; the house was grander than his, or even his brother's. Whoever the Gauleiter was, he was someone important.

The car pulled around the back, and Tischer killed the engine. Volger didn't wait for them to open his door, but got out on his own and took several steps toward the house before he stopped with his back to the car and waited for the Gestapo men to join him.

"Major, you will remember that while you are in Switzerland, you are in our custody," Karol hissed as he approached from behind.

Volger didn't look at him. He stood and stared at the house with his hands clasped behind his back.

"You will come with us. March!" Karol said.

Volger still didn't look at him, but followed him inside the back door.

He found himself in a spacious hallway, with walls of dark paneled mahogany. A tall butler in a black tuxedo jacket with tails hurried to them. "Messrs Tischer and Karol, you are expected. And this must be Major Volger?"

Volger nodded.

"I will announce you. Follow me, please."

Volger noted with mild amusement that this Swiss butler spoke finer German than any of the Gestapo officers he'd met that day.

The lanky butler opened a large door and stepped into a high-ceilinged library. "Messrs Tischer and Karol are here, sir. They have brought Major Volger."

"Excellent. Show them in, Anton."

Volger strode into the library with his back straight, and his head high. He removed his peaked hat and held it between his left arm and his torso. Across the room in a high-backed chair sat a man in dark business suit, with long thin limbs, thin dark hair slicked back from his long face, with a narrow hooked nose protruding prominently. He stared back at Volger from deep-set eyes.

"Greetings, Major. I'm glad you could make the trip."

"I wasn't given a choice, sir. I am here on the Reich's business," Volger replied. "I understand that you are to explain my presence in Switzerland."

The Gauleiter chuckled. "Direct and to the point. I like you already, Major. A fine example of German efficiency—we could use more of that in Switzerland. But we mustn't ignore the niceties of polite society. I understand you were raised that way."

Volger said nothing.

"I met your father once, years ago in Frankfurt. A shrewd businessman. He was still working at Deutschebank at the time, and my bank did business with him. I understand he's retired now, and your brother Johann has risen though the ranks at Deutschebank. Is that so?"

"Yes."

"I'm afraid I have not had the pleasure of meeting your brother—though I was in Frankfurt last month, and met other executives at Deutschebank while I was there. Perhaps next time."

"Perhaps so."

"Please be so kind as to give my regards to your father when you see him next, will you Major?"

Volger's patience was wearing thin. "And who should I say sends those regards?"

The Gauleiter smiled. "I'm not sure he would remember me anyway."

Volger's lips tightened, and he kept the anger from his tone with difficulty. "A moment ago you reproached me for ignoring the niceties of polite society, and yet you have failed to introduce yourself, sir. Hardly polite."

The Gauleiter laughed out loud for a moment. "How bold of you, Major! You are just the sort of man I need. Very well. Would you leave us please, gentlemen?"

Tischer and Karol looked startled. "Sir?" Tischer asked.

"I'd like to have a private conversation with Major Volger. Please leave us." A coldness had come to the Gauleiter's voice, and the Gestapo men nodded in acquiescence and exited.

"Much better. Now, have a seat please, Major. Do make yourself comfortable. It is important that guests feel comfortable in my home, and you are an honored guest."

Volger took a seat opposite his host and set his hat and gloves on the desktop, but kept his back rigidly straight.

"I am Ernst Zubler, your host while you are in Switzerland. I am also the internal leader of the movement to join our little country to the greater German nation—from which we originated, of course."

Volger nodded. "A pleasure to make your acquaintance, Mr. Zubler. How am I to assist you?"

"Do you know who General Henri Guisan is?"

"Of course. He is the commander of the Swiss Army."

"Yes," Zubler replied, a note of distaste in his voice. "General Guisan is a French-speaking *Romand*, and unlike General Wille during the last war, he is not as favorable to the German Reich. He is a leading member of the *Schweizerischer Vaterlandischer Verband*— the SVV—which, much like your Nazi Party, is against immigration, and militaristic."

"I have heard of it," Volger replied.

"Many of the highest officers in the army belong to the SVV. Any of them could have been made commanding general—including Colonel Ulrich Wille, Jr., General Wille's son. But alas, we have Guisan instead. You know what happened last July, I'm sure."

"I know that he mobilized your army against the possibility that the Reich would invade Switzerland. But we never did."

"He did far more than that!" Zubler practically spat the words. "Before the fall of France, he had been secretly making military preparations with the French, despite our neutrality. The Leader and his generals are aware of this treachery. Then in July of last year he called six hundred officers to the Rutli meadow—the very site where the Swiss Confederation was formed in 1291, a base appeal to their patriotism—and he called upon them to resist German invasion. If they ran out of bullets, he urged them to resort to the bayonet, and above all to *never surrender*. After rallying the army at Rutli, he went on the radio and addressed the nation, calling upon all citizens to resist invasion and occupation to the last man, if necessary. He instructed Swiss citizens to regard any surrender broadcast as enemy lies, and to continue resistance to the end."

Volger listened without a word, grateful that he had never been part of any invasion of Switzerland.

A bitter smile came to Ernst Zubler's mouth. "And the loyal citizenry of this otherwise disorganized republic rallied to him. Guisan has become a symbol of national resistance, and is revered by every stratum of Swiss society, across all cantons, language groups, religions, and across the political spectrum. Protestant, Catholic, Jewish; German, French, Italian, or Romansch; leftist, centrist and rightist—all adore him.

"Well, almost all. There are some of us who see him differently, as a dangerous threat to the Volk. He betrayed the movement in Switzerland, and for that he must die. That is where you come in, Major Volger."

Volger went cold. "You want me to assassinate the commanding general of the Swiss army?" His mouth hung open.

"I have a dossier on you," Zubler said with a thin smile. "Let me point out specifically that you received high marks for your marksmanship during SS training. Your accuracy with an automatic rifle is incredible. Don't be modest, Major—I have seen the reports of your superiors. You are an excellent marksman! And that is why I need you to assassinate General Guisan when he emerges from a meeting with the Federal Council in two weeks."

Volger took a deep breath and regained his composure. "What is the plan?"

Zubler chuckled. "You are to take a position atop the building across the platz from the Bundeshaus, and shoot the general when he emerges."

Volger swallowed. "How am I to escape? The police will swarm the area looking for the shooter. I'll never get out of Switzerland!"

"Relax, Major. We have more planned than that. General Guisan must be killed, that is certain—but it will take a grander gesture than that to accomplish our larger goal of integrating Switzerland into the German Reich."

"There's more you want me to do?"

"You recall January 1933, I'm sure—the fire at the Reichstag?"

"Of course."

"It's still unclear whether the Communists actually set the fire, or if the Leader's minions did it to frame them. Probably we'll never know. But either way, the Leader screamed that Red Revolution was upon Germany, and the people rallied to him. He would never have been able to curtail civil liberties the way he did without that sudden explosion of support from the people."

Volger was shocked at Zubler's suggestion that the Leader would have been party to the arson at the Reichstag, but he held his tongue with some effort.

"We need something big like that to have the same effect on the Swiss people. The assassination of General Guisan is a start, but not enough by itself. If the government itself were attacked—by Communists—that would have the desired effect."

Volger frowned. "You want me to set fire to the Bundeshaus?"

Zubler laughed out loud. "No, my dear Major, not arson. In the confusion that will ensue the moment after the general is shot, six Russian agents—recruited by you—inside the Bundeshaus disguised as custodians, will shoot all seven members of the Federal Council. Attention will be drawn away from you, and you will make your escape. I will see to it that they are kept silent."

"How can I recruit six agents and train them in less than two weeks?"

"Russian POWs, Major. Get six big strapping young men, preferably blonds who can blend in. Brutish young men who can hold their own in the Stalag will make the best assassins. Our Gestapo office here in Zurich will provide you with false papers to get them into Switzerland."

"How can I be sure they'll complete their mission once we get them here?" Volger asked. "They might disappear into the Russian émigré community."

"Arrest their families! Select only POWs who hail from towns that are already under occupation of the Wehrmacht, and then arrest their families and bring them to see the men. Show them that you have their families, and tell them that if they do not complete their mission, their families will be killed. No margin for error."

Zubler handed Volger an envelope. "This is a letter to Colonel Von Bernuth, the Commandant of Stalag II-B in Pomerania. Go there and deliver this to him. It instructs him to take you to the Russian prisoners. There you will select your six agents. You are to learn everything you can about them and their families, to make the coercion easy. They are to pose as Russian émigrés living in Switzerland for several years, since at least before we restricted our refugee policies, so it will be best if you choose men who can speak some German, to make it believable. Besides, unless you can speak fluent Russian—which we both know you do not—you will need for them to understand German. They must be completely clear that they are under your total command, or else their families will die."

"How will you keep them quiet after the assassinations?"

"We have agents within the police force, and they will be present at the scene and will ensure that none of the Bolshevik assassins leaves the building alive. It goes without saying, Major, that you are not to give the Russian prisoners the slightest hint that they will not survive. In fact, you should give them assurances that our agents in Switzerland will take care of them." His cold smile grew wider.

Volger shifted in his seat. "And will your agents also 'take care of' me in the same fashion?"

"Don't be absurd," Zubler replied with a wave of his hand. "You are a patriotic German officer, performing a patriotic service to the Fatherland. No one questions your loyalty to the Reich, and you are intelligent enough to understand that your silence about the mission will best serve the interests of the Fatherland. And we will have you swear an oath of silence."

"How can I be sure that you won't kill me anyway?"

"We are on the same side, Major. You will have to trust me. You have no choice."

"If I refuse?"

The smile faded from Ernst Zubler's face. "Then you will be sent to Buchenwald as a prisoner, with the pink triangle to identify you for the pervert that you are."

Volger felt a cold shiver, wondering how many people knew this secret. He raised his chin, kept his expression proud, and stared into Zubler's deep-set blue eyes. "And what will you do for me if I agree to complete this task?"

"Do for you?" Zubler frowned. "I suppose we could arrange for a medal of some sort, for your meritorious service to the Reich."

Volger nodded. "That, and I want papers for Michael Kaim."

Ernst Zubler appeared stunned for the first time. "Michael Kaim? That Jewish boy you've been fucking? You can't be serious."

"Yes—papers that indicate his racial status is Mischling, not Jewish."

Zubler scowled. "I don't have that authority."

"And yet you have the authority to arrange papers for Russian POWs to enter Switzerland."

Zubler stared at Volger for several seconds. "Very well. You shall get your wish. By this time Monday, your catamite will officially be a first-degree Mischling. And you will be on a train for Pomerania."

"I'd like to deliver the new identity papers to him myself," Volger said.

"As you wish."

"And a passport—a German passport."

Zubler frowned. "That could take a bit longer. But I'll do my best."

"Thank you, Gauleiter Zubler." Volger removed a photograph from his inside breast pocket, looked at it for a moment, and tossed it onto Zubler's desk. "That is a recent photo you may use." Volger had taken the picture himself five months before, and kept it in the breast pocket of his uniform jacket.

"Very well."

"What am I to do now?"

"You will take the overnight express to Berlin. Even with the inevitable delays, you should be in the capital by this time tomorrow. Then take the morning train to Hammerstein, Pomerania. The SD will have a car waiting for you at the station to take you to the Stalag. The Commandant will be expecting you."

Zubler put on a charming smile, and began playing the host again. "Shall we have some port to toast to your success? Perhaps we should invite in our friends in leather?"

"I have no desire to drink with your Gestapo thugs, Mr. Zubler. My apologies for the candor."

"No apology necessary, my dear Major. I feel the same. They are unfortunately a necessary evil." Zubler raised his glass of port. "To your success."

"And to the eternal German Reich. Heil Hitler!" Volger said, tossed back the glass, and downed the port.

He set the glass down on Zubler's desk, straightened his jacket, and gave his host a curt nod. "Now if you'll excuse me, I'd like to make my own way back to the train station. No Gestapo escort will be necessary, I assure you."

Ernst Zubler took a sip of port, and set the glass down. "As you wish, Major. There is a ticket waiting for you. Come back here when you have finished in Pomerania, and I shall have Mr. Kaim's new papers ready for you. Good day."

Sunday,
October 5, 1941

28

Basel

Franz caressed Jason's back, a slight smile on his lips. Jason slept with his head on Franz's bare chest, his hand on Franz's shoulder. His body leaned against Franz's left side, his torso half on top, his left leg wrapped over and around Franz's left leg.

Jason had dozed off after they finished making love for the second time yesterday. Then they stayed up half the night exploring each other's bodies. Franz didn't wonder he was so tired.

After a little coaxing yesterday afternoon, Jason had abandoned his reticence, and the two of them had gone at it like insatiable animals. Twenty hours later, their clothes still lay scattered on the floor in front of the couch.

Franz's smile turned to a frown a moment later, when a knock at the door echoed around the apartment. When the knocking repeated a few seconds later, he nudged Jason off his shoulder and hauled himself out of bed.

"What is it?" Jason asked, rubbing one eye. Franz caught Jason staring at his buttocks while he tugged on a pair of trousers.

"Someone's at the door." And as if on cue another series of knocks echoed off the walls. "Stay here."

Franz pulled a shirt over his head and hurried barefoot out of the bedroom, pulling the door closed. A fourth set of knocks began as he reached his front door and yanked it open.

"Mr. Lemiel, I'm sorry to disturb you," his portierfrau said, glancing over his shoulder into the living room. "I know you have a guest…"

Franz suppressed his irritation, knowing there wasn't a portierfrau in the world who didn't know all of the comings and goings in her building. Of course Mrs. Statweiler knew that Jason hadn't left.

"Yes?"

She looked back at him and handed him an envelope. "A telegram arrived for you a few moments ago, marked 'Urgent.'"

"Thank you, Mrs. Statweiler," Franz said, taking the telegram and closing the door before she could say anything else. He tore open the envelope and read the message, then swore under his breath.

"What is it?"

Franz looked up to see Jason standing naked in the bedroom door, a concerned look on his face.

"I told you to stay in the bedroom."

"I heard the door close," Jason said.

Franz tossed the telegram onto the table. "Bad news."

"What happened?" Jason approached Franz and put a hand on his shoulder.

"I have to go to a phone booth and make a call to Fribourg. It can't wait. I shouldn't be long."

"Can I go with you?"

Franz shook his head. He retrieved the telegram from the table. "From Mireille Casson, one of the young women in the Fribourg group. Several of the young men in the group have been arrested. I have to find out why."

Jason touched Franz's cheek. "I have to leave in a couple of hours."

Franz gave him a quick grin, and patted his bare butt. "I'll be back in thirty minutes. You don't even need to get dressed!"

*****

There was a bookstore two blocks away that had two phone booths in the rear, of which Franz made frequent use. It was also one of the few stores open on a Sunday afternoon. The store owner nodded when he entered, but stayed behind the counter and left him alone.

He asked the long distance operator for Fribourg, and gave her the number. He drummed his fingers while the line rang several times.

"*Allo?*"

"Mireille, this is Franz," he said in French. "What's happened?"

"We're not certain. The police have accused them of defacing buildings. Someone has painted anti-German slogans on the front of businesses owned by German-speaking *Freiburgers*, including the butcher shop around the corner from Jacques' apartment. Someone claimed to witness Jacques and the others running from the scene with buckets of paint in their hands, but it's a lie."

"*Merde!*" Franz cursed in French. "What kind of slogans were they? Political?"

"Some. There was an anti-Nazi slogan spray-painted on the wall of the city hall, but all of the others were just anti-German, not really political, and on private property owned by German-speakers."

"*Merde!*" Franz repeated.

German-speakers were a minority of about twenty percent in the city of Fribourg—which had been a German town known as Freiburg in the Middle Ages—but they were a close-knit community, concentrated in the Old Quarter of the city near the river. Perceived attacks such as this could easily boil over into violence.

"Has anyone posted bail?"

"No. We're not sure where they are. We have been to City Hall, but the police refuse to tell us anything." There was a hint of panic in Mireille's voice. "Why would someone want to frame them?"

Franz took a deep breath. There was nothing he could do. "Send me another telegram when they have been released. I'll call you back then."

He hung up the phone, and cursed under his breath.

29

Berlin, Brandenburg, Germany

The late afternoon sun cast long shadows in the woods of the Grunewald as the train slowed on the outskirts of Berlin. The large villas of the western suburbs glided past Rudolph Volger's window, but he stared ahead, lost in thought.

The overnight express from Zurich had been delayed several times to allow military trains to pass, and the trip that would have taken eight hours during peacetime stretched to twenty-two hours.

But this allowed him plenty of time to sit in the club car, gathering his thoughts over a stein of beer. He planned what he would say to the Russians when they were presented to him, and what kinds of men he would pick.

His mind always came back to the troubling questions of how he would train them for the mission, and what on Earth to do once they got into Switzerland.

He barely noticed when the train pulled to a stop inside Zoo Station in central Berlin. He sat in silence while the occupants of the car exited, finally picking up his hat from where it rested on the seat next to him and standing when the conductor gave him a quizzical look. He retrieved his suitcase from the rack, and stepped down onto the platform.

The other passengers had lined up for a Gestapo check point near the exit, and he strode past them. A dark-haired man in a black leather coat appeared behind the check point and motioned him forward.

The civilians in the line glanced at his SS uniform and avoided eye contact.

"Papers please," the standing Gestapo man asked him as he passed the table where two other men in leather sat, checking identity papers. Volger retrieved his papers from his coat pocket and handed them over.

"Yes, Major Volger. We were told to expect you. You may go through." The standing man said, his expression humorless, thrusting the identity papers back. Volger nodded as he put the papers back inside his coat pocket, and strode through the exit.

On the street, he hailed one of the waiting taxis. "Adlon Hotel, please."

It was a short ride through the center of the city, and past the imposing Brandenburg gate. On the sidewalks, phosphorescent badges glowed in the gathering twilight, pinned to coat lapels to stay safe in the black-out.

The taxi stopped in front of the hotel's grand entrance. On previous visits, the sidewalk had been awash in light from the elegant lobby. Now, only hints of the soft warm glow could be seen around the edges of the black paper taped to the windows, and to the glass of the revolving door. But the red-coated doorman still stepped out and opened the taxi door, then closed it behind Volger before taking the suitcase from the driver. "Follow me please, sir."

"May I help you, sir?" the willowy blond woman said when he came to the front desk. It was requisite in Germany these days that front-of-the-house staff at any establishment look suitably Aryan, and this young woman certainly did. She was about twenty, the age Volger had been the first time he'd stayed at the Adlon. She flashed him a smile that didn't extend to her cool blue eyes.

"I believe you have a room reserved for me. Major Rudolph Volger."

She glanced at a large open book on the desk, and made a small mark next to an entry. "Yes, Major, we have your reservation. The fee has already been paid." She handed him a brass key. "Room four-fifteen. I'll have a porter carry your valise."

She motioned toward the porter's station, and a young man of about eighteen, with perfectly parted light brown hair, sprang forward and took the suitcase.

"Room four-fifteen," the young woman said to the porter. Then to Volger, "Enjoy your stay, sir."

"Right this way, sir," the porter said, and strode toward the elevator.

Volger stole a glance at the young man's backside, where the burgundy fabric of his uniform pants stretched tightly across his buttocks. They weren't the fullest or roundest Volger had beheld, but they appeared firm, and he felt the involuntary twitch in his crotch. That always happened, a Pavlovian response to hotel porters.

The Adlon had once been notorious—but that was before the Night of the Long Knives in the summer of '34. Now, things were different. Or at least, far more circumspect.

"Set the valise beside the bed," Volger said as he followed the porter into the room. He cast a long glance at the young man's backside, his eyes lingering long enough that the young man would notice when he turned around.

The porter stood straight-backed, and stared at the wall. "Will that be all, sir?" There was a tension in his voice that told Volger his glance had not been missed.

He took his time opening his wallet, removing several thousand Reichsmarks in cash and holding them where the lad could see them. Then he removed a single hundred-mark note and held it out. A generous tip.

He allowed his fingers to linger around the young man's hand when he took the tip, and noted with pleasure the widening of the youth's gray eyes, and the rosy flush that came to his cheeks. For a second, he thought the young man would stay. But then the warm hand jerked away, the porter cleared his throat, muttered a quick "Thank you, sir," and hurried out the door, closing it a touch too hard.

Volger sighed. Yes, things had changed.

Rudolph Volger had first come to the Adlon Hotel in 1926, with the Gymnastics squad from the University of Frankfurt-am-Main. When he'd tipped the porter who carried up his luggage, the gray-haired man made a surprising offer.

"You seem like a gentleman that could use a little male companionship. I can find that for you. What kind do you like, sir?"

"I'm not sure what you mean."

The middle-aged porter chuckled. "I can guess what you like, sir." He looked Rudolph up and down. "A big strapping blond like you, I'm thinking a petite brunette. For forty Reichsmarks, I can send up one you'll like very much."

A while later, there was a knock on his door. An adolescent page boy stood in the hall. "I have a telegram for you, sir. May I bring it in to you?"

Rudolph stepped aside, and the short, thin boy walked in. He handed him the envelope. Rudolph looked at the paper in his hand and almost laughed. It was made to look like a German Poste telegram, and anyone looking at it from a distance would have been fooled.

"Open it, sir," the page said, his voice boyishly high.

Rudolph tore open the "telegram" and read the hand-written note.

> *Take off your clothes, relax.*
> *The boy will do whatever you like.*

Give him forty Reichsmarks when finished with him.

He looked up from the spurious telegram, and the boy was already unbuttoning his gray uniform, and then stripped it off, revealing a thin, pale torso.

"How old are you?"

"Fourteen, sir."

"You've done this before?"

"Yes, sir. Many gentlemen pay for it."

Visions of that night merged with the fantasy of tonight's porter naked, his lithe body pressed beneath Volger's own, knees clamped around Volger's shoulders. The fantasy deepened the ache in his belly and heightened the physical sensations as he pleasured himself.

Plopping onto the pillows, Volger wondered where that page-boy was now. He'd be grown up, twenty-nine years old, probably had a wife and children. Maybe he'd joined the Party. Perhaps he was a civil servant somewhere, or a shopkeeper. More likely he made a living on the Black Market. If the Gestapo hadn't killed him.

Volger hauled himself up from the bed with a grunt, and stepped to the wash basin on the table. He paused to look at his naked form in the mirror. He was still lean and muscular, though his once-narrow waist had squared with age. Very fit for thirty-five. That porter tonight didn't know what he had missed.

He poured water from a pitcher into the wash basin, dipped a washcloth into it, and ran it across his torso and down to his groin. Perhaps it was just as well—he needed rest before tomorrow's impending trip to the Stalag. And no distractions.

Monday,
October 6, 1941

30

Bern

"Mr. Schuller, you have your private meeting, as requested," Ambassador Harrison said. "I take it this is a matter of some importance and urgency? To disrupt my schedule first thing on Monday morning?"

Martin hid the wave of nervousness that swept through him at the ambassador's annoyance. "There is a security threat among the embassy staff, Ambassador."

Harrison's eyebrows rose. "Oh?"

"I've recruited a Swiss agent with a considerable network of anti-Nazi operatives in Switzerland, France, and inside Germany itself. An artist in Basel. This weekend, I learned that he's engaged in a sexual affair with one of the Americans in the embassy."

Ambassador Harrison took a long breath. "What reason do you have for thinking this a security threat, Mr. Schuller?"

"The American in question is not female."

There was a long silence. Both men seemed to be waiting for the other. "Go on," Harrison finally said.

"I feel that you should dismiss Jason Bachman immediately."

Harrison arched one eyebrow. "On what grounds?"

Martin heard Reginald Sloan's words in his head. He ignored the irony and delivered them with less bluster than the grizzled FBI agent. "For fraternizing with a foreign national who is acting as an agent of the Intelligence Community; and by his homosexual activities he has opened himself to blackmail by hostile operatives."

Martin hated himself for channeling Sloan's predjudices. But it was necessary, damn it.

The ambassador was silent for a moment before leaning forward and speaking in a calm and measured tone. "I ca—*will* not dismiss Jason Bachman. You won't speak of his involvement with your agent, nor of his alleged unconventional morality, to anyone. I will speak with Mr. Bachman personally, and instruct him to avoid contact with your agent. You are not to speak of this to Mr. Bachman, is that understood?"

The reaction stunned Martin for the barest of seconds. Then his back stiffened, and his jaw tightened. "May I ask why?"

Harrison leaned back in his chair. "Switzerland is a plum post in the Foreign Service, Mr. Schuller. Surely you're aware of that. We have hundreds of FS officers in Washington who would give their eye teeth to be assigned to this mission. I'm sure you're also aware that most of our Berlin staff was recently sent back to the States, and the embassy there is operating on a skeleton crew.

"Any of the FS officers sent home from Berlin would have been more than qualified for a post here—but four months ago we accepted young Mr. Bachman for a position. A *new* position here, not a replacement. He is the only newly-minted FS officer at any American mission in this country. Why do you suppose that is?"

Martin thought for a few seconds before shaking his head.

"At the beginning of the summer I received a personal request from Congressman George Paddock, of the Illinois 10th. Congressman Paddock sits on the Foreign Commerce committee. He asked me to hire the son of Dr. Walter Bachman, a surgeon in Evanston to whom the congressman owed a few favors. Jason Bachman had recently begun his training in Washington, and while it's true that he passed his

FS exam with exemplary marks, it's still unlikely he would have been accepted for a post anywhere in Europe—let alone in Switzerland—without the congressman's good word. More likely he would've started his career at some minor colonial legation in Africa or the Near East."

Martin stared Harrison in the eye. "I believe you are also from Illinois, aren't you, Ambassador?"

A faint smile came to Harrison's lips. "Yes, I am."

Martin nodded.

"Then we understand each other," the ambassador said.

"Nearly," Martin said, sitting forward. "You asked me not to say a word to Jason Bachman about any of this—I'd like to know why."

"To my knowledge, Mr. Bachman is not aware that his father asked the congressman to intervene on his behalf. My belief is that it could be uncomfortable for Dr. Bachman if his son were made aware of his inquiry. Which would also be uncomfortable for the congressman. I see no need for that, do you?"

"No—as long as Mr. Bachman stays away from my agent. I also request to be present when you speak with him about it. I'm sure you understand why."

The ambassador stiffened. "Perhaps you should speak to your agent, Mr. Schuller, and allow me to handle my employee privately."

Martin hid his irritation behind a stony expression. "Of course. Thank you, sir." He stood, giving Ambassador Harrison a polite nod.

Martin fumed the whole way back to his office. How could the ambassador not understand what a security threat this was? *How could he not get it?*

"What's got you so happy this morning?" Amanda asked when Jason arrived at her desk with his morning pastry and newspaper.

"I had a fantastic weekend!"

"It must have been."

"Why do you say that?"

"Honey, did your feet even touch the ground when you came down the hall? And you're beaming as if you just won a million bucks."

Jason blushed. "Can you keep a secret?" he whispered, leaning down.

"Of course. You know I don't tell anyone anything."

Jason leaned closer. "I spent the weekend in Basel with Herr Lemiel. And it was fantastic! *He* was fantastic!"

Amanda's jaw dropped. "Get out!"

"It's true," Jason said. Then he leaned in toward her ear and added, "He did things to me no man has ever even tried to do. And it was *amazing*!"

Amanda didn't look scandalized, but her eyes were wide, and a smile twitched the corner of her mouth. "Well I'll be damned. Who'd have thought it? Guess I had him pegged all wrong. And I'm *never* wrong about men, honey. If anyone knows men and what they want, it's me."

"Nobody's perfect," Jason said with a huge grin.

They looked up at the sound of footsteps coming from behind the desk, and the ambassador himself appeared. He looked surprised to see Jason sitting on the side of Amanda's desk.

"Ah, Mr. Bachman, just who I need to see. Would you come to my office for a moment?"

Jason nodded, and glanced at Amanda. She gave him a slight shrug and bewildered look.

"Have a seat, Mr. Bachman," Ambassador Harrison said as he closed the door behind them. He took his own seat, leaned forward and folded his hands on the desk. "Do you have any idea why I called you in here?"

"No, sir."

"It has come to our attention that you have had homosexual relations with a Swiss national."

Panic raced through Jason, and every muscle in his body tensed.

"Don't bother denying it. I have no desire to pry into your private affairs. But I must insist that you desist at once, and do not cavort with this individual ever again. If you disregard that order, I will have no choice but to dismiss you from the Foreign Service. Is that understood?"

Jason's stomach dropped. His mouth was dry, and he could barely muster his voice. "Yes, sir."

"Good. You may return to work."

Jason broke out in a cold sweat, and his hands trembled. "Does anyone else know?"

Ambassador Harrison sat silent for a moment before responding. "Only one other, but you have no need of his identity. Rest assured that he will be as discreet as I. Now go back to work."

"Thank you, sir." Jason's voice was still quiet. He kept his eyes down as he stood and left the room.

"What's wrong?" Amanda asked when he approached her desk.

Jason's voice quivered. "They know about this weekend. I don't know how, but they know."

Amanda looked around, then motioned him close. She whispered as he leaned in. "Listen, that Herr Lemiel spent several hours on Friday talking with that new man, Mr. Schuller. I told you, there's something going on here, and they're being extremely secretive about it. I'd stay far away from all of it if I were you."

Jason said nothing and walked away.

31

Hammerstein, Pomerania, Germany

"Ah yes, Major Volger. The Commandant has been expecting you," said the SS sergeant at the gray-painted metal desk. He pressed an intercom button and spoke into the speaker, "Major Volger, sir."

"Send him in," the metallic voice echoed in reply.

The sergeant opened the door, standing aside, and then closed it behind Volger.

"Good morning, Major. Welcome to Stalag II-B." Colonel Von Bernuth stood behind a large wooden desk, and extended a hand. He was a portly officer, and his belly strained the buttons of his SS jacket. His thin dark hair was slicked back. Volger accepted his hand and gave it a firm shake, noting with distaste that it felt cold and clammy.

"Please have a seat. I received a telegram from Berlin, informing me of your visit, and instructing me to cooperate fully with anything you request. I was informed that you are on a sensitive mission for the Reich."

"Yes."

Von Bernuth attempted a smile. "Yes, well then, how may we be of service to you?"

Volger reached inside his jacket and removed the envelope that the Zurich Gauleiter had given him. He handed it to the Commandant without a word. Von Bernuth removed the letter and read in silence for a moment.

"You are in luck, Major. We are overrun with Russian prisoners. As I'm sure you are aware, Army Group South had a major victory at Kiev on the 26th September, and captured more than six-hundred-thousand enemy combatants. We received several thousand of them last week—far more than we can handle at the Lager Ost camp, I'm afraid. We already took several thousand after the victory at Smolensk last month, and could barely house them. We would be more than happy for you to take some of them off our hands." Again the over-eager smile.

"I need six men, uninjured and in good health. No cuts, no visible bruises, no diseases. You have some like that, I presume?"

"Yes, of course."

"When may I inspect them?"

Von Bernuth shifted in his seat. "I've taken the liberty of ordering us some lunch. The telegram from Berlin said to expect you at eleven o'clock, but naturally with the way train schedules are kept these days, I did not expect you to be so precise."

"I had a driver." That had been a surprise to Volger as well.

"Yes, well, as I said, you arrived a bit earlier than I anticipated, and I'm afraid that lunch won't be ready for nearly an hour. I shall leave it up to you, Major, if you would like to inspect the prisoners before eating."

Volger ignored the implication. He wouldn't lose his appetite. "I should like to get started right away, Colonel. My mission for the Fatherland is urgent. I'm sure you understand."

"Yes, of course. I shall take you to the compound personally."

Volger followed the Commandant from the Headquarters building, in the center of the twenty-five-acre camp, and they turned toward a fenced compound on the east side of it. The sign above the gate read "Lager Ost." Several wooden huts stood in rows, occupying most of the space. A small yard stretched in front of them, mostly dirt with some scraggly brown grass scattered about. Hundreds of skinny men in dirty faded green uniforms wandered around, while armed guards watched from wooden watch-towers at the four corners of the compound. The unmistakable odor of human waste hung in the air.

Four armed guards stood at the compound gate, mirroring the guard detail at the gate of the camp, and one stepped forward to open it. All four guards extended their arms in salute until they passed, and the gate slammed shut behind them.

"Have the prisoners assemble in the yard," the Commandant instructed one of the guards. "New arrivals in front."

Within a minute whistles blared, echoing off the wooden slats of the huts. Guards barked orders to come out, line up, stand still, be quiet. Once they had lined up, Von Bernuth turned back to Volger with the same stiff smile.

"We might as well have a general inspection, eh Major? Care to join me?"

Volger was aware of thousands of eyes on him as he walked beside the Commandant. Most of these men were painfully thin, with sunken cheeks and sallow complexions. Even the newest arrivals in the front wore the haggard look of men who had not slept or eaten well for some time.

Still, these were far from the "ugly Mongol hordes" that the Leader warned against. Most were pale-skinned, and not a few were fair-haired. Many of the newest arrivals were well-built. As they walked down the rows, Volger pointed out several promising candidates, and motioned for the guards to pull them from the ranks. This continued until he had perhaps eighty prospects standing in a new line off to the side. He stopped before they'd inspected the entire collection of prisoners, but they were getting scrawnier the farther back he went.

"Dismiss the others," he instructed Von Bernuth, ignoring the Commandant's superior rank.

Von Bernuth stiffened, then turned to the head guard. "Those will stay. Dismiss the others."

Volger stood in front of the group, his hands clasped behind his back, looking them over. He stayed that way until the other prisoners had been squired away inside the huts, and Col. Von Bernuth had rejoined him.

"Which of you can speak German?" Volger demanded in a loud voice. Nine of the selected prisoners raised their hands.

He suppressed his disappointment. "Stand aside! Over there, beside the gate. Quickly!"

The nine hurried as instructed, and gathered in a huddle near the gate, looking at one another apprehensively.

Volger walked up and down the row of those who remained. He stopped in front of a blond youth with rosy cheeks and bright blue eyes. "Can you understand me?" The youth stared at him with frightened, uncomprehending eyes. *Pity*.

He took a step away, but then thought again and turned back to the youth. He motioned for him to join the others at the gate. He would need something to amuse himself for the next few days.

"Send the others away," he said to Von Bernuth.

The Commandant relayed the order to the head guard, and the others were herded back to the huts.

"What do you feed the prisoners, Colonel?"

Von Bernuth looked surprised. "A bowl of potato soup for breakfast, then a bowl of vegetable soup and a piece of dark rye bread for lunch. Dinner is more soup and bread. On Sundays they are given a meat pudding for dinner as a weekly treat."

"That is all?" He knew prisoner rations were paltry, but the specifics still shocked him.

Von Bernuth stiffened and scowled. "It is eleven-hundred calories a day, which the Red Cross doctor says is adequate to sustain them. You can't expect us to feed them as well as our own soldiers, Major."

Volger nodded. "What are you serving us for lunch today, Colonel?"

The Commandant smiled. "I have a Wurst platter waiting for us, Major, with sauerkraut and fried potatoes. I'm sure that you will find it quite satisfactory."

"Yes, I'm sure I will." He nodded toward the ten prisoners clustered near the gate. "See that these men are served the same lunch we are, Colonel."

"I beg your pardon?"

"These men will leave with me in one week's time. They are to be well-fed and tended to until then. They have been selected for a special mission, and for that mission I need for them to be strong. Is that clear, Colonel?"

"We have limited supplies, Major—"

"Colonel, my orders have come down from the High Command. The Leader himself has given his blessing to our mission. I trust that I will not have to report a lack of cooperation from Stalag II-B."

"No, no, of course not!" the Commandant sputtered.

"I will need a place where they can be sequestered away from the other prisoners. Can you accommodate this?"

"Yes, of course. As you wish, Major."

"Good. See that they are separated from the others immediately. I shall like to begin questioning them after we have all eaten. And see that they are given beer with their lunch, not water. Shall we then?"

"Yes, yes. Come with me, lunch should be ready. Will your driver be joining us?"

Volger considered a moment. The driver had been a surprise. He'd been told to take a train from Berlin. When he'd stepped off the elevator that morning to check out of the Adlon, a young man in an SD Lieutenant's uniform had approached him and saluted.

"Major Volger, sir! I am Lt. Minnich, and I am to drive you to Hammerstein this morning. I'll take your valise, sir." The words had rolled off his tongue in a rich Austrian accent.

Evidently the SD didn't want to trust his arrival to fate. Or to the unreliable train schedules.

The driver was a handsome young man, with neatly-combed light brown hair, bright blue eyes, and a nicely chiseled jaw-line. A bit slightly-built for an SD man, but he proved a capable driver, who kept the black Mercedes' speedometer near one-hundred-fifty kilometers per hour the entire trip.

"Yes, Colonel, I think that would be appropriate. Thank you." Something more pleasant to look at than the commandant.

32

Basel

Martin flashed his FedPol badge at the portierfrau as he stormed past, silencing her with a look. He took the stairs two at a time, and reached the top floor in less than a minute. Barely winded, he marched down the hall and pounded on the door of number sixteen.

Franz Lemiel's irritated look when he opened the door melted into a smile. "Mr. Schuller! I didn't expect to meet you until this afternoon."

"I need to speak with you now." Martin pushed his way past Franz and stood in the middle of the room.

Franz scowled. "What's this about?"

Martin removed a manila envelope from inside his coat, tore it open, and removed three black-and-white photographs. "Here." He almost threw them at Franz's outstretched hand. "I snapped those on Saturday afternoon." He pointed at the large window.

Franz glanced at the photographs, of he and Jason Bachman kissing and removing each other's clothes on the couch, and set them aside. "Yes?"

"Mr. Lemiel, you have been too indiscrete at every step of this process. You revealed my identity without my permission to Sonia Rubenstein, you took Mr. Bachman to a political meeting in Bern, and then you brought him here to seduce him. You have jeopardized my mission."

"I don't see that I have jeopardized anything." Franz's eyes were unwavering, his voice firm. "Where would you be right now without my assistance? Do you think Sonia would have allowed you to review her father's papers? Would you have found anyone like Reverend Kuntz, who could give you contacts inside the German Reich that may be able to give you information about the things happening in this country? No, you'd still believe the Communists were behind the assassinations, and you'd be off chasing red herrings, as the Nazis hoped."

Martin's eyes narrowed, and he took a step closer, glaring down at the shorter Franz. "Are you a homosexual, Mr. Lemiel?"

Franz stared right back, unwavering, his expression calm. "I am bisexual, Mr. Schuller—as are many of my friends and acquaintances. There has never been anything secret about that."

"That is a security threat."

"How?"

Martin exhaled hard. "You could be blackmailed by enemy agents." He pictured the curly-haired young man watching from a dormer.

Franz laughed out loud.

"Is there something funny?"

"Mr. Schuller, you can't blackmail someone who has nothing to hide!" Franz said, still laughing. "How could anyone blackmail me? I hide nothing! I am not ashamed. Besides, I am an artist, and for artists there is nothing more logical than bisexuality. As Cicero said, *'a true lover of beauty must be equally drawn to both sexes.'*"

But Jason Bachman was no doubt less shameless. "Stay away from U.S. Embassy staff."

Franz shrugged. "You should know by now that I never bow to tyranny."

Martin's face flushed. "Your assistance will no longer be required."

Franz looked startled. "With your imminent mission into Germany, I think that is unwise. You'll need my expertise."

Martin snarled as he repeated, "Your assistance is no longer required. Good day, Mr. Lemiel." He stormed out of the apartment, slamming the door.

"Ah, Mr. Schmidt!" Rev. Gerhard Kuntz greeted Martin in his office. "I have your introduction letters. Each is addressed to a different pastor. Different denominations—Reformed, Lutheran, and Union—but all active in the Confessing Church movement. There are two in Stuttgart, one in Heidelberg, three in Frankfurt, two in Koln, two in Dusseldorf, one in Essen, and two in Hamburg, if you should need to go that far. An even dozen. I'm certain at least a few of them can provide you with information or contacts that will be useful to you. If you should need to go as far as Berlin, ask one of the other pastors to write you a letter of introduction to Dietrich Bonhoffer."

"Thank you." Martin took the twelve envelopes, tied together with a ribbon, and put them inside his coat pocket.

"I expected my young friend to accompany you again."

"He won't be able to join me."

"Oh! Then do be careful, Mr. Schmidt. I often worry about my young friend, but I also know that he is quick-witted and resourceful. I know little of what he does—which is a blessing, I am sure—but I have no doubt that he is well-suited to it."

Martin nodded; he agreed with the assessment, but kept his thoughts to himself.

"Yes, well. Godspeed, Mr. Schmidt. Do be most cautious inside Germany, the walls have ears there. I shall pray for you."

Martin cringed. "Thank you for your help."

"I hope we shall see each other again," Rev. Kuntz said, clasping Martin's right hand in both of his.

Martin took a step backward. "Thank you again." He bolted from the office.

The board in the grand hall of the Basel train station indicated that the afternoon train to Stuttgart would depart on-time. Martin joined the line at the ticket booth.

"May I see your passport please?" the ticket agent requested.

Martin handed over the forged Swiss passport, and remained outwardly calm while the clerk glanced between the photo and his face, then handed the passport back with his train ticket and his change.

"Enjoy your trip, Mr. Schmidt."

Martin went directly to the platform. He had almost thirty minutes before the train departed, but it was already boarding. He entered one of the middle cars and took a seat in an empty section.

His stomach felt like it was tying itself in knots. He'd been on many clandestine operations, but never inside Nazi-controlled territory. He had to admit to himself that he was terrified. And it was only made worse by the fact that he was unarmed. But he knew better than to try to sneak a gun into a police state.

He set his hat on the seat across from him, as much to stop himself from fidgeting with it as to hold the seat open. He took the time to mentally run through the details of his fake identity, to be certain that he wouldn't accidentally contradict anything on his forged passport or identity papers. Once he'd assured himself his memory of the details was perfect, he rehearsed in his mind what he would say if stopped by a Nazi official questioning his business.

The car was less than half-full when steam emerged with a hiss from the wheels of the train. A few men in business suits ran across the platform, as the train's whistle announced its imminent departure.

Just as they started to creep forward, Martin heard and felt someone plop onto the seat next to him. He turned from the window to see Franz Lemiel beside him, a big grin on his face.

"What are you doing here?"

"I couldn't let you blunder into this by yourself," Franz whispered, and patted Martin on the shoulder.

Martin said nothing, but a wave of relief rushed through his belly while the station slipped away.

33

Hammerstein, Pomerania, Germany

"Name?" Rudolph Volger sat stiff-backed in a chair opposite the Russian prisoner, and stared him hard in the face.

"Captain Feodor Popov, Soviet 26th Army."

"Age?"

"Twenty-six years." The man's voice was husky and heavily-accented. His thick brown hair had been hastily finger-brushed into a side-part, but his icy-blue eyes didn't waver under Volger's intense stare.

"Where did you learn to speak German, Captain?"

"At school."

"Where was this school?"

"In Orsha, in Byelorussia."

"Is that where you are from?"

Feodor Popov looked wary. "Yes, I am from Orsha."

"Was your teacher a German?"

Popov looked surprised for a moment. "Yes, he was a German."

"Was this teacher a member of the Communist Party?" Volger kept his voice level, not accusing.

Popov shrugged.

Volger put on a disarming smile. "Come now, Captain! Do you expect me to believe that you didn't know if your teachers were members of the Communist Party?"

Popov relented. "Yes, he was a member of the Party."

"Are you a member of the Communist Party?"

"No."

Volger grunted. This was his ninth interrogation of the day, and all of them claimed to not be members of the Communist Party. It didn't really matter—these questions were mostly meant to test their fluency in German, and to give him a feel for their personalities.

He leaned back, stretched his legs out, folded his hands across his abdomen, and put on the disarming smile again. "How did you enjoy your lunch, Captain?"

Popov looked surprised at the question, and at the friendly nature of the SS officer asking it. "It was good."

"How did you like our German sausages? Our fine German beer?"

"It was good, thank you."

"Would you like another stein of beer?"

The prisoners had been given steins of dark autumn bock beer with their lunch, very strong. As expected, it served to loosen their tongues a little during the interrogations—at least, the first five. For the last few, Volger had been obliged to order the prisoner another beer to sustain the effect.

"I would like some water, please."

A crafty one, Volger thought, observing the veil come over Popov's eyes. "Why don't we both have a beer? Be social, yeah? Two officers conversing over a beer." He motioned to the guard, who opened the door and disappeared.

"I ordered that lunch for you, Captain—you and the others I selected. I could see to it that you get meals like that from now on."

"That would be kind of you. But why?"

"The war will soon be over, Captain Popov. There is no reason for me to treat you as an enemy when we need men such as you who can speak German and Russian."

"I don't understand."

Volger grinned, and launched into the same speech he had made eight times already that afternoon, with its practiced lies and half-truths. "The German Wehrmacht is advancing on Moscow. We expect to be there soon. Comrade Stalin is preparing to abandon the capital and withdraw to the Urals, leaving the countryside open to our victorious armies.

"It is a vast country, is it not? We will have a very big job on our hands once the fighting has finished. Many men will be needed to administer such a huge country, with so many millions of people. We will need to rebuild the factories, to distribute food to the displaced masses, to organize all of the workers. We are not so naïve as to think that the SS can do that alone. We will need Russians such as you—intelligent men who know German, who can learn our system and teach the Russian people how to live in the new order."

"I am not interested."

The guard reentered the interrogation room, two steins of dark beer in his hand. Another guard in the hall closed the door, and the inside guard set the beer steins on the metal table before resuming his position beside the door.

"The Reich rewards those who serve it, Captain Popov," Volger said, taking one of the steins. "You would never be hungry or thirsty again. You would have nice, warm clothes, and much nicer lodging."

"I'd rather stay with my men, and share their fate." Even as Popov spoke those words, his voice firm, Volger detected the hint of indecision behind his eyes.

"A good officer!" he said, flashing Popov a wide smile and raising his stein towards him in a toast. "Sharing the fate of your men—I admire that, Captain. Come, have a drink with me. *Prost*!"

Popov nodded and took a swig of beer.

"Ah, that's good beer!" Volger said with a grin, setting the stein back on the table and wiping his lips. He leaned back and cocked his head, giving Popov a thoughtful look.

"How would you like to see your family, Captain?"

Popov looked startled. His voice was cautious as he replied. "Yes, of course I would."

"I could see to it that they are brought here, and they could stay with you while you train for your new role. Not here at the camp, of course—on an estate nearby." He noted with satisfaction the growing conflict in Popov's eyes, and continued to lay it on. "They would be well-fed, the same as you were today. They would not continue to go hungry in Byelorussia—and we both know that they are cold and hungry, Captain. Do you have children?"

The Adam's Apple in Popov's throat bobbed up and down, and his eyes filled with emotion. "Yes—a boy and a girl."

Volger leaned forward. "I have children myself, back home in Frankfurt. I know what it is like to worry about them, to want a better life for them. I know what it is like to be separated from them, to miss them so. I cannot imagine how troubling it must be for you to know that yours are suffering. And now you have been given an amazing opportunity—you can end that suffering tomorrow. How could you not help them?"

Tears had begun running down Feodor Popov's cheeks. Volger stood and walked around the table, placing his hand on Popov's shoulder. "I understand, Captain. You are a good father. I know you will do the right thing. Come now, take a big drink, wipe your eyes."

Popov did as directed, taking a large fortifying gulp of the beer.

Volger returned to his seat. "The Reich needs good men like you, Captain. Won't you accept our offer?"

Popov nodded in silence.

A satisfied smile spread across Volger's lips. "Excellent! We will begin your training tomorrow. Give me the names of your family members, write them down here on this paper, and I assure you that we will fetch them from Orsha this very evening. You will see them here tomorrow, I give you my word."

A light of hope shone in Popov's pale eyes. He took the pen and paper, and began furiously writing names. "My parents, too?"

"Of course."

Popov's face broke into a grin as he pushed the paper back across the table to Major Volger. "Thank you, Major! Thank you very, very much! How can I ever thank you enough?"

"You can show your appreciation to the Reich, Captain. We will have important work to do."

"Yes, of course." Popov's expression clouded. He stood and extended his hand toward Volger.

Volger shook Popov's hand, suppressing his distaste for Slavs. "You may go back to the others."

After the Russian captain left with the guard, Volger took the page of names and put it inside his attaché case with four others. Popov was the fifth one of the prisoners who hailed from a town behind the front, in territory occupied by the Wehrmacht. Five out of nine—about as good as he could expect, Volger figured. He needed six for the mission, however.

He still had one more prisoner—the young, rosy-cheeked blond boy who spoke no German. Ideally, all of the six should speak German, to pass as long-time residents of Switzerland. But it was not a challenge he couldn't overcome. Rudolph Volger would find a way to make it work.

34

Stuttgart, Württemberg, Germany

"Wake up! We're here."

Martin jolted awake as Franz jabbed an elbow into his side, and he silently cursed himself for falling asleep on the train. It was careless, the kind of mistake he could ill afford in this uncomfortable role.

The aisle was full of passengers exiting the train, which gave him a moment to clear his head before standing and retrieving his suitcase. He took a deep breath before following Franz to the exit.

What should have been a two-and-a-half hour ride to Stuttgart had stretched into five hours. The train had departed Basel on time, and made its first stop after crossing the German border five kilometers north of the station. The conductor had all of the passengers exit with their luggage, and stand in line to be checked by the German border guard.

Franz had stood in front of Martin in line, and Martin listened carefully as he was interrogated by an official with a permanent sour expression after comparing Franz to the photographs on his passport and his identity papers. "Franz Lemiel. You are Swiss?"

"Yes."

"It says here you are from Basel."

"Yes."

"Basel is German-speaking. Your surname is clearly French."

"Yes, it is."

"You are not originally from Basel, then?"

"I've lived in Basel my whole life."

The official's sour expression crinkled up in a scowl, as if this were too much for him to understand. "Your family came from France?"

"Yes, I believe so."

"When?"

"About two-hundred-fifty years ago. They were Huguenots, I understand—religious refugees from France."

The official made a condescending snort and scribbled something in his log. "What is your reason for visiting the Reich?"

"To attend the Stuttgart beer festival, of course!" Franz smiled at the official, who did not return the friendliness.

"You have been to Stuttgart before?"

"Yes, I attended the festival last year, and the year before."

Apparently satisfied, though with an unsatisfied expression, the heavy-set official stamped the passport, slapped it closed, and handed it and the identity papers back to Franz. "Enjoy your stay in Germany. Next!"

Martin stepped forward.

"Papers, please."

Martin handed over his forged passport and identity papers, and the official gave them the same scrutiny as all the others. "You are Swiss, Mr. Schmidt?"

"Yes."

"From Bern?"

"Yes."

"What is your business in the Reich?"

"I'm here to tour churches."

"Churches? For what reason?"

"I'm a divinity student. I'm here to meet with German pastors, to get the German theological perspective."

The official looked him over with a suspicious expression. "You are a bit old to be a divinity student, aren't you? It says here you are thirty-three years old."

Martin wondered if it was a mistake to use his real age. Too late now. "Yes, I'm thirty-three years old. I had a job I didn't like, and I've always been interested in theology." The lie almost got caught in his throat. "I'm not the only man to come to the ministry later in life."

"Which divinity school do you attend?"

"The school in Basel."

The official's scowl deepened, and his brow furrowed so much it looked like hillocks above his eyebrows. "Isn't that agitator Karl Barth on the board there?"

Martin didn't know the answer, and cursed himself for having not learned more about the school he was supposed to be attending. He let silence be his answer.

The customs official took advantage of Martin's silence to pronounce his own judgment. "Karl Barth gives encouragement and support to dissident clerics, some of them criminal. He has written the most spurious accusations against the Fatherland. I hope you are not coming here to speak with enemies of the Reich, Mr. Schmidt?"

"No, sir."

The official scrutinized Martin's face for another moment, then slapped the passport closed without stamping it, and thrust it and the identity papers toward Martin's chest. "Take your luggage and report to the office behind me. Karl! Inspection!"

A young man in a black leather coat emerged from a doorway behind the customs official, and motioned Martin forward. "Come!"

Martin's stomach dropped as he picked up his suitcase and walked around the table toward the door. A shiver ran down his spine when that door closed behind him, and he was alone in a cold room with two Gestapo officers.

"Open your luggage."

Martin put his suitcase onto the table and opened it.

"Step back." The two Gestapo men began pulling clothing and personal items from the suitcase and tossing them onto the table. Martin's face flushed as his spare underwear was scattered in plain view. He remembered with some relief that all of the labels were Swiss.

He kept silent while the two Gestapo men poked and prodded the sides of his now-empty suitcase. One was a skinny young man of about twenty-five, plain-looking and pale, with mousy brown hair, dull gray eyes, and a nose that was a bit too big for his face. The other was a stockier man of about fifty, with thin dark hair and a high forehead. This one removed a stiletto from his jacket pocket and ripped the lining of the suitcase on all four sides.

Martin had to stop himself from protesting.

Apparently disappointed at not finding any secret compartments, the older man grunted and instructed his younger companion to "Put those things back in." As the young man threw Martin's belongings haphazardly into the suitcase, the older one turned to Martin and demanded that he remove his hat, coat, and shoes.

This was far more extensive than the only other time Martin had entered the Third Reich, in May 1933 with Becky and Marty. He could feel his upper lip sweating. He did as instructed, and handed over his hat and coat. The older Gestapo man searched the pockets, removing the envelopes that contained the introduction letters.

"What are these?"

"Letters of introduction to German pastors, from Reverend Gerhard Kuntz in Basel."

The man grunted again, and ripped open the envelopes, removing the letters one at a time and perusing them, then stuffing them back into the envelopes and tossing them aside.

"Empty your pockets."

Martin removed the keys to his apartment and the Ford, several coins, a money-clip with several hundred Swiss francs in cash, and his train ticket to Stuttgart.

The older man turned to his younger coworker, who had finished stuffing Martin's suitcase, and ordered, "Search him."

The young man ran his hands up the sides of Martin's legs all the way to the groin, reached inside all of his pants pockets, and then patted down his back and sides. "Arms out."

Martin held his arms out as the young Gestapo man felt their entire length.

Meanwhile, the older man picked up Martin's shoes and checked the insides. Martin breathed a sigh of relief that he hadn't torn the soles with his stiletto. He didn't have a spare pair. Finding nothing, the officer tossed the shoes onto the floor near Martin's feet.

Turning back to Martin's coat, he inspected the stitching—no doubt looking for signs that something had been sewn inside the lining. Then he gave the same scrutiny to the lining of Martin's hat. Finding nothing amiss, he thrust the hat and coat at Martin. "You may go."

Martin almost smiled at the man's obvious disappointment. He kept his eyes down while he put his coat and shoes back on, retrieved his suitcase, and left the room.

The other passengers still in line at the customs desk avoided looking at him as he strode back toward the train.

One hurdle cleared, he thought when the train pulled away a half-hour later.

The train had made one more scheduled stop at Freiburg im Breisgau, then two unscheduled stops on a sidetrack in the middle of the Baden countryside, to allow military trains to pass on their way to Strasburg in Alsace. The second unscheduled stop had lasted forty-five minutes, but none of the passengers uttered a single word of complaint.

Now it was past ten o'clock.

"We'll have to find a cheap room at a hostel, then see to our business in the morning," Franz said in a low voice as he stepped down onto the platform of the Stuttgart station.

As they exited the train, Martin inwardly groaned at the sight of a long line waiting at a Gestapo checkpoint. *Here we go again.*

He was singled out again for inspection. *Apparently the Gestapo don't care for clerics.* He almost wished he'd posed as a policeman instead. But the possibility of official police "assistance" with his investigative work was a risk not worth taking. Besides, if what Franz and Kuntz said about the Confessing Church pastors held true, he was more likely to learn what he was after this way. He would deal with the Gestapo checkpoints the way the ordinary German people around him dealt with them—with silent perseverance and outward patience.

"The lining of your suitcase is ripped, Mr. Schmidt," remarked the Gestapo man searching his bag, with an obvious note of accusation.

"Yes, your colleagues at the border were very thorough with their search."

The scowl that came to the man's face brought Martin amused satisfaction, but he kept his poker face.

"I'm sure they were. Arms up!"

A few moments later he put his hat back on, took his sloppily-repacked suitcase, and exited the Gestapo inspection room. A quick glance around, and he spotted Franz standing outside the exit, not looking at him. Martin could see the corner of Franz's eye, however, and knew that the younger man was watching for him. He held a burning cigarette between two fingers of his left hand, though Martin had never seen him smoke.

Franz began to move before Martin reached him, not looking back. Perhaps the young activist was better at this than Martin had surmised.

"The cigarette was a nice touch," Martin whispered when he came up beside Franz.

Franz made no visible reaction to the compliment. "I always bring a couple of packs with me when I come to Germany. They come in handy whenever I need to loiter someplace," he whispered. Then, in a regular voice, "Yes, of course you may have one, sir." He stopped and handed one to Martin, then struck a match and held out the flame.

Martin took the cigarette between his lips, held it to the flame, and puffed long enough to light it. He had to force himself not to make a face as the taste hit his tongue.

"Just walk with it in your hand," Franz whispered.

Fifteen minutes later, after a short tram ride, they arrived at the door of a hostel Franz knew, in a shabby-looking part of Stuttgart. They had not sat together on the tram, and Martin waited several seconds after Franz got off before he also stepped down onto the sidewalk.

The front room of the hostel was plain, with bare wooden floors and bare walls. One shabby green couch with worn material sat facing a scratched-up coffee table. Two plain wooden chairs sat across from it. A plump middle-aged woman with gray-streaked dark hair pulled back into a bun greeted them at the desk. She was pale with dark circles under her gray eyes, and droopy cheeks that had probably once been plump and pink and round before gravity and sorrow had taken their toll.

"One bunk, please," Franz said.

She requested two reichsmarks. "Dormitory number 8, third floor."

"One room, please," Martin requested.

"I'm sorry sir, but we're out of vacant rooms. We're full-up, with the Volksfest going on. I can put you in a bunk in one of the dormitories on the third floor."

He would've much preferred to be behind a door that he could lock.

After climbing three flights of stairs they came to a dark hall, lit by a single uncovered light-bulb at the top of the stairs. Upon locating the assigned dormitory in the dim light, Martin found an empty bunk in one of the corners.

He removed his coat, folded it in two, and placed it under the thin pillow. He slid his shoes under the bunk, then removed his tie and stuffed it inside one of the shoes. He kept the rest of his clothing on.

After wedging his suitcase between the bunk and the wall, he slipped under the sheet and thin blanket. Trying to ignore the snores all around the room, he closed his eyes.

Welcome to the Thousand-year Reich. And then the exhaustion swept over him, and he fell into a shallow sleep.

He woke Franz before dawn. "It's six-thirty. Let's check out before the others."

Several of the bunks in the room were still filled with sleeping men, while a handful of others quietly dressed. In the hallway, three men in boxer shorts and undershirts waited outside the communal bathroom, shaving kits in-hand. No one made eye contact with anyone else.

The first gray light was gathering in the eastern sky as they stepped out onto the sidewalk. "We should split up now," Franz said in a low voice, then paused to light a cigarette for each of them. "You can get a shave at the train station. Lots of traveling businessmen do it, you won't be noticed. You can get a good breakfast at Froegger's on Konigstrasse, a few blocks from the station. It's on the tram line, so you can get around from there. If you can't find the churches, don't be afraid to ask for directions—the Germans may be paranoid that the Gestapo are listening to their every word, but they're still more than happy to help a lost stranger. Just don't ask a policeman—he might ask more questions than you'd like."

"I thought you didn't want me to 'blunder into this' by myself." Martin let his scowl speak volumes.

"You'll be fine. If you've been paying attention to my lead, and I'm sure you have, you know how to get along inside the Reich now." Franz grinned, the first time he'd smiled since they'd entered Germany. "Besides, I'm not wasting an open trip into Germany. I have my own work to do."

"Will we meet at the station later?"

Franz shook his head. "We shouldn't stick together at all. You never know who's watching. We entered on foreign passports; it wouldn't be unheard of for the Gestapo to have informants keeping an eye on our activities."

Martin nodded, his stomach jumping with nerves. So he was traveling on his own.

Franz continued "I'll meet you tomorrow at four o'clock, in front of the train station in Koln. Then we'll go to Frankfurt. If you get into trouble before then, call Lange's Bakery in Heidelberg—tell them you brought Emmentaler into the country, but now you can't pay the duty. They'll arrange to pick you up."

Franz turned away without another word, stubbed out his unsmoked cigarette, and walked off into the Tuesday morning dawn.

Tuesday,
October 7, 1941

35

Hammerstein, Pomerania, Germany

Rudolph Volger lounged in the comfortable armchair with a glass of after-dinner brandy, listening in satisfaction as five of the six prisoners conversed in German, and attempted to teach a bit of the language to the sixth one.

They'd spent the day in a spacious house a few kilometers north of the Stalag, practicing their German language skills under Volger's close supervision, eating three full meals, and drinking plenty of dark beer. Volger found that their conversations, awkward and forced at first, became more natural the more food and beer they consumed. Twice that day, they had been given an hour-long exercise session on the grounds of the estate, led by an army trainer. Volger wanted them fit and strong.

After dinner, they'd been bold enough to request some vodka. Volger had suggested they try German schnapps instead. The schnapps arrived, Captain Popov pronounced it "nearly as good as vodka," and now they were on their way to inebriation. One thing you could say for the Russians—they could hold their liquor.

The unmistakable rumbling of army trucks neared, and his smile widened. He stood and raised his arms for silence.

"Gentlemen, your families have arrived. If you will all stand, and line up in front of the fireplace, I shall take you to them."

The Russians nearly fell all over each other to get in line in front of the immense stone hearth.

303

The house belonged to a Pomeranian *Ritter*, a member of the old-fashioned knightly class that still dominated the countryside of the eastern provinces. The owner, once a member of the DNVP—the monarchist party that had formed the short-lived coalition with the Nazi Party, until the Leader disolved it—was currently serving on the Eastern Front, a colonel in a panzer unit, Volger had been told. His wife and children were moved to their townhouse in Berlin, while the SD had taken temporary custody of the estate.

Outside in the chilly night air, the Russians' expressions became confused at the site of four green army trucks, their canvas covers the only shelter from the cold for the ragged civilians now scrambling out of the backs. These civilians ranged from small children to gray-haired men and women. All of the adult women wore scarves tied around their heads, and everyone wore frightened expressions.

These expressions changed from fear to shock, then sudden joy at the sight of their loved ones standing in Soviet uniforms in front of the big house.

Cries of joy filled the air, and the six prisoners broke rank and dashed toward their families. The snap of rifles cocking echoed all around, and the guards pointed their guns at them. "Halt!" several shouted.

The POWs appeared stunned, and looked toward Volger. From his position on the front porch, Volger waved off the guards, who shouldered their rifles.

For a few moments, Volger allowed the POWs to embrace and kiss their families, and whisper soothing words into the ears of wives and mothers. Best to let them experience this, to increase the impact.

After three or four minutes, Volger stepped off the porch, raised his arms and called for attention. "Gentlemen, before I can allow you any private time with your families, we must have a meeting to discuss your training. If you will line up and follow me inside, we will commence."

While the POWs got into line, he called the lead guard to his side. "Take our 'guests' to their quarters."

Once he'd gotten the POWs back inside the house, he told them to sit. He stood in front of them, hands clasped behind his back.

"Before we can send you back to the east for your new roles as leaders in the new Russia, you must prove your worthiness to the Reich by completing an important mission. You must help the Reich to bring down those who would oppose the new world order in Switzerland. Then, you will be deemed worthy to lead the new Russia."

Concerned looks darted between the POWs, and whispers of Russian.

"German only!" Volger barked, his face flushing.

Feodor Popov raised his hand. "Please, Major. Someone must translate for young Petrov."

Volger beheld the handsome blond youth sitting in the middle of the group, his bright blue eyes dazed with incomprehension. He looked so German, that one, right down to the rosy pink cheeks. Only the slight Slavic slant to his eyes hinted that he was actually Ukrainian.

The Slavs were an inferior race, Volger knew that. The Reich's official racial theories were born out in the backwardness of Soviet society. But Volger also knew that Viking traders had made their way up and down Russia's rivers a thousand years ago, portaging through Russian forests on their way from the Baltic to the Black Sea. Of course they'd fathered bastards along the way. No doubt plenty of Viking blood ran through the veins of young Alexi Petrov. Doubtless some Viking blood ran through the veins of all of these Russians he had selected for the mission—that was obviously the reason they displayed more intelligence than their countrymen, not to mention fairer looks.

"Captain Popov, you may translate for Petrov. Everyone else shall remember to speak German only. Anyone else speaking Russian will be punished."

His eyes locked on young Petrov's, and held them while Popov whispered his translation. He would summon him tonight.

He looked to the group. "A week from today, you will be taken to Bern, Switzerland, where you will pose as members of the Russian émigré community. One week from tomorrow, you will enter the Federal Palace dressed as janitors, with identification badges that we will supply. You will go to the West Wing, where you will meet the seven members of the Swiss Federal Council at noon when they emerge from their weekly meeting. You will shoot them all. You will shoot them dead."

The only sound in the room was the hushed whisper of Feodor Popov into young Alexei Petrov's ear, and even that fell into stunned silence for a few seconds before resuming at a faster, more agitated pace. All of them stared at Volger with wide eyes, stunned and terrified.

"Successful completion of this mission will dispel any doubts about your loyalty to the new world order, and confirm your worthiness to serve the new Russia."

Volger allowed the news to fully sink in.

Feodor Popov raised his hand. "Major? How are we to do this? Surely we'll be arrested the moment we reveal our guns!"

"Our people there will ensure that you are not interfered with. They will take care of you."

Another hand raised in the back—Nikolai Sokolov, a tall, ghostly-pale lieutenant from Pskov in the north who had a Russian Orthodox cross hidden in his pocket when he was captured; a handsome young man of twenty-two with thick black hair and the deepest blue eyes Volger had seen on anyone besides Alexei Petrov.

"Major, you cannot ask us to kill innocent people!" There were murmurs of agreement from the others.

A smile spread across Volger's lips. This was the moment he'd looked forward to all day. "Why do you think we brought your families here? For happy reunions? No! We brought them here to ensure your loyalty. Do as we ask, and no harm will come to them. Do as we ask, and they will be well-fed and cared for, as I promised. Refuse the mission, and you will watch the guards kill your family members one at a time. You will wish you had accepted our offer, right before you wish for death. Am I clear?"

"God have mercy on us!" Sokolov exclaimed, almost under his breath.

"The choice is yours. You have five minutes to decide." Volger strode to the table where he'd left his brandy. He beheld them from a distance, huddled together and whispering. "Remember, German only!" he shouted. He received a sullen look from Feodor Popov in response.

Five minutes ticked by on the wall clock, then Volger strode over to the huddled POWs. "Time is up! Stand, all of you. Give me your decision now."

When they'd stood and lined up in front of the hearth, Captain Popov stepped forward and spoke for the group.

"We have decided to act together, for the good of all. We will do as you ask of us, Major Volger. You have been most 'persuasive.'" He said the last word with a bitter sneer.

"Excellent!" Volger clapped his hands together once and gave them a broad smile. "Your training will begin in the morning. You will practice your marksmanship for eight hours every day. Tomorrow, you will be given dossiers which you are to memorize.

These will be the identities you will assume while in Switzerland. You will speak nothing but German from now on. Any sound of Russian from any of you, for any reason, and the guards will punish you."

"What about Petrov?" Captain Popov demanded.

"No translations, Captain," Volger insisted. "He must learn German by listening to the guards and figuring out what they are saying. He must watch and learn. In your leisure time, speak to him only in German and use gestures to help him understand. Make him repeat to you. He will learn."

Volger's expression softened as he looked at Alexei Petrov's angelic face. "Captain, you may translate that. Then, no more Russian—only German."

Popov translated quickly, got a nod of understanding from Petrov, then turned back to Volger. His expression was cold. "Where are you keeping our families?"

Volger chuckled. "Your families have been made comfortable. We are not monsters. They have been quartered in the stable, on the far side of the estate. There are plenty of empty stalls and clean straw, since the horses have been commandeered by the Wehrmacht for the Eastern Campaign. Would you like to see them?"

"Yes."

"Come with me. I will let you look in on them. You will remain silent. Don't make me regret my kindness."

Volger led them on a hike across the estate, armed guards beside and behind them. It was half a kilometer to the stables, a large wooden building on the edge of a fenced-in pasture, with woods behind it. SS guards stood at the doors and patrolled the perimeter.

Volger led them to a side door, also guarded, and motioned for it to be opened. It led into a tidy office, where the *Ritter's* account books still sat in perfect order where he had left them months before.

Another door on the opposite wall contained a window into the stables, and Volger instructed the POWs to step up to the window one at a time.

Feodor Popov went first. The interior of the stable was spacious, and he could see ragged civilians in the process of bedding down in the stalls. He spotted his wife's head above the wall of one of the stalls, in the act of spreading a blanket. She had removed her scarf, and her dirty blond hair fell long around her shoulders. He couldn't see his children, but they must be there with her.

He stepped aside, allowing Lt. Nikolai Sokolov the next look. Popov strode up to Volger and stood in front of him with his back straight, staring directly into his eyes.

"Major, you can assure us that they will be well-cared for while we are on this 'mission?'"

Volger gave him a crisp nod. "I have promised, Captain."

Wednesday, October 8, 1941

312

36

Cologne, Rhineland, Germany

Martin got the lucky break he'd been looking for on the fourth try.

He'd met with two pastors in Stuttgart yesterday, and while they had tried to be helpful, and provided a few intriguing insights into the German underground opposition, there was little information they could provide which could help him.

By the second meeting, he'd figured out that the letters of introduction from Gerhard Kuntz must contain some code word or phrase, since each time the pastor's expression changed mid-way through reading the letter. Something clued them in that his mission was clandestine and anti-Nazi.

His first meeting this morning in Koln—known as Cologne in English and French—had gone much the same as the two meetings in Stuttgart yesterday. Then at his second meeting, with Reverend Jan Jakob Issay at eleven o'clock at St. Paul's Evangelische Kirche, his luck changed.

Changed for the worse, it seemed at first. The white-haired pastor, with round florid cheeks and wise brown eyes, had stopped and scrutinized him for a moment after he'd spoken. "You are not Swiss, Mr. Schmidt," he said quietly.

"I live in Bern," Martin said by way of protest.

The fifty-something pastor shook his head. "But you are not from there. I have made more than twenty trips into Switzerland since reaching adulthood, Mr. Schmidt—if that is your real name—and I'm very familiar with Bern, and Solothurn, Basel, Zurich, Luzern, and

Interlaken. It was once quite easy to make the trip, when travel visas were easier to acquire. You are not Swiss. So who are you, then?"

Martin said nothing, but stared back at him.

The pastor's voice dropped to a whisper. "If you are British, leave now. I may not like the current government, but I am not a traitor."

"I am not British."

"Canadian?"

"No."

A look of relief flashed across Issay's face. He continued to whisper, "Then, you must be an American."

Martin said nothing, letting his lack of denial serve as confirmation.

The pastor continued to look at him for a moment, a finger beside his mouth and a thoughtful expression on his face. Then he slapped his hands onto his desk and smiled. "Come, let us take a walk in the fresh air."

After they reached the park across the street, the pastor explained in a quiet voice, "I am certain the Gestapo have the church bugged. That is the only way they could know to pay me a visit every time I venture to say anything remotely 'seditious' in my sermons."

"You could have an informer in the congregation."

Rev. Issay's doubtful look and exaggerated shrug dismissed the possibility.

"I understand you're taking a great risk speaking with me," Martin said. "I want you to know how greatly I appreciate your time."

"We have no quarrel with the United States. In fact, many people in Germany hold much admiration for your country. I myself have cousins in Indiana. My uncle and aunt emigrated more than forty years ago. I know many Germans with relatives in America. Our countries should be friends, you see."

Martin left that alone. "I'm interested in making contact with the local underground, specifically those who are in the position to know things that aren't public knowledge."

The pastor cocked his head and gave Martin a curious stare.

"That's an interesting request, Mr. Schmidt. Most of the underground is comprised of clandestine printers who create protest leaflets, and the young people who leave them on trams and buses. Or booksellers who have secret rooms with banned books. But those don't sound like the kind of people you are interested in."

"Perhaps," Martin replied. "Such people can sometimes learn things that aren't meant to be known."

"Yes," the pastor said, but his mind appeared to be somewhere else.

Martin waited, strolling in silence for a couple of moments.

"There is a man I know…" the pastor began, then hesitated.

Martin nodded in encouragement. "Go on."

"A member of my congregation. You understand, I must be cautious what I say…I would not want to compromise him. He is a man of some importance. A man who is most definitely in a position to know things that are not public—secret, even. Not that he ever speaks of it to me, of course. I know little of his work, and prefer to keep it that way. We keep our discussions to faith, but our talks have frequently been about the injustice of the current situation."

"Who is this man?"

The pastor looked around, assuring himself that no one was near. His voice dropped to just above a whisper. "I won't tell you his name. I can only say that he is in the military, and I believe his role is in the Intelligence apparatus."

"Abwehr," Martin said. The word spat from his mouth.

"Don't be afraid of the Abwehr, Mr. Schmidt. I think you will find that you have many common interests."

Martin left his doubt unspoken. He considered carefully for a moment. Certain risks were necessary. "How can you be certain he won't entrap me, have me arrested?"

The pastor stopped walking and turned to face Martin. His brown eyes were full of compassion. "I understand your fear. I live with that same fear every day. I was first detained in the summer of '33 for preaching against the book-burnings. I proclaimed from the pulpit that knowledge is a gift from God, and that Germany's gift to the modern world was our contribution to the body of knowledge as the country of Goethe, Nietzsche, and Freud. Then I was detained again in '35, after the Nuremburg Laws. I reminded my congregation that not only was our Lord Jesus a Jew, but his blessed mother the Virgin Mary was a Jewess, all of the Apostles were Jews, and almost all of the Saints in the New Testament were Jews—Paul, Barnabas, Silas, Mark, James and Jude. Even St. Timothy was a first-degree Mischling."

Martin felt his throat constrict. "The difference is that if I am arrested, I will be shot as a spy."

"All I can tell you, Mr. Schmidt, is that if I were you, I would meet with this man."

Martin considered for a moment, then nodded. "Thank you. How shall I meet him?"

They resumed walking.

"I'll arrange it. First, buy a newspaper, and a white carnation for the lapel of your coat. Go to the Hoffman Haus restaurant for lunch. It will be crowded, but wait until you can get a table by yourself. Then order the Jaegerschnitzel and spaetzel. Have the newspaper open to the sports page. After your food arrives, a man in military uniform will ask to sit at the empty seat across from you. You will let him, saying that your lunch companion has been unable to join you, and he will ask the score of the FC Koln game. You will hand him the sports section and say, 'Read about it for yourself.' That will be his signal. Then he can arrange to talk somewhere more private."

"You're sure he'll do this?"

"I will give him these exact instructions. I'm sure he will meet you. If he's not there by one-thirty, pick up your newspaper and leave."

It was almost twelve-thirty by the time Martin arrived at the Hoffman Haus, a newspaper under his arm, and a white carnation in the lapel of his dark blue coat. Every table was occupied, but at least no one else was waiting for a seat.

"I have no open tables, sir; but there are empty seats that I can offer you," the maitre'd said.

"Thank you, no. I'm meeting a young lady for lunch, so I'll wait for a table."

A commotion arose from a nearby table for two.

"Why do you need to see my papers? This is a restaurant, not a police check point!" a young man shouted. His tanned cheeks flushed red, and his dark eyes glared at the man standing before him, dressed in a business suit.

The man in the suit pointed to a sign in the window with "*Judenfrei*" printed in large black letters. "We do not serve Jews here."

The outrage in the young man's face deepened. "*I* am not a Jew."

"Then let me see your papers please, *sir*."

The young man opened his mouth to protest again, but the pale, red-haired young woman sitting across from him put her hand on his arm and said something, too quiet for Martin to hear. The young man reached inside his coat and handed the manager his identity papers.

The manager took one look at the papers and thrust them back. "We no longer serve *Mischlings* here, either."

The black-haired young man pounded his fist on the table and shouted so loudly the entire restaurant fell silent. "So because I had a Jewish grandfather, my money is no good here? I am somehow not good enough to breathe the same air as these other people? Do you think that because I am a *quarter* Jewish I will somehow *infect* you?"

The manager stretched a tiny bit taller. "Leave now, or I will call the police."

The young man jumped from his chair so hard it tumbled to the ground with a loud crash. In an instant the pale red-haired woman, who was as tall as he, stood in front of him with her hands on his chest, between him and the manager.

"We'll go," she told him with a note of authority that silenced him.

The young man retrieved his hat from the table, and thrust it on his head. He took the young woman's arm, and with one final glare at the manager, strode out of the restaurant.

"An outburst like that will get us a visit from the Gestapo," the young woman said to her partner under her breath as they passed Martin.

The manager forced a smile, and held out his arms, palms up. "Please, everyone, go back to your meals. We apologize for the disruption."

A waiter righted the overturned chair and wiped off the table more thoroughly than was necessary. A moment later, the maitre'd nodded at Martin and told him there was a table available.

Martin laid out the newspaper and turned to the sports page. An article about the FC Koln soccer game at the top of the page bore the largest headline. He made a show of checking his watch and looking toward the door. He ordered the Jaegerschnitzel with Spaetzel and a beer, then pretended to read.

His plate arrived a few minutes before one.

A minute later, a tall man in the gray uniform of an army colonel strode into the restaurant, hat under his arm. He appeared to be in his early forties, his light brown hair graying at the temples, and he had creases at the corners of his eyes. When the maitre'd offered to find him a seat, he replied that he could find one for himself. He surveyed the restaurant, then strode toward Martin.

"May I have this seat, sir?"

"Of course. The young woman who was supposed to meet me for lunch has been detained."

The colonel sat and motioned to the newspaper. "What was the score of the FC Koln game yesterday?"

Martin slid the newspaper across the table. "Here, take it, you can read about it yourself."

"Thank you, most kind of you."

The waiter approached, presented Martin with his bill, and then asked the colonel what he would like. Martin counted out the money for the bill while the colonel placed his order. As he set the money down on top of the bill, the colonel's arm came across and knocked over Martin's glass, spilling the last of his beer across the table.

"Oh, I'm terribly sorry," the colonel said, jumping from his seat. "Do allow me." He took his own napkin from his lap and laid it across the spilled beer, wiping it up with one swift motion, while slipping a piece of paper under Martin's hat with his other hand.

After the waiter retreated with Martin's payment, Martin thanked the colonel, and retrieved his hat, careful to hold it so that the hidden paper lodged between his fingers and the lining.

Martin rounded the corner before removing his hat to wipe his brow with his handkerchief, and carefully removed the paper. He turned toward the wall for a few seconds to read it.

14:30 outside the Claudius-Therme in the Rheinpark.
Ask me for change.

Martin tore the paper three times, and held the fragments in his hand for several blocks before dropping them into three different garbage cans.

Martin stood partially concealed behind a large oak tree near the entrance to the Claudius-Therme, the reconstruction of the Roman Bath on this site. The memory of the modest Roman *colonia* here had given the modern city its name.

Many off-duty Wehrmacht soldiers lounged on the grassy knolls of the Rheinpark, either in groups, or in pairs with smartly-dressed young women. The whole city of Koln was crawling with soldiers— not only was it the headquarters of Military District VI, it was also home to the 211th Infantry and 26th Artillery regiments. The ubiquitous military presence made Martin uneasy, and he held the tension inside his gut, not showing any of it on his face. It was hard to believe that only five years before, the Rhineland had still been a demilitarized zone.

At precisely two-thirty, the colonel from the restaurant came striding down the path toward the entrance.

Martin stepped forward. "Pardon me, sir. Do you have change?"

"I'm afraid not, but I will show you where the exchange is. Come with me."

Martin fell into step beside the colonel.

"You are American?" He spoke in a low voice.

Martin glanced around to reassure himself that no one was near. "Yes. You're with the Abwehr?"

"Yes. I understand you are interested in the underground."

"I am."

"How can I assist you?"

"My government wants to ensure the continued neutrality of Switzerland. It's a vital channel for diplomacy in these chaotic times. I'm sure you can appreciate that."

"Yes, of course. We also want to ensure Switzerland remains neutral territory."

"Who is 'we'?"

The colonel hesitated a moment. "The Abwehr. It is vital that we can use Swiss channels to communicate with the British government."

Martin scowled. "I have no interest in maintaining your channels to spy on the British."

"No, not to spy on the British—we have more sophisticated channels for that, which do not require neutral territory. We communicate with the British using Swiss intermediaries."

Martin hid his surprise. "What do you communicate to them?"

The Abwehr colonel glanced around. "Are you certain you weren't followed?"

"Reasonably so."

The colonel continued to hesitate. He appeared to struggle with how much to trust Martin. "First, let me stress that I am a patriot. Everyone in the Abwehr is a patriot. I served in France during the last war, for more than a year. I was barely eighteen. And I continued to serve the Fatherland in the Abwehr after the war, through the Republic and the current regime. My love for my country has never wavered, even in its darkest days."

"Understood."

"There are many in the Abwehr who believe the Fatherland is in danger, from the very men who claim to act in its interest. We are not Nazis. I don't know a single man in the Abwehr who is a Party member. I would even say there is a great distaste for the Party. We serve our country, though we harbor reservations about the regime.

But now we find ourselves at a dangerous crossroads, and many in the leadership believe we should act to save our country from the maniacs who would run it into the ground."

Martin couldn't hide his shock, and he looked at the colonel with wide eyes. "What do you mean by 'dangerous crossroads'?"

The colonel sniffed in disgust. "The Leader should never have invaded the Soviet Union. Foolish man! He pays no attention to history. And he fought in the last war. He should *know* that our worst fear in the Wehrmacht is a two-front war, and yet he started one deliberately. It can only end in disaster."

The two men walked in silence for a moment, Martin processing what he'd heard. Suddenly the nameless colonel stopped, and faced Martin.

"The Leader must be eliminated, and there are those in the Abwehr who are prepared to take that action—but we will need foreign support in the crucial hours after it is done. *That* is why it is vital that we have a communication channel to the British—and to the Americans."

He resumed walking, and Martin followed suit, his mind reeling.

"Unfortunately, Winston Churchill is a stubborn man. He refuses to deal with *anyone* in Germany, always suspicious that it is a trick. So while he sends agents and arms to the Resistance groups in France, Belgium, Holland, and Poland, he leaves the German underground to wither and be picked off by the Gestapo."

Martin's mind raced. Churchill might be stubborn, but he was also shrewd. "If you did what you just said, he would have no choice but to support you."

The colonel shook his head. "There is too much fear, and the uncertainty paralyzes everyone. No one wants to act without guarantees of support. It is too probable that the unsupported Patriot would find himself shot for treason."

"What do you want from me?"

"Only that you pass along to your government that there are those in the upper ranks of the German military who would take action to overthrow the regime—if provided the proper support from abroad."

Martin wondered if anyone would believe it. "I will do my best."

"Thank you. And now you may ask me what you want to know about the situation in Switzerland."

"Someone is attempting to destabilize Switzerland by assassinating its military leaders, and framing the Bolsheviks for—"

"Yes, we know."

"I believe this serves the purposes of the Nazi regime in driving Swiss opinion toward the German Reich. And it fits with Nazi tactics."

A bitter smile crossed the unnamed colonel's lips. "Indeed."

"I have come to Germany to learn who is behind this, and what they have planned next, so that we can stop them before the situation gets worse." He searched colonel's face.

"We have kept close watch on the situation, Mr. Schmidt. There is much that we know. As I told you, it is vital to us that Switzerland remain neutral territory. It is much easier for us to slip in and out of Switzerland than it is to get to Sweden or Portugal."

"What can you tell me?"

"The Gestapo have been operating in Zurich and Bern since at least the spring. We have agents who keep them under surveillance. It isn't difficult." He added this last with a condescending sneer.

"And?"

"The Gestapo are the ones who execute the assassination orders, but they are not the ones who choose the targets."

"Who does?"

The colonel snorted. "If we knew that, we would have already taken care of him. But our belief is that he is Swiss."

"What makes you think that?"

"There has been an increase in chatter between Zurich and Frankfurt from a secret group that calls itself the League of Swiss for Greater Germany. Their goal is to join Switzerland to the Reich. We've intercepted a few messages, copied them, and allowed them to pass on. But their methods keep shifting, and we have never been able to prevent an attack."

"One of your informants in Switzerland uses the name Corkscrew?"

The colonel looked at Martin in surprise. "Yes, he is one of our informants. One of many. I do not entirely trust his motives, but I do trust his information. You have spoken with him?"

"Yes."

The colonel's eyes narrowed. "What did he tell you?"

Martin had no intention of revealing how much he knew. "I'm sure less than what he has told the Abwehr."

The colonel grunted but said nothing.

"How can I get in touch with you?" Martin asked.

"Through the German embassy in Bern, office of the military attaché. My code name is Falkenkopf. And how can I reach you?"

No, you're still Abwehr. "I'll be in contact," Martin said, and walked away.

37

"You're late!" Franz said under his breath. It was almost quarter past four. His voice was stern, but relief flashed across his eyes.

"I had business to attend to," Martin replied.

"I hope it was worthwhile."

"It was. I'm going back to Bern tonight."

"Tonight?" Franz's brows bunched together.

"Yes."

"I could use your help. The Gestapo have broken a link in our communication chain, and I've got to find out where."

Martin shook his head. "I can't help you."

Franz's scowl deepened. "Why not? I've helped you."

Martin didn't have the patience to explain. His job was not to help the German underground. "My mission here was a success, and now I've got to get back to Bern."

Franz's face flushed. "I helped you with your mission! I got you the connections. I've taught you how to blend in here. I think you owe me some assistance with *my* work."

Martin glanced around. He was reasonably certain he hadn't been followed, but having met with an Abwehr officer still made him anxious. "I can't stay in Germany any longer. I've got to get back tonight."

Franz glanced around himself. "If you have to get out of Germany in a hurry, and you're afraid someone's watching for you, then I have people in Heidelberg who can help. I know people there who can smuggle you out."

Martin shook his head. "I'm fine. When will you return to Basel?"

Franz didn't mask the irritation on his face. "I'm not sure. Two days, possibly three."

"Contact me then."

Martin walked away without a glance back.

Martin's train was almost full when it pulled out of the station. He'd taken a seat near the back of a car, an elderly couple across from him, and an empty seat beside him. The couple talked softly to one another in a strange accent, and Martin had trouble understanding their dialect. It was not Swiss, but it was just as distinct from Standard German.

A fairly short man in a dark gray business suit approached, his fedora in his hand, and motioned to the empty seat next to Martin. "May I?"

Martin nodded, and the man sat down. He was a thin young man, about thirty, with thick dark brown hair, a tanned complexion, and green eyes that were striking in contrast to his dark looks. He had a narrow face, with a small nose, and a narrow chin. Something about his looks and his manner indicated patrician origins.

"Do you mind?" the man said, removing a pack of cigarettes from inside his jacket. Martin shook his head.

He lit the cigarette and took a long drag, held it in a moment, and then leaned his head back to exhale. "Ah!" he said, softly.

Martin turned his attention to the couple across from them. They were both plump and white-haired, but the woman was the plumper of the two. The man wore a tweed suit and a dark green hat with a little feather on the side, which he had not removed from his head. He had a full white mustache, and heavy white brows over hazel eyes. His wife's hair was pulled back in a bun, but curly white tendrils had escaped around her ears, and her light blue eyes sparkled in the light.

The door opened to Martin's left, and the conductor stepped through from the adjacent car. "Tickets please."

The young man beside Martin handed over his ticket to be punched, and then Martin did the same. The elderly man asked his wife for her ticket, then handed them together to the conductor. Hearing their accent, the conductor said "Your papers, please."

"Why do you need to see our papers?" the man asked.

"Show me your papers, please."

The man handed his over, and waited as his wife dug in her purse. The conductor tapped his foot, and finally the woman removed her identity papers and handed them to the conductor. He handed the papers back to them without another word, and moved on. "Tickets please."

The elderly man looked at Martin and the smoking man beside him, and attempted a sort of smile. "We are Luxembourgisch. They've told us that we are part of the German Volk, that Luxembourg is now a Gaue in the Reich—and yet everywhere we go, they hear our accent and ask to see our papers." He shrugged and looked at his wife.

"Our youngest son lives in Stuttgart now," the woman said. "He got a job at the Bosch factory there. We're on our way to visit him. We haven't seen him in four months."

"I apologize for our countrymen," the young man beside Martin said. "You should be made to feel welcome wherever you go, as citizens of the Reich."

Martin wondered if the Swiss would someday feel the same as the people of Luxembourg. *If I fail to stop it.*

The four of them sat in silence for a while, and eventually the elderly couple resumed their quiet conversation. A porter came through, and instructed them to lower the blackout blinds.

"Are you getting off at Stuttgart, or going all the way to Bern?" the man beside Martin asked, stubbing out his cigarette in the little tin ashtray between their seats.

"Bern."

"I am also. Business."

Martin nodded and said nothing.

"What takes you to Switzerland?"

"I live in Bern."

"Ah, you're Swiss. I noticed your accent. I hope you've had a pleasant stay in Germany."

"Thank you." Martin doubted there was any such thing these days.

"I'm thinking of heading to the club car for a drink—care to join me?"

"Thank you, but no."

"Come! I'll buy you a drink, and you can tell me what there is to see and do in Bern. I've never been. Come on!" he patted Martin's shoulder and stood.

Martin acquiesced, and followed the man down the aisle toward the far door.

As soon as the door had closed behind them, and they stood on the little platform between adjoining cars, the man turned back to Martin and leaned close. Martin's hand instinctively grabbed inside his jacket for his Luger before he remembered it wasn't there.

"Don't be alarmed," the short young man whispered. "I'm here to make sure you get safely out of Germany and reach Bern. You met with my colonel today in the Rheinpark, and I watched from a distance. I'm Captain Wolfe. While we're on the train, you will call me Mr. Mueller."

He turned around and opened the door to the next car, and motioned for Martin to follow.

Martin's gut clenched as he wondered if this Captain Wolfe had seen him speaking with Franz outside the station. Was Franz compromised? There was no way to know, and he had no way of sending him a warning. Martin silently cursed his carelessness.

Five minutes later they sat at a small table in the club car, two glasses and a bottle of white wine between them.

"I feel terrible for that old couple," Wolfe said, pouring wine into their glasses. "Luxembourg is not an occupied country, any more than Alsace. There was no formal annexation, but both are administered as part of the Reich, and their people are free to travel. They are Germans, and they should be treated as such, not with suspicion—but, alas, it is not always so."

Martin couldn't resist. "And Switzerland?"

Wolfe smiled, swirling the wine in his glass. "Switzerland is a unique case."

"Yes, Falkenkopf said the same."

"I understand the colonel explained our position in some detail."

"Yes."

"So you understand that we share a common goal."

For once. "I understand that it is in both of our interests for Switzerland to remain independent, and neutral."

Wolfe leaned closer. "That's why we must work together. That's why Falkenkopf asked me to make sure you get out of Germany without any interference from the Gestapo."

"I'm sure your assistance won't be needed."

Wolfe shrugged. "In addition to our common goal, it is important to us that you are not compromised. The Gestapo and the SD have been trying to discredit the Abwehr for some time. They believe we are a nest of traitors. Of course, they cannot prove their claims. We are very careful. My job is asset security, and you fall under that category.

We cannot allow you to tell the Gestapo what Falkenkopf told you. And if they capture you, well—sooner or later, everyone talks."

Martin had no doubt Wolfe would kill him as a last resort. "How long do you plan to stay in Bern, Mr. Mueller?"

"Difficult to say. Until my work is done, Mr. Schmidt."

The car suddenly lurched, the brakes squealed, and they slowed rapidly. A conductor switched off the overhead lights. As they came to a stop, the sound of air raid sirens rolled in from a distance, echoing over the hills.

"Our nightly visitors from the RAF," Wolfe said, and snuffed out his cigarette.

38

Frankfurt

Franz stood in the shadows of the alley for more than an hour, watching the garage behind Major Volger's house. He'd peeked inside the windows as soon as it was dark enough to sneak up to the garage; Volger's Mercedes was not inside. Since then he'd hidden in the shadow of an arbor some twenty meters away, but no car had come.

A sliver of light was visible behind the black air-raid curtains on the tiny upstairs window, but Franz saw no shadow of movement. Apparently, the major's gunsel was all alone.

The garage door was locked, but Franz wasn't prepared to break a window to get inside. He'd never actually seen the boy, aside from photographs. He had no idea what he was like. Sometimes these slaves fell in love with their captors, reveling in the slightest acts of kindness—and if that were the case, Franz would be in danger. He had no idea if the boy was capable of sounding an alarm, but it was a risk he wasn't prepared to take.

If only he knew the identity of the servant in the household who was the link to the Underground. He'd never wanted to know such details before, but right now it would be helpful.

He debated how long to wait. This would be easier with someone else watching the front of the house. He silently cursed Martin Schuller for leaving him to do this alone.

He'd fumed all evening. He'd hated going all the way to Koln in the first place. He rarely went that far north during his forays into

Germany. He'd gone only to meet Mr. Schuller and bring him back down to Frankfurt. He'd seethed as he sat on his train, waiting for it to depart. The sight of a smaller train beside his, facing the opposite direction down the westbound tracks, full of soldiers probably going to relieve occupation forces in the Netherlands or Belgium, made his mood worse.

He supposed he should be glad Mr. Schuller had found the information he'd desired. But he also knew the American wouldn't share any of that with him. Switzerland was *his* country, damn it! He had as much right to know what was happening there as some American agent.

On Tuesday and Wednesday, he'd checked all of his contacts in Stuttgart and Heidelberg, and assured himself the missing link wasn't in either of those cities—it had to be in Frankfurt. He supposed there could be a link in the chain somewhere between Heidelberg and Frankfurt—perhaps Darmstadt—but he knew no one there, and Frankfurt made the most sense.

After a while he decided it was pointless to remain in the alley. But what to do next? He briefly flirted with the idea of going to the front door, as he had the first time, but abandoned that thought. He had nothing to bargain with, and besides, they would tell him that Major Volger wasn't there, which he'd figured out for himself.

He eyed the six-foot brick wall that surrounded the yard. To get inside, he could either break into the garage, or he could scale that wall. He had no doubt the yard itself was protected by dogs, and breaking into the garage would leave too much evidence, so his eyes moved to the heavy oak tree that stood just inside the wall in front of the garage. He could reach those branches from the top of the wall.

Of course, the dogs would still raise an alarm. He cursed his lack of foresight in not bringing along some raw meat.

Taking a quick glance up and down the alley, he darted across and reached the wall a few feet from the garage. He raised his hands to grasp the top, and heaved himself onto it.

He sat there for a moment and held his breath. Total silence. The coolness of a slight breeze caressed his left cheek, and he thanked the heavens that it was blowing from the direction of the house, carrying his scent into the alley.

He crouched low, and moved as quietly as he could along the top of the wall, cat-like, towards the side of the house a hundred feet away. Other large oak trees shaded the wall the entire distance, and the gentle rustling of their dry leaves helped mask any little sounds he made.

As he got closer to the kitchen, he noticed two Doberman Pinschers lying beside a shiny metal bowl, facing toward the kitchen door. *God bless Dr. Pavlov!* The dogs must be distracted because they were always fed this time of evening.

He sat still and waited for ten minutes. From time to time, the dogs would whine—a little bit at first, but gradually getting more insistent. Then one of them let out a single high-pitched bark, almost a yelp, and scratched at the door.

A moment later, the kitchen door opened half-way, and a fat man in a dirty white jacket stuck his bald head out. The dogs both growled menacingly for a second, but stopped the instant they saw the two bowls of scraps he gingerly set on the stoop.

"There, beasts! Now shut up!" The man grumbled something else as he thrust the door closed.

The pieces fell into place in Franz's mind. *The cook! Of course!* With the kitchen facing toward the garage, only the chauffer would have been in as good a position to know about the sex slave living in the upstairs room. And these dogs weren't yet used to this particular cook, who clearly disliked them equally. He *had* to be new to the household.

So then, where was Volger? If the Gestapo had arrested the cook, which direction would their 'questioning' of him go? Were they more interested in his connections to the Underground, or were they more interested in the major? Neither direction boded well, but Franz figured Volger was a more immediate personal concern, given their arrangement.

But there was still a light on in the garret over the garage. If the Gestapo had arrested Volger as a homosexual, they would have also arrested the Jewish boy above the garage. That didn't seem to be the case. So what was the angle?

The dogs finished licking their bowls clean, then their noses twitched in the air. Deep, low growls rumbled from their throats as they turned Franz's direction, their eyes glowing in the sliver of light that escaped the edges of the black-out paper on the kitchen window.

Then they began to bark.

Franz looked down on the other side of the wall. It was the neighbors' garden. His eyes searched in vain for the garden gate, but didn't see it. Then the neighbors' Dachshunds took up the Dobermans' alarm from inside their own house.

The pounding of heavy footsteps came from inside the kitchen. He had to get off the wall fast. He sprang for a nearby Oak branch and scrambled into the cover of the leaves.

The Dobermans had moved toward the wall by the time the kitchen door opened, and two men emerged, shining flashlights around the yard. They saw the direction the dogs were barking, and shone their lights toward the wall.

Franz held his breath, hoping his dark clothing would hide him in the tree's foliage.

"Must be a cat. Stupid dogs!" one man said.

The other shook his head. "No, they have a different bark for cats and squirrels."

"Maybe Mrs. Habersham had her Dachshunds out."

"They don't bark like that at the Dachshunds, fool! Go inside and call the police."

The second man continued to scan his light across the top of the wall for another half-minute after his companion had gone inside. "I know you're there! The dogs know you're there. You can't steal anything from this house! Get out of here now, before the police catch you."

He clicked off his light and went back inside.

Franz exhaled in relief. The police they were calling were the Kripo—*Kriminal Polizei*—not the Gestapo. They thought it was a prowler!

He scrambled out of the tree and hurried along the top of the wall, leaping back down into the alley. From the corner of his eye he caught a tiny shift in the blackout curtain on the upstairs garage window, but it quickly dropped back into place.

He sprinted down the alley, the sound of the dogs' barking echoing behind him.

"Down with Hitler!"

Franz had found the handiwork of the Edelweiss Pirates, freshly-painted in large red letters across the Schmidtstrasse bridge where train passengers were certain to see it, no matter how much they pretended they didn't. Now to find the Pirates themselves.

Volger was the only person he knew in Frankfurt, and the Edelweiss Pirates were the only obvious opponents of the regime. Outside of the highly-secretive Communists, they were the only organized resistance inside the Reich.

Dozens of tracks came together in this gritty industrial section of Frankfurt, with lots of bridges—the perfect after-curfew hiding places for the illegal gang. He finally encountered them hanging out in the shadows under the Strasse der Nationen.

A tall, lanky youth with stringy blond hair took several menacing steps forward. "This ain't the place for you!" he shouted in harsh working-class German. "Scram!"

Several knife blades glinted in the moonlight. About forty teenage boys lounged with perhaps twenty girls, and the boys all stood and slowly approached. They wore long hair, except for a couple whose heads were shaved bald, and most held knives.

Franz held his hands out where they could see them. "I'm looking for the Edelweiss Pirates. It seems this is the place."

"No grown-ups allowed!" one boy shouted.

"Yeah, get lost!"

The first youth, the lanky one with the stringy blond hair, took several steps toward Franz, his knife at the ready. He had patches on his filthy trousers, and his dingy shirt was threadbare. "You come to spy for the Gestapo? They'll find you in the morning by those tracks, holding your guts in your hands!"

"I'm not Gestapo, I'm with the Underground. I want to hire some of you for a job tomorrow."

"What kind of job?" the apparent leader asked, his eyes wary.

"To help me watch a house in the Nordend. It belongs to an SS Major who's been away, and I need to know when he returns."

"What's it pay?"

Franz hesitated. He didn't have much on him. "Ten Reichsmarks apiece for four of you."

"Ha! We get more than that for showing up at the factory!"

"Making parts for the Nazis."

The boys looked stung. "Yeah, well, we've got to eat, you know."

"You can eat off ten marks."

"Slop, maybe. Make it fifteen."

Franz didn't have enough. "Twelve. And you'll be helping to strike a blow against the regime."

The headboy looked back at the youths behind him. Several shrugged. He turned back to Franz. "Thirteen apiece, and you have a deal."

Franz nodded. This would almost clean him out, but he held out his hand.

"Rolf," the leader said, shaking Franz's hand. "Rolf Metzger."

"Franz. Who else is taking the job?"

Rolf picked out three others, all skinny waifs in filthy clothes, and introduced them. "Bart Fuhrmann, Peter Koch, and Josef Kruger."

Franz shook their hands. It felt strange to be recruiting sixteen and seventeen-year-old boys. He was used to being only a few years older than the college students he worked with. These were still children. He nodded at Josef Kruger's shaved head. "Why don't you have long hair like the rest?"

Kruger stiffened.

Rolf explained. "Big brawl last weekend with the Hitler Youth. We kicked their asses, but a bunch of them got hold of Kruger and Feldman, and shaved their heads. Bastards!"

Franz nodded. Street brawls between the HJ and the independent-minded Edelweiss Pirates were common in these industrial cities.

"Tomorrow I'll need two of you to hide in the hedges and watch the doors of the house. The other two should go from door-to-door up and down the street, pretending to look for work."

"What if someone offers us work?"

"Then strike a hard bargain, one they can't possibly accept. The important thing is for you to let me know if this SS major drives by."

"Where will you be?"

"In the alley, watching the garage."

"When do we get paid?"

"When we see the major. Or seven o'clock if he never shows up."

Rolf and the others nodded.

"Good, we'll set out at first light, and get to work at dawn. Now, where can I find a safe place to stay tonight?"

Thursday, October 9, 1941

39

Zurich

Volger arrived at the Zublers' front door at seven-thirty in the morning. The butler Anton showed him into the study, and a moment later Ernst Zubler stepped in and closed the door. He was dressed for work in a pressed dark gray suit with pinstripes, starched white shirt, and black necktie.

"Welcome back, Major. I understand you've completed the first part of your mission."

Zubler's cold smile made Volger's skin crawl. "Yes, I've selected six Russian POWs, in good physical shape, all with families behind the front lines, and I have had the families brought to them and used as persuasion. They have all chosen to accept the mission."

"Excellent! Well done, Major."

"The only inconvenience is that one of the six barely speaks German. I could only find five German-speakers who fit all of the necessary criteria. The sixth one fits all of your requirements except proficiency in German."

A scowl crossed Zubler's face, but then he smiled politely and inquired if anyone was bothering to teach this Russian any German.

"Of course, Gauleiter."

"Good."

Volger held the Gauleiter's gaze. "I believe you have something for me."

Zubler chuckled. "Yes, of course." He walked toward his desk, removed a key from his pocket, and unlocked a drawer. He took a small package wrapped in brown paper, and handed it to Volger. "As promised, Major."

"I'm sure you won't mind if I check it—for accuracy, of course."

"Of course," Zubler replied with a curt nod.

Volger tore off the heavy brown paper and opened the box, then emptied its contents onto the desktop. He opened the passport first. It was an official German passport, with Michael Kaim's photograph, correct name and date of birth, and Rudolph Volger's home address. This last detail startled him for a moment, but he said nothing. Under race, it had the code M1—First Degree Mischling.

Next he opened the identity papers, which were more important on a daily basis. They also appeared official, with the same photograph and all of the same information to match the passport, including the racial code M1.

"It was fortunate that the boy's features lack the uglier hallmarks of his race, such as the tell-tale nose. I think he'll pass as a Mischling." There was no mistaking the note of condescension in Zubler's voice.

"You have kept your end of the bargain, Gauleiter. So far, at least."

Zubler's cold smile turned icy. "I'm sure you'll want to get back to Frankfurt as soon as possible. Your family will have missed you during your trip, no doubt. And I'm sure you'll want to hand-deliver those new documents to your 'Mischling' right away."

Volger took the curt dismissal with a nod. "Thank you."

"There is a ticket waiting for you at the station. Anton will show you out."

"I'm sure I can find my own way, Gauleiter. Good day."

**

Zubler seethed for a moment, then marched to his desk and picked up the telephone receiver. He gave the operator a phone number.

Tischer answered.

"This is the Gauleiter. Major Volger is on his way back to Frankfurt. See to it that he gets on the right train. Then call our associates in Frankfurt and tell them to expect him this evening."

344

40

Bern

Martin's neck and back ached from sleeping in a seat on the club car.

He'd been awakened a little past four in the morning, when the conductor announced that they were at Customs. It turned out to be German Customs. He stood shivering in line, waiting for the officials to approve his exit from the Third Reich. He spotted Captain Wolfe in a parallel line. Martin had no doubt the Abwehr agent was keeping him in the corner of his eye.

He had almost as much difficulty leaving as he'd had entering the country. The unsmiling Customs official waved him over to the office, where another pair of Gestapo agents searched his suitcase. Finding no contraband being smuggled out, the lead agent handed back his passport and said, "I hope you had a pleasant stay in Germany, Mr. Schmidt." His voice was as humorless as his expression.

When he left the Gestapo office, Wolfe was standing twenty feet away, smoking a cigarette and looking casual.

Once a cadre of other Gestapo officers had finished searching the empty train, the passengers were ushered back onboard. The train crept forward, and the heavy red-and-white border gate across the track was raised. Then once the last car was across, the train stopped, and everyone was ordered to exit again to go through Swiss Customs.

"Welcome back to Switzerland, Mr. Schmidt," the young official said as he stamped Martin's passport, attempting a friendly smile in spite of the sleepy look in his eyes. Martin supposed the young man was nearing the end of a long overnight shift.

On this side of the border they were allowed to reboard individually once they'd been checked out, and Martin leaned back against the wall in the club car and put his hat over his eyes.

He'd almost drifted off when Captain Wolfe took the seat opposite him. "You're nearly home free, Mr. Schmidt."

Martin nodded without a word, and replaced his hat over his eyes. He was vaguely aware of the train starting in motion again, and then he drifted off. That entire process had taken two hours.

It was almost eight o'clock by the time Martin stepped down onto the platform at Bern, with Captain Wolfe behind him. He started to walk away, but Wolfe's hand clasped his shoulder.

"It was a pleasure to meet you, Mr. Schmidt. Perhaps we'll meet again someday." He nodded toward a line of phone booths, and Martin accompanied him there.

"I'll be at the German Embassy for the remainder of the day, should you have any difficulties," Wolfe said. "Then I'll return to Germany on the overnight to Koln. You can ask for me by name at the Embassy."

"I'm sure that won't be necessary." Martin walked away without another word.

He took a tram to Kirchenfeld, and walked to the American Embassy.

Amanda Overstreet looked pleasantly surprised when he passed her desk, smiled, and arched her back. She wore a fuzzy green sweater, form-fitting as seemed to be her norm. "Welcome back, Mr. Schuller! I have messages for you." She handed him two slips. Sonia Rubenstein had called on Monday morning, and again on Tuesday afternoon. The second message said to call her as soon as possible.

"She spoke English," Amanda added. "I said you were out, and I didn't know when to expect you."

"Thank you."

Amanda had taken two phone numbers. The first, presumably Sonia's home phone, rang without answer. At the second number, a woman's voice announced "Chemistry Department." Martin asked for Sonia.

"Miss Rubenstein is in the lab with Dr. Karrer right now. May I take a message?"

"Have her call Inspector Schmidt. She has the number."

He spent the next hour drafting a report of his trip, including the intelligence he'd gathered. Another ten minutes encoding it, and he sent it over the wire to the COI in Washington.

He glanced at the clock. It was ten o'clock—only four AM in Washington. It would be at least four hours before he heard back from anyone.

He knocked on Colonel Legge's door.

"I heard you were back. Productive trip?"

"Yes. I need to know if you've ever heard of an Abwehr agent—a colonel—code-named *Falkenkopf.*"

Legge's brow furrowed. "'Falcon Head?' No, I'm sure I haven't."

Damn. "You've never seen it mentioned in any of the chatter you monitor?"

"No, I'm sure of that. I'd remember."

"Thanks."

The military attaché leaned back. "May I ask why you want to know?"

"I met him in Cologne. They've been monitoring the situation here, and he said the Gestapo are doing the dirty work. He's not sure who's the brains of the operation, but whoever it is is Swiss."

"That's intriguing."

Martin nodded. "Yes—if it's true. I need to find out how trustworthy this *Falkenkopf* is, and how reliable his information could be."

"There's a chance someone in Washington knows who he is."

"Already sent my report to the COI. It's early."

Legge glanced at the clock on his wall. "Yes, it is. Be a few hours at least 'til you hear from them. I can make a call to my counterpart at the British embassy, if you're in a rush. Of course, he'll be curious why I'm asking, but I'll make it as casual as I can."

"No thanks, I'll wait for Washington."

Martin stopped at Ron Witherspoon's office. "Did you learn anything for me while I was away?"

"I sure did. I managed to put together a partial dossier on that Irina Minskaya you asked me to inquire about. I had to speak with almost a dozen bureaucrats in five different agencies just to get tidbits—but when put together it's a bit suggestive." Witherspoon handed him a thin folded booklet. "Take a look."

Martin opened the dossier, and nodded as he read through it. "Very interesting."

Amanda Overstreet's voice came across the intercom on the desk. "Mr. Witherspoon, is Mr. Schuller in your office by any chance?"

Martin nodded. Witherspoon pushed the button and responded that he was.

"He has a phone call. That Fraulein Rubenstein again."

Martin leaned down to respond himself. "I'll take it in my office."

The phone on his desk was ringing when he entered and closed the door. He took his time answering. "Yes?"

"I've been trying to get ahold of you all week!" Sonia said in German.

"I understand you can speak English," he responded in English. "You never mentioned that."

"Of course I can speak English!" she replied in German.

Martin chuckled. He could imagine it riled her that his German was better than her English. He switched to German. "What is so urgent that you've been trying to get ahold of me since Monday?"

"Peter Kraus has been missing for a week."

It took Martin a few seconds to remember the young banker who'd appeared so out-of-place at the meeting in Zurich the previous Tuesday night. "Missing?"

"Yes. Elena hasn't heard from him since last Wednesday. They've been, um, spending a lot of time together, so she knew right away that something was wrong. She's been to his apartment every day since then, but he's never home. His portierfrau hasn't seen him since last Thursday morning, when he left for work. Elena called for him at the bank on Monday, and they only said that he no longer works there. She's worried."

"I'm not sure I understand why you're telling me this."

"He disappeared right after he assisted our group. Information he provided was published in a leaflet we distributed on Thursday, and then he disappeared. Do I have to spell it out for you?"

Martin tapped his finger against his chin. "Remind me—which bank did he work for?"

"The Zurischer Kredit Bank."

"And it was one of the banks you 'exposed' in your leaflet?"

"Yes, of course!" The irritation in her voice drew to mind an immediate image of her scowl.

Martin couldn't help a tiny smile. "I suppose you want me to impersonate a police inspector, and find out what's befallen him?"

"Would that be so hard? You've done it for lesser reasons."

"Why don't you report him missing to the real police."

"You think we haven't done that?"

"And?"

"Nothing, of course. The police in this country are on the side of the Fascists. They've spent about as much time on Peter's disappearance as they did on my father's murder."

Martin let the silence linger a moment. He could hear her breathing on the line, could imagine the flush of anger in her cheeks. "I could help you, if you help me."

"What do you want?"

"I still need to meet with Pavel Minskayev. Will you arrange it?"

"Yes, of course." She sounded surprised. He wondered what she'd expected.

"Tomorrow evening, at six. Just us. You make the arrangements."

41

Frankfurt

The whistled signal came from the road, and a moment later Major Volger's black Mercedes turned into the alley.

When Franz hadn't seen Volger leave in the morning, and there was no sign of him at lunch-time, he'd begun to give up hope. At one point in the middle of the afternoon he'd flirted with the notion of going to the Gestapo office and pretending to be a relative looking for the major. He dismissed the idea as foolhardy.

The Mercedes passed his hiding place; Volger was alone. When the car stopped in front of the garage, and Volger got out, Franz stepped from cover. "Major Volger, I've been waiting for you."

Volger's eyes widened in surprise, but then narrowed into a deep scowl. "Get away from here, you stupid fool!" he hissed, but not too loudly.

"A word with you first."

Volger looked around, then motioned for Franz to get inside the garage. He went back to the car and drove it in, and hurried to close the door behind him.

"Fool! They could be watching."

Franz shook his head. "I have my own people watching. We'd know if the Gestapo were around."

A strange smile came to Volger's lips, but he said nothing.

"I know about your cook, Major. It's unfortunate, but it doesn't mean your services are no longer required. We'll find other ways to contact you when you're needed."

The strange smile stayed in place. "I can no longer help you, Mr. Franz."

"We both know you still can, Major." Franz pointed at the ceiling, and the room above it with its hidden occupant.

Volger's strange smile widened. "No, I'm afraid not."

Franz frowned. This boldness was unexpected. "Are you forgetting the photographs we have? Don't make me use them."

Volger chuckled. "Go ahead, send them to the Gestapo! Play your cards, and see what they get you."

Franz stood frozen in place for a moment, unsure what to say or do. *They must already know*. That was the only explanation. Perhaps the cook had given away Volger's secret instead of his contacts in the Underground, something to bargain with—but if so, why wasn't Volger in custody? He should be in a concentration camp, wearing a pink triangle.

Unless they cut a deal. "You didn't come home at all yesterday. Where have you been, Major?"

Volger chuckled. "You shouldn't be here."

Realization dawned with the veiled warning. The Gestapo had used the information to turn Volger, to use him for their own purposes, at least in the short-term.

Then the full realization hit Franz like a ton of bricks—this could be a trap.

"You wouldn't," he whispered.

Volger wore a full grin now. "Leave now, Mr. Franz, while I still have the choice."

Franz flung open the door and sprinted down the alley.

*

Volger chuckled as he closed the door. Then he retrieved the small box from the car, and ascended the stairs.

Michael Kaim sat on a plain wooden chair in the corner, staring at him with a vacant expression.

"Hello, my sweet," Volger said in a soft voice, giving the boy a smile.

"You've been gone a long time." The expression on Michael's face was unreadable.

"Were they unkind to you while I was away?"

"No."

Volger walked to the boy, and put a hand on his shoulder. "You missed me, then."

Michael looked up, and Volger saw fear behind his dark eyes. "I was all alone."

"I know, and I'm sorry for that. I had to take a trip. I went to Switzerland, Berlin, and Pomerania. I came back as soon as I could."

"I had nothing to do—no work, no new books." The boy's voice trailed off.

"You must have been terribly bored. I'm sorry, my sweet. Truly I am." He put both hands on Michael's shoulders and pulled the boy up. "I have something for you. Come, sit with me." He sat on the bed and patted the mattress beside him. Michael sat. Volger handed him the box. "Open it."

Michael took the box, a curious look in his eyes. He opened the end, and poured the contents into his other hand. He stared at the cover of the passport for a moment.

"Go on! Take a look inside." Volger grinned.

Michael opened the passport, and stared in silence at his photograph and the information on the first page.

Volger pointed to the racial code. "First degree Mischling. And identity papers to match. With these, you can move around freely. You will no longer be confined to this garage."

Michael looked at him, his expression a bit dazed.

"See? You are no longer a Jew! You don't have to hide any more."

Michael's expression changed to anger. "No longer a Jew?"

"That's right. To the world now, you are a Mischling."

Michael's face flushed. He stood, and took a step back. "I *am* a Jew!"

Volger smacked him across the face. Michael touched his reddened cheek, his jaw hanging open.

"Is that the thanks you give to me? Do you know what I had to do to get that for you? Those are official documents. I thought you would like being able to go out without fear. You won't have to sit here alone, bored, anymore! Doesn't that mean anything to you?"

Michael cast his eyes on the floor, and his hand dropped to his side. "I hadn't thought of it like that." His voice was flat and lifeless.

"I would think you could show me more gratitude."

"Thank you."

Volger grabbed the boy's backside, giving it a hard squeeze that made him wince. "What I've done for you calls for more gratitude than that." He reached for the front of his own pants, unfastened them, and tugged them down. He pushed Michael onto his knees.

The butler approached Volger the second he stepped into the hall. "There are men to see you, sir. They arrived ten minutes ago, and I showed them into your study to wait."

Volger suspected the identities of his visitors before he walked into his study.

"Welcome home, Major," Colonel Schakenberg said. "Have a seat. You remember Captain Axethelm of the SD, and Captain Rohrman of the Gestapo."

Volger sat at his desk, not acknowledging the other two men, keeping his gaze locked on Schakenberg.

"We understand your mission has been successful thus far. Congratulations, Major. Your service to the Fatherland is most appreciated—so much so that we are willing to overlook past indiscretions."

Volger thought he knew what Schakenberg meant, but soon learned he was mistaken.

"Whatever your new cook is making for dinner smells wonderful! Wienerschnitzel, perhaps?"

"I have no idea."

"Well, it's enough to make me wish I were staying for dinner with your family," Schakenberg said, and paused. Volger made no response, so he continued. "We'd like to inform you that your former cook died yesterday while in Gestapo custody, but not before providing us with much valuable information."

Captain Rohrman of the Gestapo interrupted. "It seems he was shot while trying to escape—though he never made it beyond his cell." His crooked smile indicated that he enjoyed the joke.

Schakenberg shot the Gestapo captain a look that silenced him. Then he glanced back at Captain Axethelm, who handed him a folded sheet of paper. The colonel opened the paper and read.

"Your former cook provided the Gestapo with the names of two associates in the Socialist Underground, claiming they were the only two individuals he knew by name. One of them was a courier between Frankfurt and Underground operatives in Heidelberg. Unfortunately, when the Gestapo went to arrest this man, they bungled the job and he fled. They pursued him too aggressively, and he opted to end his own life by jumping in front of a commuter train. Now we are unable to learn the names of his contacts in Heidelberg."

The colonel shot Rohrman an even more scathing look before returning to the page. "The Gestapo have been unable to locate the second individual, who has apparently gone into hiding somewhere outside of Frankfurt. They are unsure where. But not to worry—I have asked Captain Axethelm to locate this missing traitor for us. I am certain he will be more successful than the Gestapo.

"But now we come to the most salient part of your former cook's information. It seems, Major, that you yourself have been blackmailed into chauffeuring a Swiss national around southwestern Germany, enabling him to work with Underground operatives in several German cities—including Heidelberg, where our trail has gone cold. This Swiss national goes by the code name Emmentaler."

Volger swallowed hard. He kept his back rigidly straight, and continued to stare at Colonel Schakenberg.

"Don't worry, Major—you are far too valuable to us on your current mission to be arrested for treason. Who could we get to replace you on short notice?" Schakenberg's smile was icy. "So we are offering you another chance to redeem yourself, and to prove your loyalty to the Fatherland. Tell us what you know of this Emmentaler."

Volger seized the opportunity. "He is in Frankfurt now! He was here fifteen minutes ago—he accosted me when I entered my garage. I sent him away, of course—I am finished with that business. I'm sure that you can catch him, he can't have gone far."

"You let him get away?" Rohrman demanded, his face flushing red.

Schakenberg shot the Gestapo officer a sharp look.

"We will need a detailed physical description of this man, Major," Captain Axethelm said, breaking his silence.

"Of course. He was wearing a dirty white shirt and a dark brown jacket, brown corduroy pants, brown shoes, and a brown newsboy cap. He's young—twenty-three or twenty-four. Not a tall man, perhaps fifteen centimeters shorter than I am. He has dark brown hair, very thick, and not well-combed. A squarish face, unshaved today, but he has the shadow of a beard even when he's well-shaved. His eyes are brown, and his face always seems sun-tanned—not like an Italian, more like a Frenchman."

"What part of Switzerland is he from?" Captain Axethelm asked, furiously scribbling notes.

"I don't know."

"Where do you usually meet him?" Schakenberg asked, looking Volger hard in the eyes.

"Outside of Grenzach in Baden, near the border."

"I know it," the colonel said. "Not far from Basel, is it?"

"No."

"Basel is a most liberal city, isn't it? It seems logical that this Emmentaler is from there, doesn't it?"

Volger flushed. "Yes, it does."

Schakenberg looked to the Gestapo officer. "Captain Rohrman, can your men handle this for tonight without bungling it?"

Rohrman stiffened. "Yes, sir!"

"Have this description sent to every checkpoint between here and the Swiss border. Place 'Wanted' posters with his description in every train station, police station, Customs office, and Rathaus before morning. But let the SD handle the pursuit, is that clear?"

"Yes, sir, *Colonel.*" Rohrman didn't bother to mask the resentment in his voice.

Schakenberg motioned with his hand, and the two captains left. "You have been most helpful, Major. Now I would like for you to help us locate this Emmentaler—but not tonight. I think our friends at the

Gestapo can handle it from their checkpoints tonight, if this Emmentaler is reckless enough to travel in the open. But I'm sure he is not. More likely he will go into hiding with the same people who are hiding our other missing suspect.

"You will report to my office at Lindenstrasse 27 tomorrow morning at eight o'clock. For now, you report to me—your commanding officer knows not to expect you until we have finished our business. We will discuss this Emmentaler, and also your travel arrangements to Bern on Tuesday. Now, I shall let you enjoy dinner with your family. Good evening, Major."

42

Bern

It was almost seven-thirty when Martin got the call.

"I'm glad I caught you," Legge's voice said.

"You found something?"

"Come to my office." The line clicked off.

"You wanted to see me?" Martin said, hiding his irritation at being summoned.

"It took us all day to find out who this *Falkenkopf* is. My counterparts in London and Berlin couldn't find anything in their files. Finally had to ask the Brits, for Christ sake. Then it took them more than an hour to get back with me. I told them it was high priority, but they had to check with London."

"Who is he?"

"A damned big-shot, that's who! How the hell did you get in contact with this one?"

"Through a Protestant minister in Cologne who's opposed to the regime. So, who is this big-shot? You have a name?"

"More than that. He's Colonel Friedrich Karl von Furstenau, and he's *very* high up in the Abwehr. A personal favorite of Canaris himself! He's forty-two years old, been in the Abwehr since 1922. His father is Baron Friedrich Wilhelm von Furstenau, and they've got a castle somewhere in Westphalia. Baron von Furstenau was in the Abwehr himself, retired in '26. When young Friedrich joined the army in 1917, the baron got him appointed to an officer's academy, and then got him posted to supply requisitioning for the lines—meaning he took grain and livestock from French and Belgian peasants, and paid pennies. It also meant he never had to fight in the trenches. Lieutenant von Furstenau had a good eye, though—he was instrumental in the capture of at least two Allied agents, one British, one French. A few years after the war, the baron got his son appointed to the Abwehr, and introduced him to Admiral Canaris. He was a captain then. He's a full colonel now, and reports directly to Canaris himself."

Martin was impressed and didn't bother to hide it. "And Canaris reports directly to Hitler."

"Exactly."

Martin took a second to absorb the implications. "This is huge!"

"*Beyond* huge, Schuller. Given who he is, Colonel von Furstenau was taking an enormous risk speaking with you. Let alone what he told you."

"If this ever got out—"

"I know where you're going. Himmler and Heydrich have been trying to discredit Canaris for years, to present Hitler with evidence of disloyalty. He's the only one in the inner circle who hasn't joined the Nazi Party, and they hate him."

"How much did you tell the Brits?"

"Not much. I said we'd heard some chatter about this Falkenkopf, but had no idea who he was. I declined to say what the chatter was— but they did make me swear that there was no imminent threat to the British Isles based on what we'd heard. That was the only way I could get them to cooperate. They're never forthcoming. And they want us to be their allies again!"

Martin made a little snort while Legge chuckled.

"Great work with this one."

"Thank you, colonel." Martin hesitated at the door, but then added, "I owe you a beer."

Legge laughed out loud. "You bet you do!"

Back in his office, Martin contemplated for a moment. It would be dangerous to get in the middle of a rivalry between the Abwehr and the SD. But if he played his cards right, perhaps he could work this to his advantage.

He crept to Ron Witherspoon's office. The door was locked, but he'd anticipated this by bringing a paper clip, and he set to work picking the lock. Seconds later he was inside, and flipped through the card file on the desk until he located the phone number for the military attaché's office at the German embassy.

The lieutenant who answered didn't sound thrilled to be taking a phone call. Martin asked if Captain Wolfe was still there.

"No, he is not. Who's calling?"

"My name is Schmidt, and I need to speak with Captain Wolfe urgently. He is expecting to hear from me."

"Then I'm sure you are aware that Captain Wolfe does not work at the embassy. You should contact him through your regular channels."

There was a click, and the line went dead.

Damn! Martin checked his watch, grabbed his coat and hat, and sprinted out the door.

Lt. Behr had not been pleased to be interrupted by a phone call, when he had spent hours trying to decrypt the most recent message they'd intercepted from the Polish Government-in-exile in London, to the Polish Military Attaché to Switzerland—who still operated in Bern under diplomatic immunity, even though his country didn't exist anymore. Lt. Behr had thought he was onto something when the phone rang and interrupted him.

But this call had been important.

The second he hung up the receiver, he scribbled down a message, then spent a moment enciphering it. He hurried to the telegraph, and tapped out the Morse code over the secure line to Berlin.

Martin made it to the train station in ten minutes flat, ignoring the honks of indignation from other drivers that he cut off in traffic. He parked the Ford less than perfectly in his haste, and ran to the main entrance. He stopped in the center of the main hall and stared up at the board.

The overnight train to Koln had left fifteen minutes ago.

363

Friday,
October 10, 1941

43

Heidelberg

It was three-thirty in the morning when Franz reached the Schuber house. Locating Ilsa's window, he tossed pebbles at it until he saw the glimmer of light turn on behind the black-out curtain.

The shadow of her face peeked around the curtain, and he stepped from the shadows into the moonlight, standing in the middle of the garden. He tossed another pebble, landing it on the frame just below the glass.

The light went out, and a moment later the window opened and Ilsa's head came into view.

"Franz? Is that you?" she called out in a stage whisper.

"Yes. Come down. I need your help."

"It's the middle of the night! Are you in trouble?"

"Just come down. I have to speak with you."

She held up her finger to indicate 'one moment,' and gently closed the window.

He slipped back into the shadows, and waited. He imagined her creeping down the stairs, every step in super-slow-motion to avoid making a sound. He was fairly certain the Schubers had a little dog—he seemed to recall Ilsa mentioning it before—and he hoped it wasn't the type to bark at its owners in the middle of the night.

After what seemed an eternity, the back door cracked open, and Ilsa slipped out, clutching a pink robe to her neck in reaction to the night's chill. "Franz, what are you doing here?"

He hurried toward her, took her hand, and pulled her into the shadow of the hedgerow.

"I'm in trouble, Ilsa. I think the Gestapo are looking for me. I couldn't think of anywhere else to go. Please help me!"

"How do you know?"

"I told you once that I recruited someone to drive me, someone above suspicion—that person turned on me. I had information on him, enough to keep me safe from double-cross, I thought. The Gestapo must have gotten to him, and made some sort of offer. I don't know, but he's not safe anymore."

"Who was it?"

"An SS officer. That's all you need to know."

"An SS officer? Franz!" She stared at him. "Where?"

"In Frankfurt."

"How did you get here?"

"I stowed away on a freight train, and jumped off at Mannheim." He described how the local Edelweiss Pirates in Frankfurt had helped him locate a southbound freight, kept watch for guards while he jumped onto a box car and hid behind crates, and promised to tear down any 'Wanted' posters with his picture.

"Edelweiss Pirates? Franz, they're nothing but a bunch ruffians. What in Heaven's name made you go to *them*?"

"I had to go to someone, and at least I knew they wouldn't turn me in." And a few extra Reichsmarks hadn't hurt.

"What are we going to do?"

He took her by the shoulders and looked into her eyes. "You have to help me get out. Can the courier at Lange's Bakery smuggle me to the border? If they can get me close, I'll make my own way across."

She hesitated a second. "I don't know. I can ask. I'll go there first thing in the morning, while it's still dark."

"I need someplace to hide until then. Is there someplace in the cellar that your father won't go to?"

She shook her head. "They delivered the coal the other day. Father will go down first thing in the morning to stoke the furnace, and again when he gets home from work."

"What about the shed?" he nodded toward the back of their garden. It was at least bigger than the rickety—and drafty—shed behind Rolf Metzger's parents' house in Frankfurt, where he'd slept thirty hours before.

"Perhaps. Father probably won't go there, until Saturday anyway. But Gretchen likes to go back behind the shed to relieve herself. She might smell you."

Damn, the dog! "Unless you can think of anywhere else, that's a chance I have to take."

"You may not have to stay long. The bakery opens in two hours. I can tell my mother I have to get to the library before classes, that I have work to do there. I can leave as soon as curfew ends, and get to the bakery while it's still dark. Then I can come back for you before anyone knows."

He kissed her on the lips. "Thank you, Ilsa. Help me into the shed."

She took his hand and led him along the hedgerow, opened the shed door, and covered him with a heavy blanket after he crawled under a work bench.

"I'll be back for you in a few hours," she whispered.

There was no sign of life at Lange's Bakery. Even with the black-out curtains drawn, it was still obvious that no light was on inside. And the sign in the window was still turned to the "Closed" side.

Ilsa double-checked the hours painted on the door. It still said that they opened at six. She checked her watch—ten minutes after.

Fear sank in her stomach. The other stores on the street all showed signs of life, with proprietors stepping out to dump buckets of dirty mop water into the gutter, light temporarily streaming out behind them, or shop girls momentarily moving aside the black-out curtains to turn window signs from "Closed" to "Open."

A look back at Lange's confirmed her fear—there was no one inside.

Several moments of indecision followed, and she shifted her weight from one foot to the other. When the university's clock tower chimed quarter after the hour, she made up her mind to leave. She would go to the library for a while, reversing the lie she'd told to her mother, and come back in an hour.

The faint gray light of an early fall morning was replacing the darkness when the Schubers' back door creaked open, followed by the padding of a small dog running through the wet grass, ever closer to the shed. Franz held his breath while it went around the back of the little outbuilding.

A moment later he could hear the sound of sniffing on the other side of the wooden slats a few feet from where he lay curled up in a fetal position under the blanket. He barely breathed.

Then came a low growl—not the deep rumbling growl of a big guard dog, but the warning growl of a terrier. He pictured a Schnauzer.

The growling continued for a minute, and then the back door opened again, and a woman's voice called. "Gretchen! Come inside. Stop bothering the rabbits!"

The dog padded off. The back door closed. Silence descended.

Ilsa returned at seven-thirty to find Lange's Bakery still closed. She hurried across the street to the butcher shop, and asked the short dark-haired lady behind the counter if she knew what had happened to the Langes. The lady said no, but averted her eyes.

Ilsa pretended to walk down the street, but crossed at the alley and snuck around behind the bakery. The delivery truck sat parked behind the kitchen, but there was no sign of the driver or anyone else. She stood on her tip-toes to peer inside the cab of the truck; pages of delivery sheets sat on the passenger seat.

"May I help you, young woman?" a stern voice startled her, and she jumped. Her heart leapt into her throat as she spun around. A burly dark-haired man in a black leather coat stood in the doorway of the Langes' kitchen.

"Oh, excuse me, sir! You startled me," Ilsa said, buying herself a moment. "I was looking for Mrs. Lange, but no one seems to be inside, and the store is still closed."

"This store is closed until further notice," the man said, regarding Ilsa with suspicious eyes, his lips pursed.

"But Mrs. Lange baked me a cake, for my father's birthday today. I was supposed to pick it up this morning. Do you know when she'll be in?"

"Young woman, the proprietors of this shop have been arrested. They will not be in today."

"Arrested? But why?"

"Good day, miss." The Gestapo man closed the door.

Ilsa walked back up the alley, her heart thumping, but she wavered at the corner. Was she in danger? The Langes knew her name, and it was said that everyone who went to the Gestapo's torture rooms eventually told what they knew.

It was a matter of when, not if. She had to get out of Germany with Franz.

44

Bern

"You're awfully quiet again this morning," Amanda said.

Jason shrugged, but didn't look up from the newspaper. "Just reading the paper." He was sitting in a chair, rather than on the corner of her desk as he usually did.

"Anything interesting?"

Jason shrugged again. He was reading a report on the continuing tensions in Fribourg and other communities along the Saane River. On Monday it had been front-page news; by Friday it had migrated to the fourth page.

"What are you reading about?"

"More vandalism in Fribourg, this time of a French bistro and a bakery. Bricks through windows, spray painted threats. The police say it's revenge for earlier vandalism of German-owned businesses. The reporter suggests it's the worst ethnic tension in the area since 1914."

"Sounds pretty nasty."

"I suppose."

They sat in silence for a moment. Amanda smiled and said in a light tone, "Hey, flip over to the Arts section, and tell me what pictures are playing at the movie house."

"I didn't think you liked foreign language films."

"I'm in the mood to see a picture tonight. Care to join me?"

"I think I'll go for a swim after work."

"Haven't you been for a swim every night this week?"

371

"Helps me clear my head."

She slammed a stack of folders against the desk, drawing his attention from the newspaper. She pointed a finger at him, and the proper secretarial speech gave way to a New Jersey accent. "Jason Bachman! You've been moping around here all week, and I'm tired of it. It's time you snapped out of it, brother."

He folded his newspaper and stood. "I've got to get to work."

"You're taking me to the movies tonight, whether you want to or not. And while you're at it, you can take me to dinner, too. A girl's gotta eat, and I don't have a date tonight. Besides, I deserve a night out for putting up with your mopey attitude lately."

Jason stared at the floor in front of her desk. "He hasn't called once, or sent a telegram, or anything." His voice was quiet, and his eyes stayed downcast.

Amanda's expression softened. "Oh sweetie, I can't tell you how many times men haven't called me. I know it's hard to believe, but it's true. It's tough, but you can't let it ruin your entire week."

Jason shrugged again. "I've gotta get downstairs."

Amanda took his hand as he stepped away. "Come and see me at lunch time. We'll go somewhere and have a talk, alright?"

He nodded. "Thanks." He walked toward the elevator, head down, and his gait barely more than a shuffle.

When Martin arrived at his office, Ron Witherspoon was waiting for him. "The Ambassador wants to see you right away," he said, an annoyed edge to his voice.

"What's wrong?"

"I don't know, I wasn't included. I was only sent to summon you to the ambassador's office." He marched off.

Martin found the ambassador's door closed. He knocked, and the ambassador's voice told him to enter. He walked in, and there sat Colonel Legge.

Ambassador Harrison wasted no time. "The COI has shared your report on the situation here, and Assistant Secretary Berle has directed us to cooperate with the office of the military attaché to break this Gestapo ring."

Legge cleared his throat. "We've been monitoring the situation on our own. I've stayed in contact with the Swiss Army command. Not much they can do on their own. Switzerland doesn't have a large standing army—it's mostly reserves—so they don't have the resources to break the Gestapo. Murky jurisdiction for that matter, since none of the attacks has taken place on a military base. It'll be up to us."

If Swiss military intelligence was worried about murky jurisdiction, where did that leave them? Martin supposed they'd be blamed if something went wrong, and ignored if it didn't. "How exactly will we do this, Colonel?"

"We need to know the extent of the Gestapo presence in Switzerland, and to do that we need to get inside their ring. That's where you come in."

And he proceeded to lay the outlines of a trap.

45

Heidelberg

Ilsa was out of breath by the time she reached the front door. She'd hurried home from the bakery, looking over her shoulder several times.

As soon as she was inside, she rushed up the stairs to her room. The Schnauzer Gretchen barked once, saw it was Ilsa, and followed her, jumping onto the bed to sit and watch her moving frantically around the room.

Ilsa grabbed a bag from the bottom of her wardrobe, and threw in two pairs of underwear, two pairs of stockings, and a clean blouse. Then she collected every container of make-up she owned. Maybe she and Franz could disguise themselves that way.

"Ilsa? Is that you dear?"

"Yes, Mother."

"What on earth are you doing home?" her mother's voice was getting closer, and Ilsa turned to see her standing at the top of the stairs, a curious look on her face.

"I forgot that today is Friday," Ilsa said, still breathless. "Instead of going to class, a bunch of us are taking a trip into the hills to go hiking and camping for the weekend. 'Good exercise and camaraderie for Germany's young people.'" She added the last in an imitation of the Propaganda Ministry's newsreels.

"There will be young men on this camping trip?" Her mother's expression was as reproachful as her tone.

"Of course, Mother."

"Ilsa! Your father won't approve of you skipping classes, and he won't approve of an overnight trip with young men present."

"Mother, stop it. I'm twenty-one years old, I can do what I want. Besides, you know the Hitler Youth and the League of German Girls go on joint hikes and camping trips. You didn't object when Georg went into the hills with his troop."

Her mother looked stung. "Ilsa, don't be cruel. You know your father and I don't approve of most of the things Georg has to do in the Hitler Youth. But what can we do?"

It was true that the Schubers had conveniently "forgotten" to enroll their son in the Hitler Youth, until a couple of Brownshirts showed up at the door last spring and pointed out their error. Now sixteen-year-old Georg participated in the HJ's afterschool and weekend activities with the rest of his classmates.

Ilsa regretted hurting her mother. This might be the last time she saw her for a long time. "I'm sorry, Mutti. I didn't mean to hurt you. I wish you'd recognize that I'm not a little girl any more."

"You still live here."

"But I'm a grown woman, and I can live my life as I please. And perhaps I'll meet my husband on this excursion."

"Ilsa! There's no need to mock me."

"I'm sorry, Mother. Now I'm in a bit of a hurry. The others won't wait for me much longer. I have to finish packing."

Mrs. Schuber's expression stiffened. "Have a good time, dear."

Ilsa watched her mother walk down the stairs, and a lump formed in her throat. She pushed the emotion away and set back to the task of stuffing her bag.

Once she'd finished in her room, she snuck into Georg's room. She quietly opened his wardrobe and removed a starched white shirt, black trousers, black shoes, and black neck tie. Georg might only be sixteen, but he was about as tall as Franz. The boy was still rail thin, though, so the clothes would be tight on Franz's shoulders, but it was the best she could do with no notice.

She spied the Hitler Youth uniform hanging in the back of the wardrobe, and briefly entertained the thought of ripping off the Swastika armband, but that would only cause her little brother trouble. She had already caused enough of that.

She snuck back into her bedroom and folded Georg's clothes as quickly as she could without wrinkling them, and placed them inside her bag. Seeing Gretchen sitting on her bed, watching her with ears perked and head cocked, she bent down and nuzzled the dog's head, gave her a quick kiss, and hurried down the stairs.

She set her bag by the back door, and walked into the kitchen.

"Mother, I'm going to borrow Father's boots from the shed, then I have to go. I'll miss you." She gave her mother a kiss on the cheek, then hurried out the back door.

"What took you so long?" Franz asked. His voice carried an unintended edge, but he'd grown more tense the longer he waited.

"Here, change into these. I stole them from my brother." Ilsa tossed him some clothes.

"It's a strange time to try to get me out of my clothes, isn't it?" Franz joked as he unbuckled his belt and tugged down his dirty brown corduroy pants, as much to lighten his mood as hers.

"Franz, be serious." Her expression said she wasn't in the mood for jokes.

"What's the bag for?"

"I'm coming with you. They've arrested the Langes. We'll have to find another way out."

Franz's gut tightened. "What did you tell your mother?" he asked as he changed into Georg's pants, sucking in his stomach so that he could fasten them.

"I told her I was going on a hiking and camping trip in the hills."

"Well then, we can't go into the hills to hide. We'll have to think of something else."

Ilsa's face flushed. "Where else can we go where we won't get stopped all the time?"

"We'll have to get to the railroad tracks through the farmland west of town, and try not to set all the dogs to barking." He struggled to get the shirt's top button fastened, and finally gave up. "I guess the necktie will cover it."

He stuffed his own clothes into Ilsa's bag. "Do you know anyone friendly to the cause who could be out driving a car without suspicion? A doctor, for example?"

She shook her head.

"Then we're on our own. Have you ever jumped onto a moving train before?"

She shook her head again.

"Don't worry, I'll help you." He took a moment to touch her cheek. "Now, let's get away from here before anyone comes looking for you."

He took her by the hand and led her out of the shed, through the garden's back gate, and down the alley behind the houses, keeping to the shadows of the fences.

46

Zurich

"Miss Krasnakovich!" Martin called when Elena emerged from one of the University buildings.

She looked startled, but quickly recovered and looked at him through cool eyes. "Yes, Inspector?"

"I'd like to talk with you again, privately."

She put on a coy smile. "Inspector, I don't know what you've heard, but you'll have to try harder than that to get me alone."

Martin ignored the inference. "Come, I'll buy you some lunch."

Her expression grew serious. "You want to talk about Peter?"

"Yes." *Among other things.*

Twenty minutes later they were sitting at a corner table inside a café in the Lindenhof district, with a beer and a plate of Rosti in front of each of them. "Tell me about Peter," Martin said.

"He's gone missing, more than a week now."

"So I understand. I'm hoping you can tell me more about him."

"I met him this summer, where I bank, and we'd talk a little. I dropped hints, and eventually he asked me out. He was a nice man. I don't meet many like that." She stared at her fork, and played with her Rosti.

"How long did you two date?"

"A little more than a month. Not long."

"So you didn't know him well, then?"

Elena shrugged. "I knew that he liked routine. He did the same things, at the same times, every day. I knew he didn't like parties, or speaking to strangers. I had to persuade him very hard to come to our meeting a couple of weeks ago."

"So for him to be gone for long is out of character."

Elena scowled. "I thought that was obvious."

Martin ignored that. "Sonia Rubenstein told me he spoke about his bank at your meeting. What did he tell you?"

Elena gave a recap of the information Peter provided, and how it was used in the leaflet they produced a few days later. "The day the leaflets were distributed was the last day he was seen."

Martin took a moment to consider his words. "Did Peter know anyone from Germany? Did he work with any customers from the Reich?"

Elena's eyes widened. "I have no idea."

"Did he ever mention seeing anyone in the bank wearing an SS uniform, or a Gestapo uniform?"

"No." Elena's expression had grown wary. "Why?"

Martin hesitated. "We believe the Gestapo are actively working in Zurich. I'm curious to know if they're working with the Zurischer Bank."

Elena shook her head in disgust. "Those bastards! It isn't enough for them to overrun almost all of Europe? Now they have to control us, too?"

"It would seem that they felt threatened by Peter, thought he could expose their connection with the bank. He may have put himself—and your entire group—in danger."

Her face was flushed, and angry tears formed in the corners of her gray eyes. "They'll pay," she whispered. "Some day, they'll pay."

He let her take a moment to recompose herself. Then he took a harder tone. "Last week you told me you didn't know any Communists."

"That's right."

"It was a lie."

She stiffened. "It's the truth! I don't know any Communists. Because I'm Russian, you policemen all think I'm a Red. I told you, my father was in the White army. We hate Communists."

"You used to date Pavel Minskayev, I understand."

"Pavel's not a Communist!"

"Did you ever meet his mother, Irina Minskaya?"

Wariness settled over her eyes. "Yes, once or twice."

"Was it once, or was it twice?"

She glared at him. "Twice."

"What did you talk about?"

"I'm not sure. Nothing important—Pavel, school, their cat. I don't think she liked me."

"Did you talk about Russia?"

Elena shook her head. "No, not at all."

Martin frowned. "You mean to tell me she never asked where your family was from? What your father had done during the Revolution? Do you expect me to believe that?"

"Yes! She never asked me anything about the past—only the present."

"What language did you speak?"

"German, mostly. I greeted her in Russian when I first met her, but she never said a word of Russian to me."

"What about Pavel's step-father, Adolf Lebler? Did you ever meet him?"

"Only once."

"Did he discuss politics?"

"No."

"Did you know he was a member of the Communist Party?"

Elena leaned back and looked away. "I might have guessed, I suppose. He's a labor organizer. The Reds always worked the labor unions."

"And Pavel?"

Elena chuckled and looked back at Martin. "Pavel's no Red, Inspector. I've heard him speak about freedom and democracy too often to suspect otherwise. He might lean left, but not far left."

"People are not always what they seem, Miss Krasnakovich."

"And sometimes they are *exactly* what they seem, Inspector. That can be the most disappointing."

Martin waited for her to elaborate. She took a swig of beer and leaned back in her chair, staring at him. They stared at each other for a moment before Martin acquiesced.

"How did you meet Pavel?"

"At university, a year-and-a-half ago. I was a first-year student, he was third-year. We met at a reading in a cafe, several students reading from various works by the brothers Heinrich and Thomas Mann. Pavel was one of the readers—he read a passage from *Professor Unrat*, by Heinrich Mann. We started talking after the reading."

"How did Pavel know Franz Lemiel?"

"Through Sonia Rubenstein. Sonia and Pavel started the group, and Sonia knew Franz from somewhere; I'm not sure how. They all knew each other long before Pavel brought me to a meeting."

"How did Franz and Pavel get along?"

A veil seemed to drop over Elena's eyes. "They were cordial. They worked together, and that was their only interaction."

He could tell she was lying. Her eyes shifted downward during that last phrase. "Have you dated Franz?"

A bitter smile appeared at the corner of her mouth. "I wouldn't say that Franz and I dated. I'm certain *he* wouldn't see it that way."

"What would you say?" he asked, staring hard into her eyes.

She stared back for several seconds before looking away and shrugging. "I suppose I wanted more than he did. He came around occasionally, but not as often as I would have liked. He had too many other girls in other places—and too many boys, too." She looked back at Martin. "Does that shock you, Inspector?"

"No." Martin's stare never wavered from her eyes.

"You must already know, then. I suppose you would—Franz isn't one to hide it."

"Did Pavel know it?"

"I don't see how he couldn't."

"He never said?"

"No."

"Did Franz know Pavel's mother or step-father?"

"I have no idea. Why don't you ask him?"

"I will."

An uncomfortable silence fell over the table, and they stared at each other with hostile expressions for more than a minute.

"Why the questions about the Reds, Inspector? I thought you'd decided the Nazis were responsible for Peter's disappearance."

"I'm investigating more than Peter's disappearance."

"Oh, that's right—you were looking into Dr. Rubenstein's murder last week, weren't you? How's that investigation, Inspector? Solved it yet?"

Martin leaned forward. "When she first arrived in Switzerland in 1927, Irina Minskaya worked as a housekeeper for the Rubensteins for a period of six months. Then she and her sons moved in with Adolf Lebler, the Communist union organizer."

Elena's eyes widened, and her mouth hung open. It took her a moment before she could speak. "Surely you don't think Dr. Rubenstein was a Communist."

Martin shook his head. "No. But the connection is intriguing, don't you think?"

"I think you should talk to Sonia, not me."

"I will. But right now, I want you to tell me more about you and Pavel." He raised his hand to signal the waitress, and ordered them two more beers.

"Why should I?"

"Because I could arrest you for not cooperating with a murder investigation," Martin bluffed. "And with your friend Peter's disappearance, I might be the only protection you have against the Gestapo."

"Like I told you, I met Pavel at a reading one night—March of '40, I think it was. He was brilliant, read with such passion, he really brought out the ridiculousness of bourgeois double-standards." She shrugged. "What can I say? I was smitten. We talked, and he was charming and handsome."

"And he seduced you."

Her eyes hardened. "I was young and naïve."

"Then he brought you into the political group."

"Yes, and I learned not to be so naïve."

"By going to bed with Franz Lemiel?"

Her lips tightened. "That was one way."

"So, why did you start dating Pavel?"

She shrugged again. "We'd become friends. Then one night last winter, Pavel asked me why I would sell myself short, waiting for a man who didn't want me the way a man should. We talked, and I realized he was in love with me. Maybe he always had been."

"Then, why did you stop dating?"

"I don't see why you need to know any of this, Inspector. I'm not comfortable telling you private details of my life."

Martin took his wallet from his pocket and counted out several bills, then laid them on the table with ration coupons.

"There are killers on the loose in Zurich, Miss Krasnakovich. Pray that I find them before they find you." He stood and strode from the café, leaving Elena sitting alone.

47

Dusk was settling when Martin and Sonia approached a café in the Lindenhof district. She walked on his arm. Darkness came early now, and there was a chill in the air. Sonia wore a wrap around her shoulders, and she pulled it closer to her throat.

Pavel Minskayev was already seated, a steaming demitasse of espresso in front of him, and he stood when they entered. As instructed, Sonia introduced Martin as a private detective who was looking into her father's death.

Pavel extended his hand. His pale blue eyes were almost icy in their intensity, and Martin got the feeling he was being measured. The young man was the same height at Martin, but easily twenty pounds lighter. He had long, thin arms, but his grip was firm. His dark brown hair was buzzed short, perhaps an attempt to look older, something that his rosy cheeks counteracted.

"I didn't know Dr. Rubenstein," Pavel said, his voice surprisingly deep for such a thin, boyish young man. Martin thought he heard the tiniest hint of a Russian accent.

"Your mother used to work for him," Martin replied.

"That was fourteen years ago. I was a little boy."

"But that's how you and Sonia first knew each other."

"Yes, but I never met her father."

"But your mother did. Sonia's already confirmed for me that your mother and Dr. Rubenstein interacted on many occasions during her tenure."

Pavel shrugged. "I'm sure that's true. Perfectly natural, wouldn't you say?"

Martin forced a smile and nodded. "Yes, perfectly natural. Sonia says her parents were pleased with your mother's work."

Pavel nodded, but said nothing.

"How did your mother come to work for Dr. Rubenstein? Did they have common acquaintances?"

"I'm not sure," Pavel said. "I was very young then, I didn't ask her such things."

"Did your mother ever see the Rubensteins after she left their employment?"

"I don't know. You would have to ask her that."

Martin nodded and moved on. "Why did your family come here, Mr. Minskayev?"

The question seemed to surprise him. "Why else? To be free. There is no freedom in the Soviet Union."

Martin noted that Pavel used the correct name, in contrast to Elena Krasnakovich, who still called the land of her birth "Russia."

"However did you escape, if I may ask?"

A distance came to Pavel's eyes. "We walked, at night—always at night."

"That must have taken weeks!" Martin faked a look of admiration.

Pavel shrugged.

"Why Switzerland? Why not Czechoslovakia or Poland? Romania, perhaps? They were much closer. Surely your parents must have known someone in Zurich, to have made the journey all the way here."

Indecision crossed Pavel's eyes, and he hesitated. When he spoke, his words tumbled out in rapid sequence. "Yes, I think they did. It was all so long ago, and I was very young."

"As you've said." Again, Martin faked a friendly smile. "But your father didn't come with you."

The distance returned to Pavel's eyes. "No."

Martin decided a bluff was the only way to break through the young man's secretiveness. He squared his shoulders and leaned forward. When he spoke, his voice was strong and deep, even a touch sharp, though his volume was low.

"Mr. Minskayev, I already know that your parents were members of the Communist Party, as was your step-father, so you can stop trying to hide that. I also know that your father was arrested in the Soviet Union, and that's why he didn't make it out with you. It's not difficult to surmise that either your mother or your step-father has contacts inside the Soviet Union, who informed her when your father died. Why else did she wait eight years after moving into Adolf Lebler's home to marry him? I don't think it was a coincidence that she married your step-father shortly after the purges began, do you?"

Pavel's eyes narrowed, his face flushed, and he pushed back from the table and started to get up. Martin grabbed his wrist, hard. He spoke quietly through clenched teeth. "Sit down."

Pavel remained motionless, his backside several inches above the seat of the chair, and stared into Martin's eyes with undisguised hostility. Even as his legs began to tremble from the strain of the awkward position, he didn't move.

Sonia reached over and put her hand on Pavel's, inches from Martin's grip on his wrist. "Pavel, please."

He glanced at her, and gave them the tiniest nod. He sat back down, scooted his chair in, and stared at Martin.

Martin released his wrist. Pavel pulled his arm back. The shape of Martin's grip was outlined in bright red. He continued the bluff. "Tell me what the Communists wanted with Dr. Rubenstein."

"How should I know? I have nothing to do with any of that," Pavel insisted. "I don't *want* anything to do with it. I don't know anything, do you understand?"

Martin gave away nothing. "Why should I believe that?"

Pavel leaned closer, and his voice dropped to a whisper. Martin had to lean in to be able to hear it. "They killed my father, for stupid ideological reasons. Why would I want to have anything to do with them? Others have gotten away, defected, but the GRU tracks them down and kills them, even here in Switzerland. Why do you think my mother married Adolf? She took his name, took Swiss citizenship. She stopped speaking Russian. He protects her."

"By working with the NKVD? Is that how he 'protects' her?"

"I don't know, I tell you! I don't know!" Pavel leaned back and folded his arms, looking more like a petulant teenager than a young man of twenty-two.

Martin took a gentler tone. "What was your father's name, Pavel? And don't tell me it was Minskayev, because I know it wasn't."

Pavel shrugged, unconvincingly. "I don't remember."

Martin leaned forward again and jabbed a finger toward the young man. "You were eight years old—I know you remember. What was your name back in Russia, Pavel?"

Pavel was silent for a moment, staring into Martin's eyes. Then the defiance softened. "It's not safe for me to say."

Sonia leaned over and placed a hand on Pavel's arm. "It's safe to tell him. Please trust us."

The look of indecision returned to Pavel's eyes, and he glanced back and forth between Martin and Sonia. He looked down at the table, and said in a voice barely above a whisper, "It was Pavel Grigorivich Smirnov. My father was Grigori Nikolayavich Smirnov."

"He was in the opposition with Leon Trotsky, wasn't he?"

Pavel shrugged. "I don't know. No one ever told me. But I think so. Mother said he was sent to Siberia about the time we fled. Then four years ago she heard he was dead—executed as a traitor. When Trotsky was killed in Mexico last year, Mother cut out the newspaper articles and read them over and over, for days."

Martin changed directions. "Your mother had met your stepfather before, in the Soviet Union, hadn't she?"

Pavel hesitated, then nodded. "Yes. He came to Moscow twice—for the Ninth Congress, and the Tenth Congress."

"When was that?"

"Summer of '24, then a year and a half later, at the end of 1925."

"He knew both of your parents, didn't he?"

Pavel nodded. "He came to the house for dinner several times. I was little, but I remember."

"Did he keep in contact with your parents?"

"I don't know. Probably."

"When you first arrived in Switzerland, did your mother go to see him right away?"

"I don't know. I was young, and it was so exhausting. I don't remember much about that time."

"How did she come to work for the Rubensteins?"

"I don't know."

"My parents placed an advertisement for a housekeeper," Sonia interrupted.

Martin kept his eyes on Pavel. "Did your mother read German back then?"

Pavel shrugged, but his silence and the downward cast of his eyes revealed that she hadn't.

"Someone was helping her," Martin said. "Who?"

"How should I know? I keep telling you, I don't know anything."

Martin reached into the breast pocket of his coat, and removed a folded newspaper clipping. He opened it and slid it across the table to Pavel. "You remember this, I'm sure."

Pavel regarded the yellowed piece of newspaper for a moment. "So?"

"The GRU shot and killed Ignace Reiss—a defector—at Chamblandes near Lausanne on the 4th of September, 1937. Here in Switzerland. That was only a week after your mother married Adolf Lebler."

Pavel said nothing.

"Reiss was an NKVD agent stationed in the west, until he wrote a letter to Stalin himself, renouncing the Soviet Union. Two months later, he was shot with a Soviet submachine gun by a French Communist."

Pavel's pale eyes were icy. "As I said, the GRU tracks down and kills defectors—even here in Switzerland."

"Reiss's wife Elsa was in Zurich when you arrived from the Soviet Union…"

Silence descended like a stone on the table, and the three of them sat as still as statues for several minutes.

"I remember meeting her—once," Pavel said, finally breaking the silence. "Mother said she'd been a great help, but that Mikhail and I were never to speak of her, to anyone."

"It would have been dangerous for all of you if anyone had known Elsa Reiss was helping the escaped family of a political prisoner," Martin said, his voice low.

Pavel nodded.

"Is there anything else you'd like to tell me?" Martin asked. "Anything else you suddenly 'remember'?"

The defiance had gone from Pavel's face, replaced by exasperation and exhaustion. "I'm telling the truth when I say that I don't know anything more, and I don't want to."

Martin nodded in resignation. He might never learn whether Adolf Lebler worked for the NKVD, or if Dr. Rubenstein's presence in Irina Minskaya's life was merely coincidence. "Thank you, Pavel." He turned to Sonia. "Shall we?"

The hostility in her dark eyes took him by surprise. "I'll stay with Pavel."

Martin felt unexpectedly stung. Irritation replaced the hurt feelings, and he scowled back at her. "Fine." His chair made a loud scraping noise as he stood. He marched from the café without so much as a backward glance.

48

Heidelberg

Rudolph Volger never tired of the startled looks that came to people's faces when they opened their doors and saw his uniform. Usually those looks came from Jewish faces, but the fair-haired woman standing on the other side of the doorway was Aryan.

"Mrs. Schuber, I am Major Volger of the SS, and this is Captain Axethelm of the SD. We are here to see your daughter, Ilsa."

"She's not here."

"We'll wait inside, then." He took a step into the doorway.

Mrs. Schuber's mouth opened for a split-second to form a protest, but then closed in a tight line, and she stepped aside. The schnauzer barred its teeth and refused to step aside, growling and barking.

Volger pushed the dog aside with his booted foot, but it snapped at the shiny black boot. He kicked it in the ribs, and it scurried away with a yelp.

"Gretchen!" Mrs. Schuber took a few hurried steps after the dog. Then, with a backward glance at the two officers, she closed the kitchen door and left the dog to lick her bruises safely locked away.

"My husband should be home any moment," she said, turning back to face them, her voice a touch too excited. "He works in Mannheim. He's a manager at the Daimler plant."

"When do you expect Ilsa?" Captain Axethelm asked.

"I don't know."

"Come now, Mrs. Schuber," Volger responded with a cold smile. "You must have an idea when your daughter will be home."

Mrs. Schuber shook her head. "No, I don't. She left this morning for a hiking and camping trip with some of her friends."

"I see." Volger stared until she looked away and fidgeted with her hands. He enjoyed this.

Captain Axethelm's expression was all business. "Mrs. Schuber, do you know Lange's Bakery?"

She shook her head again. "No. Our bakers are the Hansens, on Bunsenstrasse."

"Do you know anyone named Lange?"

"I don't think so. No, I'm sure I don't."

"The Langes were arrested yesterday. Your daughter was a regular customer."

"Oh, I see." Mrs. Schuber's voice was quiet. "I didn't know that. I don't know what stores Ilsa visits during the day. She studies at the university, you see."

"Yes, we know."

Volger had been surprised how quickly the Gestapo made the connection to Ilsa—and to Franz. He'd expected the baker's wife to be the first to crack, but she remained resolute in the Gestapo basement. Their delivery driver, on the other hand, squealed everything he knew at the first sign of pain.

An awkward silence descended on the room. Then the front door opened, and a middle-aged man in a blue suit walked in. He removed his hat, and was about to toss it onto the hat stand in the corner, when he spotted the two men in black SS uniforms. He held his hat in front of him.

Volger introduced himself and Captain Axethelm. "We are here for your daughter, Ilsa. Do you know where we might find her?"

"I already told them she's gone camping and hiking with her friends," Mrs. Schuber interjected, too quickly.

A second's confusion crossed Mr. Schuber's face, then he nodded and smiled. "Yes, that's right. She was going camping this weekend. I forgot."

"No, she hasn't." Volger took several steps toward Mr. Schuber, staring down at him. "Your daughter has been identified as a member of the Socialist underground, and a traitor to the Fatherland. Where is she hiding?"

Mr. Schuber's mouth hung open for a few seconds. "There's been a mistake! That's impossible. Someone has given you false information."

"No, we have it on good authority. Your daughter betrayed the Fatherland by delivering information to a Swiss spy called Emmentaler. Her actions have resulted in the deaths of German soldiers in France at the hands of terrorists."

Mrs. Schuber had come towards her husband, and now both of them stared at Volger in incredulity.

"That—that can't be!" Mr. Schuber finally said, stammering.

Volger took another step toward the Schubers, towering over them. "Where is your daughter?"

Mr. Schuber looked to his wife. Her eyes filled, and she wrung her hands. "I don't know! I swear, I don't know! She left this morning, said she was going hiking and camping with her friends. They were skipping classes today. She packed a bag. She borrowed her father's boots. I believed her. Why wouldn't I believe her?"

She began to shake. Mr. Schuber put an arm around his wife to steady her.

"Where is your son?" Captain Axethelm asked from the other side of the room.

Mrs. Schuber took a deep breath. When she replied her voice was steadier. "He's at a meeting of the HJ."

"Are you certain?"

"I—I think so. There was an activity tonight."

Captain Axethelm started to say something, but Volger raised his hand and silenced him. "Mr. and Mrs. Schuber, we require clothes from your daughter's laundry. I'm sure you have no objection."

Mr. Schuber shook his head. His voice cracked as he said "No."

"Show us to your daughter's room please, Mrs. Schuber."

The woman nodded without a word, and led them upstairs, her head down. She motioned toward Ilsa's door.

Volger motioned with his head, and Captain Axethelm marched across the room and lifted the lid of the laundry hamper in the corner. Finding dirty laundry in the bottom, he nodded and picked up the hamper, carrying it out of the room.

"Thank you, Mrs. Schuber," Volger said with a nod. "And the dogs thank you. They will enjoy tracking her scent. Good evening."

Saturday,
October 11, 1941

49

It was shortly after midnight when they awoke to dogs barking.

It took a few seconds for Franz to register that these were not farm dogs, barking at something moving in the night. No, this was the deep, insistent barking of German Shepherds, and they were coming closer.

His insides went cold. Somehow, they'd tracked them down.

He roused Ilsa from where she dozed across a couple of crates. "We've got to get out of here!"

In the darkness of the box car, he couldn't see her face, but he could hear the confusion in her voice. "Did the train stop?"

"Yes, a few minutes ago. Now come! We've got to get up top."

He reached for her hand, and pulled her toward the metal rungs along the wall. "Follow me up." He felt his way up the rungs, and ran his hands along the ceiling for the trap door he'd seen when they first got on.

His fingers found the lever, and the door swung up, letting a blast of cool night air into the stuffy box car. He could see the stars and the silvery glow of moonlight, and he scrambled onto the roof. He reached down into the darkness for Ilsa's hand.

"Stay low!" he whispered as she climbed up. The barking of the dogs had grown close.

He closed the trap door as soon as she was beside him. He motioned for her to follow, and he crawled toward the front of the car.

Reaching the edge, he crouched low, and then sprung onto the roof of the next car.

He looked back to make sure she was following. She was hesitating at the edge. "Hurry!" he whispered, motioning with his arm. The dogs were close now.

She leapt across, her foot slipping on the edge as she landed, but Franz grabbed her wrist and held her.

They repeated the process, making it to the next car as the door of their original box car squealed open. They scrambled to the end of the car before bright beams from numerous electric torches cut through the darkness.

Franz flattened against the cold metal, and glanced back to make sure Ilsa had done the same.

The shouts of several men joined the endless barking of the German Shepherds. They seemed to be all around. Franz's heart pounded in his throat.

He wasn't sure how much time passed—it seemed eternal, waiting to be discovered—but then the high-pitched whine of air raid sirens rang across the countryside from the north, from Mannheim or Heilbronn.

All of the beams switched off.

Franz glanced back at Ilsa and motioned for her to follow him. He slid forward, careful not to make any noise. Reaching the front edge of the car, he peered around for sign of soldier or dog. He reached for the next car, stretching as far as he could to bridge the gap, then hoisted himself across. He turned and waited for Ilsa to join, and reached his hand across to help her over.

He spied a patch of heavy undergrowth along the track not far ahead, and he crept forward until he reached the front edge of this car, almost parallel with the vegetation. He helped Ilsa over, then crept to the side of the car and peeked over the edge.

The nearest soldier was a ways back, forty or fifty meters. He didn't have a dog, and he faced away from them, a rifle slung over his shoulder.

Franz crept back to Ilsa, and whispered in her ear. "We've got to jump, and hide in that vegetation. We've got to be quick, while no one's looking. Jump clear of the gravel or you'll make too much noise. Do you understand?"

"Yes."

He motioned for her to follow him to the edge. He leaned forward as far as he dared, and looked both ways down the track. The soldier hadn't moved from his spot, and no others had joined him. He wasn't sure where the dogs were, heeled beside their handlers, but there was no time to find out. He took Ilsa's hand in his left, and held up the fingers of his right hand, counting out one-two-three.

A cloud covered the moon, and darkness covered the landscape.

They leapt on the count of three, landing in the tall grass at the edge of the gravel rail-bed. Franz landed squarely and rolled into the vegetation in one swift movement.

Ilsa didn't land as well. She twisted her ankle and crumpled onto her side, letting out a muffled cry.

Footsteps crunched on the gravel. The soldier had heard. Franz scrambled toward Ilsa, put his arms under her shoulders, and hauled her into the vegetation.

A moment later the shadowy figure of the soldier walked slowly past, peering into the vegetation. Franz and Ilsa stood still, holding their breaths.

"What is it, Hans?"

"I thought I heard something."

"Heard what?"

"A sound like a voice, over here somewhere."

The soldier switched on his torch and turned it toward the vegetation, but his companion slapped it down.

"Are you crazy? Do you want the RAF to know where the train is?"

"They're not after the train, they're bombing Mannheim, or Heilbronn."

"That doesn't mean they wouldn't love to drop a few bombs on a train if they spotted one. Now shut that thing off before we get in trouble."

From a nearby tree, an owl hooted and launched into flight.

"See? There's your 'voice.' Now shut that thing off!"

The torch went dark, and the crunch of footsteps on gravel grew distant.

They sat in silence for a long time, neither daring to move, both unsure what to do.

It was a long time before the distant air raid sirens fell silent. *A real raid, not a false alarm.*

The dog barks resumed a moment later. Franz tensed, listening for the barking to grow louder, closer.

It did.

"Run!" he hissed.

Branches scratched at their faces. The sound of the dogs grew ever closer, and now were accompanied by the shouts of men.

Franz ran behind Ilsa, and his chest ached from the exertion. Torch beams cut to and fro across the branches all around, and he pushed his legs even harder for a bit more speed. A beam of light cut across his back, casting a stark shadow for a split second; then the beam came back and rested on them.

"There they are!" a voice shouted, probably only twenty meters back. Other beams converged on them, and gunshots rang out.

Ilsa crumpled to the ground.

"Halt!" another voice shouted, this time to the left rather than from behind.

Franz stopped. It was pointless. They were all around. He raised his hands above his head and panted in exhaustion, his chest heaving.

The soldiers stepped aside when Volger approached, and a path cleared for him. He strode forward until he stood in front of the panting Swiss man, who looked up at him with defiant eyes.

Volger slapped Franz across the face with his gloves, the smack echoing in the woods.

He stepped back several meters to the sprawled figure of the girl. They had turned her onto her back, and he stared into her face. The blood had pooled around her, flowing from the gaping exit wound at the side of her abdomen. Her eyes blinked once, and he could hear the rasping from her throat as she struggled for breath.

Damn! It would be pointless to ask her anything. She would be gone within minutes, if she could even speak now. He un-holstered the Walther pistol at his hip and fired directly at her forehead.

He stormed off. "Bring him to my car!" he barked, and disappeared in the darkness.

50

Zurich

The early morning shadows still stretched long when Martin left the Ford in an alley not far from the city center, and went in search of a suitable messenger.

He found one emerging from a tenement building in a working class district, a boy of twelve or thirteen wearing dirty brown trousers with a patch on one knee, and a well-worn brown jacket with patches at both elbows.

Yes, the boy was interesting in earning ten francs. Martin handed him an envelope and a ten-france note, gave him specific instructions, and told him to tell no one about this.

"No, sir! No one! Thank you sir!" The boy dashed off toward the north.

Ernst Zubler sat at breakfast, in a pressed pair of slate gray pants, starched white shirt, and a necktie that matched the pants, but no jacket. A soft-boiled egg sat in an egg-cup in front of him, open on top, and he occasionally took bites with a spoon while reading the newspaper. His wife Sophia sat at the opposite end of the table, also with a soft-boiled egg, reading letters.

The butler entered with an envelope. "This arrived for you, sir."

Zubler took it, muttering a "Thank you." His name and address were typed on the front, but with no return address and no post-mark.

"Who delivered this, Anton?"

"A young boy, sir. Judging by his dress, not a professional courier."

Zubler scowled and tore open the envelope. He unfolded the single sheet of paper, and read the brief typed message.

```
I know what you've done. Go to the Haus
zum Rüden restaurant at 1:00. Give your name
to the maitre'd and tell him you have a
reservation for lunch. I will join you.
```

It was unsigned. Zubler stuffed the note in the envelope and rose from the table. "I'm afraid I have some business to attend to, my dear." He gave his wife a curt nod and strode from the room.

The Rolls Royce limousine arrived a few minutes before one, and Ernst Zubler stepped out and entered under the archways of the gray 14th century building.

Martin kept to his hiding place in the shadows, keeping an eye on the street. A delivery truck stopped a half-block away, and two figures in workingmen's clothing and brown jackets stepped down from the cab. One was tall and thin, the other shorter and stouter—the two men in black leather coats who had tailed him the night he inspected Dr. Rubenstein's files.

The men opened the back of the truck and began unloading boxes onto the promenade. The back of the truck was full of boxes. No doubt the act of unloading would take some time, and could be followed by reloading if necessary. And the two men looked around while pretending to work.

He waited another moment before stepping from the shadows and walking toward the Haus zum Rüden. He pretended not to pay any attention to the spurious deliverymen unloading their boxes, though he kept them in his peripheral vision until he was inside.

Ernst Zubler sat alone at the table in the farthest corner from the entrance, as Martin had instructed the maitre'd. Every table around it was empty, with a "Reserved" notice posted on each. It had cost one hundred Francs, but there would be no one close enough to eavesdrop.

Zubler stood when Martin approached. Martin extended his right hand, and spoke under his breath. "Shake my hand as if you were expecting me, and pretend to offer me a seat."

Zubler did as instructed, faking a polite smile and gracious manner.

"Mr. Zubler, I'm Federal Inspector Max Schmidt," Martin said when they had taken their seats.

The smile never left Zubler's lips, but his eyes took on a cold gleam, like a serpent preparing to strike. "No, you are not."

Martin said nothing. His stomach felt as if it were falling off a cliff, but he kept his expression stony.

"I know who you are, Agent X, and who you work for, though I don't know your name. I'm afraid you have the advantage there."

Martin silently cursed *Korkenzieher*. How else could Zubler have learned his identity? It wasn't out of the realm of possibility that *Korkenzieher* was a double-agent for the Gestapo. He might also have been tortured into revealing what he knew.

"I must say, you were clever meeting here, in plain view, and arranging for our privacy," Zubler continued. "Now, how may I address you? I can't very well continue to call you Agent X."

"You may call me Mr. Schmidt."

"Of course."

"I know what you've been doing, Mr. Zubler. I know you command the Gestapo agents who assassinated the colonels, and Dr. Rubenstein, and Friedrich Zindorf. I know that you selected the targets, and the dates for their assassination. I even know why."

"Oh? And why is it, do you think?"

"To destabilize Switzerland, and to push public opinion in favor of the Third Reich, by making the assassinations appear to be the work of Communist cells or Soviet Intelligence. Your goal is to unite Switzerland with Germany."

Zubler's eyebrows rose. "Well then, you have been busy. American Intelligence is more skillful that I imagined."

Martin stared at the banker, saying nothing.

"Tell me why American Intelligence is interested in any of this."

"It is in our interest that Switzerland remain neutral."

"Yes, of course. *Neutral*." Zubler said the word with a condescending sneer. "No doubt it's also in the interests of the British and Soviet governments for Switzerland to remain neutral—and the American government is the lapdog of the British, isn't it Mr. Schmidt?"

Martin couldn't let that lie, but he carefully measured his response. "The United States is not involved in the current conflict."

"Spare me the technicalities! We both know where your government's loyalties lie. Your military provides tanks, planes, and bombs to the British—and lately to the Soviets, as well."

"On lease only."

"Come now, Mr. Schmidt! Neither of us believes that either the British or the Soviets will ever *return* those armaments, do we?"

Martin kept silent.

"So what is it that you want? What does the United States government want of me?"

"Ideally, for you to stop betraying your country for Germany. Or if not, then for you to be brought to justice for your crimes."

"There is no crime in serving your country, Mr. Schmidt. Sometimes that calls for unpleasant action."

Martin couldn't hide his surprise. "*Serving* your country? How can you say that?"

Zubler's expression turned cold. "You and your government have no real care for Switzerland, Mr. Schmidt. Your aim is to use Swiss neutrality for your own purposes, nothing more. I am the one with my country's best interest at heart."

"By killing its people?" Martin made no attempt to hide the hostile incredulity in his tone.

The cold smile returned to Zubler's lips. "By saving the German people of Switzerland from themselves."

"I don't know what you mean."

"One of the greatest strengths of the German *Volk* is efficiency; efficiency and discipline. This holds true for the German people of Switzerland as well. And yet, our system of government is chaotic and disorganized, completely inefficient. It leaves too much discretion to the local and cantonal authorities. We end up with a cacophony of petty squabbles and competition.

"The Reichs-Germans have a much more efficient form of Federalism. Their central government leaves just enough authority to the state and local governments to keep them occupied. The Reich is highly efficient—and that is what Switzerland needs, Mr. Schmidt. I will see that my country takes its rightful place inside the German Reich, sharing the leadership of the new world order."

The pieces of the puzzle were falling into place. "With you as the leader of the new Switzerland—is that it, Mr. Zubler? You're killing people for the sake of vain ambition?"

Zubler stiffened, and his lips pursed. "I am doing what is best for my people. You are an enemy, Mr. Schmidt, and I will treat you as I would any enemy."

"As you treated Peter Kraus? Before you attempt my disappearance, Mr. Zubler, you should know that everything I have learned has already been reported to my superiors. There are others in Bern who know that I am here with you, and my disappearance will be noted. I'm not sure who has been protecting you from investigation so far, but they won't be able to protect you if you kill me."

Zubler chuckled. "Come now! Would you have me believe that the United States government would provoke an international affair over the disappearance of one secret agent? We both know that they would disavow any knowledge of you. I'm not a fool, Mr. Schmidt."

Martin hid his apprehension. "Then we have both been warned."

"Yes, we have indeed."

Martin stood. "You have forty-eight hours to send your Gestapo thugs back to Germany, and no action will be taken against you. We will be watching."

That last was part bluff; Martin wasn't sure how many Gestapo agents were operating in Switzerland, but his voice and posture oozed confidence as he placed his hat on his head and walked away.

They were following him. He didn't even have to glance behind him to know they were there.

Rather than returning to the alley where he'd left the Ford, he walked north, out of the medieval quarter, then across the river toward the train station. As the streets widened and the traffic increased, he paused beside a tan DKW F8 Kastenwagen that idled in front of a machine shop. The sidewalk was unoccupied, and he pretended to pat the pockets of his suit coat and look around.

The two men who had been unloading boxes from the truck beside the Haus zum Rüden looked away, and changed course toward the front door of the machine shop. "Excuse me!" Martin called to them, waving his arm. "Do either of you have a cigarette?"

The short one nodded, and the two of them walked toward Martin, standing on either side of him. The short man removed a pack of cigarettes from his pocket, tapped one out, and handed it to Martin without a word. The tall one stepped close and held out a lighter.

"Thank you." Martin put the cigarette in his mouth and leaned toward the flame. As he did so, he slapped his left palm against the fender of the Kastenwagen saloon.

The back of the Kastenwagen flew open, and two U.S. Marines launched themselves at the men flanking Martin. The element of surprise was on their side, as were forty pounds of muscle, and they had the men pinned in seconds.

Martin took two sets of handcuffs from the back of the Kastenwagen, knelt, and cuffed the men's hands behind their backs. The marines hauled them off the pavement and threw them into the back of the vehicle, climbed in and closed the doors behind them.

The entire event had taken less than a minute.

Martin opened the passenger door and got inside. "Take me back to my car, Corporal. I'll follow you back to Bern."

"Yes, sir," Corporal Lawrence said, shifting the gear stick.

51

Bern

"Hello?"

"Miss Rubenstein, this is Martin Schuller." He paused, but she said nothing. "I thought you'd like to know that we captured the two men who killed your father. One of them has confessed, and we recorded his confession on magnetic tape."

There was silence on the line for several seconds. Finally, Sonia asked, "What are you going to do with them?"

"We'll hand them over to the police, with the taped confession." *After Swiss Intelligence is finished with them.*

"How did you get a confession?"

"I wasn't part of the interrogation," Martin lied.

It had been surprisingly easy. The short one actually seemed boastful, as if he were proud that he could finally reveal his role. "Of course we shot that filthy Jew! We shot him in the heart, and rid the world of him!"

It had taken little prodding to get him to reveal the entire sequence in detail. He only became reticent when Martin asked who had ordered the killing. He appeared stunned when Martin mentioned Zubler by name, but refused to confirm or deny it.

"Did you—" Sonia's voice cracked. "Were you the one who caught them?"

"Yes, I was."

"Thank you." Her voice was softer, the gratitude genuine.

"You're welcome. I thought you should know."

"Yes, thank you Mr. Schuller."

He hesitated, then said, "You can call me Martin."

The line was silent.

"Sonia?"

She sniffed, and his own chest seemed to constrict. "I'll stop by and talk to you tomorrow." He replaced the receiver in the cradle. He stared at the black telephone for a moment, then cleared his throat and squared his shoulders. He stood and strode from his office.

"Good bit of work," Colonel Legge said when Martin rejoined him in the basement of the embassy. He sat in a large wooden chair behind a desk in a drab concrete room. "Your first joint operation?"

"Yes," Martin said, taking a chair from the wall and sitting across the desk from the military attaché.

"Won't be your last, I'm sure."

Martin nodded. He'd been taken by surprise at how far up the chain of command his intelligence had traveled, and how quickly. "How long are we going to keep them?"

The colonel shrugged. "Swiss Intelligence is arranging their transfer."

"But they'll turn them over to the police when they've finished with them?"

"Of course," the colonel said with a dismissive wave. It was insincere and Martin knew it, but he let it go.

"I understand the COI plans to send additional agents to Switzerland," the colonel continued, leaning his chair back and folding his hands across his belly.

Martin nodded.

"It'll take 'em a while, I'm sure. With any luck we'll have this whole thing taken care of before they get here."

That depends on how many Gestapo there are here, and if we can find them all.

"Sooner or later we're going to get dragged into this war, you know," Legge continued, his gaze never leaving Martin. "Bern's going to become very important. The COI's going to want top men operating here."

"I'm sure he will."

"I'm just saying, you did good work today, Schuller. I wouldn't mind if you were one of the men we got to work with next time."

Martin thought of his kids. He said nothing, just stood to leave.

"I wouldn't turn it down if I were you, Schuller. Important work to be done here." the colonel called as Martin walked out the door.

Two images flitted across his mind's eye, taking each other's place in the forefront of his thoughts—an image of his kids back in Philadelphia, and an image of Sonia Rubenstein.

Sunday,
October 12, 1941

52

Bern

Violin strains floated through the air from the string quintet sitting in the corner of the open-sided tent, near the fountain. Empty glasses clinked as waiters in white jackets took them from guests and carried them away on trays. Conversations in English, German, French, and Italian wafted through the air, mingled with laughter.

Jason stood with a group of other young Americans, low-ranking embassy grunts like himself, munching on hors d'oeuvres and sipping white wine. Normally only a skeleton crew worked on the weekends, but attendance at the Columbus Day reception that afternoon was mandatory.

Most of them were ambivalent toward the new holiday, which had become a national observance only four years before. They stood off to the side of the large tent that had been erected on the embassy's back lawn, watching the diplomats and their wives mingling.

"Some of the Italian societies in Chicago put on a parade for Columbus Day," Jason volunteered.

"They do in New York, too," Devon Wolcott said. "Never really sure why."

"Because Columbus was Italian, fool!" Mark Hodges said, smacking the back of Devon's head.

"I thought he was Spanish."

"No, the Spanish hired him. He was from Italy."

Jason turned to Devon. "Didn't you wonder why there were so many people here from the Italian embassy? And why'd you think the Italian ambassador is wearing all those medals today? You suppose he pins them on for every lawn party?"

"I don't know…because he's having dinner with Mussolini later? How the hell should I know?" Devon said, defensiveness giving way to a sheepish grin. "Can it, would ya, fellas?"

They had a good chuckle, and returned to watching the goings on.

Amanda Overstreet strolled by on the arm of an American businessman in an expensive suit. She leaned into him enough that her bust brushed his arm. She wore a stylish gray skirt that hugged her hips, and a baby-blue sweater. She didn't so much as glance at the grunts.

Brad Harris let out an appreciative whistle at her swaying hips, eliciting the briefest of scowls from Amanda. She returned her gaze to the tall American escorting her, who was too wrapped up in whatever he was saying to have noticed the impertinence.

The young men chortled like overgrown adolescents.

As he chuckled too, Jason caught the eye of a young man across the tent with dark curly hair, his round cheeks dimpled in an amused grin. Something about him looked familiar, but Jason couldn't place him. The young man returned his attention to the circle of men in dark suits among whom he stood, but cast a glance back at Jason a few seconds later, caught his eye, and winked.

Jason felt the heat in his cheeks, and glanced around, to be sure none of the other grunts had noticed the exchange.

The group split up a few minutes later. Some went to fill their plates, others to fill their glasses, while others conversed with the Swiss girls from the embassy typing pool.

Jason wandered toward the other side of the tent, alone, pretending to seek a spot closer to the string quintet. He stood near the fountain, sipping from his wine glass.

"Do you like Verdi?" a voice asked in a German accent.

Jason turned to see the curly-haired young man standing beside him, his head cocked in expectation. He had large brown eyes, the color of milk chocolate, which stared at Jason with a twinkle that could have been amusement—or something else.

"Is that what they're playing?" Jason asked, embarrassed. "I didn't recognize it."

"Yes, Verdi's Quintet in E-Minor." He smiled, and his large round cheeks dimpled again. He had a rich tenor voice. "I'm Liev Klein; I'm with the German Embassy." He extended his right hand, and gave Jason's hand one firm shake.

"Jason Bachman. Pleased to meet you."

"Yes, likewise. I have seen you before, though we have never met." Seeing the questioning look on Jason's face, he bowed in apology. "Forgive me. I should have said that I enjoy the occasional dip in the water, and I have often seen you at the public pool. You swim many laps, yes?"

That was where Jason had seen him! He'd been among the casual bathers at the pool a few times. Jason grinned. "Yes, I swim a lot of laps. I was on the swim team in high school, and also in college. I enjoy it."

"You are no longer competitive?"

Jason laughed. "No, not any more. Just for fun these days. And exercise."

"You are a fast swimmer."

Jason shrugged in mock modesty. "I suppose."

"Yes, you are! Very impressive." Liev Klein's eyes lowered and roamed back up—an unmistakable once-over.

"Thanks." Jason could feel himself blush again. He looked around at the little crowds of people scattered around the lawn, relieved that no one was looking.

Liev seemed to sense his embarrassment. "Shall we go inside? I have been told there are comfortable chairs in there, and I have been standing for a long time."

They found a couple of armchairs in a corner of one of the parlors.

"You're with the German embassy?"

"Yes."

"Liev Klein—that sounds almost Jewish," Jason said.

Liev's expression became unreadable. When he spoke a few seconds later, his voice was quieter. "My father's name is also Liev Klein. He was a doctor in Berlin until a few years ago. He was born of Jewish parents, you see. My mother has a Certificate of Aryan Blood, but that didn't stop enforcement of the law against Jews practicing medicine. Fortunately, my father is an old acquaintance of Admiral Canaris, and he got us exit visas. Now my parents live in Zurich, and my father practices medicine again. The admiral also gave me a post at the embassy here."

Admiral Canaris—Jason knew that name. But he couldn't remember exactly why.

"I heard Switzerland doesn't grant entry to Jews."

"They will if Admiral Canaris requests it. He has for many." Liev glanced around, then leaned close. "Your friend Franz is in terrible danger," he whispered.

Jason's mouth opened, but no sound came out.

"Franz was working with an American agent—it is important that we speak with him immediately."

We. Jason's mind raced. What was going on? "Are you a spy?"

Liev cringed. "I am with the Abwehr. I am not undercover—well, not usually." He added the last with a shrug.

Jason's heart raced. "How do you know Franz?"

"I volunteered to make contact with him several months ago. His work was deemed to be of interest, and I agreed to learn as much as I could." A crooked smile came to his lips, dimpling his right cheek again. "I'm not a clandestine operative, but I knew that I would be best able to get close to Franz. Men talk much more freely in bed."

A pang of jealousy ripped through Jason's belly. He stared back at Liev with undisguised hostility.

Liev recoiled. "We're not the Gestapo. We're not trying to arrest anyone. We needed an asset in Switzerland with eyes and ears in many places, as Franz does. Our intention isn't to infiltrate the Resistance—Franz would have never given me those names—but to keep in contact with networks here in Switzerland, should they be of use to us. But now the Gestapo have taken him, and we need to speak with your agent immediately."

"The Gestapo have Franz?" Jason's heart skipped, and a terrible feeling of dread rose up from his stomach.

An exasperated look came to Liev's face. "Yes, the Gestapo! Franz is in danger, and I need for you to help us save him. We must speak with your agent immediately."

Mr. Schuller—that's who he means. It all made sense now. But how to reach him? Jason hadn't seen him at the reception—not surprising, since he rarely saw him anywhere. "I don't know how to get ahold of him."

"You know people who do." Liev's large brown eyes seemed to bore into him.

Jason supposed that he did. The ambassador would know, and Mr. Witherspoon would probably know. He nodded at Liev and stood. "Come with me."

He started to step away, and felt a warm hand on his wrist. He turned back to see Liev smiling at him, the twinkle back in his milk-chocolate eyes. "I can see why Franz likes you." His glance went down and rested for a second on Jason's posterior before returning and locking on Jason's eyes again. His grin stretched wider, and he winked.

Jason turned away. "Come on, I'll take you to someone."

He found Ron Witherspoon outside, conversing with the President of the Canton of Ticino and several other Swiss dignitaries.

Jason cleared his throat to get Mr. Witherspoon's attention.

"Excuse me, sir. I have someone who needs to speak with you."

Ron Witherspoon scowled, but turned toward the Swiss dignitaries with an apologetic smile and a quick bow of his head. "Please excuse me for a moment, gentlemen."

He followed Jason to where Liev Klein stood just inside the door. Mr. Witherspoon's rigid posture, stern expression, and clipped tone revealed his irritation. "Mr. Bachman, what is this about?"

Jason introduced Liev Klein.

"How do you do, sir?" Liev said, extending his right hand and giving Witherspoon's a single firm shake.

When Witherspoon pulled his hand back, there was a slip of paper in it. He glanced around, and turned toward the wall.

He read for a few seconds and turned back toward them. "Yes, I see. Come with me please, Herr Klein." Glancing at Jason, he added, "Thank you, Mr. Bachman. That will be all."

Liev Klein didn't move. "No, I will wait here with Mr. Bachman until you have made the arrangements." He gave Witherspoon a hard stare that Jason imagined to say, *I'm not stupid enough to go with you alone.*

Witherspoon's scowl deepened. "Very well, I will come for you when it has been arranged." He stormed off.

Liev smiled at Jason and motioned toward the nearby parlor. "Shall we have a seat and wait together?"

"Have you been watching me?" Jason asked after they sat.

"Of course."

"For how long?"

Liev shrugged. "A while."

"Is that why you went to the pool? To spy on me?"

"That was one of the reasons." Liev's hand settled on Jason's arm.

Jason pushed his hand away and looked around.

"Don't be angry," Liev said. "We have informants around Bern who keep an eye on the comings and goings of diplomatic staff. It's best for us to know who sees whom, and how often. We wouldn't normally keep such a close eye on you, except that you were seen with Franz, going to one of his meetings."

"How much do you know?"

"About Franz and his work? Or about you and Franz?" The twinkle was back in Liev's eyes, and Jason had the feeling he was being toyed with.

"Both."

"We know all about Franz's network. As for you and Franz, well—" he brushed his fingertips across the top of Jason's wrist. "—you should have drawn the curtains. Franz has large windows. Not that I minded."

Jason's stomach contracted. He looked at Liev, with his crooked smile and dimpled cheeks, and felt violated. He pulled away, and crossed his arms over his chest. He stared straight ahead. "I suppose everyone in the Abwehr knows, then." He felt cold inside.

"No—only a few, whose business it is to know such matters. Your secret is also my secret, you see."

"What do you mean?'"

Liev shrugged. "There are many small minds who would no longer see your value, or Franz's value, if they knew that you've had his cock up your ass."

The vulgarity, spoken outloud, hit Jason like a brick. His face flushed, and he sprang from his chair. Liev grabbed his wrist, but Jason tugged his arm away and fled.

Martin found Jason sitting alone at his desk, writing on a report. The front office was dark, the blinds drawn in all of the windows.

"Mr. Bachman."

Jason looked up toward where he stood at the entrance from the foyer. It took a second for Jason to recognize him in a pair of glasses and a false mustache. He motioned for Jason to join him. "Tell me what Herr Klein said to you."

"He said that Franz was in danger, that the Gestapo have him, and that he needed to speak with you right away."

"Did he ask for me by name?"

"No—he said he needed to speak with our agent who was working with Franz."

Martin's eyes narrowed. "And how did you know that was me?"

Jason swallowed. "I didn't for certain. I went to Mr. Witherspoon, he knew."

Martin did his best intimidating, unrelenting stare, as if to drill a hole through Jason's forehead and into his brain. "Did you ever mention my name to Herr Klein?"

"No, sir."

One small blessing. "What did Franz tell you about me?"

"Nothing, sir. I only know that he met with you, nothing else."

Something didn't add up. "How did Herr Klein know to come to you with this?"

Jason looked away. Martin grabbed him by the shoulders and shook him. "Tell me the truth!"

"He's followed me. He saw me with Franz."

"Damn!" Martin cursed under his breath. He stared at Jason, who looked back with wide, frightened eyes.

"What you don't know about this business could've gotten us both killed! That could have been a Gestapo agent. They play tricks like that, you know. That's how they catch their prey. And they're well-practiced."

Jason appeared to feel the intended intimidation—but only for a moment. Then he squared his shoulders and stared back into Martin's eyes. "The Gestapo wouldn't use a half-Jew, Mr. Schuller."

"How do you know he was a half-Jew?"

Jason hesitated for a second. "I guess I don't, not for certain. But I believe it."

"Why?"

Jason's eyes shifted. "He looked like one. Plus something more. Just a hunch, I suppose."

Martin was silent. Following your instincts was vital in this business—but occasionally fatal. And there was more Jason wasn't saying.

He spun on his heels and marched toward the rear of the embassy.

53

Martin recognized Liev Klein immediately—the incautious young man who'd watched the meeting that Franz had attended with Jason Bachman. And who had later spied on Franz's apartment from the opposite roof.

"Who sent you?" Martin demanded in German when they were alone in his office.

"A mutual acquaintance."

"Who sent you?" Martin repeated slowly, emphasizing each word.

The young Abwehr agent held his hands up, palms out. "No need to be hostile. You understand my need for caution. How am I to know if this conversation is being recorded? I give you a name, or even a code name, and your associates attempt an interception—like yesterday in Zurich."

So that hadn't escaped the Abwehr's notice. Martin was only a little surprised. "Why is it so important that I know the Gestapo have captured Franz?"

A coldness came to Liev Klein's eyes, which now appeared quite dark. "I would think you would be concerned, considering Franz Lemiel knows who you are. He's been in Gestapo custody for more than thirty-six hours. Sooner or later, everyone talks."

That was the trump card. "Why does the Abwehr care about protecting my identity?"

"If the Gestapo learns your identity, they will come for you. If they capture you...let's just say certain individuals in the Abwehr don't want you to talk."

Falkenkopf. "How do I know I can trust you?"

"You don't."

Martin nodded. That was true; still, he had doubts. "I was told your father is a Jew—what is a Mischling doing working for the Abwehr, given the racial policies of the current regime?"

"Admiral Canaris got us out of Germany after Kristalnacht. For that, I'm grateful. He's gotten many Jews into Switzerland."

"Gratitude? There's got to be more reason than that for you to serve a country that hates you."

Klein shrugged. "I am a German citizen. I serve the Fatherland."

"You are a *second-class* citizen, Mr. Klein. I have been inside Germany; I have seen how Mischlings are treated. Why would you serve a country that treats you poorly?"

Liev Klein's expression was unreadable. "How does the United States treat individuals who are half-Negro? A quarter-Negro? Are they not second-class citizens? And if the United States went to war, would they not fight for their country?"

Martin didn't reply. Of course they would. And the comparison wasn't entirely unfair, though it still stung.

Klein leaned forward, face flushed. "Remember what your Christian Bible tells you. 'Why do you see the speck that is in your neighbor's eye, but don't consider the plank in your own eye?' Hypocrisy is an ugly thing."

Martin suppressed the defensiveness welling up, forcing himself to focus on the task at hand. "I'm sure the people who sent you have a plan of action. Shall we discuss that?"

**

Jason answered the knock at his apartment door that evening, and was stunned to see the handsome Marine Corporal Lawrence standing in the hall, dressed in street clothes. Even out of uniform, he stood with his back rigidly straight, almost at attention.

"Mr. Bachman, I need for you to come with me, sir."

"What's going on?"

"I just need for you to come with me, please, sir."

"Do I need to bring anything with me?"

"I've only been told to get you, sir. I don't have any more information."

Jason closed the door without a word to his roommates, and followed the blond jarhead downstairs. A black Ford with diplomatic plates idled at the curb, and Corporal Lawrence opened the back door for Jason.

Darkness was falling, and the remnants of a deep blue twilight in the west faded to black as they drove toward the U.S. Embassy. Corporal Lawrence parked the car in the back, and opened Jason's door. "Come with me, sir."

They approached a back door that Jason hadn't known was there, hidden from the street by high hedgerows. Corporal Lawrence removed a key from the front pocket of his jeans and unlocked first the deadbolt, then the door lock. He held the door open for Jason, and closed and locked it behind them.

They stood in a small vestibule, illuminated by a single overhead bulb. To their right was another door, also dead-bolted. Directly in front of them was a staircase, and Corporal Lawrence began climbing.

The staircase was mostly dark. Each small landing was illuminated by a single overhead bulb. At each landing was another door, all bolted. They climbed three flights to the top, and Corporal Lawrence unlocked and opened the door.

Jason recognized the hallway. They stood at the opposite end from Amanda Overstreet's desk. The door they'd passed through was regressed on one wall, rendering it not visible from most of the hallway. He wondered if Amanda knew it was there.

Corporal Lawrence walked a few feet to the closest door, knocked three times in rapid succession, waited two seconds, and then did it again. The door opened and Martin Schuller appeared.

"Mr. Bachman, come in please."

Jason walked in, and Martin closed the door. "Congratulations, you've been assigned to an intelligence operation. Have a seat."

Once Jason sat in a chair in front of the desk, Martin crouched behind the desk and brought up a piece of electrical equipment, setting it atop the desk with a thud. "Do you know what this is?"

"It's a radio."

"A short-wave radio. Do you know how to work one of these?"

Jason shook his head.

"You're going to learn, now. I'm going to Germany tonight, and I'll transmit messages back at specific times. You're one of the few people who know what my role here is, so you've been assigned as my assistant. I'll send radio messages so that we can coordinate Franz's escape. You'll be my courier to Herr Klein while I'm away. Besides the two of us, the only person allowed to touch this radio or know of its existence is Corporal Lawrence out there—he can send messages in an emergency.

"Here's how you work it—switch this to receive. You turn this to tune it to different frequencies, just like on your radio at home. You'll switch this to transmit, and then you tap out your message here." He paused and looked Jason in the eyes. "You know Morse Code, don't you?"

Jason swallowed hard. "If I can remember it. I learned it in the Boy Scouts."

Martin suppressed his irritation. "I'll have Corporal Lawrence practice with you. My first transmission will be at four tomorrow morning. I'll transmit the phrase '*Cautious in all things*.' That sounds like this—" he tapped it out on the desktop. "Then you'll reply with the phrase '*examine and consider*,' which sounds like this—" he tapped it out on the desk. "That lets me know you're listening. I'll start transmitting my message. Do you have it?"

"I think so."

Martin exhaled hard. "I need you to know so. If you vary your response in the least, I won't know if it's you or the Gestapo answering, do you understand? It has to be exact. I need you to be certain you know it."

"Can I write it down then?"

"No!" Martin's voice was harsher than he intended; he saw the startled look on Jason's face and regretted his sharp response. *He's new to this.* "You must never write these things down. Paper can be taken, read by anyone. You *have* to memorize it. Now, let's go over it again."

Four hours later, Jason sat alone in Mr. Schuller's office. He was exhausted, and slumped in the chair. One thing was certain, he would never forget their code phrases if he lived to be ninety.

Sitting alone, inactive for the first time in hours, he had time to think over the events of the evening. Martin Schuller's life—perhaps even Franz's life—might depend on how well he recorded and passed along the messages sent back. His stomach tied itself into knots.

54

Frankfurt

Franz awoke with a start. He sat in total darkness, and had no idea if it was day or night. He didn't know how long he'd been here, but suspected it was longer than a day based on the number of times guards had brought him a plate of stale bread and dry cheese, and a glass of dirty water.

There was no toilet—only a bucket in the corner. He'd held out as long as he could before relieving himself, but eventually he'd had no choice. Now the closed space reeked of stale urine and human feces.

He shivered, and hugged his knees to his chest to keep warm. His buttocks had gone numb on the cold floor, but at least he could feel a little heat when his thighs came into contact with his chest.

One of the times they'd brought food, two guards had made him strip naked, and then threw buckets of frigid water on him. They'd taken his clothes when they left.

The most surprising thing about this whole experience was how little had happened. He'd arrived at the Gestapo office prepared to face torture immediately. They did beat him before throwing him into a basement cell with concrete walls, illuminated by a single bare bulb dangling from the ceiling—but then nothing. The only interaction he'd had, besides the icy bath, was the four or five times a guard brought him food and water with a single word—"Food."

The light would stay on for a while sometimes, then switch off and leave him in darkness. Perhaps this was their torture, softening him up with the isolation and sensory deprivation.

His mind drifted to Ilsa, as it had countless times in the last however many hours he'd been here. The shock of seeing her shot in the head while she lay defenseless on the ground—and by Major Volger, no less—had left him numb the entire drive to Frankfurt. The grief hit him hours later, alone in the cell, and he was wracked with sobs that left him curled up on the floor. That had long since passed, but as he sat now with his knees hugged against his body, a tear trickled down his right cheek and splashed onto his thigh.

The heavy thud of booted feet outside his cell, then the metallic clank of a key in the lock, followed by the grinding of metal on metal as the door slid open, sent a shiver through him. Bright light from the hallway flooded in, and he had to shield his eyes with his hand.

"Rise!" a guard ordered. Franz moved, but apparently not quickly enough, and sharp pain radiated from a boot kicking him in the right hip. "I said rise!"

Franz scrambled to his feet.

"Come with us!" the guard ordered, and marched into the hall. A second guard prodded Franz's shoulder with the butt of his rifle, then fell in behind him as they traversed the corridor.

They passed several steel doors before coming to one that stood open. The first guard stepped aside and stood next to the open doorway, while the guard behind Franz prodded him in the back with the butt of his rifle.

Franz entered a room with brick walls, illuminated by a single naked light bulb dangling from the ceiling.

Major Volger sat in a metal chair behind a long steel table. A second officer in SS black sat in another chair, a pad of paper sitting on the small table in front of him. This officer had ridden with them in Volger's Mercedes after he was captured.

A shiver ran through him at the sight of the umbrella stand near Volger's chair, with its large wooden clubs and steel bars. A cabinet hung on the far wall, and a metal head-clasp extended upward from the end of the table. Leather wrist straps were bolted to the sides midway, and leather ankle straps hung from the other end. In the corner sat a large padlocked box. Franz didn't want to think about what frightful items might be inside that box.

The guard prodded Franz toward the far wall, where a pair of shackles hung from the ceiling. He positioned Franz with his back to the wall, raised his arms one at a time and clasped them in the shackles, so that he stood with his arms raised slightly higher than parallel with the floor.

"That will be all, sergeant," Volger said.

After the door closed, Volger stood. He slapped a riding crop against his palm several times as he took slow, deliberate steps toward Franz.

"Good evening, Franz," Volger said, a wicked smile on his lips. "Yes, it is evening, in case you were wondering. It is eleven-thirty. I'm sorry to have kept you waiting so long."

You're not sorry at all, you bastard!

"Have you been comfortable? No? That's a pity. At least you've had a bath." An evil gleam came to Volger's eye at his own joke. "We can end all of this right now, you know—if you're willing to cooperate with us."

Volger pointed with his riding crop at the other officer, who still sat at the table. "This is Captain Axethelm, of the SD. He will be observing."

Axethelm didn't move. He stared at Franz, his cool blue eyes never seeming to blink.

Volger stepped closer. "We want the names of all of your contacts, in Germany and France."

Franz kept his mouth clamped shut, and stared back at Volger.

Volger waited a few seconds, then swung the crop across Franz's abdomen, leaving a red welt across his midsection.

Franz cried out and tried to double over, but the shackles kept him upright.

"You're not being cooperative, Franz. I asked you for the names of your contacts in Germany and France."

Franz kept his eyes downcast this time, focusing on the shine on Volger's black boots.

The back of Volger's hand slammed into Franz's chin, sending his face flying up. He felt a painful crack in the back of his neck at the sudden force, and he tasted blood in his mouth; he'd bitten his tongue.

Volger was close now—close enough that Franz could smell the sourness of his breath, feel the heat of it on his cheek. "I'm going to keep asking. Every time you fail to answer, the punishment will get worse. Now, tell us the names!"

Franz kept his gaze to the side. A nauseating pain suddenly ripped through him and his vision went black for a few seconds, as Volger's knee slammed into his unprotected testicles.

Franz had no idea if he'd screamed or not. His ears rang, and he couldn't hear anything else. He was dimly aware of Volger repeating the question. Then came the searing pain of the crop whipping against his left shoulder and down his chest.

He steeled his resolve. Others might talk, but he would not.

He was jolted then by the splash of another bucket of cold water. An involuntary shiver racked his body, and Volger chuckled.

"Don't think you can avoid the pain by passing out, Franz. We have plenty of cold water with which to wake you up."

*

A sadistic pleasure oozed through Rudolph Volger while watching the pain he inflicted on Franz's naked form. There was an intense thrill to this, and his cock twitched every time he lashed Franz with the crop.

He'd never had the opportunity to take over a torture from the Gestapo. While Colonel Schakenberg had insisted that Volger and Axethelm be in charge of the interrogation, Volger had taken it upon himself to take it over. This was personal.

Soon he gave up all pretext of asking questions, and indulged himself in the beating. The thought of what lay ahead was even more thrilling.

After a while, he asked Captain Axethelm to unlock the prisoner. The captain unlocked the shackles, and Franz slumped to the ground. "Stand him in the corner," Volger ordered.

Captain Axethelm put his hands under Franz's arms, and hauled him off the ground, shoving him face-first into a corner. Then he stood back.

Major Volger retrieved a wooden club from the stand—the smallest of the three available—and sauntered toward where Franz stood, bare buttocks exposed. He hauled back and swung the club at those buttocks, landing it with a crack that doubled the young man over. Volger couldn't help but smile at the bright red welt he'd left, so vivid and exposed.

"Stand up!" he ordered, then swung the club again. This time Franz crumpled to the ground, his knees beneath him. Volger kicked him in the ass, and brought the club down on the middle of his back. He grinned when Franz screamed.

"Put him back in the shackles," he instructed Captain Axethelm.

While Franz was shackled again, Major Volger strode to the padlocked box and took the key from his pocket. He opened the box and removed an electric shock machine. He set it on the end of the table in front of Franz, and let it sit there for a moment in plain view.

It took a minute for his victim to focus on the machine, and then his eyes grew wide with fright. Volger switched the machine on. Its hum reverberated off the brick walls.

He put his gloves on, took one of the wires in his hand, and stepped close to Franz. "How did you know my cook?"

"I didn't know your cook."

Volger touched Franz' side with the end of the wire, sending a jolt of electricity through him.

"You were in touch with my former cook, Franz. How did you come into contact with him?"

"I don't know! I never knew your cook."

Volger touched Franz's bare hip with the end of the wire, and enjoyed the cry of pain that escaped Franz's lips.

"If you didn't know my cook, how did you get those photographs?" He held the wire between Franz's thighs, barely an inch below the testicles.

Franz stared into Volger's eyes. "What are you afraid of, Major?"

"It is not I who should be afraid, Franz." He touched the wire to the back of Franz's scrotum, and leered as the young man screamed and dropped his head. At the sight of the tears streaming from Franz's eyes, his stomach fluttered with pleasure. "Tell me how you got those photographs."

Franz lifted his head and gazed at Volger through watery eyes. "You are so full of hate. Hate for the Jews, hate for dissidents—but mostly hate of yourself."

Volger slapped Franz's face with the back of his gloved hand.

Franz turned back to him and stared directly into his eyes, his gaze steady now. "It's yourself that you hate the most, isn't it Major? You hate the queer that you are on the inside."

Volger drew back his fist and punched Franz across the jaw. "Shut up, you filth!" He spun toward the door, his face hot with rage. "Guards!"

The door slammed open, and two guards stormed in. "Strap the prisoner to the table."

Axethelm and the guards hauled Franz onto the table, face up, and strapped down his ankles and wrists. Volger himself fastened the head clasp across Franz's forehead.

"Leave us." The guards exited, and Volger turned to Axethelm. "You too."

The captain looked startled. "Major! I should be here, recording the prisoner's answers."

"Leave us! That's an order, Captain."

Axethelm came to attention. "Yes, sir!" He marched from the room, slamming the door behind him.

"This could all end now, Franz," Volger said, the soothing tone of his voice making Franz's skin crawl. He ran his fingertips down the length of Franz's torso, sending shivers through him, and then resting them on his left hip. "All you have to do is tell me what I want to know. You're going to tell me sooner or later; and the sooner you do, the less painful it will be. We might even be able to spare your good looks." The major reached up and stroked Franz's stubbled cheek.

He strode around the table. "And I can do far more than end the pain, Franz. I can make sure you are rewarded for your cooperation. Change is coming to Switzerland. You could still be part of the future, it's not too late. I know movement leaders there. They would be grateful to you for any assistance in identifying enemies of the Reich. I can negotiate with them on your behalf. I'm sure they will have tangible ways of showing you their appreciation."

Franz said nothing, gritting his teeth against the pain.

Volger took hold of Franz's chin, turning his face toward him. "I have that power, you know. I can negotiate great rewards for you. After Wednesday, they will owe me more favors than you can imagine."

After Wednesday? What was he up to? Franz's mind raced. What did they have planned?

Volger's face hovered inches above his, and he stroked Franz's cheeks and chin, stared into his eyes and spoke in a soothing tone. "You'll be able to go home. I can take you myself. We'll help each other out, you see."

Franz averted his eyes and turned his face the little that he could in the clamp.

Volger grabbed his chin hard, and yanked his face back. He forced Franz's mouth open with his fingers, then leaned in and gave him a crushing kiss, forcing his tongue down deep into Franz's mouth.

Franz bit down. The Major cried out and jumped back, blood dripping down the corner of his mouth. His face contorted, and his pulled back his hand and slapped the back across Franz's face, then the palm, and then backhand again. He slapped him over and over, faster and faster.

Franz felt blood trickling from his forehead where the metal strap rubbed his skin each time his face moved with a slap.

Only after Franz's face was bright red and purple did Volger stop. He took two live wires from the shock machine and jabbed them into Franz, anywhere and everywhere—stomach, thighs, armpits, nipples, soles of the feet, penis—anywhere he thought of in the moment.

Franz's screams grew louder with each shock. Volger's erection grew ever stiffer, and a grin spread across his lips.

Monday,
October 13, 1941

55

Frankfurt

He marched into the lobby of the Gestapo office with heavy steps, a tall, broad-shouldered blond wearing a stern expression and the black uniform and hat of an SS officer, with the insignia of *Gruppenfuhrer*—Groups Leader, an SS General—on each shoulder.

Martin strode through the empty lobby, his boot-falls echoing, and stopped before the high wooden desk where the on-duty guard— the only other person in the room—slept slumped back in his wooden chair, his mouth hanging open and drool dribbling onto his cheek. The clock on the wall read one-thirty-five.

Martin removed the Walther pistol from his hip holster, and banged the butt-end on the desk, causing the guard to jump awake. He hurriedly wiped the drool from the corner of his mouth and sat up straight.

Martin made his scowl and his voice as stern as he could. "Do you sleep on duty often, sergeant? Is Gestapo security always this lax?"

"No, sir! It's just—I mean—Heil Hitler!"

Martin scowled so deeply it made his forehead ache. "My name is General Max Stengel, with the SS in Strasburg. I have come for a prisoner you have in your possession, who is wanted for terrorist activities in Alsace. Here are my orders to take him."

The sergeant lifted a pair of glasses off the desktop and shoved them onto his nose. He took the forged papers that Captain Wolfe had given to Martin at the border crossing, and appeared to be reading them in great haste the orders to take Prisoner Franz Lemiel, a Swiss national, in shackles to Strasburg for questioning there in relation to "terrorist attacks on military transport trains."

Liev Klein had given Martin the SS uniform and identity papers at their rendezvous outside of Bern. Making Martin's fake identity Alsatian had been ingenious—the accent and dialect were so close to those of Switzerland as to be indistinguishable to most people inside Germany.

Klein drove him to an isolated border-crossing bridge over the Rhine somewhere between Basel and Solothurn. He had pulled to the side of the road a kilometer shy of the border, exited the Mercedes and instructed Martin to drive it across the bridge, where his escort would be waiting on the other side of the border check.

Martin crossed the bridge, and gave the border control guards the story that he had been in Switzerland on official SS business, and had to get to Frankfurt immediately. The guards had not questioned the story, not even asked him to get out of the car; merely stamped his forged German passport, reminded him to place the black-out shields over the headlights, and waved him through.

A kilometer north of the border a figure stepped out of the brush and flagged him down. Captain Wolfe opened the driver's-side door, motioned for Martin to slide over, and took the wheel. He drove them to the A5 Autobahn—the Fuhrer's pride and joy—and they raced north on the deserted superhighway at one-hundred-eighty kilometers per hour.

They made it to Frankfurt in just over two hours.

Now Martin glared at the Gestapo sergeant behind the desk. "Who is in charge here?"

The sergeant looked up, his eyes shifting. "Captain Rohrman is in charge tonight, General—but the prisoner you want isn't in our custody."

"He is not here? When did you release him? You idiots!"

The sergeant's eyes grew wider. "No, he's here, General. What I meant is that he's not in Gestapo custody—one of your SS officers is in authority over him, a Major Volger, sir."

"Where is this Major Volger?"

The sergeant gulped. Perspiration beaded his forehead and upper lip. "Major Volger is here now, sir. He and Captain Axethelm—also of the SS—are, um, interrogating the prisoner as we speak."

"Have Major Volger bring me the prisoner at once!" Martin barked the order in a heavy staccato, as these Nazis were fond of doing.

The sergeant's hands trembled, but his voice grew steadier. "I'm sorry sir, but we've been ordered not to disturb them for any reason."

Martin snarled at him. "I don't care what you've been told, sergeant. I have orders to take that prisoner back to Alsace tonight, and I want him brought to me immediately."

"I'll have to get Captain Rohrman for you, General," the sergeant said, looking relieved to call on the shift commander to do the interruption.

"Then get him here now." Martin jabbed his finger onto the desk top.

"Yes, sir, General!"

Captain Rohrman bustled into the lobby, having hurriedly tucked in his shirt and straightened his tie before leaving his office. He had never encountered an SS General, and never expected one at this hour.

The unknown General thrust his orders at Rohrman without ceremony as the captain hurried to salute. "Captain, I need for you to take me to this Major Volger immediately, so that I can retrieve my prisoner and take him back to Strasburg. I understand you are the only one who can interrupt them for me?"

"Um, yes, General, that's correct." Rohrman skimmed the orders, noting the name of the prisoner as that Swiss man the SS had brought in on Saturday morning. Regaining his composure, he handed the orders back to the SS General, gave him a curt nod, and motioned toward a door. "Come with me please, sir."

Martin followed the captain through a doorway and down a flight of stairs. At the bottom, a small room opened into a narrow corridor with concrete block walls. A guard at a desk stood and saluted as they walked by, and Rohrman returned the salute without pausing.

A man in a black SS uniform leaned against the wall midway down the hall, his arms crossed and an irritated look on his face. One look at the insignia on Martin's shoulders and he snapped to attention.

Captain Rohrman cleared his throat. "Captain Axethelm, this is General—" he looked to Martin.

"Stengel."

Rohrman continued. "General Stengel. He has orders to take Mr. Lemiel to Strasburg tonight."

A stunned look crossed Axethelm's face, but then his expression went back to military attention. "Major Volger is interrogating that prisoner as we speak, General."

"So I understand. Bring him out here at once, Captain."

Captain Axethelm opened his mouth as if he might protest, so Martin repeated louder, "At *once*, Captain!"

"Yes, sir!" Axethelm took two steps to one of the steel doors, and rapped on it several times.

There was a shuffling sound inside, then the metallic scrape of the lock opening, and the door swung open. An angry face thrust out, and hissed, "What is the meaning of this, Captain?"

"General Stengel is here for the prisoner, Major." Captain Axethelm delivered the news in a flat tone, then stepped aside, remaining at attention.

Major Volger looked toward Martin with a startled expression, then stood at attention and saluted. Martin returned the salute, then thrust his orders at Volger. "You have a prisoner in your custody, a Swiss national who goes by the alias of Emmentaler. I have orders to take him back to Strasburg, where he is wanted for acts of sabotage and terrorism against the Reich."

Volger closed the door behind him before taking the papers from Martin's hand and examining them. "These orders are from Berlin—from the office of Reichsfuhrer Himmler himself."

Martin wasn't sure if Volger's tone was impressed, or suspicious.

Volger looked up and stared into Martin's eyes. "Forgive me my ignorance, General—but why is the Reichsfuhrer's office concerned with this prisoner?"

Martin held Volger's gaze with a haughty expression. "This prisoner, this Emmentaler, is a notorious terrorist—a *leader* of terrorists, not only in Alsace, but also in Occupied France. He is a most wanted figure, Major."

"He is also wanted in Frankfurt."

"We are aware of no terrorist activity in Frankfurt, Major. Certainly none that would compare to what we face."

Volger broke the stare. "I'm sure you wouldn't mind, General, if I had a bit more time with the prisoner before you take him. I am close to getting information from him, information about underground networks here in Germany."

Martin stiffened, and stretched taller. He raised his voice to a near-shout. "I suppose that is meant to imply that Alsace is not Germany?"

Volger's face went pale. "Certainly not, sir! I meant no disrespect. I meant only to contrast our underground networks here with Occupied France, not with Alsace."

Martin curled his lip in a sneer. "I am not concerned with your underground networks here in Hesse, Major. I *am* concerned with the underground networks in Alsace, and in Occupied France. I am taking this Emmentaler back to Strasburg so that we can break those networks once and for all. Do I have your cooperation? Or do I have to report to the Reichsfuhrer's office that Frankfurt was uncooperative?"

Volger stood at attention. "That won't be necessary, General."

"Stand aside, Major."

Volger hesitated a second, then nodded in acquiescence and opened the door.

Martin strode through without waiting for Volger. He approached the side of the table, looked over the naked body of the prisoner, with its numerous dark bruises and bright red burn marks, then stared down into Franz's face. "Are you the prisoner Franz Lemiel, called Emmentaler?"

Franz's eyes registered recognition, and he nodded the tiny bit that he was able to in the head strap. "My name is Franz Lemiel," he croaked, his voice barely audible.

Martin turned toward Major Volger, who stood in the open doorway.

"Get him dressed and shackled. I want him in my car in five minutes." And he strode from the room.

*

Volger turned to Captain Axethelm. "You heard the General. Get the prisoner's clothes and get him dressed. And Captain—" he reached out and clasped his hand on Axethelm's shoulder as he turned, and said in a quieter voice—"call Berlin as soon as the prisoner is on his way upstairs. Check out this General Stengel from Strasburg."

"Yes, sir, Major." Captain Axethelm's faint smile said that he understood.

Franz kept his eyes down while the Gestapo guards escorted him out the door and down the steps to the waiting Mercedes. Walking was painful due to the burns on the soles of his feet, but he gritted his teeth and tried not to limp.

Mr. Schuller's voice ordered them to put him in the back seat, but Franz didn't look at him. He shuffled his feet, as much from the pain as from any effort to not look relieved. Only after he slid to the far side of the car, and Mr. Schuller took the seat next to him and closed the door, did he dare to look up.

"Thank you," he whispered.

The car pulled away, and he allowed himself to slump back.

For a moment all he could do was sit there, limp as a rotten cabbage leaf. Then the emotion flooded over him, and he began to tremble. Seconds later, he was sobbing in relief.

56

Bern

The shortwave radio crackled into life at precisely four o'clock. Jason recorded the Morse code signals, and once the expected salutation had finished, he tapped out the requisite response. It took longer than it should have, but he was terrified of making a mistake, and tapped out the code deliberately.

The radio sat silent for a few seconds, and then jumped to life as Mr. Schuller's message came across.

Jason jotted down the message, several lines, then rushed to the nearby copy of Kafka's *Amerika* in the original German, sitting open to the first page. His finger ran to and fro, picking out letters as quickly as he could and writing them down.

Several moments passed before he completed the decryption—several agonizing moments. Mr. Schuller had drilled into his head the absolute importance of keeping the radio connection no longer than fifteen minutes. Less if possible. The Gestapo operated three tracking stations—at Augsburg, Nurmburg, and in Brest, France—which homed in on any unauthorized radio signal. Coordinating their goniometers, they could angle the precise location of wireless broadcasts in fifteen to twenty minutes. They could determine the general vicinity even sooner.

Painfully aware that each passing second placed Mr. Schuller— and Franz—in greater danger, Jason hurried to finish the translation. Finishing the final sentence, he sprinted back to the radio, switched to transmit, and tapped out the phrase that would indicate the message had been received and understood.

Switching back to receive, a brief series of clicks told him Mr. Schuller was signing off.

Jason slumped in the chair and breathed a heavy sigh of relief. He became aware that the back of his shirt was soaked with sweat, and he felt suddenly chilled. He glanced at the clock—nine minutes had passed.

He'd done it.

The first part, anyway. There was no time to relax. He read through the message a dozen times to be sure he had it memorized. Then he threw on a dark gray overcoat and bolted out of Mr. Schuller's office, pausing only to lock the door and pocket the key. He sprinted down the back stairs and rushed out the door.

He walked toward the hedgerow a few feet away, and pulled a brown bicycle from where it was hidden in the bushes. He leapt on and pedaled away.

The streets were deserted. *No one out at this hour except criminals. And spies.* The thought both thrilled and terrified him. The night was cold, but he found himself sweating in spite of the chill.

The streets were deserted as he sped past darkened buildings. It was slightly uphill, and he was out of breath when he reached the Kirchenfeldbrucke—the bridge over the Aare between the Old Quarter and the Kirchenfeld district, where the embassy was located.

He dismounted at the start of the bridge, and walked the bike a hundred meters toward the center of it. He glanced over the railing at the dark waters of the fast-flowing Aare, more than one hundred feet below. He instinctively stepped off the sidewalk and waited at the edge of the street.

He only had to wait a moment. Liev Klein stepped out of the shadows of the nearby column and joined him in the street. He wore a long black trench-coat, buttoned up to his neck. He smiled and said in English, "I've been looking forward to seeing you again."

"I have a message for you, from the wireless."

Liev's face grew serious. "Were you followed?"

"No."

"Go on."

Switching to German, Jason repeated the message verbatim.

"Excellent. I'll finalize the arrangements. We'll have Franz out of Germany by first light. He'll be safe. Then perhaps the three of us can spend some time together." He put his hand on Jason's upper arm and held it there.

Jason's mouth set in a thin line. "I'm not sure that will be possible." He gave the round-faced young agent a curt nod, and turned the bike around. He jumped on and pedaled to the Old Quarter.

Turning off the bridge at Kochergasse, heading west toward home, he nodded at Corporal Lawrence standing watch in the shadow of an alley entrance. The marine touched his forehead with two fingers, the all-clear signal, and disappeared into the shadows.

57

Frankfurt

"You should be shot! Both of you, shot!" Spittle few from Colonel Schakenberg's mouth in his rage.

Captain Axethelm flinched, but Major Volger was unperturbed. "If he had been a real general, and we had forced him to wait hours for verification from Berlin, *he* would have had us shot. What would you have had us do differently?"

"You should have called me immediately!"

"We have issued an all-points bulletin for Emmentaler's escape. Every Gestapo office in the Reich is on alert for him, and every border control station."

Colonel Schakenberg glared at Volger, and pointed a menacing finger at his face. "Your failure is unacceptable. I could have you stripped of your commission, and hauled off to Buchenwald with a pink triangle."

Volger's stomach tumbled, but he kept his expression blank and said nothing.

Schakenberg turned away from him. "As it is, your mission in Switzerland is too critical, and there is no time to replace you. Your Russian agents will be transported today. They are expendable, of course—but you must succeed in killing General Guisan. All depends on that man's death." He spun back around, and took three steps toward Volger, stopping a foot from him. "If you fail in your mission to kill Guisan, I will shoot you myself, you miserable pervert."

Volger didn't flinch. "I won't fail, Colonel."

"You had best not."

"I am due in Zurich this afternoon, for a meeting with the Gauleiter."

Schakenberg waved his hand. "Yes, you are dismissed. Your visa is waiting on your desk."

"I requested two visas."

Colonel Schakenberg's mouth pursed in distaste. "*Your* visa is waiting for you, Major. Your focus should be on your mission for the Reich, not on your perversions."

The betrayal was a punch in the gut. "My understanding is that I shall be in Switzerland for some time. I'm sure the Gauleiter would approve. After all, he granted Michael Kaim a passport. Or were you not aware of that, Colonel?"

Schakenberg's lips pursed tighter. "Then perhaps you should take that up with the Gauleiter himself. You are dismissed, Major."

Bavaria

Captain Wolfe drove through the woods for a long time, and Martin wondered where they were being taken. They had kept to back roads, making two stops—once at a derelict barn far off the road so that Martin could make his four AM transmission, and the second time at a phone booth in a small town where Captain Wolfe made a brief call. He volunteered no information about that call, and Martin didn't ask.

They rode in silence, eventually coming to a crossroads with a directional sign indicating Sipplingen was ahead four kilometers. Instead, Captain Wolfe turned onto a narrow and deeply rutted dirt road through dense woodland. It was a dark and bumpy ride, and the car's springs groaned with the strain. Numerous times the undercarriage scraped on something, and Martin worried they might break down in the middle of nowhere.

The road sloped downward, and after several minutes the woods fell away. A deep blackness stretched before them.

"Lake Konstanz," Wolfe said.

The Mercedes pulled to a stop on a patch of gravel, and the landward side of a wooden pier appeared at the edge of the dull beams cast by the headlights through their slitted blackout covers. Wolfe flashed the beams three times, paused three seconds, and then flashed them two more times.

A moment later a red bulb flashed in the same sequence about thirty feet out, briefly illuminating a wooden speedboat tied to the end of the pier.

"Our escort to the Swiss side," Wolfe explained, killing the engine. "Come quickly."

The three of them exited the car, and Wolfe removed a valise and an attaché case from the trunk. "I'm coming with you. My job is to see you safely back to Bern. Someone else will retrieve the car. Now come, quickly. We have only an hour until first light."

"You're late!" a voice called from the boat as they hurried down the pier, its Swiss accent thick. A small red and white Swiss flag fluttered in the breeze off the stern. Martin figured he was probably a local entrepreneur in one of the resort villages on the south shore of the lake, smuggling people out of the Reich for cash.

The boat cast off, and steered out into the lake without the benefit of lights. The cloud cover was thin, and the quarter moon cast enough light that the outlines of the shore were dimly visible.

The boat operator eased up the throttle, accelerating without excessive engine noise. Soon they were in open water, and he opened the throttle all the way, surging forward. Cold spray dampened their faces, but no one uttered a complaint.

A neck of land to their right fell away, and now they could see clusters of lights in the distance on the Swiss side. About five miles, Martin judged—seven kilometers or so. They should be there in ten minutes.

A few moments later, the boat operator switched on the red light that stood atop a short pole in the center of the boat.

"We should be safe now," Wolfe said to Martin and Franz.

Martin cocked his head, straining to hear above the whine of the boat's engine. He wasn't sure at first, but he continued listening. Yes! There was a low rumble to their right, drawing closer. He tapped Wolfe on the shoulder.

"I think we're not alone!" he shouted over the engine. He pointed his thumb to the right. "I hear another boat, a big one."

Wolfe shook his head. "It's only your imagination. Don't worry! There are no patrols this far out. Impossible to know exactly where the border is, and neither side will risk an intrusion into the other's waters."

Almost on cue, a bright spotlight broke the darkness and illuminated the water off the port bow. A quick adjustment, and the beam locked onto their boat.

"Halt!" a Bavarian voice boomed from a loudspeaker. "Halt at once, or we will open fire."

"What are they doing out here?" the boat operator shouted.

"Faster!" Wolfe shouted back.

"This is top speed!"

The sound of machine gun fire erupted from the deck of the patrol boat, and numerous flashes illuminated the railing of its deck a dozen feet above the surface of the water.

"Down!" Wolfe shouted, but Martin and Franz had already hit the floor. The boat operator scrunched as low as he could in the seat and still be able to see over the prow.

Captain Wolfe had his Walther pistol aimed over the side of the boat, and he fired off carefully-aimed shots. Martin unsheathed his Walther and crawled across the floor to join him.

Machine gun fire from the patrol boat splashed in the water mere feet from the speedboat's bow. The first round had been warning shots, and now they were aiming closer. Martin fired at the center of the spotlight beam, but the choppiness of the water shook his aim.

His fourth shot hit the light's operator. The beam lurched away, upward and to the right, just as another round of machinegun fire strafed across the back end of the speedboat, sending splinters flying.

Franz cried out, and Martin looked over his shoulder to see the young man gripping his right leg below the knee.

It was a moment before someone else on the patrol boat took control of the search light. Its beam moved back and forth across the water, looking for the fleeing speedboat. The boat operator swerved dozens of times, always avoiding the beam.

The lights of a Swiss town grew steadily closer. It couldn't be more than a mile, Martin estimated. They had to be in Swiss waters by now.

"Hang on, we're nearly there," he assured Franz, patting his hand and feeling the thick wet blood oozing from beneath Franz's fingers.

Another spotlight sprang from in front of them, and locked onto the German patrol boat. "Munsterlingen police! You are in Swiss waters. Desist at once!" Two rifle shots echoed as they fired into the air in warning.

The police boat was smaller than the German patrol boat, but nonetheless the rumble of the German boat's engine diminished as it throttled down, and Martin glanced back to see it turning away.

The boat operator thrust a flashlight at Martin and ordered him to shine it on the Swiss flag at the stern. Martin did as instructed.

The police boat commanded them to continue to the port. "We'll follow you in."

Several minutes later, they stood on the pier at Munsterlingen, while several police officers searched the boat's compartments for smuggled contraband. The police captain interviewed the four men, asking to see their passports. He cast a suspicious eye at Martin, who still wore an SS uniform.

Wolfe stepped between them and flashed a German diplomatic passport. "These two men are under my protection. That one is a Swiss national who was tortured by the Gestapo on a false denunciation. This officer helped him escape, at great personal risk. That is why we came under fire."

The police captain faced Franz. "Can you prove that you are a Swiss national?"

Franz shrugged. He was pale, and wobbled as he leaned against Martin. "The Gestapo took my passport and my identity papers. I no longer have them."

The police captain noticed the blood soaking Franz's right pant leg from the knee down. "Have you been shot?"

Franz nodded.

"We'll get you to the hospital." He motioned for his men. Two of them carried Franz to shore.

Franz grew disoriented as they placed him into the back of a police car, and his head began to spin. Then he blacked out.

58

Bern

Martin had never been so glad to be back at the U.S. Embassy.

It had been a chaotic morning. At first he'd wondered how long the Munsterlingen police would detain him. While Captain Wolfe's diplomatic passport made him untouchable, Martin was carrying a German passport with no visa to visit Switzerland. Theoretically they could send him back to Germany, or detain him indefinitely.

Fortunately, Wolfe had insisted that "General Stengel" was under his protection. "It is of vital importance that I get this man to our embassy in Bern."

The police captain had looked unconvinced. "If he helped a prisoner escape from the Gestapo, why would the German embassy want him?"

"That is an internal German matter," Wolfe replied, his voice cold. "If you do not release him to me, I will file a formal complaint with the Ministry of Justice."

That had worked.

Martin had to give Wolfe grudging respect for the efficient way he handled everything. Within ten minutes of leaving the police station, Martin was back in civilian clothes. Not his own clothes, but exactly his size. And Wolfe also gave him an official-looking visa to visit Switzerland, in the name of Martin Stengel. "In appreciation for your service," he whispered as he slipped it into Martin's hand. "Keep this in your German passport until you get back to Bern."

"You're going back to Bern as well?"

"Yes. But best if we travel there separately."

"What about Emmentaler?"

"He's been taken to the local hospital. He is no longer our concern."

"He is *my* concern," Martin said.

Wolfe nodded. "Then we shall leave him to you."

"And if what he told us is correct?"

Wolfe touched the rim of his fedora. "I shall be in touch."

Dawn was breaking when Martin purchased a train ticket to Bern, and found a phone booth. Ron Witherspoon wouldn't be in his office this early, so Martin asked the operator to call his home.

"I have no time to explain, Ron, but I have an agent in the hospital at Frauenfeld in Thurgau, and I need him transferred to the hospital in Bern—this morning, if possible. Can you arrange that for me?"

"I'll see what I can do."

"This is important. His name is Franz Lemiel. I need him in a private room. And keep this as quiet as you can."

"I'll take care of it."

Martin arrived at the U.S. Embassy a few minutes before ten, and went straight to Witherspoon's office.

"It's been arranged," Witherspoon said. "Herr Lemiel will be at the hospital here in Bern within the hour, a private room as you requested, paid for by the embassy, all hush-hush."

"Thanks, Ron."

Martin went to his office and found Jason Bachman sitting at his desk. Jason's eyes lit up when Martin entered.

"Is Franz safe?"

The eagerness in his voice bespoke more than professional concern, and Martin fought back irritation. "The mission was a success." He immediately regretted his cold tone, and softened his expression. "Your efforts were invaluable in our success, Jason. Thank you."

A cloud seemed to come over Jason's eyes, and he nodded with a blank expression before walking out.

Martin stopped him at the door. "Herr Lemiel was shot in the leg. He's here in Bern, at the hospital." Jason's face lined with worry. Martin felt sorry for the young man. "If you speak to no one about any of this, you may go see him this afternoon."

A thin smile crossed Jason's lips. "Thank you, Mr. Schuller."

As soon as Martin closed his office door, he plopped onto his chair and exhaled hard. He allowed himself a moment to relax. He stared up at the ceiling, lost in thought. Then he picked up his phone and gave the operator a phone number in Zurich.

The woman who answered at the Polytechnic said that Miss Rubenstein was in the lab. Martin told her it was a family emergency, and asked the woman to interrupt her.

Sonia's voice was breathless when she answered.

"Sonia, this is Martin Schuller."

"What is the meaning of this? I was told it was a family emergency."

Martin ignored her hostility. "It is, of a sort. I believe Franz Lemiel is like family to you. He's been hurt, shot in the leg. I've arranged for him to have a private room at the Bern hospital."

"Shot? Is this your doing? Did you have him do some work for you that got him shot? What have you done?"

Her accusation stung. He grew irritated with himself for reacting so personally, and lashed out. "He was *not* working for me at the time; he was doing his own work. I was the one who rescued him." *And I was the one who captured your father's killers.*

The line was silent, and he regretted his harsh tone. "I just thought you'd want to know."

"Thank you."

"And one more thing—for Franz's safety, please don't mention this to anyone until he's recovered and left the hospital."

There was a pause before she answered. "I understand. Thank you for calling."

The line clicked off.

Rhine River crossing, German-Swiss border

Rudolph Volger crossed the border at Hohentengen am Hochrhein shortly after noon. The border control on the German side made only a cursory inspection of his exit visa, passport, and identity papers. The border officer gave a suspicious look to Michael Kaim, though, seated in the passenger seat, and took his time examining his passport. At length he addressed himself to Volger.

"For what purpose are you taking this *Mischling* into Switzerland?" He said the word as if it were a disease.

"My nephew has never been to Switzerland," Volger lied smoothly.

"Your nephew?"

"Yes."

"You are an SS officer, and you have a nephew who is a *Mischling*?"

Volger feigned embarrassment. "Yes. You see, my sister was seduced by a Jew when she was much too young and I to know what they are like. He left her, of course, as soon as he learned she was with child. Our parents threw her out, but I let her stay with me and my wife. We cared for her and the child."

The border control officer gave him a knowing nod. "You are a most charitable man, Major." And he waved their car through.

On the Swiss side of the river, the customs official at Kaiserstuhl examined their papers and asked how long they planned to stay on holiday in Switzerland.

"Through the end of the week."

"Where are you going?"

"Zurich, then Bern."

He stamped their passports and waved them through.

Volger smiled at Michael as they drove away. "I'm sure you'll love it in Switzerland, Michael. We'll be staying a while. I have work to do, and after that Switzerland will come home to the Reich. I expect to earn a post here, and we'll have a home together in Bern. We'll be very happy." He placed his hand on the boy's thigh and gave it an affectionate squeeze.

The sign at the entrance to Highway 7 announced thirty-six kilometers to Zurich. Volger pressed his foot against the accelerator, and the black Mercedes sped forward.

Bern

Martin's phone rang, and he picked it up before the first ring had completed.

"A Mr. Mueller from the German embassy is calling for you, Mr. Schuller," Amanda Overstreet said. "He said you're expecting his call."

"Put him through." There was a click as the call connected. "What have you got for me?" Martin asked without preamble.

"Emmentaler was right—Volger is in Switzerland," Captain Wolfe said. "He crossed the border at Kaiserstuhl twenty minutes ago. He told Swiss customs that he was bound for Zurich, and then Bern. We have informants in both cities watching for him."

"What will you do when you spot him?"

"Keep him under surveillance."

Martin doubted the Abwehr would share much about what their surveillance uncovered. He thanked Wolfe and hung up.

He unrolled a map of Switzerland on his desk, and ran his finger along the border with Germany until he located Kaiserstuhl seventy-five kilometers east of Basel. It was possible that the alleged stop in Zurich was a diversion, and he could be bound directly for Bern. But there was no direct route. He traced his finger along the roads that would connect that crossing to Bern via Aarau, Zoflingen, and Solothurn—about one-hundred-forty-five kilometers. Surely, if he were coming directly to Bern, he would have crossed the border at Basel or someplace near there. That would be half the distance.

Of course, the "Gauleiter" was in Zurich.

Martin grabbed his coat and sprinted out the door.

59

Zurich

"I trust you know how to work one of these?" Ernst Zubler said as he handed the 1940 Model Tokarev semi-automatic rifle—the SVT-40—to Rudolph Volger.

"I've been trained on them, yes."

"Excellent! It wouldn't do for General Guisan to get assassinated with a German rifle, would it? We must make it believable."

"I thought you said the police would be on our side."

"Relax, Major. I have been assured that every policeman who will be at the entrance to the Bundeshaus on Wednesday at noon is one of ours. But we mustn't pretend that FedPol won't call out its best inspectors. The autopsy *must* show that the general was killed by a bullet from a Soviet rifle."

"How am I to escape before the inspectors arrive?"

"You'll have five minutes. That's as long as our men on the scene will be able to keep your escape route open. But that should be plenty of time. See here." Zubler unrolled a map of Bern on his desk and pointed. "We have reserved a room for you at the Hotel Bern, here on the Kochergasse—next-door to the Bundeshaus. Your room is on the northwest corner, overlooking the Bundesplatz.

"The general will exit the Bundeshaus from the central hall onto the Bundesplatz, right here. The hotel will not provide you with a good shot, so you must be on one of the rooftops across the square, over here. I recommend this one—it is one of the buildings of the

471

Swiss National Bank, and I can arrange for the roof to be open to you. How will you conceal the rifle?"

"Inside my overcoat," Volger replied. "I have a strap sewn into the right side, which will hold the rifle in place. The coat is bulky— I've had padding sewn in to make me look portly."

"Very good. Hopefully it will not be too warm on Wednesday. We wouldn't want you to look conspicuous. You will enter the bank at eleven o'clock, and say that you have an appointment to see Mr. Dietrich Hagen. You will go with Mr. Hagen to his office, and he will explain the finer details of getting onto the roof. Are we clear, Major?"

"Yes, Mr. Zubler, very clear."

"Now for the other half of your assignment. Your Russian POWs will arrive in Bern tomorrow, via train from Berlin, changing trains at Zurich. They will be accompanied by several Gestapo agents." A frown crossed Zubler's mouth. "We have unfortunately lost two of our Gestapo agents in Zurich, so this serves a double purpose. Your POWs have been given their new identities, and have been instructed to 'be in character' during their entire trip. The Gestapo will keep a close eye on them, and will stay in Switzerland when the operation is finished. They, too, have only recently learned of their permanent transfer.

"You will meet the Russians at the Bern station tomorrow, the 12:04 arrival from Zurich. You will notice the Gestapo agents, I'm sure, but do not acknowledge them.

"Take your POWs to the Hostel Schenck on Spitalgasse, here. It's four blocks from the station, and as you see it is only two blocks from the Bundesplatz. The proprietor of the hostel is one of ours. He is expecting you and your POWs, but he knows no other details. We have asked him to reserve a private room for the six Russians, with empty rooms all around—so you will be able to give them their final instructions without being overheard. There, you will give them these."

Zubler pulled two large valises from beneath his desk and heaved them onto the desktop. He clicked open the latches, and turned them toward Volger.

Inside were six janitorial uniforms; six identification badges bearing the Russians' photographs, which indicated the bearer was a custodian at the Bundeshaus; six pairs of work boots; and six Tokarev TT-33 semi-automatic pistols.

Zubler chuckled, and regarded Volger with a proud smile. "You will find that we have taken every precaution. The uniforms have been tailored to the prisoner's sizes, the names on the uniforms match the respective identity badges—which match the identity papers they were given today. And naturally, Soviet handguns for the assassinations."

Volger was impressed. "You have thought of everything, Mr. Zubler."

Zubler chuckled again, closed the valises, and unrolled another paper on top of them.

"This is the layout of the ground floor of the Bundeshaus. The Federal Council holds their meetings here, in the west wing, every Wednesday morning. This is their chamber, and this is the corridor they will take to the central hall. That is where the Russians must meet them.

"The custodial station is all the way over here. This is where the Russians will go when they enter the Bundeshaus, where they will take a broom and a rubbish bin. Then they must make their way all the way down this corridor to the central hallway before noon, to be in place when the councilors emerge."

Zubler rolled up the chart and handed it to Volger. "Timing is of the essence. You must shoot General Guisan precisely at noon. Any earlier, and the councilors will still be in their chamber, and they won't emerge if they've heard it. Your shot will be the signal to the Russians to begin shooting the councilors." Zubler snorted. "We are not so naive as to believe that they will be able to kill all seven councilors in the short time they will have available. Our hope is that they will kill at least four of them, perhaps five. That plus General Guisan's death will be enough to shake this country to its foundations."

"And if they don't succeed? If they lose their nerve at the last minute and don't carry through with it?"

Zubler's expression became stern. "You will not allow that to happen, Major. Let me remind you that you are responsible for these Russians, and for their success. If they do not succeed, you will find yourself in a concentration camp wearing a pink triangle."

Volger's stomach lurched, but kept his posture rigidly straight. "Understood, Mr. Zubler. I will remind them that their families' lives depend on the success of the mission."

"Excellent. I'm sure we can count on you. Now, I must return to the bank. Anton will show you to a room where you may change into civilian clothes. Good day, Major."

60

Bern

"I brought you some flowers," Jason said after knocking on the hospital room door and taking a tentative step inside.

Franz lay in the bed wearing a white hospital gown, and had been staring at the ceiling with a faraway look, but he turned at the sound of Jason's voice and grinned.

"I hope you don't mind," Jason said, handing him the bouquet of autumn flowers that he'd bought from a street vendor.

"Of course not. Thank you, that's sweet of you." He took the flowers and set them on the table next to him.

Jason pulled up a wooden chair next to the bed and sat. "I'm sure you've had a lot of visitors."

Franz shook his head. "I've not been allowed to tell anyone where I am. Your Mr. Schuller insisted."

"Oh, I didn't realize. I should have come sooner."

Franz smiled and patted Jason's hand. "Nonsense. I hear you were instrumental in my rescue."

Jason blushed. "A little bit."

"A lot, from what Mr. Schuller told me."

A smile crept across Jason's lips. "I just passed messages, that's all."

"Like me!" Franz said with a grin, tapping a finger on his chest. "I pass messages."

Jason laughed. "I think you do a fair bit more than that!"

Franz's expression grew serious. He took Jason's hand and held it. His golden brown eyes staring deep into Jason's. "Thank you."

The words were so soft, so quiet, and yet they echoed in Jason's head. He looked away. "I wanted you to be safe, that's all. I was afraid for you. Afraid I'd never see you again."

They sat in silence for a moment, Franz holding Jason's hand and looking into his face, Jason staring down at his hand.

"When did Mr. Schuller come to see you?" Jason asked, sitting up straight and pulling his hand back.

"This morning, not long after I arrived. They removed a bullet from my leg in Frauenfeld, but he arranged for my transfer to Bern. I'm sure he also arranged for me to have this room by myself. He's very thorough, your Mr. Schuller."

"Yes, he is."

"I asked him how he knew where to find me, and he was vague. The one thing he wasn't vague about was that you brought the information to him in the first place, and then acted as his liaison while he was away. He didn't say much, but I could see that he was pleased. You must have done a very good job."

Jason shrugged. "I hope so."

Franz took his hand again. "I'm here now because of you."

A tingle ran up Jason's arm and down his spine. He looked back at Franz, at those beautiful golden eyes staring deep into him, and this time he didn't look away.

From his car parked in the shadows of an alley off Kochergasse, across the street from the Hotel Bern, Martin watched Major Volger get out of his Mercedes and hand the keys to the valet.

Martin had waited in his car down the block from Ernst Zubler's house in Zurich that afternoon, hoping his instincts had been correct.

His suspicions were confirmed when Volger's black Mercedes pulled out from Zubler's driveway.

Martin had followed at a distance, keeping the Mercedes in sight through the Zurich traffic, then southwestward into the countryside on the highway to Bern. After reaching the capital an hour later, Volger drove to the hotel on Kochergasse, just off the Bundesplatz.

Now Volger opened the passenger-side door, and a dark-haired youth of perhaps sixteen or seventeen exited the car and walked with Volger into the hotel. A porter carried their bags behind them.

Martin lowered his binoculars. Who was the boy? And what was his role in this?

Martin glanced at his watch—almost four o'clock. Where would Volger go after this? And would he have the boy with him?

He settled in for a long wait.

Tuesday,
October 14, 1941

61

Zurich

Pavel Minskayev was perfectly willing to help a friend, but he didn't like what she'd asked him to do.

"Franz is in the hospital in Bern. I can't get away right now, so could you take something to him for me?"

Pavel would do almost anything for Sonia, a fact that he was certain she knew. Still, the thought of standing face-to-face with Franz Lemiel again after he—Pavel pushed the memory away. He would do what Sonia asked of him. It was important, she had said. Something about the Gestapo presence in Switzerland.

He'd wanted to ask about that, but the look on her face had said quite clearly, '*Not now.*' He trusted that if she said something was important, then it was, and he accepted the small package she gave him without question.

Now as Pavel stood on the platform at the Zurich station, waiting for the 11:08 train to Bern, he kept sinking deeper into a foul mood. The thought of Franz in a hospital bed, helpless and weak, barely quelled his irritation.

"We're hungry. May we get something to eat while we wait?" a nearby voice said in an unmistakable Russian accent. A group of six men in workingmen's clothes—dingy white shirts, worn brown pants, tattered newsboy caps—stood in a tight circle to his right.

That's curious. The Russian community in Zurich was small, and he didn't recognize any of these men.

"You will eat when you get to Bern, not before." The harsh words, spoken with an Austrian accent, came from a stern-looking man in crisp tan pants, off-white shirt and tan tie, and a black leather coat who stood ten feet behind the group.

Something about that seemed off—an Austrian in a black leather coat, giving orders to a group of Russians on their way to Bern. There were plenty of Austrian refugees who'd come to Switzerland in the last three-and-a-half years, most of them intellectuals—but this one didn't seem that type. And that leather coat…

He told himself he was being silly, and turned away. Anyone could wear a black coat. It was probably Sonia's unexplained reference to Gestapo being in Switzerland that made his imagination run wild.

He tried to mind his own business, but his ears kept straining to hear the whispered words between the six men clustered a few feet away. Mostly they whispered in German, which was curious; but then the youngest one, a baby-faced blond boy, whispered in Russian.

"What if we don't go through with it?"

One of the others cast a quick glance at the Austrian in the leather coat before replying in Russian, "Then they'll shoot your mother."

"They won't really, will they?" the boy asked.

The other's expression was deadly serious. "Yes, I'm certain they will. Now try to speak only German."

Pavel glanced back at the Austrian in the black coat. His eyes were scanning the crowd, but kept the group of six Russians always in sight.

Pavel scanned the platform. There were three other men in black leather coats scattered through the crowd. They all stood with the same posture, hands clasped in front of them in an attempt to look casual in spite of their straight posture. Their positions encircled the group of Russians, and all of them scanned the crowd while keeping a close eye on the Russians.

This was not his imagination. These four men in leather were Gestapo agents, they had to be, and they were transporting these Russians. But why would they be taking six Russians on a train to Bern?

Something sinister was going on, he could sense it. His thoughts jumped to all of the military officers who had been assassinated over the last two months, purportedly by Communists or Soviet agents. He'd never believed that—his stepfather had been adamant each time a news report blamed "Bolshevik agents" for the attacks that it was all lies, "Fascist propaganda" as he put it. Could it actually be the Gestapo who were behind the violence? Were they using Russian prisoners so that the press would blame the Reds?

The train arrived, and the crowd on the platform lined up to board. Pavel deliberately inserted himself behind the six Russians, in front of the Austrian in the black leather coat. He took a seat across the aisle from them, and noted the scowl he received from the Austrian as he sat in the seat facing Pavel.

Pavel picked up the copy of the Bern newspaper that had been left on the seat next to him and perused it, only half-reading it while keeping his ear trained on the hushed conversation amongst the Russians across the aisle. What little conversation there was, anyway—mostly they sat in silence.

Then an inconspicuous little item, an article of just two short paragraphs buried several pages deep inside the paper, caught his eye. It was a simple, matter-of-fact announcement that General Guisan was scheduled to meet with the Federal Council at their weekly meeting tomorrow morning, to report on the military preparedness of the country.

A chill raced through him, and the tiny hairs on his arms stood on end as if the atmosphere were suddenly charged with electricity.

He had to speak with Franz, immediately. For the first time in more than a year, he was eager to see Franz, knew that he would know what to do.

Only Franz would know what to do.

62

Bern

"Are you certain?" Franz arched an eyebrow in doubt.

"What else could it be?" Pavel panted, still out of breath from his sprint to the hospital from the train station.

"If you're right, it would plunge the whole country into chaos!"

Pavel nodded vigorously. "Fascist elements in the police or the army could seize power, suspend civil liberties to 'restore order,' and bring in more Gestapo to help them."

"Just like Germany in '33," Franz mumbled.

"What?"

Franz stared hard at Pavel. "It would be just like in Germany after the fire at the Reichstag. Hitler blamed it on the Communists, and declared martial law. They clamped down on civil liberties so that they could 'restore order,' but never reinstated them."

"What are we going to do?"

Franz stared off into the room, lost in thought for a moment. "I have to make a phone call."

"How are you going to do that? They won't let you leave the hospital until your leg heals. If it gets infected—"

Franz's face snapped back toward Pavel. "You have to help me get out of here."

"How?"

"I don't know—bribe an orderly to take me in a wheelchair to the front door, and turn away so I can walk out."

"I don't have enough money to bribe anyone."

A mischievous smiled spread across Franz's lips. "Then we'll have to tie sheets into a rope and climb out the window."

One of the Swiss girls from the typing pool dropped a note on Jason's desk. It was unsigned, but Jason recognized Amanda's handwriting.

"Come upstairs right away."

"I'll be back in a few minutes," he said to Mark Hodges at the next desk, and hurried toward the elevator.

Amanda regarded him with a raised eyebrow as he approached her desk. "Herr Lemiel is on the phone. He asked to speak with Mr. Schuller, but he hasn't been in all day. Then he asked to speak to you, and said it was urgent."

"I'll take it in Mr. Schuller's office."

Amanda's other eyebrow shot up, and her jaw dropped. "Excuse me?"

"Put it through to Mr. Schuller's office. I'll take it in there."

"Did you pilfer a key? Jason, you're gonna get yourself in such deep trouble you won't even know it when it hits you!"

"No, I didn't pilfer a key, I was given one. Now would you please put the call through to Mr. Schuller's office for me, Miss Overstreet?"

He instantly regretted his harsh tone, but it was too late—a stung look passed across her face, followed immediately by feminine wrath.

"Right away, *Mr. Bachman*." She nearly spat the words.

There was no time for apologies, though he wanted to. He turned away and hurried down the hall toward Mr. Schuller's office.

The phone was already ringing when he opened the door. "Jason Bachman."

"Jason, it's Franz. We must speak with your Mr. Schuller right away."

"I don't know where he is. I was told he hasn't been here all day."

"You must reach him somehow. There is something about to happen, something terrible, and we need his help to stop it."

Jason's mind raced, trying to think of how he could get ahold of Mr. Schuller. He could try the two-way radio, but he had no way of knowing if Mr. Schuller had it with him. And besides, to send an unauthorized broadcast like that could be dangerous.

"Where are you calling from?"

There was a hesitation before Franz answered. "A phone booth at the train station."

"Can you meet me in half an hour, at the cafe where we met the Bern group the other night?"

"Yes. Say no more until we meet." The line clicked and went dead.

Jason locked Mr. Schuller's office and hurried down the hall to Amanda's desk. "I've got to go do something outside the embassy. If Mr. Schuller shows up while I'm gone, have him wait until he hears from me."

The icy look on Amanda's face could have turned him to stone. "And what shall I tell anyone else who might ask where you've gone?"

"Say you don't know. But whatever you do, don't mention Herr Lemiel's call to anyone but Mr. Schuller. Got it?"

She stared at him in icy silence.

"C'mon Amanda! Be swell, would ya? I can't explain right now, but you know I would if I could. Just promise you'll watch for Mr. Schuller for me, OK? It's important."

She pointed a finger at him. "I'll watch for him, and I'll tell him what you asked me to—but you'd better never talk to me like I'm beneath you ever again, you understand me, mister?"

"I'm sorry, Amanda. I just—I'm in the middle of something, and I'm not really sure how I got here, but I'm in it now so I've got to see it through, you know? You thought something was going on, and it is—I just can't tell you."

Her expression softened a bit. "You be careful. I hope you know what you're doing."

"I don't. I'm making this up as I go."

She looked like she was on the verge of tears. "Then be extra careful. Don't end up lying face-down in a ditch somewhere, OK?"

He nodded and raced toward the elevator.

63

Bern

Martin stood across the street from the Hostel Schenck, pretending to read the newspaper. After ten minutes, he folded the paper, held it under his arm, and strolled to the front door.

The man behind the desk gave him a polite nod. He was about fifty, tall and slim, with thinning dark brown hair and gray eyes deep-set in a long and narrow face. "May I help you, sir?"

Martin held out a fifty-franc note. "Seven men came in here ten minutes ago. Six of them were wearing workingmen's clothes, and the seventh was a tall blond in a tweed suit. What did they say?"

The man didn't touch the money. "They're here to do some work on our kitchen. The grease has clogged the pipes."

Martin didn't hear the sounds of plumbers banging on pipes. He added a second fifty-franc note. "Why don't you tell me where I can find them?"

"Why don't you leave and stop insulting my integrity."

Martin held out his FedPol badge. "Why don't you cooperate with me, and I won't arrest you."

The man didn't flinch. "On what grounds would you arrest me? Having clogged pipes?"

Martin's patience snapped. Maybe it was the restless night spent in the front seat of his Ford, watching the front of the Hotel Bern after Major Volger checked in. Maybe it was his frustration at not having the first idea what Volger was up to after following him for twenty-four hours. Or maybe it was just the smug look on the face of the hostel proprietor that set him off.

He grabbed the man by the throat with his left hand, while grabbing his Luger with his right hand, cocking it, and aiming it inches in front of the man's face. "What are they really doing here?"

The man's breath wheezed from his constricted throat, and Martin felt him trembling, but his eyes remained steady, locked on Martin's. In a raspy voice he said, "You're going to have to shoot me."

Furious that his bluff had been called, Martin struck the man against the temple with the butt of his Luger, and pushed him back, sending him sprawling against the wall. He leapt over the desk and kicked the man in the stomach as he struggled to get up.

"There are laws against police brutality!" the man screeched as he crawled backward.

Martin stood over the cowering figure and glowered at him. "Do you think those laws will mean anything when the Nazis are running things here?"

"I don't know what you're talking about!"

The man's eyes shifted, betraying the lie. Martin leapt on top of him, pinning his arms to the ground with his knees, gripping his throat in his left hand while bringing the butt of the Luger down hard on his forehead.

The blow knocked him out cold.

Damn! Martin stood, catching his breath. *Well, now what?* He still didn't know where Volger was with the six other men, or what they were doing.

After the night watching the front of the hotel in case Volger went anywhere under cover of darkness—he didn't—Martin finally saw Volger leave this morning shortly after eleven-thirty, alone, and retrieve his Mercedes. Martin started his car and followed him to the train station. He almost lost him while struggling to find a place to park without blowing his cover. He managed to keep on Volger's trail all the way to the platform where the train from Zurich arrived a few minutes after noon. Here, six men in tattered workingmen's clothing exited the train and gathered around him.

Several men in black leather coats surrounded the six men at a distance, corralling them. Gestapo, of course. Like Franz had said the night they'd met, it was not hard to identify the Gestapo once you got a feel for them.

Martin bought a newspaper from a nearby stand, and was careful not to keep too close of an eye on Volger and his six joiners.

The men in leather had all followed at a distance as Volger led the six newcomers to the grand hall and across the Bahnhofplatz to the tram stop. They tried to appear casual and disinterested, but Martin wasn't fooled.

He waited until the tram arrived, and Volger boarded with his six companions. Martin hurried to his car, noting that the four men in leather all went back into the station. That was curious.

He caught up to the tram several blocks later, and hoped that Volger hadn't exited already. It was possible that he'd sensed he was being followed, and used the tram as a diversion. Martin had evaded the Gestapo in Zurich that way not long ago. But then at a stop on Spitalgasse, Volger stepped down, followed by the six men, and walked half a block to the Hostel Schenk. Martin breathed a sigh of relief. He'd pulled the car onto a side street, parked, and took up position where he could watch the front of the hostel.

But now he'd knocked out the hostel's proprietor, and the only thing he'd learned was that the proprietor was somehow involved in the plot.

Whatever that plot was.

64

Jason was startled to find Franz not alone. Franz appeared not to notice as he introduced Pavel Minskayev. "Pavel is with the Zurich group," Franz added under his breath.

Jason shook Pavel's hand. He seemed stiff, uncomfortable.

"What is it you need to see Mr. Schuller about?" Jason asked quietly, taking a seat at their table. The tables surrounding them were empty. It was nearly two o'clock, and there were only a few customers in the cafe.

"Pavel witnessed some Russians being escorted from Zurich to Bern by Gestapo agents," Franz said.

Pavel wore a scowl. He whispered at Franz with a pronounced note of irritation, "You never told me the person you called was an American. I won't speak to spies! I want nothing to do with that business."

He pushed his chair back, but Jason shook his head. "I'm not a spy. I work at the American Embassy, I'm a Foreign Service officer."

Pavel's lips tightened. "Spies always say they are just in their country's Foreign Service."

"Well, I'm not a spy. I'm a friend of Franz."

That brought a deeper scowl to Pavel's face.

Franz nodded. "He is not a spy, Pavel. He tells the truth."

Pavel still looked doubtful. "Then why should I tell him what I saw? What can an American diplomat do?"

"He knows someone who can help."

"And who is this 'someone'? A spy?"

Franz leaned in close. "Pavel, this is for Switzerland, and the preservation of our freedom. I'm afraid we can't trust the police. You'll have to trust Jason."

Pavel sat in silence for several seconds. Finally, he nodded and leaned over the table. When he spoke, it was in a low whisper, and Jason leaned in to hear. When Pavel had finished, concluding with the news of General Guisan meeting with the Federal Council the next morning, Jason stared back at him in disbelief.

"How would they possibly be able to do that?" His jaw hung open.

"We don't know that part," Franz said. "But one thing is certain—there is someone on the inside who is working with them. That is the only way they could have plotted such a thing."

It took a moment for the enormity of the situation to sink in. When it did, Jason's stomach tied in knots, and he broke into a sweat. He took a deep breath and tried to remain calm. What would Mr. Schuller do in this situation?

He looked at Pavel. "Where did they go when they got off the train, these Russians?"

"I don't know. I went to see Franz, I didn't follow them. I did see they gathered around a man who was waiting for them on the platform. He was a tall blond man, very big." Pavel puffed out his chest for emphasis.

"Was he Swiss? Or German?"

"I don't know. I couldn't hear him speaking."

Jason pondered this a moment.

Franz had a curious expression, his head tilted to the side. "I think I know who that man is."

Jason frowned. "How could you?"

Franz explained what Major Volger had said about going to Switzerland.

"Then we need to find Mr. Schuller right away," Jason said, and rose from the table. "Do they have a phone here?"

"There's a booth in the back," Franz said, nodding over his shoulder.

Jason found the phone, inserted a coin, and asked the operator for the U.S. Embassy. The Swiss receptionist who answered transferred him to Amanda. He asked her if Mr. Schuller had been in yet.

"No. He hasn't called to check in, either."

Damn! "Listen, if he comes in or calls or anything, be sure to tell him I need to speak with him right away. You can tell him Herr Lemiel called for him earlier."

"Will do. And be careful, you hear?"

"I will. Don't worry." He hung up, knowing she would.

He stood there a moment, unsure what to do. Then he called the operator again, and asked for the German embassy.

"I hoped I'd hear from you," Liev Klein said when the call was transferred to him.

"I need your help," Jason said. "I can't explain over the phone, but I'm with Franz, and we can't find Mr. Schuller."

"Does this have to do with a certain SS Major who's in Bern right now?"

Jason didn't answer, stunned that Liev Klein already knew that.

"We've been observing him," Liev answered Jason's unspoken question.

"Where can you meet me?" Jason asked.

"Where are you?"

"Where can you meet me?"

Liev chuckled. "Very good, Jason! They'll make a good spy of you yet. Meet me at the fountain in the Rathausplatz in thirty minutes." The line clicked off.

Jason hurried back to the table. "I've got to go. Meet me at the Bundesplatz in an hour?"

"Where are you going?" Franz asked.

"I have to meet someone. *Alone.* Can the two of you hide out somewhere for an hour, and then meet me in the Bundesplatz?"

"Whom are you meeting?" Franz asked, frowning.

"Someone who can help me."

"Not Mr. Schuller?"

"No. I don't know where he is."

"So, just whom are you meeting?" Franz pressed.

"I told you, someone who can help us."

"Abwehr?" Franz asked.

Jason was stunned that Franz had guessed. He didn't answer.

"I don't like you going alone. You're too new at this. You could walk into a trap."

"I'll be fine."

"I can guarantee the person you're meeting won't be alone. You may not notice, but he'll have others with him."

"Franz, don't try to follow me. Please stay hidden somewhere. If I'm going to walk into a trap, I'd rather not endanger you again. If I don't meet you at the Bundesplatz by four o'clock, go look for Mr. Schuller without me."

"I don't like it."

"I'll be careful."

Jason gave Franz his most determined look, and Franz didn't argue further. "Then we'll see you in the Bundesplatz in an hour."

Franz's eyes followed Jason, hurrying out of the cafe and turning.

Pavel stared at him. "You're going to follow him, aren't you?"

Franz ignored the flutter in his stomach at being caught. "Yes."

"You love him."

Franz's face snapped left, and he stared hard into Pavel's face. "Don't be ridiculous."

"You do," Pavel said. "Just as I loved Elena."

Franz stiffened. "That was a misunderstanding. I wasn't trying to come between you. I didn't realize you didn't know..." his voice trailed off.

Pavel opened his mouth to say something, but he stopped. He looked away and nodded toward the door. "Go on, before he gets out of sight."

"You're coming with me." Franz grabbed Pavel's arm and pulled him along.

65

Bern

The clock on the front of the Rathaus, nestled between two gothic arches above the entrances, indicated it was quarter to three.

Jason found Liev Klein waiting beside the fountain, beneath the armored standard-bearer. He wore a heavy brown suit and a brown hat with a small feather in the side. His hair curled out from beneath the brim of the hat. He smiled as Jason approached, dimpling his round cheeks. "Very good to see you again, Mr. Bachman." He extended his right hand and gave Jason's one firm shake.

"Thank you for meeting me."

"It's my pleasure." The twinkle in his eyes made them seem to laugh.

Jason felt an involuntary flutter in his stomach. He managed to keep his expression serious. "Let's walk."

They turned and strolled toward the park a block north of the square.

"Tell me about this SS Major who's in Bern," Jason said as they left the square.

"What do you already know?"

"I know his name—Rudolph Volger. I know that he was the one interrogating Franz in Frankfurt. And I know that he's now in Bern, where he met six men this afternoon at the train station."

"What else do you want me to tell you?" Liev asked.

"What he's doing in Bern."

"We'd like to know that ourselves."

"You're being very coy," Jason said, allowing an irritated edge to his voice.

"I don't mean to be," Liev said, touching Jason's shoulder as they entered the shady park stretched along the left bank of the Aare, and followed a trail that descended downhill toward the river.

"Don't pretend that your people don't know more about this Major Volger than I do!" Jason said, shaking his shoulder away from Liev's hand. "I'm sure there's more you can tell me."

Liev looked down, his expression serious. "I'm afraid I'm not at liberty to tell you much. Our mutual friend Franz was the one who told us Major Volger was coming to Switzerland on some sort of official business—but I'm sure you already knew that."

Jason stiffened. "I knew he told Mr. Schuller. I didn't know he'd told *you*."

"Well, not me *personally*. One of our people helped your Mr. Schuller to get Franz out of the Gestapo's grip, and safely back to Switzerland. When Franz revealed what Volger said, it was to both men."

Jason considered this for a moment. "You've been watching Major Volger, then?"

"Yes, of course; ever since he arrived in Bern. So has your Mr. Schuller."

Jason tried not to let the surprise show, but his eyes widened involuntarily. "Where are they?"

"A little while ago they were at the Hostel Schenck, a few blocks from here on Spitalgasse. Volger took the men there from the train this afternoon."

"Is that where Major Volger is staying?"

Liev laughed. "No, he's staying at the Hotel Bern on Kochergasse, near the Bundesplatz. A much nicer establishment." He paused a second before adding, "He's staying there with his boy."

This time Jason couldn't hide his surprise. Liev laughed out loud.

"Don't be so shocked! Hypocrisy and self-loathing are regular hallmarks of Nazi thugs. That's why they're so angry at everyone."

Jason took a moment to ponder this revelation.

Liev continued. "The boy might be the key to finding out what Volger is doing here. He's Jewish—though his papers now say he's Mischling. Volger oversaw the deportation of the boy's family almost a year ago. It might not be hard to turn him."

"You think Major Volger told him anything?"

Liev shrugged. "Perhaps. Men say all manner of things when they're in bed with a lover. That's why prostitutes are a spy's best informants."

Jason changed the subject. "Who are the six men the Major met at the station?"

"We don't know exactly."

Jason had little doubt that while Liev was being technically honest, he knew more than he'd revealed. "What do you know about them?"

Liev didn't say anything.

"I thought you wanted us to cooperate with each other."

Liev stopped, and turned to face Jason. "I haven't been authorized to tell you anything. I'm sorry. Of course, I *can* use my own judgment when the situation calls for it..." his voice trailed off, and he put his hand on Jason's shoulder. "You'll find that I can be a good friend to you. How friendly are you willing to be with me?" Those smiling brown eyes roamed downward and back up.

Jason couldn't help the flutter of excitement that rippled through him, alongside a shiver of revulsion. It was a confusing feeling. He wasn't used to this kind of seduction—at the University of Chicago he'd had a dozen encounters with a half-dozen fellow students, always in the backseat of a car after two or three bottles of beer had loosened inhibitions; and always the next day the other fellow made a point of saying he'd been "so drunk last night" he couldn't remember what he'd done.

"I'll consider it," Jason said. He wouldn't. "Perhaps you can give me a little something in good faith, some piece of information I don't already know, to let me know it will be worth my time."

Liev grinned. "Very good! You're learning quickly. I knew I liked you. Let's see—I already told you about Volger's boy, you want more? Alright then, I'll tell you that before he arrived in Bern yesterday, Volger may have made a stop in Zurich; presumably to meet with the man they call the Gauleiter. Do you know about the Gauleiter?"

"I don't know what that is," Jason said.

"In Germany, a Gauleiter is a regional Nazi Party leader. The Party doesn't operate outside the Reich, however, so for someone in Switzerland to use it..." Liev's voice trailed off.

"Who is this person?"

"We don't know. We've heard much about him from our informants, but never his identity. Whoever he is, he's very careful."

"But Major Volger met with him yesterday?"

"We believe so. We're not certain."

Jason scowled. What kind of vague information was this? "So what does that mean?"

Liev hesitated a moment. "We don't know exactly, but we do know that the Gauleiter—whoever he is—has been the mastermind of Gestapo activities in Switzerland, including the assassinations of the colonels that have been blamed on the Communists."

Jason nodded as a picture came together in his mind. "Thank you."

Liev smiled. "For you, it's my pleasure. Now, when will I see more of you?" His eyes twinkled and glanced down again.

Jason ignored the question. "What are you going to do next?"

Liev glanced behind Jason. His eyes were serious, distant even. "I need to check in and find out if Volger is still at the Hostel Schenck. If he is, then I'm going to pay a visit to the Hotel Bern, and call on his boy." The twinkle came back to his eyes. "Care to join me?"

Jason disliked being toyed with. His voice was sharp as he replied. "Perhaps—but not for the reasons you're implying."

Liev appeared stung, but then he chuckled and the adorable dimples returned to his round cheeks. "I wasn't implying what you think. Unlike Major Volger, I'm not excited by teenage boys. I was only suggesting that we might work together. I'd like us to be friendlier."

He reached his hand out and squeezed Jason's arm below the shoulder, then turned to leave.

"If I decide to join you, where should we meet?" Jason called after him.

Liev looked around. He took a couple of steps back toward Jason and said in a low voice, "Meet me on the corner of Kochergasse and Inselgasse, a block east of the Bundesplatz, in one hour." He turned and walked back the way they had come.

Jason watched him for a moment, then walked west through the park, making a wide arc on his way to the Bundesplatz.

As Liev Klein exited the park and stopped for traffic on Brunngasshalde, he stood next to a park bench where two young men sat with newspapers in front of their faces.

"Hello Franz," Liev said without glancing over. With a mischievous half-smile he added, "How's the leg? Healed already?"

There was a break in the traffic, and Liev hurried across the boulevard and disappeared into the medieval quarter.

66

Bern

The bell clanked as the front door opened. "I'll be with you in a moment!" Martin called. He finished the last of the knots, and stood above the gagged and hog-tied proprietor, who was still unconscious. It had taken several minutes to locate a long enough stretch of rope from the Hostel's supply closet, along with a rag for gagging. He still didn't know where he was going to stash the man so he wouldn't be discovered for a long time.

He'd deal with that in a moment. First he had to see who had entered the hostel.

He stepped out behind the front desk. Captain Wolfe stood in the lobby with another man, a young blond with slicked-back hair and an intense look on his face. Both men held their fedoras in their hands.

Martin nodded at Wolfe. "I'm not surprised to see you, Captain. I assume you've been watching our friend the Major?"

"Yes, and you as well."

"Who is this?"

"An associate. You can call him Hermann."

The young man nodded at Martin but remained silent.

Wolfe continued. "Volger will recognize you if you're here when he leaves, or if he spots you on the street. He won't recognize either of us. You should leave now, before he comes downstairs."

"I'll make sure he doesn't see me."

Wolfe nodded toward the door. "There are two Gestapo agents who arrived a few minutes ago. One went around to the back, presumably to keep an eye on the backdoor. The other is watching the front of the building from the very spot you stood watching a little while ago. He might not take much notice of you leaving alone, but he'll notice if you follow Volger."

"What about you? Won't they notice you following him?"

"We can deal with the Gestapo. We've been doing it for years."

Martin stared at Wolfe. He wasn't certain he could trust the Abwehr's motives, and he doubted they'd tell him anything they learned by following Volger without him. "There's a cafe down at the corner. The three of us can leave together and make it seem you came here to meet me. From there we can keep an eye on all of them. When Volger leaves, the three of us can split up if necessary to keep the Gestapo busy. You know as well as I do that they're here to keep an eye on those Russians, not to follow us."

Wolfe glanced at his companion, and the younger man shrugged.

"Alright," Wolfe said. "We'll go with you."

"In a minute," Martin replied. "Captain, will you come with me a moment?"

The young blond stepped forward and opened his mouth, but Wolfe put his arm in front of him. "It's alright." He followed Martin into the back.

The proprietor's eyes were open, and he began to make noise and wiggle around when he saw Martin and Wolfe.

"We need to do something with him," Martin said. "We can't have our friend upstairs find him."

Wolfe exhaled hard through the nose, his lips a thin line. "We can't take him out of the building without the Gestapo seeing. We'll have to lock him in an empty room. I'll get a key."

Wolfe went back to the desk, and returned a moment later with a key. "There's an empty room on the first floor. We'll only have to carry him up one flight."

"And hope no one else is using the stairs or the hallway."

"I'll have Hermann keep watch for us."

"While you were looking for an empty room, did you check the guestbook to see where Volger's friends are staying?"

Wolfe's expression grew guarded. "Of course. All of the rooms on the second floor are marked 'Reserved,' but with no name."

A moment later, Hermann signaled all clear from the top of the first flight of stairs, and Martin and Wolfe proceeded up to the first floor, Martin holding the proprietor's shoulders while Wolfe carried the legs.

The room they were looking for turned out to be midway down the hall, and the floor creaked with every step they took. Hermann unlocked the door. They placed the proprietor on top of the small bed, and Wolfe turned back to Hermann at the door.

"See if you can find more rope. We'll tie him to the bed."

Hermann closed the door behind him, and Martin went to the window to peer behind the curtain. The window looked onto the alley behind the hostel, and he spied a man in a black leather coat lounging at the far end, smoking a cigarette.

Martin figured Volger and his men were directly above them. He entertained the idea of going upstairs to eavesdrop at the door, but the creaky floor gave him pause.

Martin and Wolfe waited in silence. Wolfe smoked a cigarette.

Hermann returned several minutes later with a length of rope, and the three of them looped it around the proprietor and the bed-frame several times before tying a firm knot. They locked the door, and Wolfe pocketed the key. They kept silent as they descended to the lobby.

The unattended desk stood accusing in its stillness.

"What if other guests come downstairs? Or come to check in?" Martin asked, hesitating by the door.

"We can't worry about that now," Wolfe snapped. Then his expression softened, and he added, "We'll send someone later." He pushed the door open.

They pretended not to notice the Gestapo agent standing at the corner half a block down the street, and walked the other direction to the cafe.

"Tell me what you've learned," Martin said quietly after they'd sat at a corner table beside the front window.

"Nothing more than you have," Wolfe said. "I should be asking you that question—you were already following Volger when we picked up the trail. How did you manage that?"

Martin kept his face expressionless. "I was just faster than your people."

Wolfe shook his head. "You know something we don't. It would be best if we worked together on this."

"If the roles were reversed, would you tell me everything you know?"

Wolfe didn't answer.

Martin pursed his lips and nodded. "I didn't think so."

"I would have hoped our assistance to now would have earned some goodwill from you." Wolfe struck a match and lit a cigarette, then leaned back and blew a stream of smoke into the air. Hermann stared at Martin with hard, unblinking blue eyes.

"It has," Martin agreed. "So I'll tell you that your informant in Zurich with the code-name Corkscrew is a double-agent. He's working for the Gauleiter."

Wolfe stared at Martin for a moment, his green eyes narrowed. "You've met with Corkscrew?"

"Yes."

"And you believe he's a double-agent for the Gauleiter?"

"That's right."

Wolfe's eyes narrowed further. "How do you know?"

"I know."

Wolfe continued staring at him for several seconds. "You know who the Gauleiter is, don't you?"

"I believe so."

"Will you tell us who he is?"

Martin shook his head.

Wolfe looked away, took a long drag on his cigarette, then stubbed it out as he exhaled smoke in Martin's direction.

"Very well, for the time being we shall concentrate on learning Major Volger's plans. But when the time comes, we'd appreciate your cooperation when we go after this Gauleiter."

"Volger's leaving." It was the first time Hermann had spoken, and Martin was surprised at the deep voice that emerged from the thin young man.

Volger stood in front of the Hostel door, looking up and down the street. He nodded at the Gestapo agent, then walked their direction.

Wolfe stood and laid a few coins on the table. "Let's go."

When he reached the corner opposite the cafe, Volger took a right turn, heading south along the Barenplatz toward the Bundesplatz.

The three men waited a moment before exiting the cafe. When they did, Wolfe whispered to Hermann, "Shake our hands, and go the opposite direction."

After the stern young man had left, Martin and Wolfe walked together into the Barenplatz. Major Volger was a hundred feet ahead of them, halfway down the square, and they kept pace at that distance behind him. When they'd gone a hundred feet, Martin glanced back.

"The Gestapo's not following us," he whispered.

Wolfe nodded. "When we get to the Bundesplatz, we'll split up. You go along the left side, and I'll go along the right side."

They kept Volger in sight from opposite sides of the square. Volger crossed in front of the Bundeshaus, and made his way east on Kochergasse to the entrance of the Hotel Bern.

Martin followed on the left side of the street, while Wolfe followed along the right, behind the Major. After Volger entered the hotel, Wolfe crossed over to Martin.

"That didn't tell us much," Martin said as he approached.

Wolfe glanced at his watch. It was a little past three-thirty. "He's probably in for the day. If he does what he did yesterday, he'll stay in his room the rest of the afternoon, and eat at the hotel restaurant at seven-thirty. We have someone inside watching the restaurant, in case anyone comes to meet him."

"Did anyone meet him last night?" Martin asked.

Wolfe shook his head. "No. He ate alone with the boy who came with him."

Martin let out an exasperated sigh. They were getting nowhere.

"Go home," Wolfe said. It sounded almost like an order. "Rest. You need it. We have many people on this; we can have him watched around the clock. You can't do that by yourself, so let us handle it. You can be back here before dawn."

He was right, but Martin hated it. His senses were dulled by fatigue, and it would only get worse if he didn't get some sleep.

Whether he wanted to or not, he would have to trust this to the Abwehr.

He nodded in acquiescence and turned back toward the Bundesplatz. His car was still at the train station, almost a kilometer away. He'd catch a tram at the Bundesplatz, he decided—and hoped he didn't fall asleep before it reached the station.

67

Jason spotted Franz standing with Pavel Minskayev behind some outdoor tables in front of a cafe on the Bundesplatz, arms crossed and scowling. He hurried across the square and joined them. "I'm sorry I'm late." It was three-thirty. "My meeting took longer than I anticipated."

"Major Volger came through here three or four minutes ago," Franz said. "I don't think he saw me. I was going to send Pavel to follow him, but then I saw Mr. Schuller already following him. He crossed the square and headed down that street." He pointed east.

"Yes, his hotel's a block that way," Jason said.

"You learned that from Liev Klein." Franz's words were clipped.

Jason's chest constricted. "You followed me."

"Of course I did!"

"I asked you not to."

"You don't know what you're dealing with."

"I'm not stupid, Franz! I know what I'm doing." That came out louder than Jason intended, and patrons at nearby tables glanced their way, some casting judgmental looks.

Franz said nothing. He continued to stare at Jason with that deep scowl.

Jason's anger boiled up. "I understand you and Liev Klein were quite friendly before." He kept his voice quiet, but the words spat out like daggers.

Pavel stepped away.

Franz glanced around and pulled Jason into the square. His voice was just above a whisper. "I didn't know he was Abwehr. He kept that from me. He told me he was a Jew from Berlin who had gotten out while Switzerland still admitted Jewish refugees. He seemed interested in my work as a fellow dissident. I had no idea that he was monitoring our activities for German intelligence. I learned that later. Thank God I never told him anything sensitive."

Jason crossed his arms. "So you're saying you wouldn't have slept with him if you'd known he was a spy?"

Franz's mouth dropped open. "Is *that* the reason you're angry?"

"That, plus the fact that you didn't trust me to do what I needed to do on my own."

Franz sighed and shook his head. "Jason, you don't understand these people. Liev Klein fooled me, and I have much more experience with this than you do."

"He didn't fool me. I knew he was Abwehr when I first met him." Jason left out that Liev had told him so himself.

"You shouldn't trust him."

"Why not? He was the one who told me you were held by the Gestapo on Sunday. If not for him, Mr. Schuller would have never gone to rescue you."

Franz's jaw dropped, and hung open for several seconds.

"We owe him your life, Franz. I know you don't trust them, and I don't either, but we need their help if we're going to stop Major Volger from assassinating General Guisan tomorrow."

"Please tell me you didn't tell Liev Klein about that."

"Of course not! Stop treating me like I'm a foolish little child!"

Franz's eyes dropped, and he nodded. "I'm sorry."

"Besides, he gave me good information—such as where Major Volger is staying. Beside the Bundeshaus, very convenient if he's going to assassinate the general tomorrow. Liev also told me Major Volger has a Jewish boy with him, and he wants to talk with him."

Franz's head snapped up. "Michael Kaim is here? In Switzerland?"

"You know about him?"

"Yes. I had photographs of Volger in bed with him. I used them to blackmail him into chauffeuring me around Germany several times. It made my work much easier. But how could Volger get him out of Germany?"

"I have no idea. Does it matter?"

"Perhaps." Franz looked lost in thought.

Martin Schuller emerged from Kochergasse into the square. "Mr. Schuller's coming," Jason said.

They hurried toward him.

"What on earth are you two doing here?"

"We need to talk right away, in private," Jason said. "Franz has learned what Major Volger is going to do tomorrow."

Mr. Shuller's eyes lit up, though his expression remained serious. "Meet me at the embassy, in my office, as soon as you can get there. And make sure you're not followed."

"Pavel Minskayev needs to meet with us," Franz said, nodding toward where Pavel stood in front of the Bundeshaus. "He's the one who brought the information to me."

Mr. Schuller nodded. "Very well. Be careful no one follows you." He hurried off, diagonally across the square.

"Let's go," Jason said. Franz waved to Pavel, and the three of them headed toward the U.S. Embassy.

From his vantage point a block down Kochergasse in front of the Hotel Bern, Liev Klein watched Jason and Franz converse for a moment with Mr. Schuller. They headed the other direction, and he sighed. He had work to do here.

68

Bern

Amanda's eyes widened in surprise when Jason approached her desk with Franz and Pavel in tow.

"I'm glad you're okay!" she said, breathing a sigh of relief. "I've been worried all afternoon. I kept picturing you lying facedown in a dark alley!"

Jason smiled and touched her shoulder. "I'm alright. Herr Lemiel and I are meeting with Mr. Schuller in a few minutes. We're not to be disturbed."

"Mr. Schuller's not in."

"He will be in a few minutes. We'll wait in his office. And don't mention this to anyone."

"Not a word." She crossed her heart.

Jason switched back to German as he led Franz and Pavel down the hall. "Mr. Schuller's not back yet, but I have a key to his office." He unlocked the door and let them in.

Martin arrived five minutes later, after retrieving his car. Franz started introducing him to Pavel, but Martin cut him off. "We've met."

Pavel glared at Martin. "You said you were a private detective."

Martin's expression was passive. "Yes."

"But you're a spy! You tricked me."

Franz interrupted. "Pavel, this is not the time."

Pavel shot Franz a look of death. "I wouldn't expect you to understand. You also deceived me."

"I never deceived you, Pavel. You misunderstood my intentions, but I never hid them from you." He paused a moment, then added, "Elena knew."

Pavel's face flushed.

Martin sensed the emotional direction this was taking, and he banged a fist on his desk. "Enough! There is no time for bickering. You said that you know what Volger is doing in Switzerland—if you're not here to discuss that, then stop wasting my time and leave."

Jason spoke up. "Major Volger plans to assassinate General Guisan tomorrow morning!"

Martin looked back and forth between the three young men. "How do you know this?"

"Pavel, tell Mr. Schuller what you saw and heard this morning," Franz said.

Pavel nodded, but his expression remained stony as he explained about the six Russians at the Zurich station, waiting with four men in black leather coats who were probably Gestapo, and what was said about their families being killed if they didn't go through with something. Then he mentioned the story in the newspaper about General Guisan meeting with the Federal Council tomorrow, and how it seemed to make sense.

"Plus Major Volger is staying in a hotel next to the Bundeshaus," Jason added.

Martin nodded, and took a moment to contemplate. This would be the perfect culmination to the series of military assassinations over the past two months.

"Wait here," he instructed the three young men.

Ron Witherspoon's door was open, so Martin walked in and closed it behind him.

"Hello, Schuller. You haven't been in for a while."

"Ron, what can you tell me about the Federal Council?"

"It's the executive in Switzerland. There are seven members, chosen by vote of the Federal Assembly. There's a rotating presidency and vice-presidency, and five heads of cabinet departments, but in fact all seven members are a collegial head of state—the equivalent of our President."

"They're the government of Switzerland, is that what you're saying?"

"Yes—on a day-to-day basis. The Federal Assembly makes the laws, like our Congress."

"So General Guisan would report to the Federal Council? The way our military leaders report to the President?"

"Yes. In fact, now that you mention it, I read in the paper that he's meeting with the Council tomorrow. Why do you ask?"

Martin ignored the question. "How often does he report to them?"

Witherspoon shrugged. "I'm not sure. Regularly, I suppose. The Council itself meets every Wednesday morning, and then they go have lunch together. The Federal Chancellor reports to them every week, but I'm not sure about the presiding general."

"The Federal Chancellor?"

"The head of the government bureaucracy. Kind of a chief of staff for the Federal Government."

A picture was starting to come together in his mind, and Martin tapped his finger on the desktop for several seconds while he thought.

"Martin? What's going on?"

"How quickly can you have some forged documents made?"

Witherspoon appeared startled. "If it's a rush, we could have some by tomorrow morning."

"Could you have them tonight? By eight?"

"I don't know. It's already four-thirty."

"It's urgent."

"I'll see what I can do. What do you need?"

"A couple of press passes for the Bundeshaus; I'll bring you the photographs shortly. Also, I'll need two of the smallest handguns you can get ahold of—small enough to conceal easily."

"That's a tall order."

"It's urgent. I'll explain later."

Witherspoon sighed and nodded. "Alright, I'll see what I can do."

"Thanks Ron, this has been tremendous." Martin sprinted out the door.

"Everyone understands his role?" Martin asked an hour later.

Franz, Pavel, and Jason all nodded.

Martin looked at Franz. "And?"

"Pavel and I will check-in to the Hostel Schenk, and keep an eye on the Russians," Franz said. "Jason will bring us our press passes and accoutrements before morning. After the Russians leave, we'll follow them and take position inside the central hall of the Bundeshaus."

Martin looked to Jason.

"After I deliver their materials to them at the Hostel Schenk, I'll join Liev Klein at the Hotel Bern and wait for Major Volger to leave, then we'll go get Michael Kaim."

Martin nodded, satisfied. "Very good. And I'll follow Volger after he leaves the Hotel Bern. If anything goes wrong, we'll rendezvous at sundown under the Kirchenfeldbrucke. Understood?"

Everyone nodded.

"And no one says a word about any of this to anyone, under any circumstances, ever. Is that clear?"

More nods from everyone.

"Good. See you all tomorrow. Mr. Lemiel, Mr. Minskayev, you may leave. Jason, would you stay a moment, please?"

Jason nodded to Franz and Pavel, and the two of them exited the office.

"Close the door," Martin said.

Once the door had closed, Martin asked Jason to have a seat. "I'm going to speak with Colonel Legge to see if Military Intelligence can offer us any support tomorrow. We're going to need it to get those Russians out of there. No need for the foreigners to know anything about that, understood?"

"Yes, sir."

"And another thing—we'll both need to be careful what we say to the MID fellas. As far as you're concerned, the less said the better. MID might try to take over, and we don't want that, understand? This is our operation."

"Yes, sir." A hint of excitement curled the corners of Jason's mouth.

"Good. Once those press passes and reporters' outfits arrive, you can go. Be careful out there."

521

Wednesday,
October 15, 1941

69

Bern

Feodor Popov kept his eyes down as he walked through the Barenplatz toward its south end, where it opened onto the larger Bundesplatz. He kept his hands in the pockets of the janitor's coverall, not so much from the morning chill as to hide their trembling.

His fingers touched the handle of the Tokarev semi-automatic, and a shudder ran through his midsection. Then he thought of his children and his dear Natasha, held at that stable in Pomerania. His back straightened with renewed resolve. So seven politicians would die today; better them than his family.

None of the group spoke a word.

Franz disliked the feel of the Fedora on his head, and he was even less comfortable in the gray suit, buttoned-up white shirt and black necktie. Pavel looked natural walking beside him in nearly the same outfit, and Franz told himself not to fidget.

The press pass in his pocket bore his photograph and the name Franz Lambert, and identified him as a correspondent for the Associated Press. Pavel's identified him as Pyotr Ivanov, with Pravda.

Franz hoped none of the real journalists in the Bundeshaus would get too nosy. Mr. Schuller had prepped them to say that they'd just been assigned to Bern by their respective employers. If asked where they'd been before, Franz was to say Geneva, and hope the person asking hadn't previously reported from Geneva. Pavel was to be newly-arrived from Moscow; that would give him the excuse to be evasive and seem perfectly natural.

Ahead, the six Russians in janitorial clothes entered the Bundeshaus. Franz took a deep breath and gripped his reporter's notepad tightly in his hand.

The padded coat was uncomfortably warm, and also heavy. Rudolph Volger's forehead and upper lip began sweating before he'd made it all the way down Kochergasse to the Bundesplatz. The heavy padding felt awkward, and by the time he reached the National Bank he was out of breath. That was serendipitous; a fat man should be out of breath.

He checked his watch before reaching the door. It was less than a minute before eleven o'clock. His timing could not have been more perfect. He entered the marble lobby and approached the desk, where a dour woman of about forty sat in front of a switchboard.

"I have an appointment to see Mr. Dietrich Hagen."

Martin had almost missed Volger when he exited the Hotel Bern. He seemed to have gained fifty pounds overnight, and wore a thick blond mustache of the type that had gone out of style ten or twelve years ago. The overcoat and the brown bowler hat were far from stylish, but the brown patent leather shoes looked expensive.

Volger had passed a few feet in front of Martin, who sat in one of the plush chairs in the hotel lobby wearing fake glasses with thick black frames, the morning paper in front of his face. Only as he came close did Martin recognize the face. His eye followed the Major through the front door, then he folded his newspaper and strolled after him.

He stayed fifty feet behind Volger's waddling figure down Kochergasse to the Bundesplatz, where it turned right and crossed the square. The buildings in front of them bore the name of the Swiss National Bank, and Volger entered one. This building sat opposite the Bundeshaus—an excellent vantage point to see General Guisan exiting.

And to take aim.

After Volger entered the building, Martin's eyes shot up toward the roof. It was steep, and would easily hide a figure lying flat beyond the peak.

He hurried toward the alley to the left, noting the numerous windows with bright green shutters on the neighboring building that stood between the alley and the Barenplatz. They couldn't have possibly crammed more windows into the available wall-space. If he succeeded in finding a fire escape that would take him to the roof of the bank building, he couldn't make it unnoticed.

He dashed around to the back of the bank building and found a courtyard with big planted pots and several tables where perhaps a dozen bank employees took their coffee breaks, some smoking cigarettes.

And no fire escape. Time for a bluff.

He strode through the back door of the building as if he belonged there, and no one challenged him. He found himself inside a long hall, and followed it toward the elevators. He found no directory next to the elevators, so he continued toward the front lobby.

He showed his FedPol badge to the middle-aged woman at the desk. "Inspector Schmidt. I need to see the man in charge of building security."

From his vantage point at a table behind a potted palm, Jason watched Mr. Schuller exit the lobby of the Hotel Bern. He set down his coffee cup on the saucer, laid a few coins on the table, and crossed to a corridor where there were phone booths. Most were unoccupied, and he closed himself in the farthest one.

He dialed the number that Liev had given him last night, and drummed his fingers while it rang three times.

"Aviary," Liev's voice answered.

"Two birds have flown away."

"I'm on my way." The line clicked off.

Jason met Liev in front of the elevator five minutes later. His brow was furrowed. "Are you certain?"

"Yes. Why?"

"Our sentinel is still in the lobby. He wouldn't be there if Volger had left."

Jason's stomach flipped. "But Mr. Schuller left, and he wouldn't have gone except to follow Major Volger."

Liev looked back toward the lobby, hesitating.

"What is it?" Jason asked.

Liev hesitated a moment longer, then turned back toward Jason. "We can't go up there yet. We can't risk running into Major Volger."

"But Mr. Schuller followed him out already."

"Did you see Volger leave?"

"No. But I've never seen him."

"Then it's unsubstantiated. We must wait for confirmation. Stay here and keep an eye on the lobby while I make a call." He disappeared down the hall.

The elevator door opened, and an elegant lady in a stylish blue suit with a matching hat and a fox wrap exited, followed by a porter carrying a large trunk. The elevator operator looked at Jason, but Jason shook his head. "I'm waiting for someone."

The operator nodded, closed the door, and the arrow above it moved up the numbers.

Jason hoped he wasn't making a mistake by not following Mr. Schuller's orders.

Franz was relieved that the press corps in the Bundeshaus that morning numbered barely more than a dozen, and most of them Swiss. The guards had given their press credentials perfunctory scrutiny, and the only curiosity they received was from a stout middle-aged British reporter with Reuters. He looked stereotypical in a tweed suit and brown bowler hat, with a thick brown mustache and gray-blue eyes. He was suitably jolly for an Englishman, and told Franz a couple of off-color jokes before wandering off to chat up a reporter from Luzerne.

Franz had little doubt he was on the British Intelligence payroll. They were notorious for using British reporters around the world as informants.

The group mostly stood around, chatting and drinking coffee until eleven forty-five, when a flurry of activity from the west wing caused them all to rush forward. Franz and Pavel found themselves hurrying to keep up, but then Franz realized that being at the back of the group might be most advantageous for keeping an eye out for the six Russians.

The cause of the activity soon emerged into the central hallway. General Henri Guisan was not a tall man, and slender of build for a man of his age—he was almost sixty-seven years old—and yet he was the image of military rigor and respectability with his straight posture, spotless uniform with high collar and numerous medals, and his white mustache with the ends waxed in a French style that had been popular several decades before. His stride bespoke the confidence of years, and the authority of purpose. He turned with stoic resolve to face the gaggle of reporters that spread before him.

Franz and Pavel pretended to scribble down notes as he answered questions, but their eyes searched the room.

After several minutes, Franz caught sight of the six Russians standing in the distance, in front of a side door. Several rubbish carts with brooms and dust-pans sat behind them. So that was how they'd get the weapons close to the Council—hidden amongst the waste paper.

He jabbed an elbow into Pavel's side, quickly to avoid notice. When Pavel looked at him, he barely nodded his head back toward the Russians. Pavel turned around, nodded to Franz, and walked toward them.

"Hey, where's he going?" the stout Reuters man asked.

Franz shrugged. "He probably wants a workers' perspective. You know the Reds."

The British reported snorted. "I'll bet the custodians in this building see all sorts of things the rest of us don't. I might take a gander at them myself."

He started to follow, but Franz put a hand on his shoulder. "You'll miss the Council. You can talk to the staff at any time, but if you're not here when the Council comes out for lunch, well..."

He made an exaggerated shrug, and the British reporter chuckled and patted him on the back. "Excellent point, my man! Very sporting of you."

Franz breathed a sigh of relief. He glanced back to see Pavel approaching the six men and speaking to them.

General Guisan gave the reporters a polite bow of the head, turned toward the front doors, and strode down the central hall with crisp military steps.

Guards at the front doors opened them wide as the general approached. Franz scanned the Bundesplatz through the open doors, but the lunchtime crowds milling around belied nothing out of the ordinary.

He glanced at the clock on the wall. It was two minutes before noon.

70

Martin grew ever more impatient as the security chief droned on about the National Bank's security. Most of it had to do with financial security—account checks and balances, rigorous privacy audits—and Martin understood almost nothing of it.

He tried driving the conversation back toward the physical security of the building, but there turned out to be little. The Swiss had few concerns about physical security, having never needed to.

Martin suppressed a sigh and glanced at his watch. It was eight minutes before noon. Time was slipping away. He interrupted whatever it was the security chief was saying. "If you'll show me the way to the roof, I can finish my work and be out of your way."

The man's eyebrows shot up in surprise. "The roof? I can't imagine what for."

"I'm sure you understand FedPol's desire to stay a step ahead of the criminal elements. They've grown more sophisticated, and have elaborate ways of breaking into banks these days. The most common methods are from the roof. I need to make a report on the condition of this building's roof, so if you'll kindly send me in the right direction..."

"I'll take you there."

"Please just show me the way."

The security chief scowled. "As you wish. This way please."

Martin followed him through the labyrinthine halls of the fifth floor—the sixth floor in the American way of counting—until they reached a plain wooden door at the end of one narrow hall. The security chief removed a key ring from his belt, flipped through them, and unlocked the door and stepped aside.

Martin walked through into the dimness of a narrow space, stuffy and thick with the smell of dust. Three steps led up to the sloped ceiling, where a one meter by one meter hatch was secured only with a hasp latch. There were fresh footprints in the dust.

Volger had been this way.

Martin turned back to the security chief. "Thank you. Please close the door. I will return to your office in ten minutes."

He waited until the door was closed before he unlatched the hasp and climbed through onto the roof.

Rudolph Volger lay flat against the slope of the roof, peering southward over the peak from behind an exhaust pipe, training a small pair of binoculars at the Bundeshaus across the square.

A black sedan had parked along Bundesgasse near its opening onto the square, in front of the west wing, fifty meters from the entrance. A young army lieutenant stood ready to open the back door.

Volger glanced at his watch. Three minutes before noon. He reached for the Tokarev semi-automatic rifle, laid the barrel across the peak beside the exhaust pipe, and sighted through the scope.

General Guisan emerged from the building a moment later, unescorted. Volger chuckled—only in Switzerland would high officials walk around unescorted as if they were common citizens.

The clock above the Bundeshaus doors said that it was still a minute before noon, but the general was walking toward his waiting car. Volger followed him with the rifle, keeping it aimed at Guisan's chest.

His finger tensed on the trigger, starting to pull it back a millimeter at a time, waiting for the clock to begin its chime. His pulse quickened, echoing in his inner ear as the blood rushed to his head. This was the moment that would make him famous.

He almost didn't notice the click of a pistol hammer a few feet behind him, but then a stern voice broke his reverie.

"Drop the gun, Volger!"

Rudoph Volger didn't move. He kept his gaze locked on General Guisan through the scope.

The Bundeshaus clock began its midday chime.

A wave of desperation washed through Martin as Volger didn't budge from his position. Keeping his Luger aimed at the back of Volger's head, he crept closer.

"I said drop the gun!"

His voice was drowned out by the sound of the Bundeshaus clock beginning its chime; but now he was beside Volger, the barrel of the Luger inches from the SS officer's left temple.

He saw the beginning of movement in Volger's trigger finger, and lunged against the Major's prone figure.

A loud crack echoed around the square as the shot fired harmlessly over the rooftop of the Bundeshaus.

The SVT-40 clattered down the roof, its butt catching in the rain gutter and stopping. It rested there at a thirty-degree angle, the barrel aimed at nothing. Martin's pistol clattered down after it, and came to rest inside the gutter several feet from the rifle.

Volger rolled, his arms flailing out to grasp at anything, his fingers finally digging into the tiles along the roof-peak. Searing pain shot through his hand as his fingernails ripped backwards, but he held on in desperation and his fall halted.

*

Martin had enough forethought to grasp the exhaust pipe with his left hand as his body slammed into Volger's, and he hung onto it with a death grip.

Volger hauled himself upward to straddle the peak of the roof, oblivious to the commotion in the square below, his eyes locked on the figure of his assailant hanging from the exhaust pipe.

The spurious General Stengel, dressed in a blue suit. He should have known.

He glowered at him, and scooted along the roof-peak toward the exhaust pipe. As he did so he reached inside his overcoat and grasped his Walther pistol.

Martin hauled himself up with his left arm, using the exhaust pipe for leverage, and got his balance on the roof-peak. Volger reached inside his overcoat. Of course! The SS officer would have his own pistol on him, as well as the assault rifle.

Martin glanced to his right, then let go and allowed himself to slide down the roof toward a dormer window. He scrambled behind it just as Volger got off a shot.

The bullet ricocheted off the peak of the dormer rooftop, inches from Martin's fingers as he crouched low.

Volger moved to go after his attacker, but then realized with a start that the Swiss police would soon start looking for the shooter. The Gauleiter had warned him that he would only have a few minutes to escape. He cursed his failure to complete his mission, but self-preservation took over, and he crept carefully down the roof toward the open hatch. He climbed through, slammed the hatch, and latched the hasp.

**

Franz reached Pavel, who was pleading with the six fake custodians in rapid Russian, seconds before the rifle-shot rang out from the Bundesplatz. The seven men of the Federal Council had only just stepped into the central hall with the Federal Chancellor.

"Shit!" Over the noise of shouts and screams, Franz yelled at Pavel, "We've got to get them out of here, now!"

"That was our signal," one of the Russians said in heavily-accented German. "We will not sacrifice our families for a few politicians."

"The SS told them they would kill their families if they didn't complete their mission," Pavel explained to Franz, breathless.

Feodor Popov nodded to the others, and they reached into their rubbish bins.

Franz stepped in front of them, spreading his legs and holding out his arms to create as large a barrier with his body as he could. The Russians hesitated, and Pavel did the same.

Suddenly they were surrounded by police officers pointing guns at them.

"Put your hands where we can see them!" one of the policemen ordered. His German carried a strong American accent. And all of them held Colt 45s. A broad grin spread across Franz's face, and he began to laugh.

Pavel seemed to have noticed the accent as well, and the two of them exchanged a look as the six Russians were herded down a long corridor through the East Wing, toward the rear of the Bundeshaus.

Franz and Pavel followed at a distance. The Russians looked stunned, their eyes wide and glassy. Then, tears streamed down one's cheeks.

Franz's gut clenched. *They know their families will be killed for this*. He tried to force the thought from his mind. Their families were not his responsibility.

They exited onto the terrace along the south wall, overlooking the river. Beyond a narrow drive, the palace gardens slopped down two hundred feet toward the Aare. A few feet from the door stood a DKW F8 Kastenwagen saloon, its engine idling. The driver's door opened, and Franz recognized the blond Marine who had escorted him into the American Embassy almost two weeks ago.

Corporal Lawrence nodded to the fake police and opened the back of the saloon. They waved their Colt 45's and directed the Russians into the back. When only Franz and Pavel still stood outside the vehicle with them, Corporal Lawrence closed the back.

The four Americans in police uniforms opened the passenger doors and climbed inside.

"You two never saw this. It didn't happen, you understand?" Corporal Lawrence said in English, then got back into the driver's seat and sped off toward the west.

Franz knew just enough English to get the meaning. He said to Pavel, "He told us that we're never to speak of what happened, to anyone."

"I'll never want to." Pavel's blue eyes were cold and distant. "Good bye Franz."

Franz sprinted back into the Bundeshaus, and raced through the central hall. The members of the Federal Council were nowhere to be seen, and the hall was deserted. He stopped at the rubbish bins and tossed out waste paper until he found one of the hidden Tokarev TT-33 semi-automatic pistols. He shoved it down his waistband, then sprinted toward the front doors.

He emerged onto the Bundesplatz to find it swarming with people. Several police blowing whistles herded the crowds back from the Bundeshaus. One pointed at Franz, and blew his whistle so loudly that Franz cringed. "You, get back! What have you been doing in there? Didn't you hear the evacuation order? The building is being cleared!"

Franz showed his press pass and mumbled an apology, and the officer waved him toward the crowd.

His eyes darted all around, watching for anyone familiar—Mr. Schuller, Major Volger, Jason. He saw no one.

Jason should have been there with Michael Kaim by now. Where was he?

His mind raced. If Volger had shot General Guisan, then Mr. Schuller was probably dead. And Volger would return to the Hotel Bern.

His mouth set into a tight line, he turned east, and ran toward the Hotel Bern.

Martin knew instantly that he was locked out, trapped on the roof with no way down. He crawled back to the dormer window behind which he had crouched a moment before, stopping to retrieve his Luger from the gutter.

Gripping the edge of the gable, he eased himself around onto the window sill, not looking down. He knocked on the glass with his knee, trying to get the attention of anyone who might be inside that room.

He got no response after a second knock, so he took a fortifying breath and swung his leg back, then kicked forward, shattering the glass. Keeping hold of the gable with his left hand, he reached through the hole with his right hand and unlatched the window. It swung out, so he eased himself around it, balancing on the window sill with his toes, and climbed inside.

He allowed himself a few seconds to lean back onto the wall of the unoccupied office and exhale in relief. Then he bolted for the door.

**

The sound of the rifle shot was muted inside the spacious hotel suite, but it was unmistakable, and Jason's heart sank. He exchanged a look with Liev, and he could read on the young German's face what they both knew—General Guisan had been assassinated.

Only young Michael Kaim seemed unaware of the shot. He stood in front of them, blocking the door to the bedroom.

Jason had waited with Liev downstairs for three quarters of an hour before managing to convince him that Major Volger must have slipped out without the sentinel recognizing him. They went to the top floor, found the major's suite, and knocked on the door.

"Room service!" Liev had announced. When no answer came, he reached into his pocket and removed a pair of pins, and picked the lock.

Michael Kaim had come rushing out of the bedroom as they stood in the center of the suite's living room. Jason was stunned at how young he was; when Liev had indicated Major Volger had a "boy" with him, Jason had imagined a twenty-year-old, not an actual boy.

Liev had smiled at the youth. "We're here to see Major Volger," he said, his tone light and cheery.

"He's not here," Michael had replied, his dark eyes wary. "Who are you?"

"I'm here from Berlin," Liev answered. It was technically true. "My friend Mr. Bachman is from the embassy here in Bern." He didn't indicate whose embassy.

For the next ten minutes they pressed the boy for details about where Major Volger had gone, but Michael was either unable or unwilling to give them any answers.

And now the shot had been fired, and an agonizing sense of failure swept through Jason. They had been unable to prevent the assassination.

Liev gave Michael a stern look. "Do you know what just happened?"

Michael shook his head.

"Major Volger has shot an innocent man, the symbol of Switzerland's resistance to the Reich's aggression. They'll come here now, and they'll do to Switzerland's Jews what they did to your family, and all of the other Jewish families you know."

Michael visibly tensed. "You don't know my family!" His tone was petulant, adolescent.

"I know all about your family, Michael," Liev said, his tone softer. Jason watched Liev's eyes soften with compassion. "Your family was locked up at Dachau last December. Your mother Berthe died of pneumonia several months ago, denied medication by the SS. Your brother Jakob was shot by the guards eight days ago for trying to stop one of them from beating a young girl who had fallen during work. Your father Simon, your brothers Mattias and Samuel, and your sister Miriam labor for starvation rations. It's only a matter of time before they share your mother's fate, or Jakob's."

The boy's eyes filled with tears. "Major Volger saved me from that!" he protested, but his voice sounded weak and unsure. "He protects me."

"How long do you think Major Volger will continue to protect you, Michael?" Liev asked.

"He is moving us here. He told me he's going to have an important position in Switzerland; and we'll have a nice place to live, and I can come and go as I please."

Michael's voice sounded so hopeful it broke Jason's heart. He felt a lump forming in his throat.

Liev shook his head. "He lied to you, Michael. The men who sent him here to kill the Swiss general don't care about either of you.

They'll kill him to keep him silent about what he did. Then what will happen to you?"

A look of confusion fell across Michael's face, and his brow furrowed in consternation. "That's not true," he said, voice trembling. The tears began to run down his cheeks.

"You have to help us find him," Liev said.

"I told you I don't know where he is. He didn't tell me. He'll be angry if he comes back and finds you here."

"And he'll beat you, won't he?"

Michael was silent, and the tears continued to stream down his face.

"You don't have to live this way."

"Please go." Michael's voice was barely above a whisper.

"Come with us."

"I can't."

"We can take you somewhere safe, someplace where no one will hit you, or force you to do any of the things that Major Volger forces you to do for him."

Michael stiffened, and his face tightened in anger. "Leave me alone! I don't want you here! Get out!"

"We want to help you," Jason said.

"Get out!"

There was the sound of a key in the lock, and they turned to see Major Volger entering.

Volger's eyes widened at the sight of two strangers in the suite.

That split second of hesitation was all the time Liev Klein needed to pull a 9 mm Glock from the waist of his trousers. He aimed it at Volger's face as the major's hand flew to the handle of his holstered Walther.

Liev cocked the hammer.

Volger's hand stopped in place.

"Close the door, Major," Liev ordered. "And drop your hands to your sides."

Volger removed his right hand from the holster at his waist, and closed the door. He let his hands drop to his sides. "You're German," he said to Liev.

"Yes, I'm German. Berliner."

"Are you with the SD?"

"You don't need to know who I'm with."

"You're going to shoot me for failing my mission." It wasn't a question.

Liev and Jason were both too stunned to reply. Volger's mission had failed?

Their hesitation gave Volger pause. Perhaps the SD intended to kill him whether the mission succeeded or not. He inched to the left, closer to the end table that stood next to the couch.

"What are you going to do with the boy?" he asked.

"That is not your concern."

Volger grabbed the heavy ceramic lamp from the end table and hurled it.

Liev put his arms up to deflect the lamp, but the impact still knocked him off balance. Then Volger was on him, pushing him to the ground.

"Liev, his gun!" Jason shouted when Volger pulled the Walther from its holster.

Liev still held his Glock in his right hand, and he started to bring it up. Volger held his arm down, while bringing the butt of the Walther down on Liev's wrist.

Jason scrambled toward the broken lamp on the floor.

Liev's hand opened, and Volger smacked the Glock away with his left hand; with his right hand he brought the butt of the Walther down hard on the side of Liev's forehead, knocking him out cold.

Jason picked up the largest piece of lamp, and brought it back to throw at Volger.

As soon as he'd knocked out the curly-haired one, Volger saw the other one from the corner of his eye and spun toward him, aimed the Walther, and squeezed off a quick shot.

His aim was rushed and imperfect, but the bullet grazed the young man's left shoulder, tearing a gash in his blue shirt. A trickle of blood stained the fabric below the tear.

Jason felt a burn, dropped the lamp to the floor, and clamped his right hand onto his shoulder.

Volger was on his feet now, the Walther aimed at the young man's chest. But rather than firing, Volger stepped back, keeping his eyes and pistol locked on him.

"Michael, pack your things quickly. We're leaving."

"What's happening?"

"They're going to try to kill me. And they might try to kill you too. Either they'll kill you, or send you back to Germany to a concentration camp."

From where he stood across the room, Jason watched the look of hostility settle over Michael Kaim's face, and the eyes fill with hate. Major Volger couldn't see it, with his back to the boy.

A coy grin had come to the major's lips. "But I planned for this, Michael. I thought they might try to kill us, so I brought a lot of money with me. We're driving to Zurich, and then we'll get on a plane to Istanbul, where they'll never find us. And we'll live like kings in Istanbul, in a villa overlooking the Bosporus."

Michael's eyes bored a hole into the back of Volger's head.

The door burst open with a loud crack. Franz flew into the room shoulder first, his gun drawn. He took one look at Major Volger with his gun aimed at Jason, and froze in place.

"Drop your gun, Franz!" Volger shouted.

Franz crouched and laid the pistol on the ground, then slowly stood with his hands up.

"Keep your hands where I can see them."

Franz's stomach plummeted at the sight of Volger's gun pointed at Jason. He knew what he had to do. He put his hands up, but stepped in front of Jason and faced Volger.

A brief look of admiration crossed Volger's icy blue eyes, but was replaced by a smirk. "What a brave fool you are, Franz. I can kill you both with one bullet." He took a step forward and cocked the hammer.

A shot rang out. Jason and Franz both jumped at the noise, and Franz felt the burn of impact in his right shoulder. Then his eyes settled on the open hole in Major Volger's throat, and the blood gushing from it, soaking down the front of Volger's shirt like a red fountain.

Rasping mixed with a sickening gurgle as Volger struggled to get a breath. Two seconds later, he tumbled forward onto his face and lay motionless.

Michael Kaim stood three feet behind where Volger had been, Liev Klein's Glock in his trembling hand. Smoke curled from the barrel.

71

Martin arrived to find the door to the suite already broken open, and Volger lying dead on the floor. Jason was leaning over Franz, who sat on the floor leaning against an armchair, blood soaking his shirt on the right shoulder. The other young man leaning forward in a chair, his head resting in his hand and his elbow on his knee, a dazed look on his face, was the curly-haired spy he'd seen before.

Martin shoved his Luger into its holster and hurried toward Jason and Franz. He touched Jason's left shoulder to get his attention, and only then noticed the small amount of blood crusted at the bottom of a tear. Jason flinched at the contact, but didn't make a sound.

"Call the embassy, and ask for Lt. Colonel Legge. Have him send the saloon back right away. We've got to get Franz out of here unnoticed. You and I will have to help him down the stairs."

"But what about...?" Jason nodded toward Volger's corpse in the center of the room.

"Let the Abwehr take care of that. We've got to get Franz out of here ourselves. Go call the embassy."

While Jason ran for the telephone, Martin stepped toward the young man in the armchair holding his head. "Are you Abwehr?"

The man nodded, grimacing at the movement.

"As soon as my man gets off the phone, call your people and have them take care of Major Volger. There mustn't be anything left for the police to investigate."

He nodded again.

Martin turned; a slender, black-haired youth sat on the end of the bed in the other room. A Glock pistol lay on the floor between his feet, and he wore a vacant expression. The boy couldn't be more than seventeen.

Franz appeared at his side. "That's Michael Kaim, Major Volger's catamite. He was the one who shot him."

Martin's eyes widened. "Jewish?"

"Yes."

"Then he'll have to come with us." Martin wouldn't entrust a Jewish boy to the Abwehr.

Jason appeared beside them. "The saloon's on its way, it'll be here in five minutes."

Martin looked at Franz. "Can you convince the boy to come with us?"

Franz nodded. He crouched down in front of him. His voice was too low for Martin to hear what he was saying. The boy nodded without a word and stood. He followed Franz out of the bedroom.

Franz leaned close to Martin and whispered. "I told him I know someone who can take good care of him, a Jewish woman. I'll call Sonia when we get to your embassy."

"I'll call her," Martin said, a bit too quickly. "You need medical attention."

The corners of Franz's mouth curled up, and he nodded. "Yes, you call her."

The curly-haired Abwehr agent—Jason said his name was Liev Klein—seemed to have recovered his faculties. He hung up the phone when Martin approached him with the Glock. "This is yours?"

"Yes, thank you." Klein took the pistol and stuffed it beneath his belt.

"Your people are coming?"

"Yes."

"Good. We're leaving." Martin turned and strode from the room. Franz followed with his arm around Michael Kaim's shoulder.

Liev touched Jason's arm as he passed.

"I've got to go with them," Jason said. "We have to go right away."

"I know," Liev said. "I'll call you tonight. We should talk. Maybe we could meet for coffee tomorrow?"

"I don't know..."

"I know you don't have much time—I just want to see you again."

"I have Franz."

Liev stared at him in silence for a few seconds. "No, but he has you. Best of luck with him."

Jason wondered what he meant, but said nothing, just turned and walked from the room.

Liev followed to the doorway. He watched Jason hurrying toward the back stairs, where Mr. Schuller stood holding the door open. He kept watching for several seconds after the door closed.

549

Thursday, October 16, 1941

72

RED ATTACK ON NATIONAL BANK FAILS

Agents of the outlawed Communist Party attempted to rob the National Bank of Switzerland on Wednesday. The attack was thwarted by members of the Federal Police, who apprehended all suspects at the scene.

One of the reds fired a gun at a FedPol inspector. The shot missed, passed through an open window, and flew harmlessly over the Bundesplatz.

Federal investigators raided a suite at the Hotel Bern shortly after the attack. A shoot-out with police resulted in the death of one of the conspirators. Authorities are not releasing names at this time.

Bern

Martin sat across from Ambassador Harrison.

"I can't tell you what a tremendous service you've been to your country, Mr. Schuller," Harrison said, beaming. "I sent a full report to Colonel Donovan, praising your actions, and the COI is going to offer you a sizeable monetary reward for your service."

That was welcome news, but Martin's gut told him it wasn't all. "And?"

"I'm sure you'll get some kind of commendation from the State Department," Harrison said.

"I meant, and what else did you want to tell me? It wasn't just to offer your congratulations."

"No, it wasn't," Harrison said. "I'm going to tell Bill Donovan that our mission in Switzerland—owing to its strategic importance in the heart of war-torn Europe—should have a permanent Intelligence office, with a full-time Intelligence Officer to monitor things over here."

"And you want me to take that job."

"Yes, I do."

"I was told when I took this assignment that I would return to my regular work when it was finished. I'm planning to return to Washington."

"And you are returning to Washington tomorrow," Harrison hurried to say. "But I'm hoping you'll come back before the end of the year."

"For how long?"

"For as long as the COI and the President see fit."

Martin leaned back in the chair and considered a moment. "Would that mean the end of undercover work?"

"Mostly, yes…but maybe not entirely" the older man said. "You'd keep the office you've been using here, and use your own diplomatic passport, and diplomatic license plates. You'll be able to live a normal diplomatic life."

"While recruiting a network of agents," Martin mused. "And if I decline the offer?"

Harrison frowned. "This is all supposition at this point. Nothing is official. Yet."

Martin nodded. "It's an interesting idea. I'll think about it." He didn't relish the idea of being half a world away from his kids again, so soon after returning to the States.

"That's all I can ask." Harrison stood. "Talk it over with Bill Donovan when you get back to Washington."

Martin stood, shook hands, and exited the large office. He walked down the hall to his temporary office—possibly his future office—closed the door, and picked up the handwritten letters that still sat on his desk where he'd left them yesterday. The package had been waiting for him when he got back after wrapping things up at the Hotel Bern.

There were letters from each of his three children, full of news about school and teachers and new friends. Then there was a single page included, unsigned, in Becky's familiar handwriting with its elegant loops and swirls.

> *It seems you've accepted an assignment overseas. Something top secret, of course. You couldn't even tell your children where you are. I hope you're happy. Your children saw precious little of you as it was. God knows the next time they'll see you. I hope this "important work" that you're doing helps you sleep at night.*

He crumpled the note into a tight wad and tossed it in the trash. He fumed for a moment. But then an idea struck him.

He hurried back to the Ambassador's office.

Jason felt strange sitting back at his desk that morning, getting back to his regular work with visa applications. The other grunts around him cast sideways glances at him, but not one of them asked where he'd been. He was sure there had been rumors.

His supervisor came to his desk right after lunch and asked him to come upstairs. Jason went with him to the fourth floor, and past Amanda's desk to the Ambassador's office. Mr. Higgins told him to go in, and then walked away.

Ambassador Harrison sat behind his desk, and Martin Schuller stood leaning against a wall. Harrison told Jason to take a seat. Mr. Schuller remained standing, watching Jason with those hard green eyes.

"You've had a busy week, Mr. Bachman," Ambassador Harrison said.

"Yes, sir."

"Mr. Schuller tells me that you were instrumental in neutralizing a threat to American interests. We're grateful, and proud of you."

"Thank you, sir."

The Ambassador smiled. "Jason, in appreciation of your recent activity, we'd like to offer you a promotion. Mr. Schuller is building an Intelligence apparatus. He would like to train you as an analyst, assisting him in his duties. Would you accept?"

It took a few seconds to sink in, but then Jason beamed. "Yes, I accept! Thank you!"

"Good. You'll leave for Washington tomorrow with Mr. Schuller, and you'll be there for six weeks while you're trained. You'll return here the end of November. Your new position is classified, so you won't be allowed to speak about it to anyone—not even your parents. Is that clear?"

"Yes, sir."

"It's a promotion from FS6 to FS5, with the standard increase in pay and housing associated with the rank of FS5. You'll be moved into a larger apartment that you'll share with one other man instead of two. Congratulations."

Jason frowned. "FS5?"

"That's right."

"Make it FS4."

"I beg your pardon?" The ambassador's eyes narrowed.

"I said make it FS4. After what I've been through the last five days, I think I deserve FS4," Jason said, his voice level. "I've worked long hours, couriered messages in the middle of the night, and I was even shot at. I think FS5 is unacceptable. If you want me to do this job, then I want FS4."

Jason looked up at Mr. Schuller. The man's lips spread in a slight smile.

"It's a matter of seniority, Mr. Bachman," the ambassador said. "It's unheard of for someone with your short tenure in the Foreign Service to be promoted to FS4."

"Give it to him," Mr. Schuller said, standing and extending his right hand toward Jason. "He deserves it."

Jason stood and shook his hand.

"It's a hard life—are you sure you want it?"

"Yes, sir."

"You'll have to learn how to say just enough without saying too much. That's a tough skill to master. You'll need to know ciphering and deciphering, and how to distinguish important pieces of information from the chatter. And it can be dangerous."

"I know."

That same tiny smile returned to Mr. Schuller's lips. "Good. Welcome to Intelligence, Jason."

"Thank you, Mr. Schuller."

Mr. Schuller nodded toward the door. "Now go home, pack for tomorrow. And get some rest—we've got a long flight."

Jason left the room, a broad grin on his face.

Martin turned to Ambassador Harrison. "FS4 is appropriate. He'll need an apartment to himself, no roommate. And he'll need an office of his own."

"We'll take care of all that," the Ambassador said. "Everything will be ready."

Martin nodded and turned to leave. Harrison's voice stopped him at the door. "Mr. Schuller—thank you, for everything. I hope you'll be back."

73

"I wondered when you'd stop by," Lt. Colonel Legge said, rising to shake Martin's hand. "I hear State's going to keep you on here."

"They want to."

The military attaché grunted. "I hope so—we've done good work together."

Martin got to the point of his visit. "Thank you for helping me get those Russians out of the Bundeshaus. Have you finished debriefing them?"

"Almost."

"How soon will they be repatriated?"

"They aren't being repatriated."

"What?" Martin instantly regretted his sharp tone. He'd need the colonel's good graces in the future, even if he stayed in Washington. "Why not?"

The military attaché snorted. "Feodor Popov and Nikolai Sokolov have provided information that Comrade Stalin would find treasonous. They would both be killed without question if they went back. The others have been debriefed as well, and though they know no vital intelligence, the NKVD would still ship them off to a Siberian Gulag if we allowed them to go home."

"Then what's to become of them?"

"We're sending Popov and Sokolov stateside. They'll be given housing and a stipend for their trouble. Lieutenant Sokolov will be able to pursue his art at his leisure. Popov has been bribed into taking a job in Washington as Russian translator, paired with one of our Military Intelligence analysts. God knows we desperately need Russian translators. The others will be interned by the Swiss until the war's over."

"What about their families?" Martin asked. "Won't the Soviets punish them for their defections?"

"Perhaps—if by some miracle the Nazis haven't murdered them already."

Martin nodded in resignation.

"Cheer up!" the colonel said with a smile. "You've been granted more than a month's leave stateside, I hear. You can see your kids for Thanksgiving. And you can catch up with your Russian friends in Washington, if you'd like. Then maybe you'll return to work here as an Intelligence Officer, not a covert operator. You'll have a bigger apartment, bigger paycheck, and the freedom of the country—not bad, eh?"

Martin forced a smile and nodded. He stood and extended his hand. "Perhaps so. Thanks again for all of your assistance."

"You bet," the colonel said, shaking Martin's hand and then looking down at his work. "Have a good trip." It was a dismissal.

"I'm surprised you're still in Switzerland," Martin said when Captain Wolfe picked up the line after three transfers. He hadn't harbored much hope that the Abwehr officer hadn't returned to Germany already.

"I leave this evening."

"I wonder if you'd do me a favor."

"What favor?"

"I assume you spy on the SS."

Wolfe chuckled. "We keep an interest in their activities."

"Can you find out what they've done to the families of those Russians?"

"By your request, can I infer that you have the Russians? They seem to have disappeared after the failed attack yesterday."

"No, I don't have them." That wasn't a lie. "But I do know where they are; at least, for now."

Wolfe was silent for several seconds. "I'll see what I can learn."

"Thank you. And when you know something, send it to me in Washington. I'll have a courier bring you the contact number."

"You're not staying in Switzerland?"

"No, I leave tomorrow." Martin figured the Abwehr would know if and when he returned.

"Then I'll have to be cautious about contacting you." The line clicked off.

Martin sighed. He wasn't surprised, though.

He dialed the operator, and asked for a number in Zurich.

"Hello?" Sonia answered.

"It's Martin."

"Oh, hello."

"Thank you for coming last night. I appreciate that you did that for us. I'm sorry we couldn't give you more notice."

"It's fine."

"Is the boy comfortable there?"

"Yes. I've given him my father's room. He seems glad to be here."

"Good."

"I don't know what he's been through, but he's very quiet."

"I don't know, either," Martin admitted. "Franz seems to know all about him. I'm sure he can tell you anything you'd like to know."

"I don't need to know anything," Sonia said. "I just don't know how best to help him."

"Let him know he's safe, and that you'll take care of him. Let him know you don't expect anything from him, just let him be a kid again." Martin took a breath. "I'm leaving for Washington tomorrow. I'm taking a plane from Zurich. Would you be able to meet me at the airport? I'd like to have a chance to say goodbye in person, buy you a cup of coffee."

"I don't think I can get away."

Martin hesitated, but then threw caution to the wind. "Please? I'd really like to see you before I leave."

The silence lasted several seconds. "If you're leaving, why does it matter?" Her voice was quiet, but with a slight quiver, a tiny note of vulnerability.

"I might come back someday. But while I'm away I'd like to remember your face from a happier moment than the commotion of last night."

"Well, I suppose—alright. What time?"

"Ten o'clock."

"Alright, then. I'll see you there at ten o'clock. Good bye."

"Thank you, Sonia."

She clicked off the line.

Martin leaned back in his chair, folded his hands across his stomach, and looked up at the ceiling. A smile spread across his lips, and broke into a grin.

THE END

Thank you for reading The Swiss Conspiracy. If you enjoyed this book, please tell a friend, update your social media, and/or write a review on Amazon, Goodreads, or other forum.

If you have not already, you can read more about Franz Lemiel's adventures in France in Gray Paree, a companion novel to The Swiss Conspiracy.

Questions or comments? Feel free to contact me at
www.garretthutson.com
You can also sign up for my monthly newsletter to find out when my next book will be released, and receive exclusive free content.

Also by Garrett Hutson:

In A Safe Town

The Jade Dragon (Death in Shanghai, Book 1)

Assassin's Hood (Death in Shanghai, Book 2)

Hidden Among Us (Martin Schuller Spy Catcher, Book 1)

Spy Tango (Martin Schuller Spy Catcher, Book 2)

Gray Paree

About the Author

Garrett Hutson writes upmarket mysteries and historical spy fiction. He lives in Indianapolis with his husband, four adorable dogs, and two oddball cats, and more fish that you can count. He has one grown daughter. You can usually find him reading about history, and day-dreaming about being there. This is where his stories are born, and he hopes they transport you the way his imagination transports him. You may contact him at his website, www.garretthutson.com.

Historical Note

This is a work of fiction. All characters, with the exception of a few historical figures noted below, are fictional.

Among the historical figures included in reference only are President Franklin D. Roosevelt; Secretary of State Cordell Hull; Assistant Secretary of State for Intelligence Adolf A. Berle; British Prime Minister Winston Churchill; German chancellor Adolf Hitler; Colonel William Donovan, Coordinator of Information (COI); British/Canadian spymaster William Stephenson; Congressman George Paddock; Dr. Paul Karrer (Swiss Nobel Laureate in chemistry); and General Henri Guisan, Commander of the Swiss Armed Forces.

I try to avoid casting real people as characters, but on occasion it is necessary for the story—historical figures that appear briefly in the narrative include Ambassador Leland Harrison and Colonel Barnwell R. Legge, U.S. Military Attaché to Switzerland. Stallag II-B Commandant Colonel Von Bernuth was also a real person. Though I have taken a certain amount of dramatic license in their portrayal, I have done my best to portray them as historically accurate as I can in a fictional depiction.

I have attempted to describe the geography of the setting as accurately as possible, including street names. Most of the buildings, restaurants, and shops described are fictitious, with a few exceptions—for example, the Haus zum Rüden in Zurich and the Hotel Adlon in Berlin.

Being a neutral country surrounded by Axis-controlled territory, Switzerland was a hot-bed of espionage throughout World War Two. And many historical sources have demonstrated that Swiss neutrality wasn't entirely even, mostly owing to its precarious position. There is evidence that they did treat downed Luftwaffe pilots better in detention camps than they treated downed RAF pilots, for example;

and the allegations of laundering Nazi gold are too numerous to mention here.

It is also true that a small minority of Switzerland's population—perhaps two percent total—favored political union with Germany. In a multinational country in which slightly more than two-thirds of the population was linguistically and ethnically German, this pro-Nazi group was probably three percent of that community.

The League of Swiss for Greater Germany was a real group that was founded by Franz Burri in 1941, with the aim of joining Switzerland to the Third Reich. Its documented activities were primarily propaganda newspapers…but I wondered what might have happened if they took a more paramilitary approach to realize their goal, and thus was born this story.

As depicted here, Hitler did have a plan to invade Switzerland in the summer of 1940, after the capitulation of France, and it was called Operation Tennenbaum, as mentioned in this story. Also as depicted here, the Swiss mobilized, and the invasion plan was set aside in favor of bombing Britain into submission instead. I began to wonder if leaders in Hitler's High Command would have been open to suggestions, from someone like Franz Burri, of clandestine terrorist attacks inside Switzerland to destabilize the country, and at the same time blame the newly-outlawed Communist Party. And what would be the larger geopolitical implications, especially to the United States? The idea intrigued me enough back in 2010 to start planning this novel.

To my knowledge, there was never any assassination plot against General Henri Guisan or the Swiss Federal Council, nor were there any attacks on Swiss military leaders. That is wholly a product of my imagination. To my knowledge there was also not any network of anti-Nazi university students in Switzerland—though there certainluy could have been. I don't believe the Swiss were working on jet technology at this time, though it would not have been impossible or implausible. I have imagined what could have been, not necessarily what was.

There was some historical basis to the idea of blaming communists for terrorist attacks. There has long been a question of who was really behind the fire at the Reichstag in January 1933 that Hitler used to suspend civil liberties, with many historians maintaining that the Nazis were behind it themselves; other historians disagree, but the idea has always intrigued me. And I thought a string of such attacks might make a good thriller.

Only much later, while doing research for another story in November 2020, did I discover that fascists in France actually did commit multiple acts of terrorism (bombings and assassinations of political leaders) that they attempted to blame on the communists in 1937. French police infiltrated the group La Cagoule (nicknamed "The Cowl" in the press), and arrested about seventy members. I've had Martin contemplate this plot when he gets the assignment in Switzerland.

Other little-known historical events referenced include the September 1937 assassination of Ignace Reiss in Switzerland, which actually happened as described. His wife Elsa's presence in Zurich in 1927 is made up for the sake of the story, as is any implied connected with Inrina Minskaya, a fictitious character. Any resemblance to any actual person is purely coincidental.

The period from 1939 to 1941 was an interesting time for American intelligence gathering. Aside from domestic counterintelligence, no formal intelligence organization existed outside of the narrow purview of the Army and Navy. As war escalated across Europe, the U.S. government saw the need to step up its political intelligence gathering, but initially without any concrete plans or organization. American embassy and consular staff around the world were given little direction and had to make things up as they went along.

Meanwhile, lawyer and retired colonel William Donovan persuaded President Roosevelt that the country needed a proper organization to coordinate intelligence gathering and analysis. Finally, in July 1941, Roosevelt appointed Donovan as Coordinator of Intelligence (COI). Donovan began putting together an organization, collecting men and women who shared his sense of action. We saw Martin join this organization at the end of *Spy Tango*. As they grew, they would later be named the Office of Strategic Services (OSS) in 1942—after the events of this story. From the beginning, though, Donovan was ambitious for his new organization, and this has left me plenty of room to imagine Martin's involvement in a secret operation to stop the destabilization of Switzerland, the lone spot of stability in the heart of war-torn Europe.

I've endeavored to be as accurate as possible in describing the political and social environment of the story, and the complicated interlocking games of diplomacy and espionage in the second year of World War Two. Beyond the premise of terrorist attacks by pro-Nazi elements (which I believe to be plausible, though entirely a figment of my imagination), I have taken only a few liberties, the biggest being the presence of Martin Schuller in Switzerland a full year before the first OSS operative was assigned there in November of 1942—the celebrated Allen W. Dulles. In doing this, I felt that it was not unrealistic for someone in Martin's role to be sent on a temporary, and limited, mission to one of the most important neutral countries of the time.

The novel's description of liberal student organizations, led by Franz Lemiel and Sonia Rubenstein, is a product of my imagination. We know that student opposition groups did exist in Germany during the Third Reich (the Swing Youth of the late 1930s, for example, as well as the White Rose group later in the war), so I believe that the Swiss groups I've imagined are completely plausible.

The Eidelweis Pirates were real, and functioned as I have described them. The individuals described are fictitious, however, springing entirely from my imagination.

During the Weimar Republic (1919-1932), Germany had a very enlightened and tolerant view of alternate sexualities and gender expressions, which would not have seemed all that strange to an American living at the start of the twenty-first century. This attitude was reversed when the Nazis took over in 1933, and then harshly repressed the following year.

In spite of official Nazi repression—and murder—of homosexuals and other "deviants," there are ample examples of Nazi officials who were themselves closeted homosexuals. Their own self-loathing fueled their hatred of others, which is what I've endevoured to portray in the fictional person of Major Rudolph Volger. And while sadism was officially frowned upon as "deviant," there are countless accounts of Gestapo torture that are clearly and truly sadistic. Hipocracy is never hard to find among fascists.

One of the biggest challenges to writing historical fiction with gay and bisexual characters is to portray a realistic stance for those heterosexual individuals who—like Martin—did not subscribe to the pervasive homophobic attitude of the time. What passed for a "liberal" attitude in those days would not seem very liberal—or even moderate—in the twenty-first century. But it would be an error to expect a social liberal in 1941 to hold modern views. I believe that Martin's attitude—accepting individuals as long as they kept their sexuality hidden—is the correct attitude for a straight ally at the time, however short it may fall from our modern standards. I feel this is important to show.

Generally speaking, large universities tended to have a bohemian subculture that challenged established mores. While not as large and visible as the famous bohemian enclaves in Paris and New York, the literary and artistic communities centered around European universities still fit the description. These bohemian subcultures tended to accept alternatives to heteronormative sexuality regardless of the attitude of the larger culture, which is why I feel comfortable placing Franz Lemiel within the social circle I've created for him.

As always, I have done my best to be as historically accurate as possible, except where noted above. Any errors are mine alone.

Acknowledgements

Contrary to appearances, writing and publishing a novel is never a solitary endeavor. This book in particular was a long time coming, and I have many people to thank for their contributions over the years.

First, my thanks go to the talented writers in the IndyScribes critique group, who got started in 2012 just when I was in need of other writers to give me feedback on the 1st(ish) draft of this story—Nicole Amsler, Laura VanArondonk Baugh, Stephanie Ferguson, Marcia Kelly, Jim Meeks-Johnson, and Jim Thompson. They patiently read and critiqued many sections of that messy draft, and provided excellent feedback. This group, with one departure and three additions, has had a hand in improving every book I've published, and the stories are better for it. You all really are the best!

My sincere thanks to my wonderful beta readers—Brenda Havens and Lisa Wheeler—who took the time to read the entire manuscript, and provided valuable insights and feedback. You both helped to bring out the best in this story, and I can't thank you enough. Thanks also to Bob Appelsies for reviewing all of the Jewish characters, and making sure I didn't make any stupid mistakes.

The U.S. Department of State's Office of the Historian's extensive archive of memoranda was invaluable in piecing together our country's aims and diplomatic efforts in this region during 1941.

Many thanks to Steven Novak for another amazing cover. It really captures the essence and spirit of this story, and I just love it.

And last, but never least, my deepest gratitude, love, and devotion to my husband David Lee. You put up with countless hours during which I immerse myself in my stories, and you never complain. Without hesitation, you give me the freedom to live this amazing and sometimes infuriating life of a fiction writer, and you are always supportive through all of its ups and downs. The high points are so much better when I can share them with you, and you make the frustrations easier to bear. I love you more than words can ever express.

-Garrett B. Hutson, March 2021